CHRONICLES
OF THE
RED KING

The Secret Kingdom

CHRONICLES
OF THE
RED KING
The Secret Kingdom

JENNY NIMMO

SCHOLASTIC INC.

New York   Toronto   London   Auckland
Sydney   Mexico City   New Delhi   Hong Kong

ISBN 978-0-545-29241-2

12 11 10 9 8 7 6 5 4 3 2 1   12 13 14 15 16 17/0

Printed in the U.S.A.   40
This edition first printing, April 2012
Book design by Elizabeth B. Parisi and Kristina Iulo

For Rhiannon, with love

CONTENTS

PROLOGUE

My name is Charlie Bone. I am thirteen years old and I live in a city in Britain that was built by my ancestor, an African king.

I have always wondered about the man known as the Red King. He was a magician, I was told, and he wore a red cloak. But no one seemed to know why he had traveled so far from his own country.

When I was ten something happened to me. Something odd. I began to hear the voices of people in photographs. Some of the people were already dead. The next phase of my peculiar "endowment" began when I looked at an old painting of a sorcerer. This time I not only heard him, I traveled right into his dingy old cell, all the way back into the sixteenth century. My grandmother told me I had inherited my endowment from the Red King, and I was sent to Bloor's Academy, a school for weekly boarders.

The Academy was run by a weird old man called Ezekiel Bloor. He was a hundred years old and a sort of magician. He was also descended from the Red King, and so were some of the students I met at the school. There were twelve of us who were known as the endowed.

In the past year there have been a lot of changes in the Academy. But we endowed still do our homework in the King's room. And the Red King's portrait still hangs in the space between the bookshelves. The paint has cracked and the king's face is shadowy and blurred, but there is a kind of light in his eyes, and I know that he is there, waiting for me.

It was my great-uncle Paton who suggested I help with the writing of this book. He had just finished reading the journals of our distant cousin, Bartholomew Bloor. Bartholomew is an explorer, and when he was traveling through Africa, he heard an ancient story about a boy and a flying camel. The same story cropped up again in Egypt. Bartholomew was intrigued. After that, wherever he went, he would ask questions about the boy and his camel. He was amazed to find the same story in Greece and Turkey and in cities all around the Mediterranean Sea. Often he was shown the caves and walls where carvings had been found, among them the image of a boy on a flying camel, as if it were a kind of signature.

Bartholomew began to draw maps so that he could revisit the places where he had heard the stories. Sometimes, when he asked about the boy and the camel, people's answers surprised him. In fact, the dates he was given for some of the sightings made no sense at all. If they were accurate, then the boy had not aged in two hundred years, nor had the camel.

In a lonely tavern in the Pyrenees, Bartholomew had the first inkling that he had stumbled on a story that was directly related to him. The innkeeper heard the tale from his great-grandmother, who knew everything about the village and its past. "There was a camel, certainly," he said, "and it could fly, no doubt about that. The boy would not be remembered, would he, if it had not been for the camel?"

An old woman sitting in a corner piped up, "Not true. Of course the boy would be remembered. He was a magician. An African king. He could bring rain and thunder; he could talk to animals. In that red cloak of his, he could do almost anything."

An African king? A magician in a red cloak? Bartholomew said that his heart missed a beat. He suddenly realized that, quite by chance, he had been following in the footsteps of his very own ancestor, the Red King.

The summer holidays had just begun when Uncle Paton called me. "It's about our ancestor, Charlie—the book I'm writing. Can you pop up to the shop this morning?"

The shop was Ingledew's Bookshop. Uncle Paton lived there with his wife, Julia, and Emma, her niece. They sold secondhand books, some of them very old and rare. The perfect place for a writer. My uncle was in the little room behind the shop. He was sitting at a desk piled high with ancient leather-bound books. Uncle Paton is exceptionally tall, but I could only just see the top of his head poking up behind them.

"Charlie," he said. "Come and have a look at this."

The sofa was heaped up with books and papers as usual, but we pushed them to one side and sat down. Uncle Paton spread Bartholomew's maps across his knees. "Look," he said. "Look at the places marked with a cross. There are carvings there, pictures the Red King drew maybe nine hundred years ago."

"Yes," I said, sort of unsurprised. I had already seen the maps.

"Suppose you were to go and see them, Charlie. Suppose you found yourself traveling into them, suppose . . ."

"Suppose I were to meet him, when he was young?" I was so excited I jumped off the sofa. I'd already met the king when he was older. But the portrait in the school was painted at a time when the king was in mourning. He was pleased to see me, but never said much about his past. Now, at last, I might get a chance to find out who he really was and why he'd come to Britain.

Uncle Paton grinned. "You've got the idea, Charlie. You see those tomes"—he pointed to the books on the desk—"they might have been written hundreds of years ago, but they could have got a few things wrong. They can only tell us that the king arrived from Africa in the thirteenth century, that he was a magician, and married the daughter of a knight from Toledo. I want this book to be as truthful as I can make it. Bartholomew's journals are invaluable, of course, especially the maps. But we don't know what happened right at the very beginning, and why the king came so far."

"And we don't know what he thought and if his cloak was really magic?"

"The cloak. Hmm." Uncle Paton scratched his head. "We need Gabriel."

Gabriel Silk is a friend of mine. Another of the endowed. He's a bit odd—he lives with fifty-six gerbils and other assorted pets. But his family still possesses the Red King's cloak. Gabriel has incredible psychic powers. I knew what Uncle Paton was thinking. Wearing the cloak, Gabriel could use his ability to reach into the life of the Red King. Perhaps he could even see the world as the king saw it; he could listen, watch, and feel as he did.

As I said, it was the beginning of the summer holidays. We hadn't planned to go anywhere. Mom wasn't too keen on traveling; we'd just moved into a new house and there was still lots to do. But my dad was up for it. "Two weeks, Charlie. That's all I can spare for now, but we could always go again — in the autumn perhaps."

"And again and again and again?" I said.

My dad laughed. "Maybe, Charlie."

So my dad and I went to Africa. It was the best holiday I'd ever had in my life. We found the caves that Bartholomew mentioned. We found the rocks and walls and underground passages marked on his maps. We saw the pictures, the mysterious lines and shapes that the Red King had carved. And when I touched them, I met the boy who made them. And every time we met, the king's voice became clearer and his face brighter, until it seemed as if I was just talking to a friend who was sitting beside me. Little by little he told me his story, and with Gabriel's help, my uncle and I learned about the enchanted cloak, where it came from, and how it helped the king to become a marvelous magician.

This is the first book that Uncle Paton wrote about the Red King. As for the next one — that's another story.

CHARLIE BONE
Diamond Corner

CHAPTER 1
The Forest-Jinni

There was once a secret kingdom. It was hidden from the world by a forest as wide and as deep as a sea. The people who lived there had never known war, but they had heard of it. Stories of terrible strife and cruelty in the outside world had been passed down from the ancestors who had founded the kingdom. And so, although the people had never fought a battle, they could imagine it. They kept their spears polished to a high degree, and they painted fierce animals on their stout wooden shields. They even posted a watch in the tall towers that stood at each of the four corners of the palace.

The king was everything a king should be. Standing a head taller than most of his subjects, he was wise and just and dignified. He favored brightly colored robes and golden jewelry, which he wore looped in long ropes around his neck and in wide brace-lets on his arms. Yet the crown he wore was a slim gold band, almost hidden in his thick black hair. It was a thousand years old and had once adorned the head of the first ruler of the secret kingdom.

The queen was a mystery. She was a very quiet woman, given to dreaming. It was believed that the king had chosen her for her exceptional beauty, but this was only part of the truth. He loved her for her fine mind, her kindness, and the magical quality of her voice.

The king and queen had one child: Princess Zobayda, who was two years old. Another baby was on the way but, for some reason, the imminent birth of this second child filled the queen with anxiety. It was the hottest time of the year, and yet the queen could not stop shivering. All day she paced the palace, muttering to herself. At night she cried in her sleep and called out, "Save him! Save my son!"

The king begged his wife to tell him about her nightmares. What was it that she feared so much? She was strong and healthy. Their kingdom was safe, and he tried to give her every-thing that she wished for. Why was she so worried about a child who had not even been born?

The queen could not say. She forgot her dreams as soon as she woke up, and did not understand why she found herself eroding the patterns on the tiled floor with her endless pacing. She had worn out one hundred pairs of shoes and now went barefoot. Her feet were sore and blistered, and still she paced. Sometimes the king felt dizzy watching his restless wife.

One night, a great storm blew up. The wind raged across the secret kingdom, uprooting trees and sending rivers of water through the streets. Thunder roared endlessly and lightning flashed across the land, turning night into day.

The windows in the palace were shuttered and barred, and the king and queen sat close together on a low couch filled with gold-embroidered cushions. For once the queen was motionless. She listened to the wind, leaning slightly, as though she were hearing voices.

"What do they say?" asked the king, half in jest. He took his wife's hand. "Do they . . . ?" he began.

"Shh!" hissed his wife. "Something is coming!"

At that instant, the shutters cracked apart and something flew into the room. It lay facedown, its ragged wings spread against the marble floor. The wings were not feathered, but as fine and delicate as a moth's. They sprouted from the being's bony shoulders; dark, earth-colored wings with pearly veins. The rest of the body was covered in a grayish silk that, at first, appeared like a fine mist, but gradually settled around the stranger's body, revealing its puny form.

The royal couple stared at the creature as it slowly folded its wings and pulled itself into a kneeling position. Even the king was speechless.

The little being raised its head and gazed at the queen. It had mottled gray skin and huge saffron-colored eyes. Its long nose was narrow, the tip overhanging its thin gash of a mouth. Its tiny ears rested in cavities on either side of its head, and it had no hair at all.

In spite of the creature's disturbing features, the queen was not alarmed. "What has happened to you?" she asked gently.

The creature crawled toward the queen and grabbed the hem of her robe. "Forgive me," he said. "I had nowhere to go, nowhere at all. They pursue me everywhere."

"Who pursues you?" asked the king, a little roughly. "My people harm no one, even . . . even . . ."

"A jinni?"

"Indeed, a jinni, if that is what you are?"

"A forest-jinni." The creature's voice had an echo, a distant cascade of tiny bells that enchanted the queen. "There is only one of us . . . now." His frail wings drooped.

"You appear to be lost," said the queen. "How can we help you?"

"Lost, lost. I am lost." Two fat tears rolled down the jinni's mottled cheeks. "I flew above the forest. I dared not stop. For days and days I traveled through the air. I could hear them below me. They would not let me rest. And then the wind caught me. It hurled me into your beautiful kingdom—" The jinni paused and took a breath. "And now I am here. At Your Majesties' mercy." He bowed his head.

The king stroked his chin and glanced at his wife. The recent lines of weariness and apprehension had left her face.

"I shall tell a servant to prepare a bed for you," said the queen. "If, indeed, you are used to such things. And some food. What do you like to eat, forest-jinni?"

"Fruit?" said the jinni tentatively. More tears formed in the corners of his orange-yellow eyes, and he looked up at the colored tiles that patterned the ceiling above him. "I have not known kindness for so long, it bewilders me."

"Everyone deserves kindness," said the queen. "Without it, we would die."

The king rang a small bell placed on a table at his side, and a servant appeared. When the man saw the jinni, he gave a gasp of horror.

"We have a guest," the queen said firmly. "Bring us a tray of fruit and have a bed prepared for him. Treat our visitor exactly as you would treat me, with respect."

"Yes, Majesty." The servant blinked at the jinni and retreated.

That night the queen had her first peaceful sleep in months. The storm rolled away, and in the morning the kingdom was bathed in a gentle, sunlit mist.

When the queen went to see if the jinni was awake, she found him curled in the very center of the large bed. His wings were folded neatly behind him, and he appeared to be fast asleep. Realizing the creature must be very tired, the queen tip-toed away.

The jinni slept for three days. When he woke up, his wings had brightened and his mottled skin had taken on a healthy tinge of brown. He was given a large tray of fruit for breakfast and a cup of crystal-clear water.

After breakfast, the jinni announced that he must return to the forest. It was his home, and he must face whatever danger awaited him there.

"But it seems that they — whoever THEY are — will do you some terrible injury," said the queen. "Why else would you try so desperately to escape them? Do not leave us, forest-jinni. You can stay here for as long as you want."

The jinni shook his head. "They will never stop searching for me. Sooner or later they would come upon your peaceful kingdom and destroy it."

"Who?" the king asked, frowning. "Who are these creatures bent on destruction?"

"They are called viridees," replied the jinni. "They live deep in the forest, in the damp darkness that breeds rot and decay. They are sorcerers. They can take the shape of trees or plants or any green, growing thing, and they can live for two hundred years or more. There is great goodness in the forest; there is beauty and kindness." The jinni put his palms together, so that one hand lay on top of the other. "And then there is the other side." He turned his hands so that the upper hand lay underneath. "Where there is one, there is always its shadow."

The king and queen stared at the forest-jinni in horrified fascination, but, throwing his arms wide, the jinni said, "Don't despair. I will leave your kingdom before they can follow, and I shall give you my treasures."

"Your treasures?" said the king. Was it possible that treasures were hidden in those thin, misty garments?

The jinni looked eagerly at the queen, his eyes alight with excitement. "You are soon to have a child," he said. "It will be a boy, and you want him to be wonderful."

"Yes!" The queen clutched the edge of her seat and returned the jinni's earnest gaze. "But more than anything, I want him to be safe. I am so afraid for him. I do not know why. My fear is foolish . . . irrational."

"You can sense what might be," replied the jinni. "But I can change the future for you." From the floating folds of his robe he withdrew a length of fine, silvery gossamer. As he turned it in his hands, each tiny thread glittered with a different color. The queen caught her breath. She had never seen anything so magical.

"This was made by the last moon spider," said the jinni. "Never again will cobwebs like these adorn the forest. For the moon spiders have all gone. The evil ones realized, too late, that they had killed something that could have saved them."

"And will this protect our son?" asked the king. "He might not be the sort of boy who wants to wear a cobweb all his life."

"No need." The jinni smiled. "Wrap him in the web the moment he is born, and do not remove it until he smiles for the first time."

"Is that all?" the queen asked doubtfully. "And will he be protected from everything?"

"As long as he carries the web when he is in danger. But there is something else," the jinni said gleefully. "Your son will also be a marvelous magician. For I have splashed the web with the tears of creatures that have never been seen, and I have dipped it in dew caught on the petals of flowers that will soon disappear from the world" — he smiled, wistfully — "just like me, the last forest-jinni." He laid the shimmering silk on the queen's lap.

The queen stared at the web for a moment, unable to speak or to touch it. And then a thought occurred to her, and she said, "We have a daughter, Zobayda. Can you give her the same protection and the same gifts as our son?"

The jinni held the queen's gaze for several seconds. He appeared to be reading her future. "It is too late for Zobayda," he said at last. "A child must be touched by the web before two years have passed. But I have this." And from his garment he pulled a tiny sliver of silk. "Wind this around the princess's finger," he said, "and she will have magic at her fingertips."

It was the king who took the proffered silk from the jinni's slim hand, and as he did so, he was suddenly aware that the jinni was offering the last fragment of his own protection. The king looked at the queen and saw that she too was aware of the jinni's sacrifice. And yet, thinking of their daughter, neither of them could resist the gift. They accepted it without a word.

"There is one more thing," said the jinni and, like a conjurer, he pulled a bottle from his clothing. The glass was shaped like a bird, the liquid inside it as clear as water. The jinni told the king and queen that it was Alixir, the water of life. One drop, taken at every new moon, would halt the aging process.

No sooner had the queen taken the bottle than the jinni was gone, slipping out into the sky like a windblown leaf.

That night, while Zobayda was sleeping, the queen wrapped the piece of silk around her daughter's middle finger. Almost immediately it solidified into a beautiful silver ring. It was shaped like a wing and engraved with pearly veins. A little head could be seen, peeping out of the top, and a tiny foot protruded from the other end. It was the forest-jinni, made miniature and frozen into silver.

Before she went to bed, the queen put the moon spider's web into a deep chest. Beside it she placed the bottle of Alixir.

Three weeks later the royal baby was born. He had large, thoughtful eyes and a fine, sturdy frame. He did not make a sound when the queen wrapped him in the web. After five days, he pushed his little hands free of the silk and gave his mother a wide smile.

"A smile!" The queen lifted her baby out of his wrapping and dressed him in the scarlet robes that had been worn by generations of royal babies.

They named the baby boy Timoken, after the first ruler of the kingdom. As he grew, his parents watched him for signs of the magical gifts he was supposed to display. But Timoken seemed to be just like any other boy. Perhaps he was unusual in that he could watch falling rain for many hours, that he was entranced by dew-filled leaves, that he touched even tiny creatures with reverence, and that he listened to birdsong with a rapturous expression. When Timoken turned nine, his father gave him a pearl-handled knife. It was meant as a protection against snakes and scorpions, but Timoken often used it to carve pictures on the rocks. He could be mischievous, and he made friends easily. More than anyone else, it was his sister, Zobayda, whose company he most enjoyed. It pleased the king and queen to see their children so devoted to each other. "They will never be alone," the queen sighed happily.

Zobayda's silver ring never became too small for her. As she grew, it always fitted her finger perfectly. The queen told her that a magic being had given it to her, and that it would keep Zobayda safe forever. But the forest-jinni had never made that promise.

Meanwhile, the jinni had returned to the forest. He had nowhere else to go.

It was not long before the viridees found him. He was sitting by a pool and singing to himself. He had been expecting them.

Slowly they began to surround him. But where was the moon spider's web? They had watched from the shadows as the forest-jinni washed the web with the tears of rare creatures. They had observed the dipping of the web into dew caught in precious flowers, and they had glimpsed the bottle shaped like a bird. The jinni had filled the bottle from a pool of moonlit water, and the viridees had listened as the jinni cast a spell. But he had spoken too fast for them to understand or remember what he said.

The viridees guessed that the web was more amazing, more precious, and more powerful than anything they possessed. Of course, they wanted it. Their lord demanded it.

"Where is the web of the last moon spider?" The gurgling tone of a viridee stopped the jinni's song.

"You killed the last moon spider," said the jinni.

"What have you done with the web?"

The jinni shook his head. "You will never find it."

The viridees threw a net of creepers over the little creature. He did not resist. They took him to Degal, lord of the viridees, in his gloomy palace under the forest floor. The great hall was lit by the phosphorescent gleam of a thousand stalactites, and Degal sat on a throne carved from black marble and inset with emeralds.

"Where is it?" Lord Degal's voice burbled like the water in a deep cavern. "Where is the web of the last moon spider?"

The forest-jinni wriggled free of the net of creepers. He spread his wings as though he were about to fly, and he said, "In a place that you will never find."

Lord Degal's red eyes flashed. Pointing his rootlike finger at the forest-jinni, he cried, "You will show us where it is, or suffer unbearable tortures."

The forest-jinni hardly flinched. In his sweet, clear voice, he declared, "I am one with the web of the last moon spider. I am one with the ring made of spider silk. I am one with the boy who will live forever." Then he flapped his delicate wings and vanished.

When Timoken was eleven years old, the unthinkable happened. The secret kingdom was invaded. Ever since the forest-jinni had disappeared from their midst, the viridees had been searching for the moon spider's web and the bird-shaped bottle. Lord Degal formed an alliance with a bloodthirsty tribe from the East. In return for their help in finding the web, he promised them untold wealth and any kingdom that, together, they might defeat. And so began years of terror as small kingdoms were invaded and crushed by the murderous tribe and the powerful sorcery of the viridees.

Like a tide of darkness, Lord Degal's army emerged from the forest beyond the secret kingdom. The viridees and the tribal soldiers were dressed alike in black turbans and black tunics. They carried long, shining sabers, and their drums and horns drowned out every sound except for the trumpeting of their massive elephants. The people who lived on the outskirts of the kingdom were the first to fall beneath the long sabers. Those who survived fled, screaming, toward the palace. Behind them their houses burned and their families died.

Timoken and Zobayda heard the thunder of the advancing army. They ran up to the palace roof and saw the fires and the dark forms rushing toward them from every side.

The massive palace doors were closed and barred. Soon, a roaring crowd surrounded the building. Inside, all was silent. The king was pondering. For the first time in his life he did not know what to do. But there was only one way out of this dire situation. He would have to offer his palace and his kingdom to the invaders. In return, they must allow his people to live in peace or leave the kingdom in safety.

The children watched their noble father ride out to talk with Lord Degal. The king wore a white robe and carried a banner of peace. Degal, in deepest green, looked like the king's shadow. A large green emerald glittered in Degal's turban, and his green sash lifted in the breeze as the two horses met.

A streak of light flashed in the air above the king's head. A second later he had toppled from his horse, his head severed by Degal's shining saber.

A deep wail from below told the children what their eyes could not believe. Their father was dead. They ran, screaming, to their mother.

When the people saw their fallen king, they rushed at the enemy, waving their spears. But they were hunters, not soldiers; they were no match for Degal's brutal army.

One of the king's guards found the golden crown, lying in the dust. As he picked it up, a soldier ran at him, waving a saber. But before he was cut down, the guard threw the crown to a friend. Another soldier leaped on that man, only to see the crown, once again, tossed through the air. And so it continued, the circle of gold flying above the roaring mass of bodies, caught and passed on, until it reached one of the queen's attendants, who took it to the queen.

Her eyes clouding with tears, the queen wiped the blood and the dust from the crown and put it on her son's black curls. But the king's head had been wide and splendid, and the crown was too big for Timoken. It began to slip down over his face. Seeing the problem, Zobayda stepped forward and lifted the crown above Timoken's ears. Then she closed her eyes and uttered mysterious words in her light, breathy voice. It was almost as if she were asking a question, unsure of herself and what to expect. Under her slim fingers, the crown began to fit itself to Timoken's head, and gradually he felt himself almost to be a king. Looking at his sister's closed eyes, he whispered, "You are a faerie."

"Yes," she replied. "I believe I am."

The queen quickly gathered together a few of her children's clothes. She put them in a large goatskin bag, and then she took the moon spider's web and the Alixir from the chest and handed them to her son.

"Take great care of these," said the queen. "The bottle contains Alixir. You must both take one drop every new moon, and you will stay as you are."

Did this mean that he would not grow? Timoken was reluctant to remain a child. He wanted to be a man as soon as he could. "I don't need the Alixir," he said, frowning at the bird-shaped bottle. "I wish to grow older."

"Not yet," advised his mother. "You might be an old man before you find your new kingdom."

"Will I find a new kingdom?" asked Timoken.

"I am certain that one day you will find a home," said the queen.

"And what is this?" asked Zobayda, touching the web. "It looks like a cobweb, but it's so beautiful. Is it magic?"

"Yes," said the queen. "There's so little time to explain, my children, but it was made by the last moon spider. Keep it with you, always." She thrust it into the bag with the Alixir. "Now hurry, hurry!"

Timoken slung the bag over his shoulder. He looked bewildered. "What now?" he asked.

"Now?" said the queen. "Now you must go." She hugged her children, kissed them good-bye, and told them to leave the palace. The warlord and his soldiers were already storming through the building.

"How can we escape?" cried Zobayda. "We are surrounded."

"Come with me." The queen led her children back up to the roof. The sun blazed above their heads. Below them, the warlord's army stood in its own shadow.

"What now?" said Zobayda. "If we jump, we shall die."

"You will die if you stay, so you must fly." The queen's voice sounded almost triumphant.

Timoken sensed that his mother had been waiting a long time for this moment. "We can't fly," he said, bemused and afraid.

"I believe that you can," the queen told him, smiling. "Zobayda, put your arms around your brother and hold tight. Do not let go until you are safe."

"When shall we be safe?" begged Timoken. "Mother, what are you saying?"

"Do as I tell you," his mother commanded. "Look at the sun. Fly to it."

"I cannot," argued Timoken. "It hurts my eyes."

"Close them. Fly upward. Feel your way through the sky. You can do it, Timoken. Now!" The queen's voice began to crack with fear.

Timoken could hear soldiers running up the steps to the roof. Their weapons scraped against the walls and their rough voices echoed up the narrow stairwell. Timoken's heartbeat quickened. He could hardly breathe. Zobayda put her arms around his waist and held him tight.

"Now!" screamed the queen.

Timoken closed his eyes and turned his face up to the sun. Bending his knees a little he took a leap, just like he did when he was jumping from one of the fallen trees in the forest. Only this time he made himself believe that his feet would not touch the ground for a while. He found himself lifting into the air. The sun burned his face and he clung to his sister. They rose higher and higher.

"Timoken." He heard his mother's voice following him. "Timoken, keep your secret. Never tell . . . never let anyone know what you can do."

Timoken opened his eyes and looked down at the palace. His mother had disappeared in a sea of black. Soldiers covered the roof of the palace, their weapons glinting in the fierce sunlight.

"Zobayda, I can't see our mother!" cried Timoken.

Zobayda wouldn't look back. Tears streamed from her eyes and she buried her face in her brother's shoulder. "Mother," she murmured.

Timoken understood that they were now alone. Their lives had changed forever. But he could fly, and his sister had magic in her fingers. They would survive. He found that he could move through the air with no more than a thought in his head — a wishing.

CHAPTER 2
The Moon Spider's Web

The forest-jinni had not told the queen the whole truth. He was afraid that she would return the moon spider's web if she knew what might happen. He did not warn her that when a newborn baby had been wrapped in the web it would always have one foot in the world of men and the other in a realm of enchantments, a realm of good spirits and of others that were not so kind. Worst of all were the viridees.

As soon as Timoken left the kingdom, the viridees sensed that the web had left with him. They could smell it.

Unaware of the viridees and their malicious intent, Timoken and his sister floated through the vast sky, astonished to be so high above the earth, though their minds were clouded with the memory of their lost parents. Brother and sister could not bring themselves to speak. They drifted in silence, hour after hour, with no thought as to where they should go, or when they should touch the earth again. Their father had told them that every day the sun moved through the sky in an arc, from east to west. Beyond the African forest — north, east, and west — there was a vast desert where nothing could live. And in the south, where the sun reached its zenith, there was a world of water. Here things could live: birds, fish, and strange creatures as large as a palace.

Timoken saw that the sun was now low in the west, and so he wished himself south where, already, the night clouds were rolling in. Zobayda was so weary her arms were beginning to loosen around Timoken's waist. He had to clutch her tight, but his eyelids were drooping and he longed to close them.

Down, Timoken thought, *I must go down.* Immediately he found himself falling through the air. He could hear waves breaking below him; he could sense the swirl of a great body of water and felt something utterly unfamiliar: a cold dampness rising up to claim him. Zobayda's feet touched the water first, and she woke up.

"Timoken!" Zobayda screamed. "Leave here! Whatever lies below will kill us." She could feel icy claws clutching at her heels.

Timoken wished himself away from the fearful world of water. He felt his feet skimming the surface of the sea, but he could not rise above it. The claws were now clinging hungrily to his feet. The cold made his head spin and he could not fly anymore.

"I cannot fly!" Timoken moaned.

"You must," cried his sister. "Timoken, you MUST fly!"

Zobayda's desperate voice roused Timoken. He knew he must make an extra effort. With all the strength left in his weary head, he willed himself away from the water. There was a deep gurgle, a furious groan, and the icy claws slowly released their grip. Below the surface of the water, two giant crabs sank to the bottom of the sea.

Timoken and his sister floated across the waves until their feet touched a bank of sand. Timoken gave a happy sigh and let himself fall onto dry land. Zobayda rolled beside him and, holding hands, they fell fast asleep.

The children had fallen onto sand that was still warm from the sun. But, as midnight approached, the air began to freeze and the earth became colder and colder. The children woke up, shivering. They had left the secret kingdom in thin clothing, and had brought nothing to protect them from the cold.

Timoken frantically pulled clothes from the goatskin bag. Every garment was made of fiber spun to a fine silk. When the queen packed the bag she had been too distressed to think of chilly nights. At last, Timoken came to the moon spider's web.

To his cold hand the web felt warm and comforting. He shook it out. A huge net of sparkling strands unfurled in the air. It fell softly over the children and covered them like a blanket.

"Our mother said it was magic," said Zobayda.

Timoken regarded the gleaming folds of the web. In the very center, where the threads formed a tight net, he glimpsed an extraordinary face. It had huge saffron-colored eyes, a long nose, and a thin mouth that seemed to be smiling.

"What are you?" asked Timoken, in a whisper.

"I am the last forest-jinni," said a voice with a musical echo. "And you are my creation. Believe in yourself, Timoken. Your road is long and perilous, but keep me safe and you will survive. My gifts are many."

"What are you staring at?" asked Zobayda, sleepily. She moved her legs beneath the web and the yellow eyes wavered, then the small face vanished.

Before Timoken could explain what he had seen, he became aware that they were being watched. The sand behind them slithered and crunched and, all at once, the children were surrounded. A group of warriors stood staring down at the children. Their painted spears glistened in the moonlight, but their faces were shadowed by tall feathered hats. Timoken could see their eyes, eyes that were fearful and amazed.

The men began to murmur to one another. At first, Timoken could not understand them, and then he began to make sense of their strange, mumbled language.

"It hurts my eyes," said one.

"It burns my face," said another.

"I cannot breathe," gasped a third.

The men began to back away, but one pointed his spear toward the children. They screamed and, instinctively, pulled the web up to their chins. The man gave a savage snort and brought his spear closer to their faces. Timoken's heart hammered in his chest; he waited for the weapon to slice through his neck. But as soon as the spear touched the web, there was a bright flash. The warrior screamed in pain and leaped away, dropping his spear. "Devil children," he hissed.

At this, the group let out a wail of terror and fled. The children could hear their feet stumbling over the deep sand until they were swallowed by the great silence of the desert night.

"The web saved our lives," said Zobayda, gazing at the shining coverlet of spider silk.

"We will always be safe," said Timoken, laying his head on the sand.

This time the children slept long and deeply. They awoke to find themselves in a strange landscape of huge, rolling sand dunes. Timoken ran to the top of a dune and looked out. On every side, the desert stretched in golden folds until it reached the horizon. Nothing moved. There was not a blade of grass, not a tree, and not even the hint of a stream. The warriors' footprints had been blown away by the wind, so there was no way of knowing where they had gone. Timoken plunged down the sand dune, stumbling, falling, and laughing as his feet sank into the deep sand.

Zobayda had found food in the goatskin bag: dried fruit and meat, beans, and millet cakes. But there was nothing to drink.

"Perhaps we'll find a stream," said Timoken, "or perhaps it will rain." He chose to ignore what his father had told him — that nothing could live in the desert.

They were careful not to finish the food. It might have to last for many days. Zobayda wrapped what was left in the moon spider's web; today the web felt cool, in spite of the burning heat.

They had no idea which way to go. Zobayda suggested they fly. From high above the earth they would have a better view, and would surely see a village or a stream, or even a forest.

Timoken slung the bag over his shoulder, and Zobayda hugged his waist. Then Timoken bent his knees a little and leaped from the sand. Up and up and up. He flew north for a while, but when he looked down there was still nothing but desert far below him. He flew west and east, only to see the same barren landscape stretching on and on for miles. The heat in the upper air was making him dizzy. He could feel the skin on his face burning up. Timoken let himself fall back to earth, but before his feet touched the ground, a great bird swooped out of the sky. Its huge talons sank into Timoken's shoulders, and it began to shake him.

Timoken nearly fainted with the pain. He could hear his sister's voice, screaming at him. "The web, Timoken. Use the web!"

He put his hand into the bag, but as his fingers found the web, a voice in his head told him, *No, no, no. That's what they want. The bird will steal it.*

"The web!" Zobayda screamed again. "It will protect us!" She slid her fingers around Timoken's waist, reaching for the bag. But Timoken slapped her hand away, crying, "No, Zobayda. Not this time. The bird will steal it."

"The bird will kill us," yelled Zobayda. "What else can we do?"

"Use your fingers," Timoken croaked, weak with pain. He knew he would soon lose consciousness.

"My fingers," Zobayda murmured. Clinging to her brother with one arm, she stuck her ringed finger into the bird's feathered underside. As she did this, she chanted:

Shrivel wing.
Flap and spin.
Wither beak.
Shrink and squeak.

With a deafening screech, the bird let go of Timoken's shoulders. He opened his eyes just wide enough to see a small feathered thing, no bigger than a mouse, spinning toward the earth.

"It worked," cried Zobayda, amazed by the success of her ringed finger.

"Just in time," her brother grunted as they plummeted to earth. Distracted by the pain in his shoulders, he lost control of his flying, and they landed on the sand with an uncomfortable bump.

Zobayda sat up and held out her fingers. A tiny yellow eye, set into the silver ring, blinked at her.

"Oh!" Zobayda jumped. "The creature on my ring— it blinked."

Timoken peered at the silver wing wrapped around his sister's finger, and at the tiny head peeping above it. "Did our mother tell you about the ring?" he asked.

"She said it would keep me safe," said Zobayda.

"It is an image of the last forest-jinni," Timoken told her. "I saw him in the web."

Before they could even think of moving again they ate some dried fruit, hoping to soothe their aching throats. After their snack, they took a pair of thin tunics from the goatskin bag and wrapped them around their heads. With their heads covered, Timoken and Zobayda struck north, away from the pitiless sun. They knew, now, that they were surrounded by thousands of miles of dead earth. And yet the warriors had come from somewhere. Perhaps they lived in caves beneath the sand? Perhaps, somewhere, there were other caves, uninhabited, where fresh water dripped from the rocks, and where they could find shelter from the withering heat.

It was not long before Zobayda sank onto her knees, crying, "I am dying of thirst, Timoken. What can we do?"

Timoken's throat was so parched, he could barely reply. Did it never rain in the desert? Did the white clouds passing high above them never consider travelers in the desert, never allow a few of their millions of droplets to fall? *We shall die*, thought Timoken, *if something does not happen.*

Perhaps it was this moment that set the course of Timoken's life. He found that he could not give in. It would have been easy to lie in the sand and never wake up. But the forest-jinni had told him to believe in himself. And so he would. Human beings did not fly, but he did. What else might he be capable of? He took the moon spider's web from the goatskin bag and spread it on the ground.

"What are you doing?" croaked Zobayda. "Save your strength."

Timoken picked up a corner of the web and turned on his heel. Around and around he spun, faster and faster. The web flew out in the torrid air and a tiny breeze fanned Zobayda's cheeks. She sat up and watched her brother. How could he whirl so fast in this heat? Timoken had become a spinning pillar, the web a circling wheel of silver.

Second by second the air became fresher. Zobayda stood and held out her hands. She could feel the breeze sweeping over her hot fingers and she closed her eyes, savoring its coolness. The air was filled with a soft humming. Was it the web stirring the air, or her brother's voice?

Something touched Zobayda's upturned hand: a light droplet, and then, another. She opened her eyes. Rain fell on her head and slid down her cheeks. It splashed her blue robe and trickled into her shoes. She threw back her head and let the rain splatter into her mouth. "Timoken!" she gurgled. "You are a magician."

Laughter came flying out of the whirling figure. "Save the water, Zobayda. I can't keep spinning forever."

Zobayda emptied the goatskin bag, scattering its contents on the sand. She opened the bag as wide as she could and let the rain tumble into it. When it was half-full, she called to her brother, "Stop, Timoken, before you turn into a pillar. We have enough water for days and days. Besides, I am getting very wet."

Timoken sank to the ground. The rain thinned and pattered, and then it stopped. Timoken lay staring up at the blue sky. "I burst the clouds," he said, laughing delightedly.

Zobayda tied their belongings in a long crimson robe that their mother had packed. She put the parcel on her head and balanced it with her hand. "You can carry the water," she told Timoken.

The goatskin bag was now very heavy. Timoken tried carrying it on his head but the water slopped about uncomfortably. He would have to use his arms. Once again they headed north. After a while, a range of mountains appeared, a wavering line of blue on the far horizon.

The rain had woken hundreds of creatures that had been sleeping beneath the dry sand. Lizards scurried over the children's feet, snakes slithered around boulders, and insects of every size and color appeared in the sky. They flew in a haze around the children's heads, buzzing and clicking. The desert was no longer dead.

Small, mouselike creatures popped their heads out of the sand. They watched the children, their black eyes round with astonishment. One of them squeaked, and Timoken had a feeling that he understood the creature. He stopped, put down the water bag, and stared at the furry head.

"Timoken, come on!" called his sister. "Those ratty things are not going to tell you anything."

On the contrary, thought Timoken. He smiled at the creature, and its expression seemed to soften. It pulled itself right out of the sand and, sitting on its hind legs, it said, "Safe journey!" Or did it?

"Thank you," said Timoken.

"Timoken!"

Zobayda was now a good way ahead of her brother. But what was the use of hurrying, when you didn't know where you were going? There might be more to be gained by talking to some-one — or something — that knew the desert.

Timoken knelt beside the creature. It gazed at him in a friendly way. Its companions were emerging from the sand. They turned their heads to look at Timoken, and sniffed the air with interest.

Timoken cleared his throat and asked, "What are you?" He was surprised to hear his words emerge from his throat in a series of soft squeaks.

"We are us," said the creature.

There was no doubt about what it had said. Timoken could understand its language.

"Other things call us sand-rats," the creature went on.

"Sand-rats," Timoken repeated. "I am human. My name is Timoken." He pointed at Zobayda, who was resolutely plowing ahead. "And that is my sister."

The sand-rat looked at Zobayda. "She goes the wrong way," it said. "Do not follow."

Timoken frowned. "The wrong way? How can you tell?"

"There are bad spirits that way," squeaked the sand-rat. "Viridees."

"VIRIDEES!" echoed the other sand-rats, and suddenly they were gone. All that remained were several small mounds of sand.

"Stop, Zobayda!" called Timoken. "You are going the wrong way."

"How do you know?" she called back.

"The sand-rat told me."

Zobayda stopped. She turned and stared at her brother. "That can't be true."

"It is, Zobayda."

Timoken's sister walked toward him, slowly. "You mean you could understand their language?"

Timoken nodded. "And I could speak it. They told me that there are bad spirits the way you were going. They called them viridees."

He watched the disbelief on his sister's face turn to astonishment. "You really can talk to animals," she said, her eyes wide with awe. "What else can you do, Timoken?"

"Who knows?" Timoken grinned. He picked up the goatskin bag and balanced it firmly on his head. "Let's go east," he said, with confidence.

Zobayda saw a pale semicircle beginning to rise above the eastern dunes. She fell into step beside her brother and together they walked toward the moon.

The light had almost left the sky when they saw the THING — a dark shape on the horizon. It wavered and grew in size as it approached them. Zobayda's instinct was to turn and run, but Timoken clutched her hand, saying, "It will catch us, and then we will be too tired to fight. Besides . . ."

"Besides?" asked Zobayda.

"We do not know what it is."

They stood and waited, while the thing drew nearer. Now they could make out huge teeth, bulging eyes, and great galloping feet. It began to make a noise, a long, snorting bellow, like a creature from the underworld.

Zobayda crumpled to her knees, crying, "We should have run!"

CHAPTER 3
Sandstorm

It was a camel, an animal that Timoken had seen painted on the walls of the palace courtyard, but never in the flesh. The huge animal appeared to be angry. It was making straight for the children, its head tossing from side to side and its deafening bellows increasing as it approached. Long strands of spittle hung from its lower jaw — and those teeth! Those feet!

"Get up, Zobayda," hissed Timoken, "or you'll be trampled. We have to face this creature." He lowered the water bag to the ground and grabbed his sister's hand, pulling her to her feet.

The camel slowed its pace. It gave a throaty bleat and stepped toward the children. Zobayda peeped from behind her hand and shivered.

"Good day!" Timoken's greeting emerged as a soft version of the camel's bleat.

The camel blinked. "Gabar!" it snorted.

"Gabar," Timoken repeated. *Possibly the camel's name*, he thought.

The camel blinked again, its long, curling eyelashes fluttering like birds' wings.

Zobayda forced herself to look up at the camel's face. Compared to a horse, this creature was ugly.

Timoken noticed that an odd sort of saddle rested on the camel's hump. It was made of intricately carved wood and looked like a shallow cradle. Inside the cradle there were brightly colored cushions braided in gold and silver. The camel's harness was made of plaited leather joined with rings of gold and hung with tiny bells, and its saddle was weighted by heavy bags. So where was the camel's wealthy owner?

"Where is your master?" Timoken asked the camel.

The animal remained silent.

"Is he dead?" asked Timoken.

The camel turned its head so that one eye looked at the boy suspiciously. Timoken felt uncomfortable. If a sand-rat could understand him, why not a camel?

"Perhaps we could ride it," Zobayda suggested. "It has fine feet for walking over the sand."

How could they climb up to the camel's lofty hump? The animal was obviously in no mood to help them. It gave a long bleat and walked around the children, heading west, away from the moon.

But the moon had vanished and a dark cloud was beginning to fill the sky: a cloud that grew every second, a cloud that filled their ears with its roar and sent a torrent of sand bowling toward them across the desert floor.

"A sandstorm!" cried Zobayda. "Timoken, run!"

They ran in the camel's wake. It was galloping again, and bellowing fearfully. It had obviously been running from the sandstorm until the children had, momentarily, held it up.

The great cloud of sand was almost upon them when the camel suddenly stopped. "Behind me!" it snorted.

Timoken grabbed his sister's hand, and they stumbled to the camel. By the time they reached him, the air was thick with sand. They threw themselves onto the ground behind the great creature, and he sank to his knees. Flying sand thundered about them, stinging their eyes, filling their noses, and coating their hair.

Timoken could feel his sister struggling with her bundle of clothes. Something cool and soft touched his face, and then covered his head. *The web*, he thought.

Holding the web before her, Zobayda stood up and faced the storm. The sand rushed past the web, never touching her. Slowly, she pulled one end of the web over the camel's head, tying a corner to his harness. Only then did she duck down, bringing the other end of the web over herself and her brother.

"That was brave," Timoken whispered, still hardly daring to open his mouth.

"I had to cover the camel's face," she said, "or he would have drowned in sand."

Timoken looked up at the glittering threads above him. The sand was bouncing harmlessly off the web, as though the flimsy strands of silk were made of steel. *We're safe*, he thought drowsily. A moment before he fell asleep, he remembered that the camel had spoken.

"The camel spoke," he told his sister, "and I understood him."

Zobayda smiled. "He's not suspicious of us anymore."

All three slept. The windblown sand stormed over their heads, and the moon spider's web kept them safe and warm.

In the morning, when the children lifted the edge of the web, they saw that they were, in fact, in a hole. They were surrounded by a wall of sand. Timoken stood up. His head came to just above the top of the wall.

"We'd have been buried alive," said Zobayda, "without this." She gathered up the web, untying the corner from the camel's harness.

The camel got to his feet, grumbling and bellowing. Sand flew off his back as he shook his great head. The children worried that he would not be able to get out of the hole. But the camel set his great feet against the sloping side and climbed out with ease.

"Now us," said Timoken.

The children began to crawl their way upward, pushing the goatskin bag and the parcel of clothes before them. The wall crumbled beneath their hands and feet as they clawed and slid in the soft sand. And all the while the camel watched their progress with a superior expression; once or twice he almost seemed to smile.

It was a long time before the children finally stumbled out, dragging their possessions with them. They lay on their backs and closed their eyes against the bright sunlight, their limbs aching from the climb.

The camel suddenly gave a long, loud bellow. Timoken answered with a small sound of his own.

"What's going on?" Zobayda asked.

"He says we must move quickly," Timoken told her, "but I said we needed more time."

The camel bellowed again, and kicked up a cloud of sand. "No time," he said. "Must go. QUICK!"

"All right, all right," moaned Timoken, getting to his feet. "But we need a drink, and so do you, I'm sure."

The camel blinked. "Water? Where?"

Timoken carefully undid the goatskin bag. Water had seeped from the top, but there was still enough to drink for all three of them — depending on how much a camel needed.

Before they could stop him, the camel plunged his head into the bag and began gulping up the water in great, long drafts. A few more gulps and all the water would be gone. Timoken seized the camel's harness and tried to drag his head away. "Stop!" he cried. "You'll empty the bag, and we need a drink, too."

"Got to fill up," gurgled the camel.

"We saved your life with our magic web," Timoken protested. "This is a fine way to repay us."

The camel stepped away from the bag. He rolled his eyes and shook his head, jingling the bells on his harness. "Drink, magic children," he said, in an awestruck bleat.

Zobayda laughed. She could not understand the rumbling camel language, but she had a good idea what was going on.

When the children had sipped up the few handfuls of water that were left, Timoken tied the handles of the empty bag and slung it over his shoulder. The sun was rising fast, the heat burning their faces. He would have to bring on another rainstorm before long, but the camel was anxious to move, and how much easier it would be to travel on his back, rather than plowing over the sand or flying through the hot air. Besides, the animal seemed to know where he was going.

"Could we . . . ride on you?" Timoken asked, in what he thought was a polite sort of bleat.

"Naturally," said the camel.

Timoken stared up at the camel's hump, so far above him. "But how . . . ?"

The camel sank to his knees and grunted, "How do you think?"

The saddle looked safe and comfortable. The children climbed up and sat cross-legged among the cushions. Timoken took the reins that lay across the pommel at the front of the saddle. He gave them a little shake and the bells on the harness gave a silvery chime.

The camel got to his feet.

"Where are we going?" asked Timoken.

"No idea," came the rumbling reply.

"I thought you knew," muttered Timoken as the camel set off. Soon he was galloping. Zobayda wrapped her arms around her brother's waist while Timoken held tight to the pommel. The wooden saddle swung and bounced beneath them, and the shiny cushions slid this way and that.

After a while, a curious conversation between the boy and the camel began. Timoken learned that Gabar was indeed the camel's name. His master had been a wealthy merchant, crossing the desert to barter fine silk from the north with gold and jewels from the south.

"What happened?" asked Timoken, his voice wobbling from the jolting of the camel's long strides.

"Viridees!"

That name again. "What are viridees?"

A low rumble came from Gabar's throat. "Killers! Evil ones! They told Master to catch children. He said no. So they sent jackals to pull him off my back. They blew their foul breath in his face, and I was afraid. I ran. I am ashamed. But I knew he would die." Gabar groaned.

Timoken patted Gabar's shaggy neck. "You are not to blame."

"Next time I will not run away," said Gabar. "I was afraid when I met you, but you are my master now, and I will not let you die."

"We have no intention of dying," said Timoken. "I can perform enchantments, and my sister has magic in her fingers."

"That is why they want you," grunted Gabar.

"The viridees want US?" said Timoken.

"Both of you," said Gabar. "They search the desert. They sent the sandstorm. They killed my master. They will do anything to find you."

Timoken shuddered. He thought, *If the viridees want us, it is not only for what we can do, but what we have: the moon spider's web.*

Zobayda asked why Timoken and the camel had been bleating and grunting at each other. Timoken repeated what Gabar told him about the viridees.

"They want the web, Zobayda," said Timoken.

"And the Alixir," Zobayda reminded him. "Who would not want to live forever?"

CHAPTER 4
Voices in the Cave

Gabar carried the children to a range of mountains in the northern desert. Zobayda and Timoken were asleep, when the camel began to bellow and stamp his feet. They woke up with a start, rubbing their eyes and stretching their aching legs.

"Time to rest," grunted Gabar. He sank to his knees and the saddle tilted violently.

Luckily, Zobayda had wound a long scarf around herself and her brother, and tied the ends of the scarf to the saddle, so they would not fall out. Before they could climb down she had to untie the knots, but her fingers were stiff with cold, and she could not loosen them.

"Help me, Timoken," she demanded, "or we'll be tied to this camel forever."

Timoken was staring at the sky. Never had he seen so many stars. Their cold light fell across the desert, making the sand glitter like ice. Shivering, he helped his sister with the knots so they could climb off the camel's back.

Gabar had remembered a cave where his master used to rest. Here it was, tucked into the mountainside, a few steps up from the sand. The children clambered into the cave. Away from the chilly air, their shivering gradually subsided. Zobayda decided to unpack some of their food, but it was so dark she could not even see her own hands. Groping in her bundle she found a candle, but there was no fire to light it.

"You can bring rain; perhaps you can make fire," Zobayda said to her brother.

Timoken flexed his fingers. Making fire seemed a step too far. "It was your hand that touched my crown and made it fit," he said. "And your hand that saved us from the giant bird."

"Yes, but I don't think—"

"Try."

"Very well." Zobayda balanced the candle on the floor of the cave. She cupped the tip of the candle in her two hands and whispered to herself. Or was she speaking to the candle?

Whatever the words she used, the thin string in the lump of wax refused to respond.

"My fingers are too cold," said Zobayda.

"Don't give up," urged Timoken.

His sister bent her head. A flutter of sound came from her, a quiet song. Her cupped fingers began to glow. "Oh!" She lifted her hands and revealed a tiny flame.

"You did it!" cried Timoken.

Zobayda seemed surprised by what she had done. As the flame grew, it filled the cave with light, and she could see her ring, sparkling as never before. She was certain the little face smiled at her.

"It was the ring," she told Timoken, "not my fingers."

Gabar's master had left piles of brushwood at the back of the cave, ready for his next visit. Timoken quickly gathered some up and lit a fire with the candle. Warmth spread through the children's bodies. Sitting close to the fire, they ate all the dried meat they had left. Now there were only millet cakes and beans. They wondered how long these would have to last.

There was a bag of grain behind the brushwood. For the camel, guessed Timoken. He carried it out to Gabar, who was sitting alone in the cold desert.

Gabar grunted his thanks and began to munch, while Timoken undid the saddle and lifted the heavy bags off the camel's back.

"In the morning, I will make rain," Timoken told Gabar, "and you will drink."

Gabar gave a snort. "Really?"

"You'll see," said Timoken. "Good night, Gabar."

Zobayda had spread a blanket of clothes on the cave floor and the children lay down, pulling the web on top of themselves. In no time at all they were asleep.

An hour later Timoken woke up. The fire was only a pile of embers, and its flickering light cast long shadows over the cave walls. As Timoken stared at the shadows he could see that they were, in fact, long, flowing lines. Were they letters, or pictures?

Timoken sat up. The shadows held voices. He stood and approached the wall. He touched the rough surface and felt the rock throb, as though it were alive.

"Who are you?" Timoken whispered.

A thousand voices rushed out at him. He couldn't tell one voice from another, there was such a babel of sound. He glanced at Zobayda, expecting her to leap up in fright. But she slept on, oblivious to the noise.

Gradually, Timoken began to make out the different voices. He found that he could listen to one and block out the rest. The owner of the first voice described a fine city where he lived with his wife and ten children; the next spoke of a market where gold and silver trinkets, exotic fruit, and rolls of cloth lay on tables, shaded from the sun by canopies of hide; another voice told of wolves in a dark forest; another of his escape from a giant sea creature that swallowed his boat.

Timoken realized that the voices belonged to travelers who had rested in the cave and written about their lives on the cave wall. Somehow the voices of those travelers had reached Timoken through the marks on the rock. He was excited by the notion that he could tell his own story to future travelers, and he took out the pearl-handled knife his father had given him and began to carve pictures into the rocky wall.

He had hardly begun his story when he became aware of another presence in the cave. Someone was watching him. He felt that the images he carved were spinning forward, traveling beyond him as he scrawled and scraped in the firelit cave. His spidery lines were reaching through the years; a message sent into the future to someone he would never know.

But suddenly there he was, staring out from the cave wall: a boy of thirteen or fourteen, with skin paler than Timoken's, and lively brown eyes. His dark hair was thick and unruly, his smile irresistible. Timoken smiled back.

The boy was wearing unusual clothing: a red garment

stretched tight across his body, and dirty trousers of some rough blue material.

"There you are!" The boy's voice was so clear that Timoken had to take a step back. He found that he could understand the boy, even though he spoke a foreign language.

After a moment's hesitation, Timoken asked, "Who are you?"

What was that? Did the boy say "Charlee"? A difficult name.

Timoken frowned. "Where are you?"

"I'm here," the boy replied. "I couldn't believe that this would happen."

"It is astonishing," Timoken agreed.

"I've tried so many times to reach you," the boy went on, "but always that other one has stopped me. Now, at last, he's gone."

"Who?"

"You must know. But then, perhaps you haven't met him yet. I can see that you are only ten or eleven years old."

"I am eleven," said Timoken. "Tell me, who is 'that other one'?"

"The shadow. Hark—"

A cry from Zobayda cut through the boy's next words.

"Timoken, you're talking to a wall," said Zobayda, rubbing her eyes. "Are you sleepwalking?"

"No," Timoken retorted, staring at the wall. The boy had disappeared. "I wish you hadn't done that."

"What?"

"You broke the link."

Zobayda yawned. "You're not making sense."

Timoken remained staring at the wall. He studied each line, hoping for the boy to return. But he never reappeared. At length, cold and shivering, Timoken slipped under the web and lay beside his sister. He wanted to tell her about the boy and the voices, but did not know how. He could not even begin to describe the emotion that had gripped him when he saw the boy's smiling face.

"What is it, Timoken?" murmured Zobayda. "Something is troubling you."

"I'm not troubled. I'm . . . I don't know. I heard voices coming from the cave wall, hundreds of them. And then I saw a boy. I think he is special to me. It sounds odd, and you probably don't believe me."

"I can believe almost anything of you, my brother," Zobayda mumbled sleepily.

In the morning, Timoken spun on the sand, whirling the web in the dawn air, and rain fell, just as he had predicted. The goatskin bag was filled with water and offered to Gabar. The camel showed no surprise. He emptied the bag, belched, and asked for breakfast.

"I'm sure you've never seen anyone else bring rain like that?" Timoken said to the slightly ungrateful camel.

"You are a rare human," Gabar replied, munching his breakfast grain. "And that is that." The camel had obviously ceased to be amazed by human behavior.

Timoken heaved the heavy saddle onto the camel's back, but before they replaced the merchant's bags, Zobayda wanted to know what they contained. Opening the first bag they discovered dried fruit and meat, and more grain for the camel. The second bag was packed with rolls of silk; the third was by far the heaviest, and it was difficult to open. When the children finally managed to untie its leather strings, they found another bag inside it, and another inside that, and then a fourth.

The stiff leather hide cut their fingers, and Zobayda would have given up, but Timoken was, by now, impatient to find out what lay inside such well-protected bags. He used his pearl-handled knife to cut through the leather, and the last bag fell open. A long, carved-ivory chest was revealed, the lid secured with a golden clasp. Carefully, Timoken undid the clasp and lifted the lid.

The brightness that lay within the chest caused Zobayda to reel back with a gasp. Timoken gazed, unable to believe his eyes.

The chest was filled with precious jewels: gold bangles, necklaces, strings of rubies and pearls, diamond rings, and emerald clasps all lay heaped together in a glittering mass.

"Gabar's master was more than a merchant," Timoken murmured. "He must have been a prince."

"We are rich," breathed Zobayda.

Why did the viridees ignore this chest? Timoken wondered. He asked the camel for his opinion.

"They don't need human treasure," Gabar replied.

"But they want what we have," said Timoken. "They want it so badly that they sent a sandstorm, and they killed your master for refusing to help them."

The camel grunted his agreement.

Zobayda took a handful of jewels from the chest before they closed it. "It will pay for our suppers when the food runs out," she said.

As long as we can find an honorable tradesman, thought Timoken.

With some difficulty, they managed to tie the chest into the three bags, but Timoken had cut the strings of the fourth, so they had to leave it open.

When all the bags were secured, the children climbed onto Gabar's back. Zobayda wrapped the scarf around herself and her brother, and tied the ends to the saddle. Timoken shook the reins and the camel stood up. It was up to him now. He had crossed the desert many times; he knew the trade routes. Timoken asked Gabar to take them to the nearest habitation.

"And what will you do there?" Gabar inquired.

Timoken did not know how to answer. "What will we do when we find a village, or a city?" he asked his sister.

Zobayda had no doubts. "If we like it, we shall make our home there."

"And if we don't like it?"

"Then we shall move on," Zobayda said cheerfully. "And one day we will find a home."

"But not a mother, not a father."

Zobayda was silent for a moment, and then she said quietly, "It's just you and me now, Timoken."

"And Gabar," said her brother.

"If you can count a camel as family."

"Three is better than two," said Timoken.

And so they began the long, long journey across the desert. Sometimes they would come upon a group of nomads traveling with their goats. The strangers would eye the children with suspicion. What were they doing, all alone, on a camel decked out in finery? And then they would remember that the desert was full of tricks: phantom voices, wavering lights, and often a mirage of trees and water. And the nomads would begin to smile, believing the children must be a sign, sent from a star, to bring good luck.

One night, as the children lay in the shelter of an outcrop of rocks, Timoken gazed up into the sky and saw a narrow sliver of light slicing the velvet darkness. "The new moon," he exclaimed. "Remember what our mother said?"

Zobayda lit a candle and searched the bundle of possessions. When she found the bottle of Alixir, she poured one drop onto her finger and licked it. She put another onto Timoken's finger, and he did the same.

"And now Gabar," said Timoken.

Zobayda frowned. "Why?"

"Who knows how long the journey will take? We don't want our camel to grow old before we find a home."

"This liquid is precious," she argued. "It should not be wasted on a camel."

"Gabar is precious," Timoken insisted. Seizing the bottle, he took it over to the camel.

Gabar appeared to be dozing. He half-opened one large eye when Timoken approached.

"Gabar, I wish to put something on your tongue," said Timoken.

The camel was silent. His mouth remained closed.

"See, he doesn't want it," Zobayda called.

Timoken ignored her. "Gabar, open your mouth."

The camel shifted his leathery knees. "Why?"

"I want to put the smallest drop, the tiniest speck . . . a driblet, a dot, if you like . . ."

"What is it?" asked Gabar.

"A liquid that will stop you from growing old," said Timoken.

"I shall never be old," said the camel. "There are old camels and young camels. I am young and will always be so."

Timoken scratched his head. It seemed that aging did not enter a camel's field of understanding. "Perhaps you could open your mouth, just for me?" said Timoken.

Without another word — or even a grunt — Gabar obediently opened his mouth.

Timoken stared at the huge teeth jutting out of the shadowy hole that was the camel's mouth. He tilted the bottle and let a drop fall on the camel's tongue, and then, because it was dark and his hand was unsteady, a second droplet slipped out.

The next day the camel seemed to have an extra spring in his step, but the Alixir appeared to have had no other effect on him.

Little by little their surroundings were changing. Almost without noticing it, they had left the barren desert and were traveling through a landscape dotted with clumps of grass and low, windblown shrubs.

As evening approached, Timoken saw a cluster of white buildings on the horizon. Both children had the same thought. Could this be their new home? They were so tired. Their minds were bruised by the punishing sweep of the brown desert, their eyes sore from the relentless sun, and their limbs aching from days in the camel saddle. They thought of the fountains in the secret kingdom, the breeze from feathered fans, and their mother's gentle hands.

Full of hope, Timoken urged the camel toward the town.

Gabar gave a nervous grunt. "I do not know this place."

"Nor do we," said Timoken, "but we are eager to find out what sort of place it is. Perhaps it could be our new home."

It had once been a fine town, but the wall that had protected it had crumbled away. Great stones lay buried in the sand, and wind had ravaged the place. Doors had caved in, roofs had collapsed, and piles of sand lined the streets.

There were plenty of people about, however, and in the center of the town they came upon a market square filled with stalls. Goats, donkeys, and camels nosed at the earth for scraps. Many of the animals were pitifully thin, their flanks scarred by constant beatings.

"Bad place," Gabar snorted. "Let us go!"

Timoken thought of the pitiless desert. He longed to sleep beneath a roof, to speak to a kind family. But there was no friendship in the glances that were thrown at them. He could see only suspicion and hostility.

"There will be another place," Zobayda whispered, "a better place than this."

Timoken nodded. "Let us leave," he grunted to the camel.

Gabar needed no encouragement. With a toss of his head, he whirled around and made for a street leading out of the square.

A loud voice called out. The language was strange, the sound deep and burbling. Timoken could make no sense of it. Other voices followed, and a group of figures ran out and barred the camel's way. Timoken clutched the reins; he was beginning to understand that these were not men. They were creatures, green and sinewy.

"Viridees!" said Gabar, snorting with fury. He shook off one of the creatures that had grabbed his harness, and bolted past him. The creature fell, screaming. Others yelled their fury. Gabar raced down a narrow alley, while the crowd of viridees roared behind him. A wall loomed at the far end of the street.

"We're caught!" cried Zobayda. "There's only one way out. Timoken, we must fly!"

"Not without Gabar," Timoken said grimly.

Zobayda screamed, "Camels can't fly!"

"Who knows?" Timoken spoke through gritted teeth.

"He's too heavy. We must leave him. They'll kill us, Timoken. I can see it in their eyes."

"I will not leave our camel in this miserable place!" Timoken shouted. "But I will have to lighten his load." He took out his pearl-handled knife and slashed at the strings that held the heavy bag of treasure. It crashed to the ground, and some of the viridees gathered around it, tearing at the straps. Others, however, were still intent on catching the children.

"Wall!" bellowed Gabar. "No way out."

Timoken leaned over the camel's neck. In a quiet, firm voice, he said, "Jump, Gabar, and you will fly."

"Camels do not fly," Gabar snorted.

"Believe me, you can," said Timoken.

"Then I will believe!"

The camel's trust in him was unexpected. Timoken had hardly believed his own words. Now he must make them come true. But what an absurd idea this was. How could he carry a camel into the sky?

The wall was now only a few yards away. Timoken closed his eyes. With one hand, he held the reins tight against his chest.

He could feel the wild thumping of his heart, and he trembled. He leaned down and, with his free hand, grabbed a tuft of the camel's shaggy hair. With his mind and with his soul, he leaped for the sky.

The pull of gravity was immense. It took his breath away. It dragged at his body and thundered in his scalp. *Up! Up!* He felt his lungs would burst and his body break apart. But just when he began to think that he had tested his power too far, the camel's jolting stride changed into an unfamiliar swaying motion. The saddle stopped sliding. Timoken opened his eyes. He could see nothing but sky.

Not a sound escaped from Gabar. He appeared to have stopped breathing. Zobayda seemed too surprised to speak. Every ounce of Timoken's strength had left him. He was content to sail through the sky in a stupefied silence.

The blistering sun dropped below the horizon; the sky became a dark velvet blue. A gentle warmth brushed Timoken's face, and a passing bird called out at the astonishing sight of a camel in the air.

CHAPTER 5
The Ring

A wonderful adventure had begun. For more than a hundred years, Timoken and Zobayda roamed through the cities of Northern Africa. With her enchanted fingers, Zobayda multiplied the jewels they had saved from the treasure chest, and so they never went hungry, nor did Gabar.

The camel was not always obedient, however. Sometimes he did not want to fly. It was undignified, he said, to fly in front of other camels. They were not impressed to see one of their number in the air. It was not a camel-like thing to do. This complicated life for the children. Very often, flying was their only means of escape.

Exploring was fun, but there was danger everywhere for two children traveling alone, two children who traded shells and precious gems for food and clothing. They were frequently set upon by bandits and chased by kidnappers, and they only narrowly avoided the knives that were hurled at them. And then there were the viridees, hiding behind trees, in wells and caves and other shadowy places. They would rush out at the children, long arms grabbing, tongues lashing.

And Timoken would cry, "Fly, Gabar, fly!" pulling on the reins and tugging the hair on the camel's neck.

Gabar would glance about him, making sure that no other camels were watching. If there was even one anywhere near him, he would snort, "Not yet!" And the children would have to wait, breathlessly, until the camel allowed himself to be lifted aloft.

Every night, Timoken and Zobayda slept beneath the moon spider's web. They called it the moon cloak and knew they were safe beneath its silken threads. If ever they were caught without it, Zobayda would use her enchanted fingers to escape. She could shrivel, burn, and tear, and if anyone grabbed Timoken or Gabar, she only had to point her fingers at the would-be captor and he would let go, screaming with fear and pain.

Not everyone was cruel. Kindness was often shown to the children. They would be given a meal for no reward and a safe bed in a house of great warmth and friendliness. And the orphaned children would begin to think of making a home in the city. But the very next day they could be chased and tormented, and they would have to forget their dream.

"We will never find a home in these heartless cities," Zobayda said one day. "I'm so tired of flying away, my heart throbbing and my breath caught in my throat."

Timoken looked at his sister, still only thirteen years old after more than a hundred years of traveling. He regarded his own small fingers and said, "If we had grown like ordinary people, they would leave us alone."

Zobayda shook her head. "Remember what our mother said. We mustn't start to grow until we find a real home." She spoke so sternly Timoken couldn't argue.

They decided to avoid the cities for a while, and traveled through the rough scrubland that bordered the desert. The nomad tribes had taught them how to bind their heads and faces with cloth to protect them from sandstorms, and they had learned how to survive the heat and discomfort. They often came within sight of a forest, but, although Gabar would go as far as the streams that trickled from the trees, he would go no farther. He was afraid of the darkness, the fleeting shadows, and the eerie sounds of birds and monkeys. Perhaps he sensed the strong presence of the viridees.

The viridees never lost track of Timoken and his sister. They tried every trick they knew to steal the moon cloak. They bribed merchants, beggars, and even beasts to destroy the children, but the moon cloak had a power of its own, and all their efforts failed.

Lord Degal had an idea. If the girl could be prevented from using her fingers, she could be captured. And for her safe return, surely the boy would hand over the web and the bottle.

"It is her ring," said Lord Degal. "That is what protects her. We must steal the ring."

He called for his best singer, a viridee whose voice could not be resisted. Lord Degal told the singer to practice the sweet tones of a bubbling stream.

Then, one achingly hot and tiring day, Timoken managed to urge the reluctant Gabar farther into the cool shade of a forest. The viridees were delighted. The singer could now lure Zobayda toward a stream. There she would dip her hands, attracted by a gleam beneath the water, something pretty — flowers like diamonds or pebbles like pearls. As soon as her fingers were underwater, a viridee could draw off the ring, rendering her fingers harmless.

And then we can catch her, they whispered with a chuckle.

After a night in the forest, the children were eating by their fire when Zobayda gave a little start, as though a mouse had run across her knees.

"What is it?" asked Timoken, licking his fingers.

"I felt something." Zobayda clutched her ringed finger. The ring seemed heavier today, and the little face looked anxious. Zobayda sensed that it was trying to warn her. "Timoken, you must never speak of your powers, never. No one must know that you can fly, that you can speak to animals and change the weather . . . no one."

"But some are bound to guess. They have seen us flying on Gabar."

"True," Zobayda murmured. Her dark eyes looked distant, and her next words were spoken as though she were receiving them from someone else. "You must not use your powers unless there is no other way."

In spite of the fire, Timoken felt suddenly chilled. His sister's tone was so solemn.

"But why?" he said.

Zobayda gave her brother a wide smile. "Don't worry, little brother. I know you will do your best to keep your secrets. Your place in the world is already foretold."

What did she mean? Timoken shivered with apprehension. He stared into the small flames, willing them to cheer him. "What do you mean?" he whispered to his sister.

"I hardly know myself." Zobayda stood up and brushed the

creases from her robe. "It is just a sense I have. I'm going to fetch some fresh water. I can hear such a sparkling, rushing stream." She turned a full circle, gazing through the trees. "It's some-where very near."

"Let me come," said Timoken.

"No. I can find it." She picked up their small clay jar and ran through the trees.

A little way off, Gabar had been standing in grumpy silence. Now he gave a loud grunt, and then another, and another.

"What's the matter?" called Timoken.

"Bad," said Gabar. "Worse and worse. Don't like forests."

All at once, Timoken agreed with him. "I'm sorry," he said. "We'll leave this forest when Zobayda gets back."

Zobayda followed the sound of the stream. It made an enchanting tinkle, almost like music. She had an overwhelm-ing thirst now, and longed to feel the trickle of water over her tongue.

The stream, when she found it, was all she could have wished for. It bubbled and rushed over glistening pebbles, deep in one place, wide and gleaming in another. She ran beside it, farther and farther, drawn toward an even greater sound: the thunder of a waterfall. Before she reached the falls, she stopped at a shal-low pool. She could see a bright sparkle under the swaying riverweeds, so bright it must be something precious. She knelt on a flat black rock beside the water and put out her hand. A sharp pain traveled up her arm. If she had looked at her ring she would have seen a grimace of fear on the small face, its mouth wide open, its eyes shut tight.

"No, no, no," came a tiny whisper.

Zobayda heard nothing but the pounding of the falls. Ignoring the pain, she dipped her hand in the water, reaching for that captivating sparkle. But as her fingers felt their way through the water, the weeds began to wrap themselves around her hand. They clasped her wrist, her arm. She put in her other hand to rescue the first, but that too was gripped by the dark weeds, and Zobayda cried out as the ring was slowly, very slowly, dragged from her finger.

As soon as the ring was gone, Zobayda's arms were released and she fell back on the rock. When she got to her feet and turned to run, she was certain that the trees behind her had moved closer. She stood, unsure, on the rock. The trees began to bend and twist, snakelike. They dipped and shivered and became tall green forms. The forms moved closer and closer. Zobayda could see the hint of a red eye, and then another. She saw arms, like vines, rippling beneath the shining leaves, and she guessed what those wicked forms wanted.

"You mean to exchange me for the moon cloak!" Her voice shook, but it carried, loud and fierce, above the noise of the falls. "And that you will never do."

The viridees stretched their sinewy green arms toward her, and Zobayda backed up to the very edge of the flat black rock. "The moon cloak belongs to my brother," she cried. "And it always will!" And turning swiftly, she jumped.

Burbling triumphantly, the viridees watched her black hair floating in a circle of silvery bubbles, as the current dragged her to the roaring falls. And then she was gone.

Timoken paced around the dead embers of the fire. The sun was rising; the forest was already steaming with damp heat. The sound of birds and beasts grew louder. Where was Zobayda? She had been gone far too long.

"I'm going to find my sister," Timoken told the camel. Draping the moon cloak around his shoulders, he set off.

Gabar would not be left on his own. He followed Timoken through the trees. The camel's feet moved awkwardly over the forest floor; he stumbled on creepers and leaves, and twigs kept entangling his head. He grunted unhappily.

Ignoring the camel's distress, Timoken bounded toward the sound of water. He found the stream and began to follow it. The stream became a river, and Timoken heard the roar of a waterfall. He halted and called his sister's name, but he found that his throat was choked with dread. Moving slowly now, he came to the flat black rock. He knew, somehow, that Zobayda had been standing there. He could almost see her.

Timoken walked to the edge of the rock. His hands were shaking, and the sound of his heart drummed in his ears. What had happened here? He knelt at the edge of the rock. Beneath his hands, the rock told its story. Zobayda's feet had been planted on its wet black surface. And then they had gone. They had leaped into the fast-flowing river. Why?

Timoken peered into the weeds that writhed under the surface of the water. Something shone there, on a narrow ledge that jutted from beneath the rock. Sweeping his hand across the ledge, Timoken touched a small object. When he brought it out, he found himself looking at Zobayda's ring. The forest-jinni's face was contorted with remorse.

"I could not stop them," came the whisper.

Tears of anger welled in Timoken's eyes. "Who?" he demanded.

A featherlight sound came from the ring. "Viridees."

That name again.

"Why?" roared Timoken. "Why her and not me?" He closed his fist around the ring and made to hurl it into the river.

"No-o-o-o!" screamed the ring.

Timoken gritted his teeth and growled, "Why should I keep you? You couldn't save my sister." He opened his fist, expecting the ring to drop into the torrent. But the ring clung to his finger and its voice carried, clear as a bell, over the roar of water.

"I tried to save her, Timoken. But they were too strong. I wouldn't let them take me, though. I belong to you, now."

"You're no use to me," cried Timoken, shaking his hand, trying to rid himself of the ring.

"You'll see! You'll see!" wailed the little voice.

There was a sudden rush of sound behind Timoken. It was as if every creature in the forest were echoing the words of the ring. *You'll see! You'll see! You'll see!*

"Keep me! Keep me!" cried the ring.

And a thousand chattering, screeching, howling voices chanted, *Keep the ring! Keep the ring!*

Timoken's hand dropped to his side. He turned and looked at the forest in astonishment. "Did you hear that?" he asked the camel.

"Keep the ring," Gabar advised.

Timoken muttered, "I suppose I will."

He slipped the ring on the middle finger of his left hand. An expression of weary relief appeared on the little face. Gently, it closed its eyes.

Timoken stepped off the black rock and leaned his head against Gabar's shaggy neck. "What shall we do without her?" he sobbed.

Gabar did not entirely understand human emotion, and yet Timoken's grief-stricken sounds echoed deep inside the camel and, to his surprise, he felt a tear trickling from one of his large eyes. Nevertheless, he had his own interests at heart. "We should leave the forest," he snorted.

"Not yet," sobbed Timoken. "Not yet." For, in the secret kingdom, those who grieved went into the forest and there they stayed until the grieving was over. That could be any time between one year and ten.

Wiping his eyes, Timoken began to stumble through the trees. Gabar followed obediently. They walked until nightfall, Timoken unable to stem the tears that streamed down his face. He could not rest. He could not eat or drink. Grief sat on his shoulders like a flat black rock, and he couldn't escape it.

They walked through the night. The cloud bats that Timoken had once found so entrancing, now seen through swollen eyes, appeared as insubstantial as floating dust. The calls of the owls that he had once listened to with such delight now sounded no more than a muttering of leaves.

They walked until dawn. As light and birdsong began to fill the forest, Timoken became aware that something was wrong. He looked over his shoulder.

Gabar was not there.

C H A P T E R 6
The Hunter

"GABAR!" Timoken's desperate voice lifted through the trees, and anxious monkeys leaped along the branches.

"Help me!" Timoken called up to them. "Help me find him!"

His grief forgotten, Timoken was like a creature launched from a spring. Bounding and flying through the trees, he called to his camel, the only family he had left.

Birds and monkeys took up the call. "Gabar! Gabar! Gabar!"

The answering grunt that Timoken longed for didn't come. It wasn't until nightfall that a weary, reluctant sound drifted toward him.

The camel was sitting in a patch of moonlight. When Timoken approached, Gabar batted his long eyelashes, but gave no hint that he was pleased to see the boy.

"Gabar, are you ill?" Timoken sat beside the camel and patted his neck.

Gabar chewed on a thick leaf. He didn't like the flavor, but everything in the forest tasted bitter. "My head throbs," he said, "my stomach churns, and my feet hurt."

Timoken sighed. "I'm sorry, Gabar."

"Sorry?" queried the camel.

"I am sad for you," explained Timoken.

"No," said the camel. "You are sad for your sister who is gone. But you are not sad for me. If you were, you would leave the forest."

"I can't," moaned Timoken. "It is the custom of my people to grieve in the forest. I can't leave just yet. I am grieving for my sister."

"Custom?" snorted Gabar. He got to his feet. "It is my custom to walk on sand, and so I shall leave you and find the desert." He began to walk away.

"Gabar, no," wailed Timoken, running beside the camel. "Please stay with me."

"If I stay here, I shall die," Gabar snorted.

"You are my family," cried Timoken. "I thought I was yours."

"Good-bye, Family," said the camel.

Timoken realized that he had no choice. If he didn't want to be alone he would have to follow Gabar. All the camel's senses were leading him back to the world he knew. Timoken promised himself that he would grieve for his sister another time. "I will never forget you, Zobayda," he muttered. "But Gabar is all the family I have."

The forest was beginning to thin. The heat of the sun intensified. Soon they would be out of the trees. The animal noises were changing. Not so many monkeys here, not so many birds. Even so, the silence, when it came, was very sudden.

Timoken was aware of a sound slicing through the air above his head, so fast it could hardly be heard. There was a strangled roar of pain and then a profound hush.

The forest held its breath, and the skin of Timoken's neck prickled with fear. Caught in the silence of the trees, he could hardly breathe. All at once, he was running. The camel trotted after him.

They came to a clearing and Timoken scanned the undergrowth. Was it here? Was this where he was meant to come? That muffled, desperate roar had led him here. Or was it fate? A movement caught his eye, in the shadows behind the sunlit trees.

Timoken gasped. The rotting branch resting against a tree was, in fact, a creature. Tall and reed-thin, its green hair dangled in vinelike strands over its slimy body. A quiver of arrows hung from the belt around its waist, and its rootlike fingers rested on the end of a large bow. A viridee.

Sounds reached Timoken at last. The forest had woken from its trance. He could hear snarls and whimpers and the crunch of bones. Behind the viridee hunter, a pack of hyenas was tearing at the carcass of a small gazelle.

Timoken felt the viridee's gaze upon him. Its eyes were red, like embers without the black dot of a pupil, without a heart. Pitiless, they bored into his very bones.

Timoken took a step back and, as he did so, he glimpsed another body. A female leopard lying on her side. There was an arrow sticking out of her neck, the tip deeply embedded. The leopard's eyes were glazed. She was obviously dead.

Anger and disgust made Timoken's stomach lurch. The hunter had killed the leopard, and yet he was prepared to let hyenas eat the leopard's prey. One of the animals carried a piece of meat to the hunter, but the tall green figure did not take it. Still gazing at Timoken, he caressed the hyena's head.

This was no place for Timoken. The hyenas repelled him,

and the rotting green figure gave off an overpowering scent of evil. The boy turned his back and began to run.

With the dreadful scene still burning in his mind, Timoken was blind to the creeper strung across his path. He tripped and fell, landing in a tangle of undergrowth. There was a weak hiss, and a tiny growl. Timoken turned his head and looked into the eyes of three small leopard cubs. They were huddled together behind a tangle of vines hanging from a fallen tree, only an arm's length from his face.

The cubs gave tiny defiant cries and, instinctively, Timoken put out a warning hand. "Hush!" He used a leopard's voice. "You are safe!"

The cubs stared at him with troubled eyes and then, one by one, approached and rubbed their heads against his cheeks. As Timoken stroked their dappled fur, he was consumed by a rage that he had never known. He felt it almost before he knew the reason for it.

These small cubs would soon die. Without their mother, they were helpless. She had been carrying the dead gazelle when she was shot. And it was her prey that the hyenas were gorging on.

Timoken pulled the moon cloak from his shoulders and wrapped it around the cubs. They gazed at him, but did not attempt to shake off the web. Their wide gray eyes followed the boy as he stood and took out his pearl-handled knife.

"What are you doing, Family?" Gabar asked nervously.

"Shh!" warned Timoken. "I am going to get some meat."

"I hope not," grunted Gabar.

"Shh!" Rage filled Timoken's throat.

Gabar had never known the boy to use this kind of voice. Never. The sound puzzled him. Afraid of what would happen next, the camel fell silent. Motionless, he watched the boy creep soundlessly through the trees, back to the hideous scene he had just fled.

The viridee had already seen him. Red eyes marked the boy's movements as he stepped into the glade. Two of the hyenas looked up from their feast and snarled. Facing those long teeth, Timoken knew his little knife could not protect him. But he did not lower it, and he did not stop or back away. The hyenas were all looking at him now, their snarls and screams filling the air.

Timoken began to speak. He hardly knew where the words were coming from, but he was aware that he was using the voice of an animal. He spoke of the hyenas' children, of horrible pain, of the end of life.

The hyenas lowered their heads. Meat slid from their bloody jaws and their snarls turned to whimpers. Timoken stepped closer. Any fear he might have felt had been replaced by his unflinching will. All at once, to his astonishment, the whole pack turned their backs and ran, whining, into the trees.

But the hunter stayed where he was, red eyes flashing. With one fluid movement, his long fingers reached for an arrow.

For a fraction of a second Timoken was afraid. Could he grab the gazelle before the arrow reached him? As the hunter lifted his bow, the boy had his answer. Pointing his ringed finger at the treetops, he cried to the sky.

The answering crack of thunder startled the hunter, but it did not deter him. He fitted the arrow to his bow and drew it back. The second crack of thunder came with a blinding flash. A shaft of lightning struck the tree beside the viridee. Before he could move, the tree crashed to the ground, crushing the viridee beneath its flaming branches.

Fire snaked along the fallen tree and crackled in the undergrowth. Seizing the gazelle carcass, Timoken carried it through the forest, while the fire snapped and hissed behind him. He heaved the length of meat toward the cubs' hiding place and laid it before them. Three small heads appeared between the hanging creepers. Cautiously, the cubs crept from beneath the moon cloak and sniffed the meat. Excited by the smell, they began to eat: tearing, chewing, and whimpering with hunger and delight.

"Look! Look, Gabar," Timoken said joyfully. "I got the meat. I've fed them, and they will live!"

Gabar had taken several paces away from the scene. What he saw worried him. He had never liked the smell of raw meat, and it unsettled him to see these three dangerous creatures tearing at it.

"Aren't you proud of me, Gabar?" Timoken asked. "I wish you had seen those hyenas slink away."

"There is a fire," the camel grunted. "Soon we will all be burned to death."

Timoken leaped up with a gasp. "I forgot!" Seizing the moon cloak, he whirled it in an arc above his head, again and again. His calls rose through the forest, and the rain answered him. It poured through the leaves and splashed against the trees, extinguishing the fire in seconds.

Timoken wrapped the moon cloak around his wet shoulders and laughed with pleasure. The rain stopped, but the cubs, now wet through, continued to eat. Even when their bellies were full they went on gnawing, their fear of hunger driving them on. When their sleepy eyes began to close, Timoken pushed the carcass into the hollow beneath the tree, and the cubs crawled in after it. In a few minutes they were fast asleep. Timoken covered them with the moon cloak and went in search of Gabar, who had wandered off.

He found the camel drinking from a stream. Timoken untied the bag of food hanging from the saddle, and pulled out some millet cakes.

Gabar turned his head and looked at the boy. "You will have to kill," the camel said. "Those cubs will grow. They'll eat you and me, unless you feed them."

"I'll steal more carcasses," said Timoken. "I'm not afraid of hyenas."

"Hmf!" The camel chewed a long twig. "It won't be enough. And what about milk?"

"Milk?" Timoken looked at Gabar. "Do you mean . . . ?"

"Don't look at me," said Gabar. "I shall never be a mother."

"But those cubs might need someone's mother, that's what you're saying. They might need milk as well as food."

The camel blinked in agreement.

"I will find a goat," Timoken said blithely. "There's bound to be a goat somewhere."

Unconvinced, Gabar pursed his rubbery lips.

While the cubs slept, Timoken lay on the fallen tree above them. In more than a hundred years of traveling he had never saved a life. The experience had changed him. If he had lived like an ordinary mortal, he would be dead by now. And so, it followed, would the cubs. Fate had brought them together, and now he felt bound to the small creatures he had saved. "Forever," he murmured to himself.

Timoken closed his eyes and began to devise a way to carry the cubs. Nomads had given him a small bag for water, and now the big goatskin bag hung empty from the saddle. The cubs could be carried in it.

Timoken chewed a millet cake and then drifted off to sleep. He woke up to find Gabar's nose in his face.

"Family," said the camel, "you have forgotten something."

"What?" Timoken answered drowsily.

"You never sleep without a cover. The viridees will come back. The forest is not safe."

Timoken smiled. "You are right. But first, the cubs." He lifted the curtain of creepers and looked into the dark hollow where they slept.

The moon cloak now covered the cubs completely. It had wrapped itself around them, and billowed gently with their heartbeats. The shining threads seemed to embrace the cubs, as though the web was claiming them for its own. One cub lay on his back; the others were curled on each side of him, their heads pressed against his. Seen through the veil of spider silk, the markings on their fur appeared like a scattering of stars.

Timoken drew in his breath and sat back.

"What?" asked Gabar.

"They have become . . ." Timoken didn't know how to describe what he saw to the camel.

Gabar waited patiently for the rest of Timoken's answer.

"Enchanted," said Timoken, hoping that the camel would understand.

He did.

CHAPTER 7
Sun Cat, Flame Chin, and Star

There were five of them now. "A family of five," Timoken liked to say. But the camel did not agree. He was not entirely comfortable when the leopards were close.

They were traveling through grassland, country that was neither forest nor desert. Gabar was happy on the dry, flat earth. There were water holes and streams and sometimes a low, tasty tree. And the camel knew that Timoken could keep dangerous animals away with the loud sounds he made, in languages that Gabar couldn't begin to understand.

The cubs enjoyed riding in the big goatskin bag. Sometimes, they would peek above the rim and watch the world go by. But as soon as they caught the scent of a big cat, they would duck down into the bag.

Whenever they passed a group of nomads, Timoken would exchange a fistful of shells for a bag of goat's milk.

The first time the cubs tasted goat's milk, they pronounced it very good.

"As good as your mother's milk?" Timoken asked the cubs.

"No," said the biggest cub. Timoken called him Sun Cat. His coat was darker than his brothers', the markings larger and closer, and in certain lights his spots took on a shade of sunset red. One of his brothers had a hint of orange beneath his chin, like a small flame. Timoken named him Flame Chin. The smallest of the three had a coat as pale as a star. He was always the last to approach Timoken, but it was this cub that he loved best. He called him Star.

Every night, Timoken slept under the moon cloak with the cubs snoring beside him. In the morning, he would tie the goatskin bag to Gabar's saddle and lift the cubs into it. But one morning they struggled when Timoken lifted them, and begged to be set free.

"We will follow," said Sun Cat.

"We will watch," said Flame Chin.

"We will listen," said Star.

Reluctantly, Timoken climbed onto the camel's back and left the cubs to run beside them. After a while they fell behind, and when Timoken looked back, they had vanished. He didn't know what to do.

"Stop, Gabar," he commanded, pulling on the reins. "The cubs are lost."

"No," grunted the camel. "You cannot see them. They are not lost."

"How do you know?" Timoken demanded. "Can you smell them, hear them, sense them?"

Gabar gave a grunt that was more like a sigh of impatience. "Leopards are not seen," he said. "They must NOT be seen. You should be proud that they have learned this so quickly."

"Oh!" Timoken was always being surprised by the camel's vast knowledge. "I am proud," he said. "Very proud."

Timoken did not see the cubs again all day. But that night, while he lay sleepless with anxiety beneath the moon cloak, three shadowy forms crept out of the long grass and crawled in beside him.

They continued in this way for several days, but one night the cubs did not return. The moon was, once again, a thin splinter in the sky, but Timoken forgot the Alixir. The new moon had almost disappeared when Gabar said, "Family, do you want to grow old?"

"The Alixir!" Timoken found the bird-shaped bottle. He gave the camel a single dose, and then poured a drop for himself.

Three weeks later, the cubs reappeared.

Timoken and Gabar had reached a range of tall, seemingly impassable mountains. For several days they had been traveling north across a stretch of inhospitable, stony ground. The nights were growing colder. Darkness was falling fast and Timoken decided to light a fire. Gabar settled himself close to the flames and began to doze. Timoken leaned against the camel and closed his eyes. How long, he wondered, and how far would he have to roam before he found a home? Gabar was very dear to him, but he sometimes longed for the companionship of another human being. He thought of his sister and tears welled in his eyes. Timoken pressed his fists against his lids. He was more than a hundred years old, so he should not cry.

A voice, close to his ear, whispered, "North."

Timoken looked at the ring on the middle finger of his left hand. The small silver face wore a frown. "North," it urged again.

"I have come north," Timoken said irritably.

"Farther," the voice implored. "Now."

There was a sudden, loud rumble from the camel: a nervous warning sound. Timoken jumped up and searched the rocky scrubland before him. Nothing moved, but it was dark and he could not see what lay beyond the firelight. The grasses beside him rustled and a dreadful stench came out of them. Timoken froze. He knew that smell. He leaped for the moon cloak, lying behind him, but he was too late.

Long, sinewy arms grabbed the web and tossed it away. Timoken could see them now: three tall figures, twisting and bending, one to his left, another on his right, and the third a few feet in front of him, waving the moon cloak like a banner.

"I have it," one of the viridees shrieked, and his laughter filled the air like the tuneless scream of a hungry hyena.

The web was not easy for him to hold. It fought back, stinging his rootlike fingers and burning his boneless arms. But he would not give it up. As Timoken reached for the web, the laughing viridee tossed it to another. They raced away from Timoken, shrieking and gurgling, as they threw the web from one to another.

Timoken's anger swept every thought from his mind. Forgetting the storms he might bring, or the swift flight he could make, he stumbled over the rocky ground while the viridees sped ahead. Blind with rage, Timoken was not aware of the rock that lay in his path until he ran full pelt into it and crashed to the stony ground.

Beating the stones with his fists, Timoken cried, "No! No! No!"

For a moment he did not notice the change of tone in the viridees' voices, and then, suddenly, he realized that their gleeful cries had become wild with fear.

Staggering to his feet, Timoken saw three dark forms leap upon the viridees. Their cries crescendoed to deafening shrieks and then died to a single moan, until the only sounds were the deep growls of the three leopards as they sniffed their victims' lifeless bodies.

As Timoken cautiously approached, Sun Cat carried the moon cloak over to him and laid it at his feet. The other cubs joined him and they stood, all three, before the boy. In a sudden blaze from the fire, Timoken could see that, in three weeks, the cubs had grown. Their shoulders were wide and strong, their tails thick and heavy, and the hair on their big feet hinted at powerful claws.

"Thank you, my friends," said Timoken. He lifted the moon cloak and threw it around his shoulders.

"You must go," said Sun Cat.

"North," said Flame Chin.

"Now," said Star.

"Now? But my enemies are dead. Can we not sleep, Gabar and I? We are so weary."

"No time," said Sun Cat.

"Fly," said Flame Chin.

"Over the mountain," said Star.

"But—"

"NOW!" said all three. "It is not safe here."

The leopards' voices were so grave, Timoken ran to his camel, crying, "We must go, Gabar. Now. At once."

"Now?" grumbled the camel, in disbelief.

The bags were still all in place, and after quickly dousing the fire, Timoken climbed into the saddle. "Up, Gabar, up!" he cried.

"Up?" Gabar slowly got to his feet.

"We must fly."

"Where?"

"Over the mountain."

"Oh, no," the camel moaned.

"Fly!" yelled Timoken, and he pulled on the camel's shaggy hair, willing him up the steep side of the mountain.

They passed jagged ledges and rough, crumbling stones, where no man or beast had ever walked, and there was nowhere to rest. Up, up, and up. The camel bellowed in fear and pain, gasping for air. Timoken looked for sky above the mountain, but saw only the rugged wall of rock, rising into nowhere.

"Rest!" grunted the camel. "Family, I beg."

"There is nowhere to rest," croaked Timoken, the cold air filling his lungs. "Up, Gabar, up!"

For a moment Gabar hung in the air, unable to rise any farther, and Timoken, feeling the dead weight of the camel, cried with the pain in his arms and chest. "We must fly up," he groaned. "We must, Gabar." He gave an almighty tug, and this time the camel came with him, farther and farther into the white drifts of clouds and out again into a radiant, starlit sky.

They flew a little way beyond the mountain peaks, and then slowly descended into another country entirely. From below came the distant murmur of waves breaking on a shore.

CHAPTER 8
The House of Bones

They landed in darkness on a small island in the center of a vast lake. Timoken led Gabar over a beach of rattling shells into the shelter of some trees. There, exhausted by their flight, they both fell fast asleep.

When he woke up, Timoken ran on to the beach. The shells looked valuable and he put some in his bag before venturing farther.

How could he know that, for hundreds of years, the viridees had lured travelers and fishermen to this solitary island? There they would be robbed of all they possessed and left to die. When the island viridees saw Timoken and the camel flying toward them, they could not believe their luck. How pleased Lord Degal would be when they presented him with the web of the last moon spider. For, this time, they had a trap that Timoken would never escape.

Timoken left the beach and wandered back into the trees. The ground was covered in a thick blanket of flowers and broad-leaved shrubs. The island appeared to be deserted; he couldn't even hear a bird. Timoken decided to explore. Leaving Gabar to rest, he picked his way through the undergrowth.

A building appeared through the trees and Timoken made his way toward it. The building was circular, with a white domed roof, and walls veined with gold that shimmered in the sunlight. The pillars on either side of the arched entrance were decorated with strange symbols. Timoken could make no sense of them.

What was inside the building? Who had built it? Timoken hesitated. Something told him not to go any farther, but his curiosity got the better of him. He mounted the three marble steps up to the entrance and went in.

He was immediately engulfed by an overwhelming darkness. There was not the tiniest scrap of light anywhere, even though the sun had been shining through the open doorway. Timoken turned around. He could see nothing. The doorway had gone. He walked forward and touched a cold stone wall. Feeling his way along the wall, he was sure that, sooner or later, he would find a door frame, a crack in the wall — anything to indicate an opening. He began to stumble on twigs or pebbles underfoot. Bending to find out what could be lying on the floor, his hand gripped a long, smooth object with a rounded, knobbly end. Timoken dropped it and felt for another. There were similar objects, like twigs, jagged and bony.

It was when he touched the skull that Timoken knew, beyond any doubt, that the crackling, crunching things beneath his feet were the bones of a human body. And there was definitely more than one. The floor was littered with bones.

Timoken opened his mouth and screamed. But there was only Gabar to hear him. And what could a camel do? Timoken tried to think of a power that could help him. He could fly, he could bring a storm, he could speak to any animal in the world, but how could he escape from this terrible house of bones? He did not even have the moon cloak to protect him.

But he had the ring. He ran his fingers over it. A frail light appeared on his ringed finger, and the forest-jinni's tiny face looked out at him.

"What can I do?" begged Timoken. "Can you help me?"

"Their power is very strong here," the forest-jinni said sorrowfully.

"The viridees?"

"Indeed."

"You said you would help me," cried Timoken, "but you cannot."

"They drain me." The tiny voice was not much more than a breath of air. "They are too strong." The ring's light began to fade.

"Fight them, forest-jinni. I beg you. Be strong."

The jinni's eyes were closing, but suddenly they blinked open. "Call the leopards," he whispered.

"I can't!" wailed Timoken. "They won't hear me. And how can they reach me?"

"The web has made them different from other creatures: marvelous, amazing, immortal. . . ." The weak thread of the tiny voice ran out. The light faded and the silence that followed was so thick and so absolute it forced Timoken to his knees. He swept his hands over the rubble of bones, and a huge anger burned inside him. How many people had the viridees tricked and killed in this dreadful place? He refused to be one of them.

He remembered the language of the leopards and a roar rose into his throat. Such a huge roar, it made him shake. It burst out of his mouth and filled the darkness.

Again and again, the voice of a furious leopard echoed up to the roof and bounced off the walls. Gabar heard the sound and stumbled to his feet. He was already worried. Timoken had been gone too long. That sound was like no other. It was a leopard's roar, but Gabar knew Timoken's voice by now.

The big camel began to plod through the trees toward the sound of the leopard. A black cloud rolled across the sky and the sunlight was gone, leaving the island in gloomy shadow. When Gabar reached the building it was no longer beautiful. It was gray and unwelcoming. He could see an open doorway, and yet the noise that Timoken was making was that of a trapped animal. Why could he not get out?

Gabar thought, *A spell!* No sooner was the thought inside his head than the palm leaves above, and the plants all about him, began to whisper and murmur and chuckle and snarl.

"Family!" bellowed the terrified camel. "Viridees!"

Timoken heard the camel's desperate call, but he couldn't help him. So he gave another roar; a roar so deep and dangerous the wicked creatures that were even now stealing toward the camel hesitated for a moment before continuing on their greedy way.

Gabar wheeled around to see a crowd of thin green creatures creeping toward him. Their wet hair dangled, their red eyes flashed, and their long arms swung like slimy vines.

"Camel," said one. "Let us take your heavy burdens."

Gabar raised his head and bellowed. But rootlike fingers were now reaching for the bag that contained the moon cloak.

Twisting his neck, Gabar bit, crunching the slimy arm between his big teeth. Then he kicked and howled, turned and turned, churning the earth with his furious feet.

Inside the house of bones, Timoken heard his camel bellowing. Angry and helpless, he slid to the floor and crouched among the piles of bones. He closed his eyes and growled in sympathy with his poor camel.

A thin light crept through his eyelids. The light grew stronger. Timoken opened his eyes and saw a flame burning outside a wall. He touched the wall, but felt only hard stone. He was baffled.

The flame outside began to circle the building, and Timoken had the impression that he was surrounded by a ring of fire. And now he could hear it, crackling and hissing. "Gabar!" he cried. "What's happening?"

He was answered by the roar of a leopard. Three roars. Three leopards.

The circle of fire grew brighter. Timoken could feel the heat of it through the walls. He could smell the scorched stones. The walls began to crumble; stones tumbled out and rolled down the steps. Through the gaps, Timoken could see trees and Gabar, his big eyes wide with amazement. But the leopards had no shape at all. They were flashes of fire, joined in a ring by tails of flame.

Timoken pushed and kicked the walls until he had made a gap wide enough to squeeze through. The stones were hot, but he managed to slip past them without burning his clothes. As soon as he was through, the building behind him came crashing to the ground. Timoken leaped away from the flying rubble and burst through the fiery circle without feeling a thing.

The flames began to evaporate into the air. And there were the leopards. They stood shoulder to shoulder: Sun Cat, Flame Chin, and Star.

"You saved my life," purred Timoken.

"Our lives are yours," the big cats purred in return.

Sun Cat said, "Go now!"

"This place is bad," said Flame Chin.

"Be safe," said Star.

"But you . . . how will you . . . ?"

"Nothing can hurt us," said Sun Cat.

"We are faster than wind," said Flame Chin.

"We will always be with you," said Star.

"So leave this place now!" The three roars came all at once, and there was no mistaking the urgency in their voices.

Gabar had already crouched for Timoken to mount.

The boy looked all about him, into the trees and lush green undergrowth. But there was no sign of the viridees. The leopards had frightened them away — for now. The dark cloud had folded back from the sun, and the house of bones was now a mound of rubble.

Timoken climbed into the saddle, and Gabar lifted himself from his knees.

"I'm sorry, Gabar," Timoken began, "but —"

"I know. We must fly again," said Gabar. "I am happy about it."

Timoken could not stifle his laugh. Gabar often lightened his mood in the most difficult situations.

"So, let's fly!" Timoken grabbed Gabar's shaggy hair and up they went, with no effort at all.

When Timoken looked down, the leopards had vanished, but their roars followed him across the gleaming stretch of water. "Be safe, Small King! Be wise! Be well!"

Soon Timoken could see a distant green line emerging on the horizon of the great blue lake. As they drew nearer, he was relieved to see not a mountain range, but lush green trees and square, flat-roofed houses.

They landed on a sandy beach, where fishing boats rocked beside a wooden jetty. Two fishermen were mending their nets at the water's edge, and a boy was balancing a basket of fish on his head as he made his way from the jetty to the trees.

No one appeared to have noticed the camel's unusual arrival.

The fishermen, intent on their nets, paid no attention to the strangers. They did not even turn their heads as Timoken led Gabar up to the trees.

It was a quiet place. The market was hardly busy. Timoken exchanged a handful of shells for some fruit and nuts. No one seemed surprised to see a boy alone with a camel. Perhaps they thought he was the servant of a rich master. He had covered his head with the striped hood of his robe, hiding the thin gold crown.

Will this be home? Timoken wondered. No, something was urging him on. He looked at the ring. It had lost its brilliance and the small face seemed asleep. Timoken wondered if the viridees had been too powerful for the little creature. Was he dead?

That evening, as he sat in a pine grove with Gabar munching nuts at his back, Timoken reached for his bag and took out a pearl. He let it roll around his palm for a minute, and then he attempted to multiply it, just as Zobayda had done. If the forest-jinni had lost his spirit, then the spell might not work. Timoken murmured simple words as he ran his finger over the pearl. "Let there be two, let there be three and four."

The pearl rocked to and fro, and then, suddenly, there were two. Then three. Then four. Timoken sensed that the forest-jinni had not taken part in the spell, but that he, Timoken, had multiplied the pearl without the help of the ring.

He slipped the ring off his finger, cupped the pearls in his hands, and held them against his cheek. "Five, six, seven, eight," he whispered. "Nine, ten, eleven, twelve." He continued counting to twenty. He could feel his hands filling up, the pearls pressing into his fingers. When he opened his hands, a stream of pearls fell into his lap.

"I can do it," Timoken breathed. "I can do it, all by myself."

A muffled sigh came from the ring. "You still need me." The forest-jinni's voice sounded desperate.

"Of course I do." Timoken picked up the ring and pushed it onto his finger. Multiplying the pearls made him feel powerful, more like the guardian of the ring, rather than the other way around.

Full of hope, he decided to continue his journey by starlight. He had already learned to use the constellations as a guide. Gabar did not object, and so they struck north. There was not even a dog awake to see the camel tread quietly through the village and out onto the sandy road that led—who knew where?

*　　*　　*

In the morning they reached another village, and the next day another. And so it went on until they got to the sea. Gradually, they made their way into a different sort of country. They passed the ruins of ancient palaces and temples. They saw pyramids and statues half hidden in the sand. And whenever he had a chance, Timoken would take out his pearl-handled knife and find a place where he could sketch his journey. He drew his pictures in catacombs and caves, on the floors of abandoned temples, on castle ramparts and the walls of monastery gardens. Very often Charlie, the boy from the cave wall, would arrive, stealing in from the future while Timoken was drawing.

"I've found you!" Timoken's descendant would mutter into his ear. And Timoken would laugh with delight, and they would talk and talk, the words bubbling out of Timoken like a fountain, while Gabar watched them with a look of disapproval on his proud camel's face.

One day, when Timoken and Charlie were sitting together in the ruins of a Roman villa, Timoken said, "I have told you about my life as it has been for the past hundred and more years, but perhaps you know my future, Charlie. Can you tell me when I will die?"

The boy beside him frowned. "No," he said, "but my friend, Gabriel, has the cloak that you wore." He touched the moon cloak that rested on Timoken's shoulders. "It is red velvet, not like this moon cloak."

"Red, you say." Timoken smiled. "What kind of red?"

"Like a sunset."

When Charlie had gone, Timoken patted his camel's neck and said, "Don't look so disapproving, Gabar. I cannot help talking so much with Charlie. I miss the company of other children, other beings like me."

The camel grunted, "Me, too!"

Timoken felt guilty. He knew that Gabar must miss the company of other camels. But what could be done about it? If he found a companion for Gabar, how could he make it fly? He and Gabar were bound to each other, by time and events, and probably love.

They had slowly been traveling into a cold climate. Winter came, and for the first time in his life, Timoken saw snow falling. He knew what it was because he had seen it on the mountain peaks, but to sit on a camel's back while thick white flakes drifted softly about him was magical.

They traveled north, and every day seemed colder than the last. Timoken stopped to exchange some silk for a thick woolen blanket to cover Gabar's back, and for himself, a sheepskin cape and a fur hat. Soon they found themselves in a rocky, barren land where the north wind blew constantly. They spent the winter in a cave, only occasionally venturing out to exchange shells and beads for food. The leopards paid them a visit. When they were sure that all was well with Timoken, they vanished into the chilly gray landscape, promising always to listen for Timoken's call.

Spring came, and the boy and the camel moved on. Sometimes they would stay on the edge of the same village for almost a year, and sometimes they moved on, swiftly. They flew over a sea that Gabar thought would never end. They soared over mountains so high that the camel's hair froze into rigid tufts of ice, and Timoken thought his cold nose would drop off. But still the ring urged them on. "Not safe, yet," it would whisper.

Fifty more years passed, and Timoken decided he could go no farther. "We have come so far north," he complained to the ring. "Surely the viridees cannot reach us now."

The eyes in the tiny face blinked. "There is something new," he said, and a note of apology crept into his voice. "They have extended their grasp."

"I don't understand," said Timoken.

"I think . . . I sense . . . that one is human."

"If this person is human, then he, or she, is not a viridee."

"But he is . . . and yet . . . in most respects, he looks like a human."

"Where is this human viridee? Am I about to meet him?"

"How can I tell?" the forest-jinni said regretfully. "Forgive?"

"Of course I forgive you. But what am I to do?" Timoken clenched his fists in frustration. "Am I never to feel safe in the company of humans? Never to have a friend?" He twisted the ring, as though it were all the fault of the forest-jinni. "How will I know this . . . this person if I meet him? Will there be a sign? Will his true nature show in his face?"

"You will know," said the ring.

CHAPTER 9
The Girl in the Cage

In his two hundred and forty-fifth year, Degal, lord of the viridees, decided to travel north. He had outlived all his wives and now he wanted another. But this time she had to be human. Lord Degal wanted a son who could survive the biting chill of the north wind, who could walk in snow, and live quite happily in freezing temperatures. A human mother could give her son these strengths; then the boy could take the power inherited from his father into realms where no viridee had ever ventured.

Lord Degal had heard of a certain Count Roken of Pomerishi, who had fifteen daughters. Naturally, the count wanted to find a husband for all of his daughters. He had managed to marry off eight of them, but there were seven left. It was proving very expensive to feed and clothe these seven girls; they were fussier and more bad tempered than their married sisters. It was rumored that the count was so desperate to find husbands for his unmarried daughters that he was prepared to overlook any unpleasant features the husband-to-be might have, as long as the man had a horse.

Count Roken lived in the mountains of northern Europe, a place where, even in summer, a snowstorm could blow up. Lord Degal braced himself. His scouts found three strong horses and, together with two soldiers, Lord Degal rode out of the forest. In his saddlebag he carried enough gold to buy the fur coats, hats, and boots that they would need to survive the cold northern climate.

By the time the viridees reached Count Roken's castle their greenish skin had become quite blue, and one of the soldiers had lost a rootlike finger to frostbite.

Once inside the great hall, the three viridees began to lose their blue looks and became their usual shade of green. Count Roken decided to ignore this peculiarity. Dressed in his forest-green robes, Lord Degal looked very impressive. There were no wrinkles on his damp, greenish skin and, apart from a few strands of white, his hair was still the color of pond weed. The count was pleased to hear that his visitor was looking for a wife. He called for his daughters and Lord Degal watched keenly as, one by one, they entered the hall. As soon as he saw Adeliza, he knew that she was the one for him.

Adeliza was the count's most beautiful daughter. She was also the most heartless. She had brown-gold hair, cold green eyes, and a Cupid's bow mouth. But ten would-be husbands had turned her down. Her voice was so chilly, her gaze so cold, that young men ran from her like frightened mice. Not so Lord Degal. He recognized a kindred spirit.

For her part, Adeliza was fascinated by Lord Degal's long, boneless arms. She found his greenish skin and flickering red eyes strangely attractive, and when she heard of the black marble throne inset with emeralds, she could hardly wait to be married.

The wedding took place the following morning, and a day later, the happy couple was on their way back to Africa.

The African forest was hotter than Adeliza expected, but she did not complain. She enjoyed wearing priceless jewels and sparkling robes, and she delighted in having a thousand servants at her beck and call.

Lord Degal was pleased with his new wife, and when their son was born, he could tell, almost at once, that the boy would be everything he had wished for. They named him Harken, after Adeliza's grandfather.

The baby grew into a fine young man. He was handsome, ruthless, and cunning, and his sorcery was impressive. A glance from his olive green eyes could freeze you in a second. He could turn into a serpent, he could create monsters, and he had a natural talent for poisoning.

When Harken was thirteen, Lord Degal sent him north. "I want you to find an African boy who rides a flying camel," said the lord of the viridees. "This boy has something priceless, something that could make you very powerful."

"I am powerful," Harken replied carelessly. "And camels do not fly."

"This one does," said his father. "And you are not as powerful as the African."

Harken pricked up his ears. "Oh? How so?"

"The boy has the web of the last moon spider. It was dipped in dew held in rare flowers, and washed with the tears of creatures that will never be seen again. It can protect the wearer from any attack, any weapon in the world."

"But not from me," Harken remarked, with a haughty lift of his right eyebrow.

His father was becoming impatient. "How do you know?"

Harken shrugged.

"You had better go and find out."

Harken groaned. "Where is this boy and his flying camel?"

"My scouts tell me that he is heading for the mountains beyond the two seas." Lord Degal showed his son a map drawn on the dried skin of a warthog. "And there is something else," he added. "We believe that the boy is still in possession of a bird-shaped bottle. We do not know what it contains, but it might be a liquid that can help one to live forever, for the boy has not aged in two hundred years."

Harken's curiosity was aroused. Accompanied by four viridee soldiers, he left the forest and journeyed north, in search of a boy on a flying camel. Harken was good at finding things. He did not think it would take him long to track down the moon spider's web and the bird-shaped bottle.

In a few weeks, Harken's search had led him very close to the area where Timoken was traveling. But a wide valley still lay between them, and in that valley was a group of children who would dramatically affect the course of Timoken's life.

Inside a covered wagon, pulled by a weary horse, sat eleven kidnapped children. The wagon rocked and jolted its way across the valley, driven by a man dressed in the hooded brown robe of a monk. But he was not what his clothes might suggest. On the contrary, he was a villain—a kidnapper. His five companions, all dressed as he was, rode behind the wagon. Their spare horse was tied to the side.

The eleven children sat tied to one another by their wrists. Their mouths were bound with rags and their ankles roped together so tightly that their skin was grazed and sore. They had all been kidnapped.

Four British boys sat on one side of the wagon, their legs stretched between the legs of the seven French children oppo-site—four boys and three girls.

At the back of the wagon, beside one of the Britons, there was a cage, and in the cage there was another girl. She wore a long sky-blue dress and a brown fur-lined cape. Her blonde hair, braided with blue ribbons, reached to her waist. She sat with her legs curled to one side; her hands were bound, but her mouth and legs were free. The kidnappers obviously thought her skin too precious to mark with ropes or rags. She was, in fact, a daughter of the most famous soldier in Castile, though her present captors did not know this.

The wagon suddenly jolted to a halt, sending its occupants rolling against one another. They struggled upright and waited for something to happen. Were they to be rescued, or tortured?

Silhouetted against the moonlit sky, the broad outlines of two men appeared at the open end of the wagon. The men climbed up and began to remove the gags from around the children's mouths. As they walked between the rows of children, they roughly kicked and pushed their legs. One of the French girls began to whimper, and the boy next to her whispered, "Shh, Marie!" The other children were silent. They knew that if they cried out they would get no supper.

Pieces of black bread were handed out. At first the children had found it difficult to eat, tied to one another by their wrists. But they had learned always to use their right hands, leaving their left to be tugged up to their neighbor's mouth. They had to take care not to spill the water, passing the jug from one to the other without tipping it up too far.

When he reached the back of the wagon, one of the men opened the cage door and put a jug of water onto the floor. He placed a hunk of bread and cheese beside it.

The two men left the children and a few moments later the crackle of a fire could be heard. The kidnappers began to murmur to one another. One said, "In two days she will be off our hands." Another voice muttered, "What price did you ask?" The reply could not be heard. Soon the tantalizing smell of roast meat drifted into the wagon.

One of the Britons clutched his stomach and rolled his eyes. He was thirteen and almost the height of a man. His father was an archer, and he was fast becoming one himself before he was kidnapped. He was broad and strong and always hungry.

The copper-haired boy beside the cage said, "Do not make us laugh, Mabon. They will punish us!"

"The smell of meat is punishment enough," said Mabon.

Little Marie began to giggle. Henri, her neighbor, choked on his bread and soon they were all shaking with silent laughter.

The copper-haired boy glanced at the cage beside him, wondering if the girl was smiling. She had only been with them for a day, and so far she had not smiled once, even when he tried to tell her his name.

The girl stared at him and, once again, he pointed to his chest, saying, "Edern!"

The girl laid a hand against her own chest and said, "Beri!"

Everyone looked at the cage. It was the first time they had heard the girl speak. Was she British or French?

First Edern, then Henri, asked the girl where she came from. She would not reply to either of them.

Henri shrugged and said, "*Mysterieuse!*"

Gereint, the smallest Briton, began to sing, very softly. He had a beautiful voice. He sang in Latin, a language his singing master had taught him. It was like magic. The girl gave a beautiful smile and clung to the bars of her cage. A stream of words poured from her, but they were neither French nor English.

"Perhaps she is a Roman," said Mabon, when the girl sat back, still smiling at Gereint.

"The Romans are all dead," said the boy beside him. His name was Peredur. With his narrow face and long, sharp teeth, he looked like a golden-haired wolf.

While they continued to argue and chatter, Beri's thoughts were far away. Gereint's song had reminded her of the cathedral in Toledo. The last time she had entered the cathedral, it was to see her cousin married. Beri did not want to get married. Not ever. She had always wanted more from life. She had wanted adventure, excitement. Only her father knew that she was already an accomplished sword fighter. Their lessons had been held in secret.

"If only I had a sword," she murmured to herself in Castilian.

"QUIET!" One of the kidnappers appeared. He was the cruelest of the six. His face was scarred and his nose flattened by years of fighting.

Mabon, who was nearest to the man, asked, "Please, sir, where are you taking us?"

The man stared hard at him. "How many times have you asked? I told you. You will know when you get there."

"Give us a clue," said Peredur bravely.

The man gave an ugly smile. "All right. You asked for it. You are going East, to a place where pale-skinned, golden-haired children like you fetch a very good price."

"Price?" Edern swallowed nervously.

"Slaves!" The man's crooked smile grew wider. "That is what you will be. And just so you know: There is not a house for miles, so you might as well save your voices."

When the kidnapper had gone a grave silence fell over the children. The French had not understood the man's words, but the Britons' desperate faces told them that things were not good.

As the wagon began to move again, Edern whispered to Peredur, "I am going to escape. I am the fastest runner, so I stand a chance. Will you use your teeth to help me, Perry?"

Peredur grimaced, showing his wolflike teeth. He lifted his hand and Edern's with it, and he nodded, putting his mouth against the rope that bound their wrists together.

"Not yet," whispered Edern. "Wait until we reach some trees where I can hide. It looks so desolate out there."

Gereint, who had overheard them, said softly, "You are fast, Edern. You can escape. But will we be rescued? Will you come back for us?"

"Of course. All of you." Edern looked at the shadowy faces around him. "All," he repeated. And then he turned to the cage. The kidnappers had been discussing Beri, he realized. "In two days she will be off our hands," they had said.

Soon, it would be too late to rescue the girl in the cage.

CHAPTER 10
"You Are a King!"

Summer had arrived, but in the mountainous country where Timoken found himself, the nights were still chilly. One morning, as he and Gabar were walking along a narrow mountain track, they heard a long, wailing call. It was in a language that Timoken had never heard, but there was no mistaking the desperate urgency in the voice.

Timoken had been leading Gabar, rather than riding him, and now he dropped the reins and, kneeling on the ground, looked over the edge of the track. At first, he could see nothing, and then, far below, he made out the small figure of a boy. He was sitting on a ledge that jutted out a yard or so above a fast and furious river. The boy had thick copper-colored hair and a face that looked all the paler for the dark blood that streamed from his nose.

"I fell!" The boy looked up at Timoken. "Can you help me?"

A strange language, thought Timoken. But he could understand it. He withdrew his head and tried to think what to do.

"Please don't leave me, I beg you!" called the boy. "I think my arm is broken, and I cannot swim."

How did he think anyone could rescue him? It was an almost sheer drop down to the ledge. Even with a rope it would be impossible to rescue the boy if he had a broken arm. Timoken had no choice. He would have to fly.

"Gabar, don't move!" Timoken commanded. "This track is dangerous."

Gabar gave a loud snort and stamped his foot, sending a shower of rocks bouncing down the mountainside.

"HELP!" came a cry.

"I'm coming," called Timoken. He launched himself off the track and floated gently down to the ledge where the boy was sitting. For a moment they gazed, astonished, at each other. And then the strange boy asked, "Do all Africans fly?"

"No," replied Timoken. "Do all your people have fiery hair and . . . and marks across their faces?"

"Only some," said the boy. "My father and my brothers are all freckle-faced."

A cascade of stones came tumbling down behind him and he yelped, "Can you lift me, African? Can you fly with me?"

"I can lift camels," said Timoken, putting his arms around the boy's waist. Lifting him carefully, Timoken easily flew up to the track.

Gabar, surprised by the sudden appearance of the two boys, stepped away nervously. One of his back feet slipped off the side of the track and, with a rumble of stones, the camel disappeared over the edge, bellowing with fear.

Without hesitation, Timoken dropped the boy on the ground and flew after Gabar. He tried to catch him as he fell, but the camel was heavy and laden with bags. He dropped like a stone into the fast-flowing river, his desperate voice gurgling up through the water in rings of muddy bubbles.

Timoken plunged after him. The river was thick with weeds and mud, but he could feel Gabar's shaggy hair just beneath the surface and, looping his arms around the camel's neck, he pulled with every ounce of his strength. Gabar thrashed in the water for a moment and then, all at once, his body sagged and he sank down to the riverbed.

Timoken pressed his face against the camel's head and, keeping his mouth closed, he hummed into his ear. "You will not drown. You cannot drown. You are my family, and I am yours. Up, Gabar. UP!"

The camel's head drooped, but Timoken would not let go. His lungs were bursting and he longed to take a breath, but he rubbed the shaggy neck and hummed into his ear again, "Up, Gabar! Up, up, up."

Gabar did not move. Timoken thought, briefly, of the boy he had just rescued. What would he do now, if Timoken drowned with the camel? Because he would drown if Gabar did not move. He could not bring himself to leave his oldest friend, his family.

There was a movement beneath him. The camel was struggling to his feet. With a surge of hope, Timoken pulled Gabar's head upward, up to the surface of the water where they both took long gasps of air, and then up again, the camel's heavy body struggling out of the river while Timoken shouted encouragement. Gabar's big feet kicked themselves free of the water, and Timoken lifted him into the air. Now they were flying, their grunts and cries of delight filling the air.

They landed on the track with a bit of a scramble. Gabar sank to his knees, water pouring from the bags tied to his saddle.

Timoken lifted the bags off the camel as fast as he could. Only when he had made sure that Gabar was safe did he notice the red-haired boy, gaping at him, almost in horror.

Timoken grinned at the boy. "I thought I had lost him," he said. "He is my family, you see!"

The boy just stared at Timoken. At last he said, "What are you?"

"I am just a boy," Timoken replied.

The boy shook his head vigorously. "No, you are a king, I think." He pointed to the gold band embedded in Timoken's thick hair, the crown that had never left his head. "A magician-king," the boy added, dropping his voice.

Timoken could not help laughing. He still felt so happy to have rescued Gabar. "My name is Timoken, and I suppose I would be a king," he admitted, "if I had a kingdom. But it is all gone." He fell silent for a moment and then said, brightly, "We must find somewhere safe to dry ourselves and talk."

The boy went first. He limped a little, from a twisted ankle, but pressed on in a very determined way, his free hand holding his injured arm against his side. Gabar followed the boy, placing his feet carefully on the rough track. And Timoken came last, so that he could watch the others. He dragged the saddle and the wet bags behind him, and he thought of the moon cloak, and how he could use it to warm Gabar's back and perhaps, even, to mend the boy's arm.

Luckily, they did not have to walk far before they came to a small grove of trees growing in an old quarry. There was room to spread the wet clothes and for Gabar to sit in the sun and dry himself.

The boy's arm was not broken after all, but badly bruised. Timoken gave him some water and then, a little self-consciously, he lit a fire. Although the sun was out, the wind was chilly and Gabar was still shivering from fright and the cold.

The boy watched Timoken for a while, and then he said, "My uncle can do that!"

"He can use his fingers to . . . ?"

"Light a fire, yes. But he cannot fly."

Timoken began to spread his possessions in the sunlight. He gave the boy some dried meat, and they sat watching the flames and each other before Timoken eventually asked the boy's name.

"Edern," the boy replied and then, unable to keep quiet any longer, he began to explain how he had come to be in such a dangerous place and so far from home.

"I come from a land many, many days away," said Edern. "My father is a poet and I lived in a castle in much splendor, because the prince of our country values poets even above soldiers. One evening a group of monks came to the castle, begging for shelter. It was our duty to let them in. But that night they stole up to the room where my three friends and I were sleeping. Before we could cry out, they had gagged us and bound our hands and feet. They carried us out of the castle, past two guards who were sleeping, drugged, no doubt." Edern's mouth formed a grim line. "We kicked and struggled but those men were no holy monks; they were built like oxen, brutal, powerful, and cruel. They put us in a covered wagon and drove us to the sea, where a ship was waiting. We were carried aboard in sacks, like so much rubbish, and thrown into the hold. There were other children there, weeping and groaning. Some lay very still, too still."

Edern rubbed his bruised arm and stared at the sky, shading his face with his hand. "When we came to this land, wherever it is, we were loaded onto carts. But some of the children got sick. They were thrown out to die on the road, like dogs."

"But you escaped," said Timoken, trying to sound cheerful. "And now you are on your way home."

Edern shook his head. "Not without my friends. I promised to go back and rescue them, when I found someone to help."

"Well, you have found help," said Timoken. "But who are these men who are not monks? Did they kidnap you for a ransom? And were your families unable to pay the price?"

Edern leaned forward. "We were to be slaves," he said in a low voice. "Rich men in the East will pay a fortune for slaves with pale skin and yellow hair" — he touched his head with a rueful grin — "and even more, it seems, for boys with hair like mine."

"Slaves?" said Timoken in horror. "Where are your friends now? Have you come far?"

"Not far," said Edern. "This track will soon descend through woods into a wide valley. The false monks hold my friends in a barn there in the trees. Every night we were roped together by our hands. I was at the end of the line, next to my friend, Peredur. Peredur is renowned for his sharp teeth; they are like the teeth of a wolf." Edern opened his mouth in a wide grin and pointed to his incisors. "And so he gnawed the rope between us, and when his jaw began to ache, I gnawed, and between us we chewed right through the rope. As soon as I was free, I stood on Peredur's shoulders and climbed through a hole in the roof. It was but a short jump to the ground."

"Were there no guards?"

"All the false monks were asleep in a stone house beside the barn. The dogs were our guards; three great brindled hounds that set up a great barking at the slightest noise."

"And they did not see or hear you?"

"They did. But we had saved a little of the meat that evening, and hidden it beneath the stones where we sat. I threw it to the dogs and they let me pass, but their first warning barks had woken the false monks, and one came stumbling out of the house. He must have thought the dogs were eating a rabbit, or some other creature, for he cursed them for their noise and went back to bed."

Timoken's mind began to race. He was confident that he could rescue Edern's friends, but he had to plan his actions. "How many of you are there?" he asked.

"There were twenty or more. But only twelve of us survived the sickness. We must rescue them soon," Edern said anxiously. "Tomorrow they will be on the move again."

"Perhaps they have gone already," Timoken said. "Would those brigands stay another night in the same place?"

"They were waiting for someone," said Edern. "We heard them talking. One of the girls was to be collected today. She is in a cage." He paused for a moment and added, with a frown, "I am afraid for her, Timoken. I am afraid for all my friends, but the way those false monks talked, I think they expect a large sum of money for this girl, and so they will guard her very closely. Perhaps we cannot rescue her."

"Nothing is impossible," said Timoken. "I have a plan already. We will wait for moonlight."

That evening he packed the bags for traveling. Everything had dried in the sun, even the woolen blankets. Gabar had thoroughly recovered, and ate a hearty meal of dried fruit and grass before dozing off. Timoken unfolded the moon cloak and laid it under the trees. The boy watched, his expression a mixture of wonder and curiosity.

"What is that?"

Timoken hesitated. Should he tell Edern the truth? The boy already knew so much about him, what did it matter? Timoken trusted him. He was certain that Edern was not the one whom the ring had warned him about.

"It is made from the silk of the last moon spider," he said at last. "I call it the moon cloak, and it will protect us. We must get some sleep before we set off to rescue your friends." Timoken lay beneath the moon cloak and beckoned to the boy.

After a moment of uncertainty, Edern crawled in beside him. The red-haired boy was soon asleep, but Timoken lay staring up at the night sky. Where was the moon? They needed a good light if they were to rescue all the children and escape. He had been gazing at a pale splinter of light for several seconds before he realized what it was. The new moon was rising in the eastern sky.

Quickly rolling from beneath the moon cloak, Timoken ran to the bags that were piled beside Gabar. The Alixir was kept in a small pouch of red calfskin. But it was not there.

"It must have been lost in the water," Timoken said to himself, "when poor Gabar fell in the river." He looked again at the thin slice of moon and shivered. He had found no home as yet, but he was going to grow. He would be like other mortals. The prospect was exciting, and a little alarming. He had been eleven years old for more than two centuries; in less than another eleven years, he would be a man.

CHAPTER 11
The Angel on the Roof

Edern woke up. A thick blanket of clouds obscured the stars, and yet there was a light in the grove where he lay.

He could see the camel, its head lowered and its eyes closed. He could see the branches of the trees, spread like a canopy above his head. He sat up, and light rippled across the cloak that covered his legs. It was like seeing the moon reflected in water. Edern ran his hand lightly over the glimmering threads. They were so soft, he could hardly feel them. Beside him, Timoken stirred in his sleep; the band of gold around his head glinted in the gentle light.

"A king," Edern said to himself. Something his father had said came into his head: "To be a king is an honor and a burden.

He cannot show fear, and he cannot shoulder the huge weight of his responsibilities without our support. Never forget that."

Edern looked at his sleeping companion. *I won't forget*, he thought.

He shook Timoken's shoulder and the African woke with a start. "I have never slept so deeply." He yawned and stretched his arms.

"I think we should go now," said Edern.

"Of course!" Timoken exclaimed. He went over to the camel and began to load him up.

"It is night," grunted Gabar.

"I'm sorry. We have a task to perform—a rescue!" Timoken lit a small lamp and hung it at the front of the saddle.

Gabar wearily lifted his rump. "Rescue?" he snorted. "At night?"

"Yes. And don't get up yet. We have to climb on your back."

"Two again," grumbled Gabar.

Timoken smiled. "We weigh hardly anything." He got into the saddle and called Edern over, telling him to climb up behind him.

When they were ready, Gabar raised himself to his feet and, at a touch of the reins, began to walk down the mountain track.

It had widened out into a rough road, and on either side trees grew thickly, keeping the camel safe from another tumble.

As they traveled, Timoken described his plan to Edern. They would stop a little way before reaching the barn, so the dogs would not hear them. When he was quite sure no animal had been alerted, Timoken would fly into the trees above the buildings. He would talk softly to the dogs, commanding them to be silent, and then he would ask the horses to be quiet and steady while he untied the ropes that tethered them to the trees.

"They keep the saddlery in a hut beside the stone house," Edern said. "Shall I saddle the horses while you are freeing my friends?"

"No," said Timoken firmly. "I will do it. I will call to you when all is safe. If you do not hear from me before dawn, it means I have failed, so you must find some other route, and continue alone on Gabar."

It had not occurred to Edern that Timoken might fail. He could find nothing to say, except, "I understand."

"Treat my camel well," said Timoken. "He is family."

"I will," Edern said huskily. "But you will not fail."

They reached a sharp turn in the road and Edern said, "We are close to the barn. It is maybe two hundred strides away."

Timoken guided Gabar into the trees at the side of the road. He took the moon cloak from a bag and swung it across his head. Edern watched in awe as the clouds rolled back and starlight filtered down through the trees.

Timoken leaped from the camel's back, and the last Edern saw of him was a pale shape, floating high in the trees. The moon cloak streamed behind him, like a pair of silvery wings.

The girl in the cage looked up through the hole in the roof and saw what she thought was an angel. One of the boys saw it, too. "Look! Look!" he cried.

Beri knew they must be quiet if the angel was to rescue them. "Shh!" she hissed. She could smell fire.

Other children were waking up now. The angel perched on the roof and looked down at them. He put a finger to his lips and whispered, "Hush!"

Silence fell. The angel had a dark face and wore a thin gold crown. The children were a little afraid of him. They had never seen an African before. Beri had seen many. Now that he was close, she doubted that he was an angel, even when he dropped lightly to the ground, as though he were borne on wings.

Timoken whispered quickly to the children while he severed their bonds. He told them he could not remove the heavy chains across the door, but he could carry them up, one by one, through the roof. They would find horses saddled and ready, but they would have to ride two to a horse. When they were all free, he turned his attention to the cage.

"How will you open this?" asked the girl, shaking the iron bars.

Timoken grinned. "Wait and see." He walked around the cage, stroking his chin like an old man.

The others began to whisper urgently. "Please, get us out. The false monks will hear. They'll catch us before we can ride away."

Timoken turned to them, frowning. "Hush!" His tone was severe. "Climb on each other's shoulders if you can't wait!" He walked around the cage again. The door was padlocked; the key, presumably, in one of the false monks' pockets.

The little pearl-handled knife would not do. All Timoken had were his hands. He put his ringed finger on the padlock and murmured, "Help me, ring! Melt! Click! Open!"

The girl couldn't understand him. "What are you doing?" she asked.

Timoken was too absorbed to answer her. His finger felt as though it was burning. The pain was almost unbearable. And now he thought his whole hand was being boiled, but he kept his finger on the padlock until, suddenly, with a loud *click*, it opened and fell to the ground.

The girl stared at Timoken in astonishment. "So you are a magician, not an angel," she said. Cautiously, she pushed at the cage door.

"Quickly!" urged Timoken. "Get out!"

The moment the girl stepped out of the cage, Timoken seized her around the waist and flew up through the hole with her. His feet had hardly touched the roof before he was floating gently down to the ground.

The girl saw flames billowing up in front of the stone house. Timoken had built a pyre against the door and set it alight. The false monks could be heard shouting inside the house. There was only one window and that too was engulfed in flames.

"They will burn," said Beri, with satisfaction.

"No," Timoken told her. "It will rain and the fire will die."

"How do you know?" Puzzled, the girl stared at his solemn face.

"Find a horse and wait for one of the others," he commanded, giving her a little shove in the direction of the house.

Some of the other children had already managed to climb onto the roof and were even now jumping to the ground. Timoken flew up to collect the others and remained on the roof while they found their horses. As soon as they were all mounted, he gave a loud bellow and Gabar came thumping through the trees with Edern on his back.

"Edern!" cried the Britons. "You found a camel."

"A camel and a friend," Edern replied.

Timoken leaped from the barn roof and landed lightly in the camel saddle. "Go now," he called to the others. "We will follow."

The six horses took off immediately, their riders calling loudly to one another, keen to put a distance between themselves and their captors.

"What are we waiting for?" Edern asked anxiously.

"There is another horse," said Timoken. "He pulls the wagon. I untied the rope that tethered him, but he would not move. The other horses listened to me. They were happy to obey, but not this one. If we left him, the false monks could follow us."

They rode into the woods at the back of the house. The big horse was standing under a tree. He had not moved since Timoken had spoken to him.

Gabar seemed uneasy. He was reluctant to go too close. But Timoken urged him forward until they were only three strides away from the horse. He was a huge beast, jet black, with hooves bigger than a camel's foot.

"Go now," said Timoken in a rough snort. "You are free."

A deep and dreadful sound came from the horse. It was more of a roar than a neigh. It made no sense to Timoken. "Horse, why won't you go?" he asked.

The great beast pawed the ground. It looked as though it was about to charge at them, and the camel stepped back nervously. The black horse thrust out its head and rolled back its lips, revealing its huge teeth. Then, from its throat, came a snarl that had no meaning.

"Let's go," cried Edern. "I have never seen such an evil creature."

Timoken was shaken. Until now he had understood every animal that he had met. They all had a language, but not this beast. *It is possessed by an evil thing*, he thought. It worried him that, even here, wickedness existed, when he thought he had left it far behind. He gave the camel's reins a light tug and grunted, "Go, Gabar. Go like the wind!"

Gabar was only too happy to obey.

As they passed the stone house, Timoken saw that the flames had reached the roof, and burning rafters were crashing into the building.

"They cannot follow us now," muttered Edern.

But Timoken could not bear the false monks' screams. Waving his arms at the sky, he called for rain, and within seconds, raindrops the size of pebbles came tumbling down on their heads.

Gabar gave a snort of disgust and galloped down the road.

Timoken did not stop the rain until he was sure that enough water had fallen to douse the fire.

Edern was disappointed. "They will follow us now," he grumbled. "They have the wagon and that brute of a horse. And they have weapons. When they catch up with us, we are done for."

Timoken just laughed. "If they follow us, then I will bring thunder and lightning on their heads. Don't be so gloomy, Edern. I have weapons, too, even though you cannot see them."

Edern grinned. "So you have. We'd better catch up with the others; they may be in need of your special weapons."

"Let's find them, Gabar," said Timoken. And Gabar's pace increased.

They trotted across the valley, past small hamlets and lonely farmhouses, through dense woods, over bridges, and below a castle that stood proud on a rocky hill. But there was no sign of the eleven children, and Timoken began to fear that they had been caught again, by bandits or worse. The children had no protection but their wits.

"Peredur Sharptooth has wits as well as teeth," said Edern, almost as though he had read Timoken's thoughts.

"Then let us hope that his wits are as sharp as his teeth," said Timoken.

In spite of the danger, Edern found himself laughing.

CHAPTER 12
Poisoned

The next day they came to a village where something odd had happened. Something ominous. The usual scent of woodsmoke was absent. There were other smells: death and decay. Night was falling fast but the houses were all in darkness. Not a light showed anywhere. The village stood in a great, hollow silence.

Timoken was reluctant to stop. He was afraid for the eleven children, and wanted to find them before it became too dark. But Gabar demanded a rest. He had seen a stone trough standing beneath a pump in the center of the village, and he made toward it. As the camel bent his head to drink, Timoken suddenly jerked the reins, forcing Gabar away from the water.

The camel bellowed furiously. "I am thirsty. Why will you not let me drink?"

"Look at the water, Gabar! Look!"

The reflected light from Timoken's lamp made the water sparkle. To Gabar, it looked delicious.

"What's wrong?" Edern peered around Timoken to get a better look. "Why won't you let the camel drink?"

"Because someone has poisoned the water." Even as he spoke, Timoken realized that Edern could not see the thin green mist rising from the trough; a mist filled with swimming shapes, diminutive forms with grotesque features. They were grinning at him, their twisted faces full of malice.

"How do you know?" Edern asked in a puzzled voice. "How can you tell that the water is poisoned?"

"I can see them," Timoken said simply.

"Them?"

"Demons."

Gabar felt something now. He could not see the tiny forms, but he could sense them, and he began to back away.

Edern could see nothing, yet he knew that Timoken must be believed. "What shall we do?"

"Perhaps the whole village has been poisoned," Timoken said thoughtfully. "Perhaps they are all dead, but then some might have lived."

Edern looked at the houses, which stood shadowed and silent

in the gathering darkness. "Should we go and look?" he said, a little fearfully.

"We must."

Gabar knelt and the two boys climbed down. The first house they entered was quite empty. So was the next. In both houses there was food on the table, a water pitcher, and several tankards. The pitcher was empty. So were the tankards. When they found no one at home in the third house, they began to think that perhaps the villagers had been frightened away, and not poisoned after all.

Timoken returned to the trough. He steeled himself to look at the water again. The tiny demons were still there, floating in their pea green vapor. Cautiously, he poked his ringed finger into the mist. The demons he touched shrieked with pain and shot upward; pinpricks of lime green light, hurtling through the dark sky.

"I saw them," cried Edern, enthralled by the shooting lights. "What did you do?"

"I am not sure," answered Timoken. "But they are not smiling at me now." On the other side of the trough he could just make out a large building, set back from the others. It was a meetinghouse, perhaps, or the home of an important village elder. Were all the villagers in there? Had they gone to seek advice, for an illness brought on by the infected water? Timoken was about to investigate the large house when Edern suddenly clutched his arm.

"Listen," Edern whispered.

A boy's voice came drifting through the air. It was very clear and sweet, and it was singing in Edern's language.

"Gereint!" cried Edern. "I know his voice so well. He is our prince's favorite singer." He ran toward the house where the singing could be heard. Timoken followed him.

The door was open and the two boys ran in. Candles flickered on a rough table where nine children sat, their faces white and terrified. But when Edern and Timoken walked into the light, the children jumped up, smiling with relief.

Running to Edern, Peredur cried, "We thought you were lost, or caught again by those false monks."

"You are not all here," said Timoken solemnly. "Where are the others?"

Peredur's face fell. "We think they are dying." He stood back and pointed to a dark corner, where two children lay on a mattress, a boy and a girl. The others had covered them with their jerkins, but the sick children looked very close to death. Their eyes were closed, and they did not appear to be breathing.

Another boy approached Timoken. He was smaller than Peredur, and his hair was very blond. "I was singing to them," he said, almost apologetically. "I thought it would ease their journey into heaven."

"They are not dead." Timoken walked over to the mattress and knelt beside the children. "He is warm," he said, taking the boy's hand. "What happened?"

"They rode ahead of us," said Peredur. "Henri was always urging his horse to go faster, and poor Isabelle, sitting behind him in her long dress, was always scared of falling off. When we reached the village, we found their horse tied to a post, and then we saw Henri and Isabelle; they were both lying beside the pump. Their lips were green and slimy, their faces pale as death."

"We thought it must be the water," said Gereint, the singer. "So we decided not to touch it."

"You were wise," muttered Timoken. He whirled through the door and ran to Gabar, who was standing patiently outside.

"Water?" Gabar inquired, as Timoken pulled the moon cloak from a bag.

"Later, Gabar," said Timoken. "The water in the trough is poisoned; be grateful that I stopped you from drinking it."

"Always grateful, Family," the camel grunted as Timoken ran back into the house.

He threw the moon cloak over the sick children and sat beside them. Edern brought a candle and held it up so that the light fell on the sick children's faces. The others gathered behind him, whispering anxiously. The moon cloak glimmered in the soft light, its threads like a pattern of stars.

"What is that thing?"

Timoken recognized the caged girl's voice. She sounded suspicious. He was not sure how to explain the moon cloak.

"Magician, tell me what you are doing." Her voice was gentler now. "I trust you, but I want to know."

Timoken took a breath and, lifting a corner of the web, said, "I call this the moon cloak. It is made from the web of the last moon spider. It keeps me safe and, sometimes, it can heal." He translated his words for the others.

The children behind him murmured in awe. The sound grew to a buzz of excitement as Henri turned his face and groaned.

"He's coming 'round," said Peredur.

They waited expectantly, watching Henri's face. Suddenly, he sat up and groaned, "I'm going to be sick!" Although the Britons didn't understand him, they had a very good idea what was about to happen and leaped back like the others, as Henri bent over and retched. A green liquid pooled on the earthen floor. Only Timoken saw the demons writhing in the puddle and slowly dying. In a few seconds, the green liquid had seeped into the earth, leaving only a small, damp patch.

"It's you!" said Henri, looking up into Timoken's face. "Did you save me yet again?"

Timoken grinned. "No. The moon cloak did that."

Henri frowned at the glimmering web. "Aw!" He swung his legs onto the floor and stood up, letting the moon cloak float down beside the girl. "Oh, Isabelle!" Henri's hand flew to his mouth. "She's still sick. And it's my fault. I made her drink the water. It was poisoned, wasn't it?"

"You idiot!" said one of the French boys. He was tall and thin, with a mop of blond curls. "Why are you always racing ahead?"

"I'm sorry, Gerard. I can't help myself. I did not mean. Oh . . ." Henri covered his face with his hands. "Will she die?"

"No," Timoken said firmly.

"She's opened her eyes!" cried Edern.

All at once, Isabelle sat bolt upright. Long strands of damp hair clung to her face, and she looked wildly about her, not understanding where she was or how she got there. "Oooooh!" she moaned, leaning across the mattress.

The others backed even farther away as Isabelle retched, and a familiar green liquid spilled onto the floor.

"What has happened to me?" cried the poor girl.

Ignoring the small demons dying at his feet, Timoken crouched beside her and laid a hand on her shoulder. "You were poisoned," he said gently. "But now you are better. You are with your friends."

Isabelle looked up. A broad smile lit her face and she said, "You are the boy who rescued us. We thought you were lost."

"No. Not lost," said Timoken. "I am never lost." He stood up and the other French children crowded around Isabelle, exclaiming with joy and relief. She got to her feet and lifted the web, gazing at the glittering patterns.

"It's magic," Henri told her. "It saved us. I'm sorry, Isabelle. It was all my fault."

While the French children chattered eagerly to one another, the Britons were searching for food. They had already eaten a loaf of bread they had found on the table.

"I am going to the big house," Timoken told them. "The villagers may have gone there."

"No!" One of the Britons swung around. He was older than the others, taller and broader. His hair was not even blond; it was a rich brown. Perhaps he had been stolen for the color of his eyes, which were a very pale blue.

"Why should we not go there, Mabon?" asked Edern.

"It is . . . it is full of dead people," Mabon said gravely. "We went there first, thinking that only a village elder would live in such a grand house."

"All dead?" murmured Timoken.

"All," said Mabon.

"They probably went there for help when the sickness came upon them," said Peredur.

Timoken lowered his head. It suddenly felt very heavy. "I was too late," he mumbled.

The children had found some dried beans and a few vegetables. There would be enough food for everyone, but there was nothing to drink, and they dared not fill the cooking pot with water from the pump.

"It is going to rain," said Timoken. "Bring every jug, every bowl and tankard outside. We will soon have water."

The children stared at Timoken suspiciously, but before any questions could be asked, Edern said, "Come on, everyone. You heard what Timoken said. It is going to rain."

There was a moment of silence, and then everyone was grabbing a container of some sort. They followed Timoken outside and, holding up their jugs and pots and tankards, watched, astonished, as the African whirled the moon cloak above his head, and rain tumbled out of the dark sky in never-ending bucketfuls. While it was still raining, Timoken ran into some of the other houses and brought out more bowls and jugs. Eventually, he found what he was looking for — a huge cauldron. He dragged it to the entrance of a stable and called to Gabar.

"I thought you had forgotten me," the camel grumbled as he came pounding over to the stable.

"Quick, get inside." Timoken ordered. "Next, you'll be blaming me for soaking you. When the cauldron is full of water, you only have to poke out your head to take a drink."

"It is all very well," Gabar muttered, easing himself under the low roof. "But thank you, Family."

When Timoken returned to the house, he found that the children had filled the cooking pot hanging in the fireplace.

As he approached them, it came to him that these children knew almost everything about him now, and he remembered his sister's warning. Yet how could he have kept his secrets? *What would you have done, Zobayda?* he wondered. A sharp pain traveled through his ringed finger, up his arm, and into his very heart. Only one of the children noticed that he was shaking.

"What is it, Timoken?" asked the girl from the cage. "Are you in pain?"

In a second, the pain had gone, and Timoken was able to answer truthfully, "It is nothing."

"Are you sure?" She touched his arm. In the candlelit room her eyes looked a deep violet blue. She was still a child, but Timoken saw that she was already beautiful. The ribbons in her hair were made of fine silk, he noticed, and her dress was edged with gold lace. *She must, indeed, be very special*, he thought. He was about to ask her name when she said, "I am called Beri."

When the thick soup was cooked, the children ladled it into bowls and then squeezed together onto the benches at either side of the table. Some were beginning to gobble it up, even before they had sat down.

"What was that?" Gereint looked at the door.

Timoken had heard it, too. A soft, shuffling sound. It was followed by a kind of scratching. Slowly, the latch was lifted and the door creaked open.

An ancient face appeared, so wrinkled and bony it was difficult to know if it was a man or a woman, but as more of its form moved into the room, they saw that it must be a woman. Beneath her gray shawl, her back was bent, and her garments hung loosely on her scrawny frame. The hem of her dress was torn and ragged from being dragged through the mud and stepped upon.

"Children!" she croaked. "Dead or ghosts?"

"We are not dead." Timoken stood up.

The old woman stared at him in horror. "It's you!" she cried. "You are the one he was looking for!"

Timoken shuddered under the accusing gaze of the old woman. "Who is looking for me?" he asked in a small voice.

The dry, wrinkled lips worked furiously, trying to utter a word. At last she managed it. "The sorcerer!" The word came out in a wheezy gasp as she crumpled to the ground.

CHAPTER 13
The Sorcerer

Mabon and Peredur carried the old woman over to the mattress and laid her down. Her eyelids fluttered, and she drew a deep, rasping breath.

Timoken knelt beside her. "Madame, who is this sorcerer?"

She gave a bitter laugh. "Who knows?" Her next breath brought on a coughing fit, and when she had recovered, she said, "I saw it all, but then I went to sleep, and so it was too late to warn them."

When she began to cough again, Marie, one of the French girls, brought her a tankard of water. The girl was smaller than the others, only six or seven years old. The old woman cried, "Poison!" and struck Marie's hand, sending the tankard crashing to the floor.

"It is pure rainwater," said Timoken.

"Oh?" The woman's eyes narrowed suspiciously.

"We have been drinking it, and, as you can see"—Timoken spread his hands and looked at the others—"we are all still alive."

The old woman uttered a wary "Hm!" And then she said, "They all died, you know. The others. When I woke up I could hear moanings and groanings from the other houses. I saw men and women and little children rolling and retching up to Monsieur Clement's house. He is a physician, and his potions have cured many ailments. Not this time. Monsieur Clement was dead already." She began to cough again, and this time she accepted the water that Marie offered her.

Timoken watched her drain the tankard. He wanted to know more about the sorcerer, but did not like to press her. The water seemed to revive her and she sat up, wiping her whiskery chin. Edern brought her a bowl of soup, and she slurped it down greedily, smacking her lips between every sip.

The children watched in silence, waiting for the old woman to speak again. At length, she handed Edern the empty bowl and sat back against the wall, folding her arms across her chest.

"Please, Madame . . . ," Timoken began.

"Grüner," she snapped. "Adèle Grüner."

"Can you tell us what happened here?" asked Timoken.

"Don't stare at me," Madame Grüner complained. "Go and sit down, all of you."

Timoken motioned the others to sit. He told them that Madame Grüner might be persuaded to describe what had happened.

The French children clustered around the table, while the Britons sat cross-legged on the floor. Beri came and knelt beside Timoken. "You will have to explain her words to some of us," she said.

Timoken nodded.

Madame Grüner had already begun to talk. She mumbled and wheezed her way through the events that led up to the death of her village, while Timoken relayed her words to Beri and the Britons in their different languages. Within a few seconds he had mastered this process so well that the others hardly noticed it. His words reached them in one seamless story.

The old woman lived at the far end of the village. Three days ago she was collecting sticks in the wood behind her house, when five horsemen rode up. They were leading another horse, a huge black beast that snorted fire and whose great hooves made the earth tremble as he passed. Four of the strangers had a green look about them; their limbs were long and appeared to have no joints. No knees, no wrists, no elbows. They wore fine clothes and their green cloaks were lined with fur, but their faces . . . "Their faces . . ." Madame Grüner stopped speaking and rubbed her eyes. It was as though she were trying to rub away the memory. All at once her hands dropped to her sides, and she said, "Their faces were not right."

The fifth horseman was not much older than Timoken. He had brown-gold hair and eyes the color of dark green olives. Madame Grüner knew this because he stopped and spoke to her. He asked if she had seen an African boy on a camel. She had laughed at him because she had only heard of such things but never seen them, and would not expect to in her lifetime. Her laughter annoyed the boy and, without warning, he pulled out a whip and struck her hands. She cried out in pain, dropping the bundle of sticks. The boy merely smiled. Leaning from his horse, he said coldly, "Old woman, this is not a joke." Then he turned his horse and led the group into the village.

"And now I have seen things that I never thought I would," murmured Madame Grüner. "A camel in our stable and an African wearing a crown."

Timoken awkwardly touched his head. He had forgotten to wear his hood. "How did they die, Madame Grüner, all those people?"

She took another sip of water and went on, "When I got back

to the village, I saw Monsieur Clement talking to the strangers. The boy was shouting, and my neighbor told me that there had been an argument. The boy sorcerer said that an African on a camel was on his way to the village." She pointed a bony finger at Timoken. "You!"

Timoken frowned. Without a doubt she was right. He twisted the ring, remembering the forest-jinni's warning. A viridee had become human. Timoken knew what he wanted: the moon cloak. And he would kill to get it. "I hope I was not the cause of all those deaths." Timoken's voice was so low, only the girl beside him heard it.

"Monsieur Clement was a brave man." The old woman's watery eyes spilled tears down her furrowed cheeks. "My neighbor told me that when the boy commanded that the African should be caught and imprisoned, Monsieur Clement refused. He was adamant. Visitors would always be welcome in the village, he said, unless their intentions were evil. It was his duty to offer hospitality, not harm. And he looked at the crowd and asked, 'Am I not right, my friends?' And they all agreed, very loudly, whereupon the boy shouted a curse at him. When he and his companions rode off, I heard him call out that we had made the wrong choice."

"And they came back," said Timoken.

Madame Grüner nodded. Her hands plucked at her skirt and she began to mumble incoherently. Timoken took one of her hands. He only meant to calm her, but when he touched her dry skin and looked into her faded gray eyes, he began to see what she had seen in the village, three nights ago. It was dark, but a lamp burned outside Monsieur Clement's house. A boy stood beside the pump. He dropped a stone into the water trough, a shining stone that gave the water an eerie gleam. The boy began to speak. His language was harsh and ugly, his voice too deep for a boy. *A spell*, thought Timoken. Before he left, the boy put his fingers on the pump, and for a few seconds the handle glowed like a hot poker. And the boy smiled.

Timoken heard Beri's voice, very close, saying, "How can you make sense of all that babbling?" And he realized that he had not been listening to Madame Grüner, but describing a scene that was in her head.

"I was with her," he said, and, beside him, he felt Beri shiver, slightly.

Madame Grüner continued to babble, and once more the things that she saw began to swim before Timoken's eyes.

It was the morning after the boy had thrown the stone. The sun had not yet risen and no one had come to the pump. But Madame Grüner was still awake, and she heard the clatter of hooves on the cobblestones. Two monks rode into the village. They dismounted and looked about them. Seeing a stable, they walked stealthily toward it. Their movements were furtive, their faces guilty. Horse thieves, no doubt. Before Madame Grüner could cry a warning, the boy sorcerer appeared, and she was afraid.

The boy spoke to the monks and they replied. Madame Grüner was too far away to hear them, but Timoken watched their lips and understood. The monks were looking for a horse to pull their wagon. The boy offered them an animal that was stronger than any horse on earth. But there was a condition. They must capture an African who rode a camel.

"And then what?" asked one of the monks. "In three days we have to deliver certain goods to a trader in the city of St. Fleur."

The boy shrugged. "Make your delivery. And then bring me the African. The horse will find me, wherever I am. He is a beast of my own making."

The monks frowned, not quite believing the boy. He disappeared from view, and when he returned he was leading a great black horse. The monks looked incredulous. Before the boy handed the horse over, he spoke to it, all the while stroking the beast's nose. He passed the reins to one of the monks, and warned them not to drink the water from the pump. As he said this, he looked directly at Madame Grüner's window. An icy light streamed from his green eyes. Its touch was so painful that she had to cover her face. She dropped to the floor and fell into a deep sleep. When she woke up, everyone else in the village was dying or dead.

Madame Grüner's head drooped. Her eyes were closed and she appeared to be asleep.

Timoken released the old woman's hand. He rubbed the back of his neck and shook his shoulders. He felt so tired, he wanted to lay his head beside the old woman's and sleep. "Did you hear all that?" he asked the others.

"We heard," said Edern. "The black horse was possessed, as we thought. Why does the sorcerer want you, Timoken?"

"It is not me that he wants." Timoken lifted the moon cloak from the mattress where Isabelle had dropped it. "It is this. And perhaps something that I no longer have."

They waited for him to say more and so, reluctantly, he told them about the Alixir that had been lost in the river. He told them about the secret kingdom and the way that his father and mother had died. He told them about the viridees, and, last of all, about his sister, Zobayda. When he had finished, the only sound in the room came from the old woman, who was quietly snoring.

Timoken's arm had begun to throb again. And again, there was a light tug at his heart. "I think we should sleep now," he said. "Tomorrow we will decide what to do."

He could feel the children's eyes on him, but still no one spoke. What could they say after such a story? *I have said it all, now*, thought Timoken, *or nearly all*. For more than two hundred years he had carried his story alone, but now children that he trusted knew it, too, and he felt lighter and happier for having shared it. The only thing that he had kept to himself was his age, his and Gabar's.

They set about preparing for bed. They would all sleep in the one room, they decided. It would be safer that way. The horses were brought in from the woods and stabled close to the house. There was plenty of hay for them, and enough left over to take into the house for pillows. Timoken hung the moon cloak across the door as a protection against the false monks, who might return. The candles were doused, and one by one the children curled up on the floor and went to sleep. Once again, the only sound in the room was Madame Grüner's quiet snoring.

Timoken had slept for only a few minutes before he found himself awake again. He had forgotten something.

Stepping carefully over the others, he unlatched the door and crept out.

Gabar was resting on the stable floor, but he was not asleep. Timoken removed the saddle and the heavy bags from his back. Finding some dried fruit in one of the bags, he laid it before the camel.

Gabar grunted his approval and ate the food.

"We have come a long way, you and I," said Timoken, crouching beside the camel. "And now we are going to grow old together."

Gabar said nothing, but when Timoken got up to leave, he grunted, "Family, please stay with me."

Timoken thought of the moon cloak, out of his reach now. But what did it matter? It would keep the children safe. He sank into the straw and, resting his head against the camel's warm body, fell asleep.

When Timoken entered the house the next morning a serious discussion was taking place. What was to be done with Madame Grüner? That was the question that worried everyone. The old woman was still asleep, and they did not want to frighten her awake.

Eventually, their noisy chatter woke her. For a moment, she scowled at them from under her heavy brows, and then she remembered what had happened and began to rock back and forth, moaning constantly.

"Madame, how can we help you?" asked Timoken.

The old woman stopped rocking. Frowning up at Timoken, she told him that she could not stay in a dead village. She would go to her cousin, who lived only a day's ride away. But there was a problem. Although the villagers' horses had not been given the poisoned water, she could no longer ride. Her hands were too frail to hold the reins, and she found it hard to sit upright.

"We will take you," said Timoken.

Martin, one of the French boys, offered to share his horse with Madame Grüner. He promised to hold her very tight, and to keep his horse under control so that she did not fall off.

It was quite a business, lifting the old woman up into the saddle. She caught her feet in her long skirt, twisted her hands in the reins, and protested loudly when Martin squeezed in behind her. But realizing it was the only way she was going to reach her cousin's village, she calmed down and, muttering directions, allowed Martin to lead the way out of the village.

They had found six extra horses, and so everyone had their own mount. The girls were very pleased about this. They looked different today. They had found clothes in the deserted houses and were now dressed as boys. Their hair was tucked into hoods attached to their short tunics. Having discarded their long dresses, they now wore woolen stockings, so their legs were free and they did not have to ride sidesaddle, which they found annoying and uncomfortable.

As the group approached a small village, half hidden in the woods, Henri began to look around him, studying the ancient trees. He twisted in the saddle, staring up at a towering pine and, with mounting surprise, declared that he thought he recognized the place, and that it was not so far from his home.

This caused a lot of excitement among the other French children. All at once their own homes seemed closer, and the possibility of seeing their parents before very long made some of them whoop with joy.

"Shush!" Madame Grüner commanded. "You will frighten everyone, and they will bar their doors."

And so they entered the village in silence, until Madame Grüner saw her cousin peeping out of a window. With a joyful cry, the old woman half slid and half tumbled off the horse and fell to the ground, while her cousin, a woman much younger than herself, rushed out and clasped her in her arms.

There followed such a babble of frantic conversation between the two, even the French children could not understand them.

Other people began to emerge from their houses. They stared in amazement at the camel. None of them had seen such a creature. But, at length, they motioned for the children to dismount and, climbing off their horses, the children stood grinning at the villagers, who all grinned back.

The cousin, Madame Magnier, invited everyone into her house, while the horses were taken to be fed and watered. Gabar, however, was left well alone.

"Well, Gabar," Timoken grunted softly. "I think you had better let me down, because I do not intend to fly."

He heard a woman say, "The African can only speak in grunts."

"On the contrary, Madame," said Timoken. "I can speak many languages. I was merely instructing my camel."

The woman gasped. When Gabar knelt, she suddenly saw Timoken's crown. "Forgive me," she said, blushing. "I am a foolish woman."

Timoken smiled. "You made a common mistake, Madame."

Soon the whole village knew the story of the boy sorcerer and the fatal poisonings. When they heard that all the children, except Timoken, had been kidnapped, they clutched their own children protectively, agreeing to never let them out of their sights.

That evening the visitors were given a grand meal in the village meetinghouse. While they ate, the villagers pressed them to tell their stories.

The children's accounts were listened to with outrage and horror. Several mothers stood up and piled even more food on their plates.

Madame Magnier's husband was a soldier, but after being wounded in battle he had returned home for good. He walked with a limp, but declared that his sword arm was still useful, and he offered to accompany the French children to the castle where Henri lived with his family.

"My father will make sure that the others are taken home, I promise you." Henri smiled around at the French children, who began to cheer and clap.

The Britons had been listening to all the chatter while they ate, but they could understand very little, and so when Monsieur Magnier leaned over the table and asked Edern where he wished to go, Edern merely shrugged and looked puzzled.

"He is asking you where you want to go from here," said Timoken.

"I go with you," Edern said quickly. He asked the other Britons.

"We stay together," said Peredur, "with you."

"And the girl there, who is not French?" asked Madame Magnier.

"Where do you want to go next?" Timoken asked Beri.

"Home," she said gravely.

"She wants to go home," said Timoken.

"Of course." Having no idea where the girl lived, Madame Magnier smiled at her.

"And you, African?" asked one of the mothers. "Where will you go, you and your camel?"

For a moment, Timoken was unable to answer her. He had given no thought to his next destination. He had no home, and he felt like a blade of grass, tossed about by the wind and having no direction. His ringed finger began to ache, and the ache spread through his body. Almost without thinking, he found himself saying, "I am going to Castile."

"Castile?" A murmur went around the table. Many had never heard of the place.

Monsieur Magnier had heard of it. "You will never get there," he said, shaking his head. "It is far, far away."

"Not too far," said Timoken. He glanced at Beri and she smiled at him.

Why had he said that name? He wondered. Castile. Where was it? He knew only that Beri lived there, and yet it seemed to tug at him. He looked at the ring, twisting it pensively around his finger.

"SHE is there," came the whisper.

"*SHE?*" gasped Timoken.

CHAPTER 14
Zobayda's Dream

Zobayda was old now and spent much of her time dreaming. There were the nightmares, too. They would always haunt her. She would see her father, in his white robes, riding out to meet the lord of the viridees, who sat on his horse like a dark shadow, waiting to kill a king. However hard she tried, she could never blot out the flash of the saber, and her father's tumbling, headless body.

Sometimes she dreamed about her journeys with Timoken, and the camel whose name she could never recall. These were the scenes that made her smile, but they always led to the day, sixty years ago, when she thought she had died, when she leaped into the river and was swept over the thundering falls. She had expected to drown, but somehow she had survived. She had tied herself to a floating log and was carried through the water for days and days. Without a doubt, any other mortal would have died, but the Alixir that Zobayda had taken for over a hundred years now kept her alive. She had been unconscious and almost dead when Ibn Jubayr, an Arab traveler, found her on the shore and saved her life. She would never forget his kind, concerned face looking down at her.

When Zobayda had recovered, Ibn Jubayr took her with him on his travels. She washed his clothes, cooked, and tidied for him. His eyes were failing and he taught her Arabic, so that she could read aloud from the large book that he always carried with him. They crossed the Mediterranean Sea to Spain, and traveled to Toledo, in the kingdom of Castile, the city that Ibn Jubayr called home. And there Zobayda met his nephew, Tariq, whom she came to love. Eventually, they were married. Her husband had died a year ago, but Zobayda still kept his workshop exactly as it had been. Tariq had made the most beautiful toys ever seen; even the king admired them, and had bought many for his children. But Zobayda could not bring herself to sell the toys that were left.

She felt unwell today. Not unwell, exactly, but troubled. The toys always soothed her, and so she descended the narrow steps to the workshop. She often walked here, her skirt whispering through the wood shavings, her fingers touching the shelves where wooden dolls sat side by side with leather animals and birds made of colored straw. She was especially fond of the camel, with its squirrel-hair eyelashes and shiny glass eyes. It stood knee-high, and when she sat down she could stroke its smooth wooden head.

She did this now, and then she took the camel onto her lap and asked it, "What was his name, that camel I rode so many years ago?" She wondered if Timoken had found a home at last. Or was he still wandering, searching for a place where he could grow old?

A sudden prick in her finger made her thrust it into her mouth. "What was that?" She examined the camel to see what could have pricked her. But there was nothing.

Zobayda had once worn a ring on the finger that was now throbbing with pain. She could still see the pale mark that it had left on her skin.

She stood up, letting the camel fall to the ground. The workshop around her began to spin and fade. Strange images swam into her head. She saw the viridees, the creatures that had forced her into the river. Now they were dressed in fine clothes, but she knew them by their strange limbs and swamp-water faces. Their powerful horses sent clouds of dust into the air as they thundered along the dry, stony road. Their leader was a boy of twelve or thirteen. He was not like them, and yet, beneath his cold, handsome face, beneath the fur-lined cloak and fine green tunic, she could see the rubbery bones and fluid sinews of a viridee.

Zobayda covered her face with her hands; the dust in her dream was so real it seemed to sting her eyes. And now she saw a great black beast, a giant horse that snorted flames and bared its teeth. It was pulling a wagon driven by a burly fellow in a brown monk's robe. Behind him in the wagon sat three others. Their faces were partially hidden by their hoods, but they were not monks. All of them wore swords in their belts, and the driver's face was scarred by knife wounds.

Why were they traveling so fast?

Now, in the very corner of her vision, something appeared that made Zobayda cry out in astonishment.

"Timoken!"

Her brother looked just as he had sixty years ago, the last time she had seen him. He was riding the camel whose name she had forgotten. Behind him came five children on horseback. They were laughing and singing, and Timoken looked carefree and happy.

"I'm glad that you are happy, Timoken." Zobayda went to the

small window in the workshop, almost expecting her brother to appear on the road below.

But, of course, he was not in Toledo; he could not be. And yet she felt he was nearer than he had ever been. As she absently rubbed the mark on her finger, she began to feel that she was floating high above the world, and her brother and his friends were now tiny dots in the landscape. As they vanished from view, something appeared on the road behind them. Zobayda might have been a mile above them, but she knew that she was seeing the black horse and its wagonload of armed monks.

"Timoken, take care!" He could not hear her. Could not see her. Probably thought she was dead. There was nothing that Zobayda could do. Besides, someone was shouting her name and banging on her door.

Zobayda's dream faded. She felt herself floating to the floor. She was back in the workshop, staring at the empty road from her small window. Somewhat unsteadily, she climbed the steps to the courtyard and went to open the door onto the street. Her friend Carmela was standing outside. She looked distraught.

"What is it?" Zobayda ushered her friend into the courtyard and closed the door behind her. "Has something happened, Carmela?"

"Didn't you hear?" Carmela lowered herself onto the stone seat in the center of the courtyard. Behind her, roses bloomed, filling the air with their fragrant scent. Carmela never failed to admire them, but today she ignored the roses and bent her head, puffing loudly.

Zobayda sat beside her friend and waited for her to get her breath back.

"Terrible news," Carmela said, patting her chest. "There has been enough fighting in our precious city, and now it is happening again. Did you not hear the shouting, Zobayda?"

"I heard nothing. I was . . . dreaming."

"Well, I heard it. It came from the river. My neighbor had the news. Strangers came over one of the bridges. They would not pay at the tollgate. When the guards forbade them entry, their leader, a mere boy so I am told, he . . ." Carmela closed her eyes. "He . . ."

Zobayda took her friend's hand. "You are distressed. Take your time, my dear."

"The boy's sword came out so fast you could not see it," Carmela cried. "Someone said he had no weapon at all. But the guard's hand was severed." She turned to Zobayda and stared into her face. "They say the boy is a sorcerer, his followers not even human."

"Not human?"

"They say they have a greenish look, arms like roots, hair like vines."

A shiver of fear ran down Zobayda's spine. "Viridees," she murmured.

Carmela frowned. "Do you know of them?"

"I have met them." Zobayda stood up and began to pace the courtyard. "What are they doing here, so far from Africa?"

"Africa?" Carmela got to her feet and made for the door. "Lock yourself in, my dear. That's my advice."

"Stay with me," begged Zobayda.

"I must be with my children," said Carmela. "Go down to your husband's workshop and stay there until it's over. They have sent for Esteban Díaz." She stepped out and closed the door behind her.

Zobayda bolted the door and pulled the bar across it. She could hear screaming now, and the clatter of hooves. "Esteban Díaz," she breathed, as she hurried down to the workshop.

Esteban Díaz was the most famous swordsman in the kingdom of Castile. He had never been beaten in a fight. Several weeks ago, his daughter had been kidnapped and Esteban had gone to search for her. But it was rumored that he was returning to Toledo, to await the ransom note that must surely be delivered.

Zobayda was tempted to look out of the window, but decided instead to sit on a bench at the far end of the room. From here she could see almost every toy, and she tried to ignore the sounds outside and think of her husband, carefully cutting and stitching, carving and painting.

The screams, the roars, and the clatter of hooves were getting louder and closer. Had the boy conjured up an army?

Zobayda waited. Waited and waited. An unlikely battle raged in the streets. If the boy was a sorcerer, what kind of dreadful power could he use against the people? But, surely, if Esteban Díaz had arrived, there could only be one outcome. Even a sorcerer could not defeat the famous swordsman of Toledo.

The sun began to sink. The toys cast long shadows on the floor. The noise outside began to fade. Silence, at last. Had the boy and his viridees left the city, or were they dead?

A sudden crash above brought Zobayda to her feet. The courtyard door had been broken. She could hear the clangs of iron on stone as the bolts and the bar hit the ground. Silence again. Zobayda waited, clutching her throat.

A figure appeared at the top of the workshop steps: a boy in a green cloak. When he descended, the viridees followed. Four of them. Their footsteps soundless, their faces sickly, their eyes red as sores. They filled the room with their awful stench.

The boy came toward her, kicking the toys out of his way. He had no use for toys. He was no ordinary boy.

"Who are you?" asked Zobayda, her mind seeing the greenish bones under his pale cheeks.

The boy's smile was icy. "My father is lord of the viridees, my mother the daughter of Count Roken of Pomerishi. I am Count Harken." He gave a mocking bow.

Zobayda glanced at the tall figures behind the boy. Her throat was dry with fear. "What do you want?" she asked huskily.

"You are awaiting your brother, no doubt. Well, so am I. We will wait together."

Timoken and the five children had been heading west for several weeks, but they were making little progress. The land was dry and rocky. Even the horses found it hard going. Sometimes Gabar would refuse to go any farther. He would sink to his knees and chew at the rough grass and thorny undergrowth, ignoring all of Timoken's attempts to move him on. There was only one way to make the camel go faster. He would have to fly.

At first, Gabar did not think much of this idea. But Timoken pointed out that there were no other camels around to embarrass him, and it was not as though he would have to fly over a mountain. So, a little reluctantly, Gabar allowed Timoken to lift him a short distance above a particularly rocky stretch of land.

The first time they saw the camel flying, the children were, momentarily, too astonished to speak, and then they all began to cheer, urging their startled horses after the flying camel.

Now, they often traveled in this way, and they began to make better progress. At night Timoken would build a fire, and they would cook the food they had managed to find during the day. When Peredur suggested they steal a chicken from one of the hamlets they passed, Timoken knew that he would have to reveal yet another of his talents.

"If we are caught, we will be hanged as thieves," Timoken told Peredur.

"We won't be caught," Peredur insisted. "How else are we going to eat? The food the Magniers gave us has all gone."

"Except for this." Timoken took the last piece of dried meat from the bag. He cupped it in his hands for a moment, and muttered a request in the language of the secret kingdom. When he spread his palms, two pieces of meat were revealed.

The others stared at the meat, and then at Timoken. No one spoke as he multiplied the meat until there was enough for all of them.

"Thank you, Magician," Mabon said at last. "We will never go hungry again." Mabon loved his food.

That evening, as they sat around the fire, Beri talked about the day she was kidnapped. She was the only one who had not yet told her story. Timoken translated her words for the others.

"My father is famous in the kingdom of Castile," said Beri. "His name is Esteban Díaz, and he is the best swordsman in the land. Whenever there is a battle, our king calls for my father. He has never lost a fight, and the king has made him very wealthy. My mother is from Catalonia, and she wanted me to marry a distant cousin who lives there. His family is rich and well connected. But my father insisted that I meet this young man first and decide for myself. And so we made a long, uncomfortable journey to Catalonia, and all the way I kept seeing two men riding behind us. Following. I told my mother, but she insisted that I was imagining it."

"And what did you decide, when you met this cousin?" asked Timoken.

Beri pouted. "I did not like him. He was older than me. Fat and boring. I ran away from him, one day. And that is when I got caught. I think that the kidnappers had followed us all the way from Toledo. They had been waiting for a chance to grab me and when they saw me alone, outside the castle, they could not believe their luck. Before I could cry out, they had run up and, while one put his hand over my mouth, the other bound my hands and feet. I was thrown over one of the horses, and they galloped off before anyone even knew that I had left the castle."

"They were not the monks, then," said Timoken.

Beri shook her head. "The monks came later. Before a ransom note could be sent, the men who kidnapped me were killed by bandits. The bandits had no idea who I was. They passed me on to another gang, who sold me to those false monks. I don't know why they kept me in a cage. I could not understand their language."

"You were wearing a very fine robe," said Timoken. "Perhaps they wanted to keep you apart from the others and try to ransom you, when they could find out who you were."

"Perhaps I stand a better chance of survival, now that I am a boy," Beri said with a grin.

The season was turning. Nights were growing chilly. When the sun went down, the sky was filled with fiery colors. For several days now, troops of soldiers had been filling the roads, and rather than pass them, the children had taken to the woods. One evening they emerged from the trees and found themselves on a wide plateau. Far below, a river wound its way through sand-colored cliffs, flowering herbs filled the air with their wonderful scent, and the setting sun made everything glow with a warm, rosy light.

They decided to stop for the night, but before he made a fire, Timoken took out the moon cloak and spread it in the sunlight.

"I believe we should arm ourselves," he told the others. "There is someone who wants the moon cloak, and your lives may be in danger, as well as mine. So I shall hide it."

Without any more explanation, Timoken began to cast a spell. Using words from the secret kingdom, he began to transform the glittering silk of the web into a soft, crimson velvet. Before their eyes the delicate threads gathered together, rippled, and spun until a fine red cloak lay at their feet.

"You shall all have one," said Timoken. "And then the moon cloak will be truly hidden."

He set about changing their, by now, ragged jerkins into warm red cloaks. He turned slim green sticks into swords, and lines of twigs into wooden shields. Later, they used charcoal from the fire to draw signs on their shields, and Timoken turned the rough shapes into fine-colored emblems: a bear for Mabon, because he was the strongest; a wolf for Peredur with his sharp, wolfish teeth; an eagle for Edern, because it was the nearest he could get to flying; and for musical Gereint, a fish from a singing stream.

"And what will you have?" Timoken asked Beri, who was deciding.

"A hare," she said at last, drawing two ears on her shield. "Because I have never been allowed to run, and I find that I love it."

For himself, Timoken chose a burning sun, the sun that had turned the moon spider's silver threads into a red velvet cloak.

When they set off the next morning, they were ready for whatever challenges they might meet. Without even discussing it, each of them knew that a challenge would very soon come their way.

It came the very next day. A passing traveler told them that they must follow the road south if they were to reach the kingdom of Castile. So they took to the road again.

Timoken was the first to feel the danger. A tremor in the earth and a distant thunder filled him with a sense of foreboding. He looked back and saw a cloud of dust on the road behind them. And out of the dust came the black beast and the swaying wagon with its load of brown-robed villains.

CHAPTER 15
The Black Beast

S hall we run, or stand and fight?" Mabon had already turned his horse.

"I have a score to settle with those villains," said Peredur, brandishing his new sword.

Timoken hardly heard them. He knew what he must do. This time he did not even wave his cloak; there was no time. In the language of the secret kingdom, he called to the sky.

He was answered by a roll of thunder louder than the roar of any beast. In a second, the sky had turned an inky black and streaks of lightning flashed across the darkened landscape, striking the center of the wagon.

The wagon vanished behind a cloud of smoke, and a tall flame rose into the air. There was a distant shriek, and an acrid scent of burning filled their nostrils.

"Are they dead?" Edern looked at Timoken in awe.

"They will not follow us," Timoken replied. He could not say if the false monks were dead. He had done what he had to do. That was all.

The others cheered heartily; even Beri gave a whoop of joy. But it was too soon to celebrate. For now the black beast, untouched by the flames, walked out of the fire. Gabar trembled and gave a bleat of fear.

"Stay still, Gabar. I can stop this creature," said Timoken softly. He brought a shaft of lightning down upon the great beast's head. But still it came on. Bolts of burning light hit the creature again and again, as Timoken desperately called to the sky. He took off his cloak and swept it through the air, still calling. The lightning came down, striking the beast on every side. And still it came on.

The others had already turned their horses and were galloping away.

"The beast is possessed," shouted Edern. "It is the very devil. You can't defeat it, Timoken. Come away. NOW!"

Defeat tasted sour in Timoken's mouth. It made him afraid. But as he turned Gabar's head, he heard the beast give a bellow of surprise. The thundering hooves were still, and there came another sound, the growl of a big cat. Three growls.

Timoken looked over his shoulder. The horse had stopped in its tracks. It faced three large leopards, their bright coats glowing in the dark. It was as if they knew one another, the leopards and the horse that was not a horse. They could recognize the power and the enchantment beneath the coarse black hair and the spotted coats.

"Sun Cat! Flame Chin! Star! You have found me," breathed Timoken.

The enraged beast pawed the ground. It lowered its great head and charged at Flame Chin, who stood between his brothers. As Flame Chin twisted away, Sun Cat leaped onto the beast's lowered neck, while Star bounded onto its back. Snorting with fury, the beast tossed its head; flames from its nostrils licked Sun Cat's paws, but the leopard clung on, his claws biting deep into the beast's skull.

Timoken was aware of the other children moving up behind him.

"What are those creatures?" whispered Beri.

"Leopards," said Timoken.

"Where have they come from?" asked Edern.

"From Africa. They have always been with me."

They watched in silent amazement as the four creatures fought. Flame Chin was now braving the beast's furious kicks. One strike of those hooves would have felled him in a second. But with astonishing agility, the leopard avoided them and leaped at a kicking hind leg, biting deep into the flesh.

The beast reared up; it shook its massive head, but the leopards clung on. Suddenly, Sun Cat leaned over and sank his teeth into the black neck. The creature stumbled; it heaved a dreadful sigh and began to sink to the ground. Its groans were almost pitiful, and Timoken had to remind himself that it was not a horse, but a creature conjured up by wickedness.

The leopards did not release their grip until the beast was on its knees, its neck twisted and its nose on the ground. Star and Sun Cat slipped off the body, lifted their heads, and growled contentedly. Flame Chin withdrew his teeth from the torn leg and joined his brothers. They might have killed the beast, but they would not eat its flesh. It was not an animal, and it tasted poisonous.

"I thank you once again, my friends," said Timoken.

The leopards purred. "The thing cannot hurt you now," said Sun Cat.

"I still have far to go," said Timoken.

"We will be with you," said Flame Chin.

"Always," said Star.

The three leopards moved out of sight so swiftly it was impossible to tell in which direction they had gone.

Timoken realized that the others were staring at him. They looked bewildered.

"Can you even speak to leopards?" said Beri.

"They are friends," Timoken replied. "I am sorry if my growls frightened you."

Beri smiled. "They were very gentle growls."

Recovering his composure, Mabon said, "That fight has given me an appetite."

"For food?" said Timoken. "Let's find somewhere safe to eat." He had no need to urge Gabar down the road. The camel could not wait to get away from the fallen beast. The sun came out again. Gereint began to sing, and everyone joined in.

They found an orchard full of ripe apples. Peredur caught a rabbit, and they ate contentedly beneath the trees. That night they slept in a deserted hut. Timoken hung his cloak across the door, as was his habit now. But he was glad to know that the leopards were close.

The children decided that it would be good to work for a living. There were ripened apples in the orchards, and grapes filling the vineyards. The farmers were glad of their help and asked no questions. For their labor the children only wanted a hunk of bread and some cheese at midday, and a square meal before the sun set.

Timoken thought he should wear a turban to hide his thin gold crown. When Beri asked why he did not just remove the crown, he replied shyly that it was something he had tried all his life to do. But it was impossible.

The others attempted to pull off the crown. One by one they tugged and twisted the thin gold buried in Timoken's hair. But eventually they gave up. Edern declared that Timoken was meant to be a king, and they had better not argue with fate.

Timoken put on his turban with a resigned expression. "Edern might be right," he said. "But a king without a kingdom seems a sorry sort of person." And then he smiled, just to let them know that he really did not mind.

After several weeks, they reached the kingdom of Castile. The country had been ravaged by war, but to Beri it was home and it was beautiful. The roads were thronged with soldiers and, once again, Timoken and his friends took to the fields, to the woods, the mountains, and the wide, sandy plains.

Gabar had been quiet and gloomy ever since the incident with the black beast. And Timoken worried that, without the Alixir, the camel would suddenly become old. But after a few days walking over the sand, Gabar's mood improved considerably. He had seen other camels on the road, though he thought them a little inferior, tied one to another in a line and weighed down with provisions and weaponry. Some had almost lost their humps.

"Pathetic," he snorted, lifting his head in a superior manner and prancing forward.

"Do not belittle them," said Timoken. "They did not ask to join an army."

The soldiers were not his only worry. In spite of the bright sun, Timoken found himself caught in a mood that he could not shake off. He would laugh and sing with the others, but his heart was heavy with foreboding. It was as though a dark cloud lay between himself and the blue sky. Every day it grew worse.

Beri appeared to know the way now, but occasionally she would stop and ask for directions. Some of the villages they passed had been abandoned and destroyed, but there were people in the small, more remote hamlets. She became impatient to get home. Toledo seemed so near and yet so far. Traveling through the wilder parts of the country took far too long, she said, and she begged Timoken to take to the road again. But he would not. "I do not like soldiers," he would say.

When they finally came within sight of Toledo, they found that it was just as Beri had described: a beautiful walled city built on seven hills and almost encircled by the river. A city that shone with welcome . . . and yet . . .

"We must take the road, now," Beri cried triumphantly. "Or we will not reach any of the bridges into the city." They were on a small rise above the plain, with the road clearly visible beneath them. Beri kicked her horse and began to gallop down the hill.

"Wait, Beri!" shouted Timoken.

"What are you afraid of?" Edern asked, looking anxiously at Timoken.

"Those!" Timoken pointed to the dark shapes sitting on the city wall. There were more on the roofs, on the arches, and on the gates.

"Statues?" said Edern.

"No." The dread in Timoken's heart became heavier every second.

"Then what?" asked Edern.

"Birds," Timoken said in a low voice. "And then, not birds."

"You do not make sense." Mabon lifted a hand to shade his eyes and stared at the city. "Surely, birds cannot hurt us."

Timoken's finger burned. He looked at the ring. The eyes in the small silver face were wide with fear. A thin voice came creeping out. "Do not enter the city."

"But I must," said Timoken. "You told me that my sister, Zobayda, was there."

"I hinted," agreed the forest-jinni.

"So why should I not enter the city?"

"HE is there also," whispered the ring.

"I thought as much," Timoken said grimly.

Peredur turned his horse impatiently. "We should be following Beri, not consulting a ring," he said.

"Hush!" Timoken said abruptly. "I must know what is happening in the city."

"We shall find out soon enough." Mabon began to follow Peredur down the road, but his horse reared as a terrible scream came from the direction of the city.

Timoken urged Gabar after the others, while Edern and Gereint galloped ahead. Mabon managed to calm his horse, and came racing behind the camel.

They found Beri's horse in a small copse beside the road. A boy was holding the reins. His clothes were ragged and his face scarred by deep scratches. Beri was lying at his feet.

"What has happened here?" Timoken slipped off the camel and ran to Beri. "Did you hurt her?" He spoke in the Castilian language that he had learned from Beri.

The others dismounted and gathered around the girl on the ground.

"He — she asked what had happened," the boy said defensively. "And so I told her."

Beri began to moan. Timoken helped her to sit up and Gereint gave her his water bag. She pushed it away, covering her face with her hands. And then she began to cry. Timoken had never heard such sobbing. He thought her body might break under the weight of such terrible grief. She rocked back and forth, hardly able to breathe, as the wails and groans poured out of her.

"What happened, then?" Timoken demanded. "Speak, boy."

"The city has been invaded," said the boy. "See those birds?" He pointed to the city walls. "They did this to me." He touched his scarred forehead. "But I was lucky. Some died. A sorcerer came, and four men, who were not men . . . greenish creatures they were, things that changed and caught and tortured. The sorcerer was just a youth, but he had magic weapons: a sword that could fly, fiery stones, and a gaze that had death in it. The people ran into their houses and there they stayed. Esteban Díaz was sent for."

"Esteban Díaz?" Timoken looked at Beri.

She had no more tears left, and sat quietly staring ahead.

"Esteban Díaz is her father," Timoken murmured.

The boy hung his head. "I am sorry. I did not know that when I told her the news."

"Is he dead, then?"

The boy nodded miserably. "The bravest soldier in all Castile — maybe the world. He killed two of the creatures when they surrounded him. But the sorcerer was indestructible. And then the birds came. They were like no other birds that I have ever seen. They were not properly feathered. Their beaks were knives, their talons . . ." The boy shook his head. "They attacked Esteban from above. He had no chance. While he struck out at them, the youth ran him through — and he died."

"You saw this?" asked Timoken.

"I was hiding in a doorway, too afraid to move."

They stared at the boy. The others had come to understand a little of the language, having listened so often to Beri. There was no doubt in their minds about what had been said.

Beri seemed to be in a trance. Timoken touched her arm and said, "I am sorry, Beri. I can find no other words. But I understand your grief."

"Let us leave this place," said Mabon. "We came to Toledo to find Beri's father. Now there is no need."

"I know what you are saying!" Beri leaped to her feet, glaring at Mabon. "You want to run away, don't you? But the murderer must be punished."

The other boys shifted uncomfortably. None of them wanted to confront a sorcerer and an army of savage flying creatures. They wanted to get away from the city as fast as possible.

In spite of the forest-jinni's warning, Timoken knew he could not run away. Getting to his feet, he scanned the distant towers and spires, the tiled roofs and the tall stone walls. "Where is the sorcerer now?" he asked the boy.

"They say he went to the house of Tariq, the toy maker." The boy's gaze drifted away from Timoken. "They say he is waiting for an African — on a camel."

"Then I shall not keep him waiting," said Timoken. "You can stay here," he said to the others. "You are not bound to me, and there is no call for you to risk your lives." Without waiting for Gabar to crouch, he took a flying leap and landed in the saddle.

"But the birds," cried Edern. "How will you defeat the birds?"

Timoken smiled. "You will see."

As Gabar trotted down the hill, Timoken was already recalling the voices of the eagles he had met on his long journey. In his head, he heard the cries of falcons, of giant owls and greedy gulls, and all the birds of prey that he had ever listened to. Lifting his head, he began to call them.

Beri sprang onto her horse and began to follow Timoken. "You do not expect me to stay behind, do you?" she cried.

Gereint suddenly sang out, "I know what Timoken is doing. I too can cry like a bird. I am going to Toledo."

Edern scowled. He wished he had been the first to follow Timoken. "Come on, Peredur, Mabon. We cannot let them go without us."

And so the company of six was together when they reached the first bridge into Toledo. Their swords were drawn, their emblazoned shields hung at their sides. The wolf, the bear, the fish, the eagle, the hare, and the blazing sun. The guards had fled and the gates were open, but as the children trotted into the city, the black birds rose into the air and began to circle above them.

The city appeared to be deserted, but weeping could be heard behind the shuttered windows. The only other sounds came from the great black birds, a high-pitched, dreadful shrieking.

Timoken searched the sky for the birds he had called, but there was no sign of them.

"Only one thing for it," he said, standing on the saddle.

"Timoken, what are you doing?" cried Beri.

"I am going into battle."

Gabar grunted, "Do you want me to come with you?"

"Not this time, my family," said Timoken, laughing. His black mood had lifted and, still smiling, he sailed into the sky, his sword pointed straight at the head of the biggest bird.

CHAPTER 16
The Sign of the Serpent

The wheeling circle of birds began to close up, and Timoken found himself sailing into the center of a densely packed flock. The wind tore at his cloak, leaving his body unprotected, but the birds seemed afraid of the billowing red velvet and tilted away, shrieking with fury.

Timoken went after them, slashing at wings and talons. They soared above him and then swooped down, so fast he hardly had time to draw breath. Razor-sharp beaks tore at his turban again and again, until it unraveled and blew away in shreds, leaving his head exposed to their vicious stabs. Timoken lifted his shield over his head, but time and again, the birds knocked it away. Desperately, he kicked out at them. He lunged at the black heads and jabbed at the fiery eyes, and as he twisted and whirled he used their own language to curse and threaten them. But they still came at him, and he felt his strength begin to ebb. His sword arm ached, his head throbbed, and he found himself dropping, helplessly, lower and lower.

One of the birds swooped toward Timoken, its beak pointed at his eye; a second later a shutter snapped across his vision, and the world went black.

Covering his face with his shield arm, Timoken felt blood running across his cheeks; blood that was mixed with tears. He did not want to die before he saw his sister again. But when he drew his arm away, Timoken realized that he was not blind after all; a dark cloud had covered the sun. It seemed to fill the sky. And out of the cloud came sounds that Timoken recognized: a thousand voices, the voices of eagles and hawks, of gulls and owls, and of every bird of prey that he had ever heard. And they all spoke with one voice: "We are with you!"

The cloud fell on the black birds, covering them like a shroud; it flew around them and beneath them, until nothing could be seen of the fearful creatures. Their furious screams rose above the cries of the thousand birds of prey.

Help had come not a moment too soon. Timoken knew that he could not have defended himself any longer. The black creatures would have torn him to shreds. His throat was parched, his head pounded, but he managed to utter a feeble, "Thank you, my friends," before he dropped to earth.

Timoken lay where he had fallen, on the dusty road into the city. His friends rode up to him, with Gabar galloping behind.

"Is he dead?" cried Beri.

"Looks like they finished him off," said Mabon.

"No!" shouted Edern. "That cannot be."

"He looks dead," said Peredur, and Gereint agreed.

Timoken raised himself on one elbow and grinned at them. "Don't believe everything you see," he said to Peredur.

They leaped off their horses and surrounded him, cheering with relief and joy.

"You look terrible, Timoken," said Mabon.

Edern said, "Without wounds, a hero is not a hero."

"I'm not a hero yet." Timoken felt strong and confident. "Let us go into the city," he said, jumping to his feet. Gabar crouched to let him mount, and he swung himself easily into the saddle.

"You are very bloody," Beri remarked, looking at Timoken's tunic. "Do you not have a clean garment in one of those bags?" She glanced at the bundles hanging from his saddle.

"I am alive," said Timoken, raising his sword. "That is all that matters."

On the street outside the toy maker's house, the sorcerer stood watching the cloud of birds. One by one, the flying creatures that he had created with such cunning dropped like wet rags onto roofs and walls and cobblestones. A bundle of bones and black feathers fell at his feet and he stepped back. One end of his mouth curled up in a grim smile. "Well, African, a new game can begin," he muttered.

Watching from their windows, others had seen the monstrous creatures fall. Cautiously, people began to emerge onto the streets. They looked at their neighbors and shook their heads, murmuring, "Is it all over? We thought the end of the world had come."

A small procession was moving up the main street. People turned to look. They saw a boy on a camel and, behind him, five children on weary-looking horses. One of them suddenly rode up beside the camel. He — no, it was a girl — swept off her battered headgear, and a mane of golden hair tumbled out.

"I am Berenice, daughter of Esteban Díaz," cried the girl, "and I have come to avenge the death of my father. Where is the murderer?"

Someone pointed to an alley leading off the main street. Others nodded, and a woman shouted, "He is in the house of Tariq the toy maker. Tariq is dead now, but his wife still lives."

"The sorcerer keeps her prisoner," cried an old man.

"Don't go there, child," said another woman. "You cannot avenge your father. He was murdered by a sorcerer. Wait for the soldiers."

"This is Timoken." Beri pointed up at him. "He is a magician, and he has just defeated the flying creatures that have been menacing our city."

The crowd stared up at the boy on the camel. He had certainly been in a fight. His white tunic was streaked with blood, his face and hands were scarred with deep scratches. There was a glimmer of gold in his hair. Could it be a crown?

Timoken slid off the camel's back, and the others dismounted. Children ran forward to hold the reins. They were proud that a boy, no bigger than themselves, had defeated the flying monsters.

One of the boys pointed to the narrow street a few paces behind him. "The sorcerer and his creatures are down there," he said. "We saw them."

"Which door?" asked Timoken.

"The sign of the camel," a small girl told him.

Timoken felt the eyes of the crowd on him. He could not fail now. But before he faced the sorcerer, he had to do something about his sword and shield. They had not protected him as well as they might have. He sat on the cobblestones and laid the sword across his lap. In the language of the secret kingdom, he begged the weapon to defend him, to be invincible against all enemies, and to end the life of any being that wished him dead.

The people listened to the African's chanting. They watched in awed silence as he ran his fingers over the sword, and they saw a silver ring on the middle finger of his left hand. The ring flashed as though it were made of fire.

Timoken put his sword aside and, laying his shield over his knees, he repeated his chant. When he had finished, he asked his friends to hand him their weapons. One by one he ran his fingers over the swords and the shields with their bright emblems: the wolf and the bear, the fish and the eagle, and the running hare.

"This means that we are coming with you," said Edern, as Timoken returned his sword.

"I want it to be your choice." Timoken stood up. He glanced at Beri.

"Do you expect me to choose safety, when I have a chance to avenge my father?" she said hotly.

"No." Timoken's face was solemn.

Beri quickly tied her long hair into a knot at the back of her head. "I am ready," she said.

Timoken had been prepared to go alone, but it was good to hear his friends' footsteps close behind him. He came to a flight of steps. The door at the top was painted with the sign of a camel, and he smiled to himself. A camel could only bring good luck. But as he looked at it, the camel became a fluid thing; it turned from gold to green, the head withered and melted into the long neck. The legs vanished and the body stretched into a narrow, writhing creature: a living serpent.

Timoken mounted the steps. The others followed. He stared at the moving green coils twisting and sliding across the wood. He had never seen magic like this. His friends took a step back, but Timoken tucked his sword into its scabbard and put his fingers on the ringed door handle. As he began to turn it, the serpent's head lunged toward his hand, its open mouth revealing lethal fangs. Timoken was quicker. In a flash he had seized the thing by the neck. It hissed in fury, its jaws widening, its yellow eyes glaring. But Timoken kept his grip until the serpent's mouth began to close. Its eyes rolled back into its head and it was still.

"I do not trust it," muttered Timoken, dropping the serpent to the ground.

Without hesitating, Edern pulled out his sword and cut off the serpent's head.

The others stared at it in horror. If this was the beginning of a battle, what could they expect to find behind the toy maker's door?

Timoken turned the handle and the door swung open. At first he could see nothing but an empty courtyard. There was a stone seat in the center and, behind the seat, a rosebush covered in golden yellow blooms. A breeze sent their fragrance drifting toward the group, but when they inhaled the lovely perfume, it turned sour in their nostrils and became foul and dreadful. The strength of the smell made their stomachs churn, and while they were reeling and retching about the courtyard, the petals on the bush withered and dropped. Behind the dying blooms, three shadowy figures could now be seen.

"At last!" called a voice.

Timoken shivered. It was the voice of a youth, but its tone was ancient and evil.

Someone came out of the shadows and walked around the rosebush. The youth was not much taller than Timoken. His golden-brown hair touched his shoulders, and his eyes were the color of polished green olives. Timoken instantly shifted his gaze to the hand that rested on the tip of the youth's sword. "Do not look into his eyes," he told the others.

"You know what I want." The sorcerer's smile was almost pleasant.

"The web of the last moon spider," said Timoken. "But you shall never have it."

"You could have added, 'while there is breath left in my body,'" said the youth. "And I would have answered, 'The breath in your body has not long to last.'"

"The breath in my body will last forever," said Timoken. Now that he was face-to-face with his enemy, he felt quite calm. He was aware of the two viridees, gliding around the other side of the bush, and, without turning his head, he said softly, "Be ready, my friends. Remember, your swords are invincible."

"We are ready," said Edern.

The sorcerer took a step toward Timoken. "I see you have your sister's ring," he said. "A pity she was left without it."

Timoken frowned. "What do you know of my sister?"

"I know that she lies dead in her husband's workshop."

"What?" Timoken clutched his chest. He could not breathe.

"Poor African. Did you not know that this is her house?"

Speechless with shock, Timoken shook his head.

"At least it WAS." The sorcerer's voice was filled with gleeful spite. "She would not be quiet, you see. She wanted to warn you, and whatever I did to her, she would still raise herself and shout and scream. So I had to —"

Timoken heard no more. His shriek of anguish drowned every other sound. His sword was in his hand and he was flying at the youth. Again and again he slashed at the bobbing head, but found that he was cutting through empty air. The sorcerer had become a column of smoke, a spinning green cloud. But his sword was still a weapon, and it came at Timoken in a lightning flash. Timoken raised his shield, but the youth's enchanted sword came snaking across his chest, and Timoken's movements had to become faster than seemed humanly possible. He whirled around, so that the red cloak covered every part of him except his head.

A voice cried, "I see it now! I see the web! You are wearing it, you foolish king."

But the sorcerer's sword could not penetrate the red moon cloak, and so he sent a shower of fiery stones raining down on Timoken. Most bounced harmlessly off the spellbound wood of his shield, but one of the burning stones caught the back of his neck. He staggered and fell. In a glance, he took in the fighting all about him. One of the viridees had curled its fingers around Edern's sword and pulled it out of his grasp. Before the creature could turn the sword on Edern, Beri sliced at its arm and the severed limb fell to the ground, leaving the creature gurgling with rage.

Almost too late, Timoken saw the sorcerer's blade coming at his chest. He parried the blow with his own sword, but now the whirling column came so close that Timoken could see the sorcerer's form behind the vapor. He could see the green sinews, the long fluid limbs, and the shifting, spongelike skull beneath the handsome face.

"What are you?" Timoken breathed.

"I am the only human son of Degal, lord of the viridees." The sorcerer's voice rose in triumph. "The dark blood of the forest runs in my veins, and mine is the only human heart that cannot be touched by love or the sword."

"You are not human!" cried Timoken, jumping up.

The cloud-wrapped form whirled around him, and the air hummed in its wake. Timoken turned with the cloud, bending, twisting, and leaping, as the sorcerer's sword sliced the air about him.

"And are YOU human?" screeched the sorcerer. "A boy who flies; a boy whose life depends on the web of the last moon spider?"

Timoken tried not to listen, tried to anticipate the next thrust of the sorcerer's gleaming blade, but his head was throbbing, and he wondered how long he could keep his eye on the spinning cloud.

All at once the shrouded sorcerer became very still. Timoken stared at the cloud, waiting. After such frenzied movement, its stillness was unnerving. When it came, the sword thrust was so fast, Timoken hardly saw it. How he avoided it, he would never know, but, twisting aside, he lunged at the cloud, sending his sword deep into its core, and he prayed that he had found, if not his enemy's heart, then whatever force it was that kept him alive.

For a few seconds, the cloud continued to spin, but gradually it dwindled. As it sank to the ground, a deathly wail came out of it. The sound was so terrible that Timoken had to drop his sword and cover his ears.

The viridees were nowhere to be seen, but a trail of thick green slime ran over the cobblestones at his feet. Edern was sitting on the ground with his head between his hands. When he felt Timoken's eyes on him, he looked up and grinned.

The others were all on their feet. Battered and bloody, they looked cheerfully triumphant.

"We have won, my friends!" Timoken raised his sword.

His eyes had left the cloud for only a moment, but in that time it had vanished.

"Did you see it?" he asked the others. "Where did it go?"

They shrugged, and Mabon said, "A sorcerer can vanish, you know."

Edern added quietly, "My uncle can do that — almost."

Timoken picked up the sorcerer's weapon. There were strange symbols carved into the blade: a sword made with magic, and yet the sorcerer could not take it with him.

As he studied the symbols, Timoken could see a small creature moving behind them. It was as though the bright steel were a mirror, reflecting objects that could not be seen by the human eye.

Timoken could make out the thing more clearly now. It was a serpent. The reflection of the shining creature darted up a wall; it dropped to the ground, slithered across a street, and vanished into the shadows.

Dropping the sword, Timoken rushed to the courtyard door. He squinted into the shadows, crying, "Did you see it? Did you see it?"

Edern ran up behind him. "See what?"

"The serpent. It was small, you could have missed it."

"There are many lizards," said Edern. "They are basking on the wall. No doubt you mistook one for a serpent."

"No," Timoken said firmly. He closed the door. "It is gone now."

The others crowded around him. "Was it the sorcerer?" asked Mabon. "There's no sign of him."

"How could he vanish like that?" asked Peredur.

"He is a sorcerer," said Timoken.

Gereint looked alarmed. "Not dead, then."

Timoken shrugged. "It is likely that he has many lives. I have taken only one of them."

"Will he come back here?" asked Peredur.

"We will soon be gone," Timoken reassured him. "And then there will be nothing for him in Toledo." He noticed that Beri was sitting alone on the stone seat. She looked drained of life. Her face showed not a spark of her former bravado. She had killed a viridee, but she did not know if she had avenged her father. For where was the sorcerer now?

Timoken sat beside her. The others looked on. They wanted to celebrate, but they could not. Beri had lost her father, so how could they expect her to smile?

"You are the bravest girl that I have ever met," said Mabon. Beri was not to know that, coming from Mabon, this was an unheard-of compliment.

"It is true," agreed Edern.

"The bravest," said Gereint.

"And the most beautiful," mumbled Peredur, his cheeks reddening.

Timoken agreed with all them all, but he had nothing to add. He could only think of his sister, lying somewhere in the house. He could not believe that she was dead. She had taken the Alixir for more than a hundred years, so, surely, even a sorcerer could not end her life.

The boys' kind words failed to comfort Beri. Their sympathy tipped her over into tears again. This time she hardly made a sound. But her shoulders began to shake and a river of tears flowed down her cheeks and dripped onto her battle-stained tunic.

Timoken did not know what to do. The sight of those tears tore at his heart and he had to close his eyes. In the language of the secret kingdom, he quietly begged the sky to show Beri that, in spite of everything, the world was still beautiful.

There was a moment of silence before he felt a light touch on his shoulder.

"Rain," said Edern. "And the sun is still shining."

Timoken opened his eyes. Raindrops were falling all about them, sparkling in the sunlight. They sprinkled the creepers on the walls until every leaf held a tiny diamond. They fell into Beri's lap and splashed onto her feet. Raindrops like pearls rolled over the toes peeping out of her sandals, and the roses behind her bloomed again. Fragrant petals, as soft as silk, fluttered onto her head. Beri breathed in their perfume and smiled. "I know this place," she said.

"You know it?" said Timoken.

"My father brought me here to buy a doll."

"Where was the toy maker's workshop, Beri?"

She nodded toward an arch set into a corner of the wall.

Timoken ran to the corner. No one followed. He saw a flight of steps leading down to an arched doorway. When he looked back, he found his friends staring at him, their faces solemn and concerned.

The steps were steep, and Timoken's legs shook as he descended. He longed to see his sister again, but he was afraid of what he might find when he reached the room at the bottom.

He took a deep breath and forced himself to hurry down the last few steps. He looked through the doorway and saw a room full of toys. Sunlight came slanting through the windows, intensifying the bright colors of wooden dolls and animals. Some, he noticed, had been smashed and broken.

A woman was lying on a bench at the end of the room. Stepping carefully over the broken toys, Timoken walked toward the bench.

Zobayda lay with her hands clasped on her chest. Timoken knew that his sister was old now, but she did not look old. Her hair was black and her cheeks unlined. Her eyes were closed, but she did not look dead. He laid his ear over her heart. A faint sound reached him, the lightest whisper. But Zobayda's eyes remained closed, her hands as still as death.

"You are not dead, Zobayda," cried Timoken. "I know it. I can hear your heartbeat. Every night, for more than one hundred years, you laid under the web of the last moon spider. A sorcerer's spell could not undo that."

Pulling off the moon cloak, Timoken threw it over his sister. "Open your eyes, Zobayda," he demanded. "You are alive!"

Zobayda's lips parted and she gave a long sigh. Her eyelids fluttered and then flew open. "Timoken!" she said, and almost laughing, she sat up.

CHAPTER 17
The Golden Castle

When brother and sister came up into the courtyard they were greeted with a huge cheer. The Britons gathered around them and, one by one, were introduced to Zobayda, whose smile grew wider every second. And then she saw Beri sitting alone on the stone seat.

"And who is this?" asked Zobayda, looking at Beri.

"A brave girl who lives in Toledo," said Timoken.

"I've seen you before," said Zobayda.

"Yes." Beri got to her feet. "My father brought me here . . . to choose a doll."

"Your father." Zobayda frowned. She knew the girl now. "I'm so sorry."

"Yes. Esteban Díaz." Beri twisted her hands together. "I am happy for your . . . recovery," she told Zobayda, "but I cannot celebrate." Her eyes roamed over the group of Britons and then came to rest on Timoken. "Good-bye," she said. "I wish you luck." Before anyone could move or speak, she stepped lightly through the door and was gone.

Only a moment after Beri's swift departure, two finely dressed gentlemen appeared in the doorway.

"The orphans told us that the menace has been defeated," said the younger man.

"Orphans?" said Timoken.

"Sadly, there are many of them in the city," said the older man. "You were unaware of them, no doubt, but they saw what happened here."

"We have come to congratulate you and to thank you." In spite of his fine clothes, the younger man had the face of an adventurer. His hair was black and curly and he wore an earring in his left ear. "I believe that one of you is — how can I put it — a magician?"

"My brother, Timoken." Zobayda proudly lifted her brother's arm.

Surprising Timoken, the two men bowed. They introduced themselves as Francisco Padilla, who was the older of the two, and Juan Pizarro. They were wealthy merchants, they explained, and would be honored to supply a feast for the magician and his friends. It would have to be a subdued affair, however, as the city was in mourning for the great and inestimably brave soldier, Esteban Díaz. Therefore, unhappily, they could not attend the feast themselves, nor could any city dignitaries. "But all of you," said Francisco, inclining his head toward the group, "all will be provided with the best food we have, attendants to wait upon you and, for each of you, a bed in my own house."

Timoken thanked Francisco. He looked forward to the feast, he said, but he would rather sleep in his sister's house, though he could not answer for his friends, the Britons.

"Britons?" said Juan Pizarro, with a puzzled frown. "They are far from home."

"They were kidnapped," said Timoken. "But they mean to return to their own country as soon as they can, and I . . ." He looked at Zobayda. "I had intended to go with them, but now . . ."

"I am not yet weary of adventure," Zobayda said curtly. "Nothing shall part us now."

By this time, the four Britons were looking quite bemused. They could only understand a few words of Castilian, and were desperate to find out what was being said. Timoken quickly translated. He could not help laughing when he spoke about the feast; his four friends' eyes widened with delight, and Mabon even rubbed his stomach.

While Timoken was translating, Juan Pizarro had been thoughtfully stroking his beard. Now he said, "I own a ship. It sails north in seven days. It carries silk and carpets to Britain. It could also carry you. But you would have to leave the city at first light tomorrow."

When Timoken told the others, they gave a loud cheer and hugged one another heartily.

"Fresh horses will be provided for you all," said Juan. "You can leave them on the dock and my man, Pedro, will bring them back."

"Thank you." Timoken hesitated before saying, "I have a camel. I cannot leave him behind."

"A camel. Ah, yes, he is being cared for in my stables." Juan frowned and stroked his beard again. "I am afraid that the captain will not allow him on the ship."

"I will persuade him," Timoken said firmly.

That evening, the five friends and Zobayda sat down to the grandest feast they could ever have imagined. There were boxes of figs; bowls of fruit the Britons had never even heard of; platters of fish, stuffed and baked; meat of every description; pickled eggs; and large green cheeses piled around crisp brown bread. And then there were bowls of almond biscuits and mounds of rich spiced cakes.

"This is even better than our prince's food," said Edern, gazing around the candlelit hall. The walls were hung with bright carpets, and the beams in the vaulted ceiling were decorated with patterns in red and gold.

"Good to have a knife and spoon again," said Gereint, who was more fastidious than his friends.

Mabon was not even bothering with his knife and spoon. He was piling food on his bronze platter and stuffing it into his mouth as though he might never eat again. The floor around him was littered with bones, and his platter surrounded by greasy bread and half-eaten fruit. He was determined to try everything.

Timoken exchanged glances with his sister, who was sitting next to him. They could both remember a time, in the secret kingdom, when they dined off golden plates and drank from goblets made of silver. And yet Timoken's mind rested on the nights he had spent with his companions, sitting together around the fire, eating the foods of the forest, with only a starlit sky for their roof. And he wondered if, perhaps, those were the best feasts of all.

When they could eat no more, and were almost falling asleep, the four Britons were shown to the beds that had been made up for them. There were two rooms with a large four-poster in each. The covers were made of linen and the curtains of heavy silk.

"We could all fit in one bed," Edern declared.

But the others decided that, for once, they would like a little more room to stretch. And because Edern did not seem to mind a squash, he was made to share with Mabon, who really should have had a bed to himself.

"I shall not sleep a wink," Edern whispered to Timoken, who had gone up to see the sleeping arrangements. "Mabon has eaten so much; I dread the noises that will come out of him."

Timoken was still laughing when he went down to join his sister.

"I always wanted children," Zobayda told her brother. "But Tariq and I were never blessed. Now, I have five children to look after. I am very happy."

"There might have been six," said Timoken, thinking of Beri.

Before leaving, they thanked Francisco Padilla's cook for the excellent food and asked him to convey their best wishes to his master. "And one more thing," said Timoken. "There is so much food left over, will you give it to the city orphans?"

"We try to do our best for them," said the cook. "Francisco Padilla will be pleased with your request."

As they stepped out into the cool night air, Timoken said, "Zobayda, do you know where Beri lives?"

"Of course. Everyone knows. Esteban Díaz has a grand house at the top of the city."

"Will you take me there?"

"Timoken," Zobayda said gently, "no one will come to the door. The family will be in mourning."

"Take me anyway," begged Timoken.

So Zobayda led her brother up the steep streets to a large house decorated with many fine carvings. Timoken mounted the steps to the tall oak doors and knocked. No one answered. He became aware of weeping behind the thick walls. It seemed to come from every part of the building.

"Come away, Timoken," said Zobayda.

Timoken stood there a moment longer, even though he knew it was hopeless. He was unaccountably sad to think that he would never see Beri again.

"I only wanted to say good-bye," he murmured, turning reluctantly from the door.

Brother and sister had so much to tell each other, it was past midnight before they went to sleep. Within a few hours, Timoken heard a pounding on the courtyard door.

"Are you not ready?" said Edern, when Timoken's sleepy face appeared at the door. "The horses are waiting. The others are already mounted, and Juan Pizarro has provided a guide to show us the way."

"We were talking." Timoken rubbed his eyes. "Horses, you say . . ." Suddenly, he was wide awake. "But my camel — what has become of Gabar? I forgot him last night, so much was happening."

Edern grinned. "Your camel is in excellent hands. The boy we met at the gates has been caring for him."

Timoken found Zobayda throwing her possessions into a large bag.

"I cannot leave all the toys," she said. "I must take something to remind me of Tariq."

Timoken watched patiently as she rolled carved animals into her shawls and dresses. When one bag was full, she began on another. They would not be able to carry so many bundles down the street, so Timoken ran off to bring his camel up to the steps.

What a strange reunion it was. Zobayda and the camel stared at each other for what seemed like minutes before she asked, softly, "Do you think he knows me?"

Gabar appeared to be concentrating fiercely. Not a muscle moved, not a whisker twitched, not an eyelash fluttered.

"Do you remember Zobayda?" Timoken asked the camel.

"I could never forget," said Gabar.

To Zobayda, it sounded like a grunt of approval. She came down the steps until she was level with the camel's head. She kissed his nose and he nuzzled her neck. It was as if they had never been parted.

They caught up with the others on the bridge, and another long journey began.

The small procession reached the coast just in time. The ship was already loaded and due to sail the very next morning. Pedro, the guide, took a boat and carried his master's sealed letter out to the captain. He came back with good news and bad. The captain would be happy to have six children and a lady aboard, but as for a camel, that would be impossible. Camels were large, heavy, and dangerous.

"He is a very obedient camel," Timoken protested.

Pedro shook his head. "They will not take him."

Timoken looked up at Gabar. Did he understand what was being said? His expression gave nothing away. His large eyes always looked sad, his mouth always a little submissive.

"I will make sure he is well treated," said Pedro. "Juan Pizarro holds camels in high regard. He will have a good life."

Timoken led Gabar to the barn where the horses had already been stabled. He watched the camel drink deeply from the trough, and he left the barn while Gabar's back was still turned. He could not find a way to say good-bye to his companion of more than two hundred years.

There was only room for one in the tavern beside the dock. Zobayda insisted she would be quite comfortable on a bale of straw, but eventually accepted the bed, while the children went to a barn beside the stable.

Timoken did not attempt to sleep. He lay in the straw with his arms tucked behind his head, staring out at the night sky. He could hear the animals moving in the stable and he thought of Gabar.

A figure, holding a lantern, appeared in the open doorway; a small person, silhouetted against the moonlit sky.

Timoken's hand flew to the knife in his belt, but a soft voice said, "Timoken, it's me."

The others were awake now. Dangerous journeys had made light sleepers of them.

"Who is it?" called Peredur.

"It's me, Beri."

"Beri?" Timoken sat up.

The lantern was lifted, and now Timoken could see her more clearly. She was dressed as a boy again, and her hair was tucked into a leather hat.

"It's Running Hare!" cried Mabon.

"Running Hare!" echoed Gereint.

"We shall be six again," said Mabon joyfully. "The wolf and the bear, the fish and the eagle —"

"The burning sun and the running hare." Edern rolled out of his straw bed and crawled over to Timoken.

Beri came into the barn and sat beside the boys. "A friend of mine was helping in Francisco Padilla's kitchen," she said. "She heard you talking about the ship, and she came to tell me. I left the city only an hour after you. My horse is stabled and now I want nothing more than to sleep."

"But you are in mourning . . . and your mother . . ."

"I have seven brothers and sisters, enough to keep my mother company." Beri gave a huge sigh. "Soon she will try and match me up with another rich and dreary man. She will not miss me."

"I am very, very glad that you are coming." Timoken's wide smile, so white in the lantern light, made Beri laugh.

"She's coming with us," he told the others.

They gave a roar of approval, causing the horses in the stable beside them to whinny fretfully.

"Our prince likes nothing so much as a new face," said Edern. "He is always happy to receive strangers from other lands. You will be especially welcome, Timoken," he added. "And then, of course, my uncle, the magician, will be very happy. . . ."

Timoken had heard all this before, but he knew that Edern was only trying to impress upon him how welcome he would be, in that distant land over the sea.

Beri's eyes were already closing. She gave great weary yawns and flung herself into the straw at the back of the barn. She was asleep as soon as her head was down.

Timoken knew he would never sleep if he avoided the task he dreaded. He got up and crept outside. He could hear the rustle of waves on the shore. Out in the bay, the big ship was clearly visible, and he felt a shiver of excitement. He went into the stable. Gabar was crouching just inside the door, almost as if he was waiting for someone. Timoken sat beside him.

"Gabar, are you awake?"

"I am not asleep."

"I have been a coward. I could not say good-bye."

"Good-bye?" Gabar lowered his head.

"They say I cannot take you with me to Britain. We have to go on a ship, and it would not be safe for a camel."

"I understand," said Gabar. "I am just a camel. I cannot help you like the birds and the leopards. You do not need me."

"Gabar!" said Timoken in a desperate voice. "You have helped me every day of my life. Without you, I would have wanted to die."

Gabar looked at Timoken. Was that a smile? It was certainly a tear.

"What a fool I am!" cried Timoken, leaping to his feet. "I cannot leave you. I will not. We will fly together. What do you think of that?"

"I think we will fly," said Gabar.

"It is a great distance . . . over water. . . ."

Gabar tossed his head and stood up. "I am ready."

"Not now," said Timoken, and laughed.

"Soon?"

"Soon."

They settled side by side in the straw, the boy and his camel, and at last Timoken fell asleep.

The others looked worried when Timoken told them his plan the next morning.

"There's so much water to cross," said Edern. "You will fall. You will drown."

"He will not fall. He will not drown," Zobayda said. "Gabar and Timoken have traveled farther than the widest ocean. So have I, come to that."

And so it was agreed. Before Edern stepped onto the boat that would take them to the ship, he described every detail of his prince's castle. It was a golden color and the highest in western Britain. The hill where it stood was surrounded by a sea of trees. They would be red and gold at this time of year.

Timoken thought of the secret kingdom. He watched the others rowing out to the ship, and when the ship weighed anchor, he climbed onto his camel and, tugging at the rough hair on Gabar's back, he said, "Fly, Gabar, fly!"

The camel rose into the air as easily as if he were a bird. They flew above the ship, sometimes losing sight of it beneath the clouds, and sometimes skimming the water right behind it. At night they would look down and see the lanterns shining in the bow, and once Timoken saw three pairs of bright golden eyes, gazing up at him from the stern. And he caught a flash of copper red, flaming orange, and starry yellow.

"I wonder how they got on board," he said, smiling to himself.

The castle was not far from the coast, and the captain got as close as he could before putting his passengers into a boat with two strong sailors.

Timoken watched from above, as his sister and his friends climbed out onto the beach. When they began to make their way inland, he followed their progress for a while, and then he flew ahead. Soon he saw the hill rising out of the autumn trees. On top of the hill stood a castle. A golden castle in a golden sea.

"There it is, Gabar!" he cried.

"There is what, Family?"

"Home," said Timoken.

JENNY NIMMO

I was born in Windsor, Berkshire, England, and educated at boarding schools in Kent and Surrey from the age of six until I was sixteen, when I ran away from school to become a drama student/assistant stage manager with Theater South East. I graduated and acted in repertory theater in various towns and cities.

I left Britain to teach English to three Italian boys in Amalfi, Italy. On my return, I joined the BBC, first as a picture researcher, then assistant floor manager, studio manager (news), and finally director/adaptor with *Jackanory* (a BBC storytelling program for children). I left the BBC to marry Welsh artist David Wynn-Millward and went to live in Wales in my husband's family home. We live in a very old converted water mill, and the river is constantly threatening to break in, which it has done several times in the past, most dramatically on our youngest child's first birthday. During the summer, we run a residential school of art, and I have to move my office, put down tools (typewriter and pencils), and don an apron and cook! We have three grown-up children, Myfanwy, Ianto, and Gwenhwyfar.

Interview with Jenny Nimmo

What inspired you to tell the story of Timoken, the Red King?

Once I had made up my mind that Charlie Bone's ancestor would be an African king, I found myself referring to this ancient king in every book in the series. But I could never decide why the Red King came to Britain. I found myself wondering more and more about this mysterious and elusive character, until I finally realized that in order to make the Children of the Red King series more satisfying and complete, I would have to write the Red King's story.

Despite your story taking place in different parts of the United Kingdom, Timoken is an African prince. Is there a particular reason you chose for Timoken to be of African descent?

I've always been interested in the features and characteristics we inherit from our ancestors. In the Magician Trilogy, my hero, Gwyn, inherits his gifts from an ancient Welsh magician. Gwyn has few friends and lives in an isolated farmhouse in the Welsh mountains. I wanted Charlie Bone to be connected to a much wider world than lonely Gwyn, so I gave Charlie an African ancestor. After all, Africa is where mankind began — so we are told.

Magic is a key element in many of your books, including Chronicles of the Red King and the Charlie Bone series, Children of the Red King. Why is that? And were you drawn to magical stories when you were a young reader?

When I was a child I didn't want to read about children like me; I wanted to read about princes and princesses, goose-girls, shepherd boys, and talking animals. For a precious half hour or so, I could identify with the principal character in a fantastic world, where, with the aid of magic, they would inevitably overcome all the seemingly insurmountable problems stacked against them. When I began to write, I naturally wanted to use the genre that had so comforted me as a child.

Chronicles of the Red King tells the story of Charlie Bone's magical ancestor, the Red King. Yet you wrote the Charlie Bone books first. Was it hard to go back and imagine this powerful king as a child born without his full strength and magic?

At first I thought that it would be easy to write about the Red King as a boy, and then I realized that I knew very little about Africa or Spain in the twelfth century. So I did a lot of research, which might not be apparent in the books, but gave me the confidence to concentrate on my characters without being held up by worries about their environment. And I really enjoyed working on Timoken's gradual discovery and understanding of his new powers.

The bond between Gabar and Timoken is one of the most powerful relationships in the story. Is there a reason you chose for Timoken's closest companion to be nonhuman?

Gabar had no place in my early notes for *The Secret Kingdom*. He appeared quite without warning, but once he had arrived, I realized how necessary his friendship with Timoken would be. I knew, from the beginning, that Zobayda would disappear, and Timoken would long for human company. But his utter loneliness needed to be mitigated and a talking nonhuman seemed to be the perfect companion. I began to enjoy their strange and funny friendship so much that Gabar sort of "took me over."

Sun Cat, Flame Chin, and Star are magical leopards that protect Timoken. However, in your other series, they appear as house cats named Aries, Sagittarius, and Leo that protect Charlie. Why did their names and form change over the centuries? Without Timoken, have they lost some of their magic?

In the prologue to Children of the Red King #5: *The Hidden King*, the Red King changes his leopards into cats. He does this to hide them from hunters who would enjoy killing leopards. As cubs, the leopards were wrapped in the web of the last moon spider. This made them immortal and, although they don't have the physical strength of leopards, they still have the magic that the web gave them. Over the years Timoken's names for them are forgotten, and from one of his many ancestors they acquire the names of astrological signs.

Do you have a favorite character in the Children of the Red King series? If so, who and why?

Uncle Paton is my favorite character in the Charlie Bone books. He reminds me of my guardian who was very tall and quiet and mysterious. He would arrive at my boarding school quite unexpectedly, but always with a book for me. I loved him very much.

If you could have any one of Timoken's or his descendents' powers, which would it be and why?

If I could have any power I wanted, I would choose to fly. It would be so good to escape from noisy crowds, traffic queues, and bad situations, and then have a bird's-eye view of the world below.

In what ways, if any, do your theater and television background affect the stories you imagine?

When I was about nine or ten, I was enchanted by the thought that actors could step into another world and, for a while, become someone different. Working in the theater was everything I had hoped for, and when I began to write, the excitement of entering another world was still with me, only now I could create that other world; and although I couldn't actually become another person in the same way as an actor, I could certainly leave my own character behind and identify with someone utterly unlike myself, a character whom I had created.

What books have inspired you the most?

Grimms Fairy Tales were my favorite stories when I was a child. They were the reason that I used fantasy when I began to write. In *The Mabinogion* — a collection of Welsh legends — I found my first real hero, Gwydion the magician. It was his story that inspired the Magician Trilogy, and now, under another name, he plays a part in the Chronicles of the Red King. Authors need a language to convey their ideas, and Bruce Chatwin's work, especially his novel *On the Black Hill*, has had the greatest influence on my writing.

Where is your favorite place to write?

My favorite place to work in is a small room with a window overlooking the river in my home. It used to be my daughter's bedroom, and the blue sky and white clouds that she painted on her wall are still there, so that sometimes, I feel as though I'm flying.

What advice would you give to aspiring writers?

To an aspiring writer I would say: Read as much as you can and use the genre that you most enjoy. Create strong characters that you — and therefore your reader — can totally empathize with. Read your work aloud — it's surprising how many mistakes will come to light. If it sounds good, it will be good to read. Have patience. Keep writing, even if your work is not immediately accepted.

What are you working on now?

Right now I am writing about the Red King's ten children. I'm having a great time choosing the moments when each one of the children begins to discover their own peculiar endowment.

THE SAGA CONTINUES IN
The Stones of Ravenglass. . . .

As Timoken's journey takes him through the northern
forests, he realizes he is being followed, and what
lurks in the trees could be more dangerous than anything
he's faced before. Is Timoken's magic strong enough to
protect those closest to him?

AVAILABLE JUNE 1, 2012!

BATTLE IN THE MOONLIGHT . . .

Sabin went running then, bending low and giving the shack as wide a berth as he could; he got behind the buildings and lost himself in the brush that fringed the clearing. He could hear the guns, the sound coming closer as he got to the far side of the place and began edging toward the men from Pitchfork. He bellied down for the last lap, worming forward upon his elbows and knees—for he could see the drifting shadows of men. They were still scattered among the stumps, and from such shelter they made their way, moving up as they could, a thin crescent of men drawing closer and closer to the shack.

Sabin thought, *This is going to be one helluva surprise,* and took delight in the thought, lifting out his gun and holding it ready, wanting the shooting to count. He tried getting one of those shifting shadows in his sights; his eyes hurt with straining. He wanted just one man—any man—to show himself, and he waited for a gun flash to mark . . .

Look for Norman A. Fox's:

Available from POCKET BOOKS

Books by Norman A. Fox

The Badlands Beyond
The Rawhide Years
Shadow on the Range
Stormy in the West
The Thirsty Land

Published by POCKET BOOKS

NORMAN A. FOX

Stormy
In The West

POCKET BOOKS

New York   London   Toronto   Sydney   Tokyo

POCKET BOOKS, a division of Simon & Schuster Inc.
1230 Avenue of the Americas, New York, NY 10020

Published by arrangement with Dodd, Mead & Co.

ISBN 0-671-64818-7

First Pocket Books printing November 1989

10 9 8 7 6 5 4 3 2 1

POCKET and colophon are trademarks of
Simon & Schuster Inc.

Printed in the U.S.A.

1

Meeting at Medicine Tree

FROM THIS HIGH PLACE where he kept his fireless camp, Sabin commanded all the broad basin, seeing the full sweep of Arrowhead's graze, wild as any country between the Musselshell and the Missouri, seeing the far hills belted with the gold of turning aspen and the dark green of everlasting pine. Nearer, the smoke of Stirrup made a halo by day and the town's lights winked at him by night. In the afternoon, all things lay like a painted picture in the stillness, the brown of grazing cattle, the ant-like movements of distant riders. Sometimes Pitchfork's spread, due west of Stirrup, stood out with startling clarity; sometimes he could have named each building that belonged to Inland's acres, abutting Pitchfork to the south. Crowfoot and G-Rafter and Star-Cross were too far to his right to give him a clear view, but he could mark the motte of cottonwoods where Grove schoolhouse stood; he could look into the heart of Arrowhead, and looking, remember.

7

Only the old place was lost to him, for it stood almost directly below his camp; a thickness of timber on the slope of this hill that was part of Arrowhead's west wall shut off the view. He'd supposed that weather and time had claimed the old place and that the rats ruled whatever was left of it, but last night he'd gone down to have a look, and the shack was still standing and light burned in its windows. He'd gone no closer.

The fools! he'd thought.

On this, the third night of his patience, he squatted with his back to the ancient pine that had once been a medicine tree where migratory Indians had hung gifts to the Great Spirit—bear claws and strips of colored cloth and bead work and bunches of white sage—a growing restlessness in him, and a feeling that an enemy was about. He had known this feeling before, and it had sharpened his wariness, for he had learned to give his strict attention to the little intangibles. Now he listened to the wind that fretted the pine tops; the wind had a sting to it, but the stars stood out clear and cold; and there'd be no snow, not tonight. He wondered about the wind; he wondered if the wind was the voice of the enemy.

He stood up, fretful with this turn of thought, and went to have a look at his horse to give himself something to do. He'd picketed the sorrel deep in the brush, a good distance from camp, and he found the mount grazing, less fiddle-footed than himself. When he returned to the medicine tree, he squatted upon his bedroll and beat his right fist softly against his left palm. He wanted a fire tonight, but a fire might draw men—the wrong men.

He stood again and began pacing the small clearing, a man high and angular of shoulder, lean-bodied and lean-faced, with a moroseness of features that showed all this thinking to be somber. He looked like a loose rider between jobs; he looked like a saddle tramp who kept his leather soaped and his garb clean because these claims to respectability were his last ace in the hole.

He got to thinking about the enemy again, and he knew then that he'd sensed such a presence before he'd reached the fringing hills overlooking Arrowhead. He'd taken a long trail out of Miles City and covered a lot of country and found little of it to his liking. The summer had been unusually hot and dry, with the breath of the wind shriveling the grass and shrinking the creeks and springs; and range fires had sprung up everywhere to put their black pall against the horizons. Creek water had got a bitter, alkaline taste to it, so strong that in some places Sabin's sorrel had refused to drink; and his campfire coffee had sickened Sabin, just as he had been sickened to see what the summer had done to the range. Many a rancher had moved his herds to the Dakotas or north into Canada. Some had complained of poisoned stock, finding in this off-season a new hazard, for poisonous plants had withstood the drought and thrived where good grass died. Sabin had seen too many carcasses of good native steers.

But now, in this fall of 1886, there were other signs that troubled him more. Such beaver as the mountain men had left were piling up great quantities of saplings, and the bark of the younger cottonwood was thicker than Sabin ever remembered finding it. The native birds, he noticed, were bunching much earlier than usual, and the wild animals were growing heavy coats of fur. These were signs for one with eyes to see them. These were the threats of the enemy that lurked faceless and bodiless in some remote place where the weather was made.

The wind, then, was indeed the voice of the enemy. He thought of the cattle who would hear this voice and know its meaning in their own brutish way. Montana was getting crowded with cattle—lean Texas longhorns pouring in from the south, their strain sometimes mixed with shorthorn blood from the fine herds of Missouri; breeding stock from the farms of Wisconsin, Minnesota, Michigan, and Illinois, those pilgrim or barnyard cattle that crowded every westbound stock train; herds that stirred the dust eastward out of Oregon and Washington and Idaho. Cattle from every direction. Sometimes it seemed as though all the world was dumping its cattle into Montana. And because Sabin had been here when a man had elbow room, he wondered about this, listening to the wind.

It was no more than the crunch of a twig beneath a man's boot, but it sent Sabin to the shadow of the medicine tree.

Then he heard the sound that the wind failed to swallow. Here he waited, making no real move toward his gun, though his fingers gave his cartridge belt a hitch that brought the holster into easier reach. This movement would have been too late, he realized, for the intruder's tallness was now a clear silhouette against the screening timber walling this clearing, and if there was a gun in the man's hand, it was already lined and ready.

Sabin said evenly, "I'm Mark Sabin."

The silhouette moved. There *had* been a gun, but now it was being pouched, and that tall-standing shadow sighed. "I'm Garth Trenchard," it said. "You can't blame me for playing it safe."

They crossed toward each other and shook hands, and there was enough starlight in the clearing's center to show Trenchard's face, strong and clean-shaven and ruggedly handsome. He wore a suit of some dark material that had been tailored for riding, the trousers tucked into high black boots, the polish gleaming in this futile light. His handclasp had the firmness of one who would show his strength in every act. He said, a trace of irritation in his voice, "I got your letter. You could have picked a place easier to reach."

Sabin said, "I got your letter first. You wanted a place where we could palaver before I showed myself in the basin. I know Arrowhead. There's only one medicine tree."

Trenchard lowered himself to a deadfall log; and though he sat there immobile and Sabin stood before him, they might have been two dogs circling each other, not yet sure. Trenchard spoke. "You said the fourteenth. I couldn't make it last night."

"I got here a day early," Sabin said. "This makes my third night. The basin looks the same from where I've stood." The surprise from last night came back to him, and he tipped his head toward the slope. "Who's down there?"

"Squatter named Teasdale. Ben Teasdale. Moved in about a year ago with a wife and a hundred children. He runs a few cattle—pilgrims mostly."

"The fool!" Sabin said.

Trenchard's hand fumbled beneath his coat, and he extended a cigar case toward Sabin. Sabin shook his head and reached for the makings, then let his hand fall. Trenchard stripped the band from a cigar and made a vague motion, perhaps using a clipper; and Sabin said, "If you can't talk without smoking, keep the match close to you."

Surprise touched Trenchard. "You're a careful man, Sabin. I wanted a careful man."

"Mostly you wanted a man named Sabin."

Trenchard's eyes looked startled in the starlight, but only for an instant. He made a show of his teeth, and they looked strong enough to bite through a silver dollar. "I asked for you when I wrote, because I wanted a man who knew Arrowhead. They'd told me about you at that meeting of the Stock Growers' Association in Miles last April. Your father had the Teasdale place, didn't he? That was before my time out here—I took over Inland the summer of '82."

Sabin thought: *One of those Easterners.* There were getting to be as many breeds of men in Montana as there were of cattle. You had the old Texans, like Morgan Lantry, who'd come in first, hazing his Pitchfork herd up the long, long trail and lighting where the grass looked the best. But now there were rag-tag ranchers like this fellow Teasdale, and there were men with big money behind them, those who came from the East or from England or Scotland or France to manage ranches for their betters. Mostly these managers knew about the book work but had no savvy of cattle. This Trenchard was still a hard one to peg. Inland had had another manager in Sabin's day, an ineffectual man scared by the bigness of the country.

Sabin said, "What's the trouble? You mentioned rustling."

Trenchard nodded. "It goes back to what happened to Morgan Lantry. You heard about that, I suppose?"

Sabin's lips drew tight and uncompromising. "I heard about it. I didn't do any crying. You've been around here long enough to know about Jeff Sabin. He was my dad. That's over and done with. Who got Lantry?"

Trenchard's shoulders lifted in a shrug. "My guess would be Reese Stringham. He's holed up somewhere in these hills."

"The Association missed him in the clean-up of '84," Sabin said. "That was where the cattlemen made a bad mistake. Reese could give cards and spades to half the rustlers they hanged. He's been hitting at Pitchfork?"

"And at me," Trenchard said. "Pitchfork might have stood it, perhaps. Rustling losses only run about three per cent. But somebody drove a bullet into Morgan Lantry right on the main street of Stirrup, and they got him where his suspenders crossed. Ginselling's the kind of foreman to make a war out of that."

"Ginselling doesn't need any help from the Stock Growers' Association."

"Agreed," Trenchard said. "It's Ben Teasdale who's had me worried. His place is the backdoor to the west hills. If Pitchfork beef is run off in the dark of the moon, it must move past Teasdale's door."

"It always did," Sabin said, a kind of laughter in him.

Trenchard still held the cigar in his hand. He cupped a match now and touched it to the cigar, and his face stood painted briefly against the night, highlighted, hard-planed as Sabin's own but not so weathered. Trenchard waved the match out, and Sabin stirred uneasily at his carelessness, the old wariness whetted fine. Far out in the basin a coyote howled, the sound remote and sad.

Trenchard said, "It adds up to this: Pitchfork's got a rustling problem that's become a personal feud since Morgan Lantry's dead and buried. You know the civil laws and the courts have been useless in this rustling thing. It's always been the Stock Growers' Association that's scotched its own snakes, and it did a fair job in '84. But Ginselling hasn't sent for outside help. One of these days he's going to pick on Teasdale. I don't want that. Teasdale has some land in alfalfa, and I've found it easier to buy feed from him than to raise it. Moreover, if there's any kind of big trouble in the basin, Inland is bound to be dragged into it. I want no war with Pitchfork."

Sabin said bluntly, "Then it's your own ax you're grinding."

Trenchard sucked hard on the cigar, and his eyes,

thus revealed, were cold. "I pay my dues," he said. "I asked for a stock detective who knew Arrowhead. I got you."

Sabin said, "I take the work they hand me."

Trenchard held silent for a moment; and Sabin waited out this silence, knowing he had ruffled the man but not caring. Then: "I'd like to know how you intend to play it," Trenchard said.

"Close to my vest. Pitchfork knows where I draw my pay. But mostly I've been chasing Indians who jumped their reservations and run off horses, or else I've been putting my heel on the necks of whisky peddlers. I could be on my own this trip; I have a brother in Stirrup. I might be visiting him. You're the only man who knows different. You want Reese Stringham's hide tacked to the wall, is that it?"

"Stringham and every man who rides with him. Stop the rustling and you've stopped the trouble before it happens." Trenchard's head lifted, and Sabin felt the sharpness of the man's gaze. "You wouldn't have a reason for going easy on Stringham?"

"I knew him," Sabin admitted, not angry. "He was a friend of the old man's. Sometimes he bunked down there at the shack when he was caught between camps. Maybe he split a dollar with the old man a time or two. That was between them. Reese took his trail; I took mine. It was a long time before the Stock Growers' thought it safe to hire a pup of Jeff Sabin's to do their work. They haven't had any complaint to make."

Trenchard said slowly, "No. You wouldn't be the kind to bite the hand that feeds you."

Sabin shrugged.

Trenchard stood up, making a tall, solid shape in the night. "If you want me, get word to Inland. You've got the facts now, and that gives you something to sink your teeth into. Any questions?"

But Sabin didn't hear the last of it, for he had cocked his head to another sound, ragged and remote and almost borne away on the wind. Then he heard it again and knew it for what it was, and he lifted his hand, stopping Trenchard's talk. Trenchard heard, too, for he stiffened.

"Guns!" he said.

"Down below," Sabin decided. "At the old place."

Trenchard shook his head, and his voice had a wilted sound. "Teasdale's," he said. "That would be Pitchfork bringing guns and a torch." He made a flat, hopeless gesture with his hands. "One day," he said. "We got together one day too late."

2

Deborah

Now THE RESTLESSNESS that had kept Sabin fiddle-footed through the early evening's vigil was gone, for he was suddenly a man with something to do. There was no way of getting down the slope but to climb down; he'd found that out last night. He went cat-footing it from the clearing, running almost, until the brush made a barrier. He went clawing through this, not knowing Trenchard was behind him until the man reached and grasped Sabin's elbow.

Trenchard said, "My horse . . . I tied him out back there." He waved his hand along the spine of the hill.

"Leave him," Sabin said. "Unless you want to break his neck and yours."

He clambered over a fallen log and gave curt warning to Trenchard, a need for hurrying strong in Sabin, a need for patience stronger. With half the slope behind them, the sound of guns lifted with fiercer intensity, yet the clamor was sporadic and indefinite and made nothing to fill in a picture. Sabin knew how it would be with Ginselling; Ginselling would drag a thing like this out, playing it safe, playing it cat-and-mouse. He struggled on downward, his boots stirring loose gravel and sending it rolling.

Sometimes he lost Trenchard in the night, but he didn't wait for the man. Nobody was paying Trenchard to go up against Pitchfork.

Near the slope's end, the timber and the brush thinned out; but there were stumps beyond, where Jeff Sabin had used an ax when ambition had been upon him. Mark Sabin had felled a few of those trees in his time, and Curly, too; but Curly hadn't been much of a hand for work, not if there'd been a horse to ride. This far Sabin had come last night, and from here he could see the shack and the barn looming behind it and the other buildings scattered in a haphazard semicircle. From here he could also see the cottonwood; it stood before the shack with its great, bare limbs gaunt against the night. Jeff Sabin had favored its shade in the long, hot afternoons of the lost summers, so he had let it stand.

Pitchfork's men were before the shack, lying low and hidden and unhorsed among the stumps, driving bullets against the log walls. Pitchfork numbered no more than half a dozen tonight; this was its contempt for a man of Ben Teasdale's cut. No light showed in the shack, but Sabin could mark a window, for gunfire came from it to hold back Pitchfork. A single gun, a Winchester, he decided.

Now he could fill in the picture: Pitchfork had come and laid down its challenge, and Teasdale had had a voice to answer that challenge, and now there was siege. Teasdale hadn't showed himself, and that was why his gun could answer Pitchfork. The sign here, Sabin decided, said Teasdale wasn't such a fool after all. But lead could knock out the chinking between the logs; lead could find the windows and riddle the door;

and when enough lead was poured, there'd be no Winchester to stay the tide of Pitchfork's rush. It added up to that. It added up to calamity.

Trenchard came again to Sabin's elbow, and he said, "What are you going to do?" Exertion had made him short of breath, but there was no fear in his voice.

Sabin said, "If you're buying in, hunker down here. I'm going around back of the barn and get on the other side of Pitchfork." He lifted his arm and made a long, sweeping gesture. "Mark my gun-flash. When I open up on them, that will be your sign. A crossfire will scare them more than a dozen bunched guns."

Trenchard nodded. "I can make a lot of racket, but I couldn't hit a barn door from twenty feet."

He's lying, Sabin thought, not knowing how he knew.

He went running then, bending low and giving the shack as wide a berth as he could; he got behind the buildings and lost himself in the brush that fringed the clearing. He began following out a wide semicircle, groping his way toward where he could angle his gun at Pitchfork without coming into Trenchard's line of fire. Always he could hear the guns, the sound growing distant during the first half of his maneuvering, then coming closer as he got to the far side of the place and began edging toward Pitchfork's position.

He bellied down for the last lap, worming forward upon elbows and knees, for he could see the drifting shadows of men. They were still scattered among the stumps, and from such shelter they made their war, moving up as they could, a thin crescent of men drawing closer and closer to the shack.

Sabin thought: *This is going to be one helluva surprise,* and took delight in the thought, lifting out his gun and holding it ready, wanting the shooting to count. He looked across the clearing to where he'd posted Trenchard. He couldn't see Inland's man, but he knew that Trenchard was still there; he would have bet on that. He tried getting one of those shifting shadows in his sights; his eyes hurt with straining. He wanted just one man—any man—to show himself, and he waited for a gun-flash he might mark; and while he waited, the door of the cabin opened, and a man flung himself out into the yard.

Here was madness beyond belief, for this must be Teasdale, this little man, indefinite in the starlight, who came out from cover with a rifle clutched in one hand and his free fist raised to the sky. He stood there, naked to the guns. He shouted, "Ginselling! You've shot a woman, damn you! Does that mean anything to you!"

Ginselling showed himself, standing up from behind a stump, a shape vague in the night; but Sabin knew that squat, powerful body, those ponderous shoulders. Ginselling said, heavy-voiced, "You had your chance to move your folks."

Teasdale was turned fanatic by a sense of outrage, a man magnificent and mad in the same moment. "You'll answer for this!" he shouted. "Every one of you! You can ride over me, but you can't do what you've done tonight! Get out of here, you sneaking dogs!"

Ginselling took refuge in anger and in action; and because Sabin had expected Pitchfork's foreman to do just this, he was ready. He saw Ginselling raise his arm; he saw the glint of gun steel in the starlight. Sabin fired then, hastily, and at the same time he shouted, "Get inside!" That was for Teasdale, and it broke the spell.

It must have told Teasdale how near he'd stood to death, for the man turned and went scurrying; and Ginselling dropped down behind the stump. Sabin wasn't sure whether he'd hit Pitchfork's man or whether the airlash of the bullet had whispered close enough to scare Ginselling. Trenchard had begun firing; his gun winked across the clearing like a malignant firefly; and Sabin let his own gun speak fast. Teasdale had got inside and was shooting from the window again, and Pitchfork had now three targets to find instead of one.

Pitchfork broke with such suddenness as to leave nothing but fleeing shadows to seek. Ginselling's voice lifted, the words indistinguishable in the bedlam, and his men retreated, moving back toward the timber at the foot of the slope. Sabin judged that was where they'd left their horses, and he feared for Trenchard until he saw that the angle the retreat was taking made no peril for Inland's man. Pitchfork was on the run, and Sabin wondered if the new guns had weighed so heavily or if the words Teasdale had flung had made the rout; and while he wondered, hoofbeats rose, thundering in the night, until the sound dimmed and was lost in the immensity of Arrowhead.

Still Sabin stayed on this far edge of the clearing; he waited, watching the shack and looking across to where he'd left Trenchard. The first move came from the cabin. The door creaked slightly, and Teasdale's voice reached him, shouting, "Hallo! You, out there!" and Sabin showed himself, pouching his gun and keeping his arms straight down at his sides so Teasdale would make no mistake.

The silence became so heavy that it pressed against him bodily. He thought to call Trenchard's name, then changed his mind and whistled instead. The slope took the sound and fashioned it into an echo and flung it back in thin shards. Sabin listened, his ears strained, until he caught the faint crackle of brush and knew that Trenchard had gone to his horse, not wanting his part in this night's work known.

Sabin came across the clearing and found Teasdale standing cautiously before his door.

"There was two of you," Teasdale said.

"The other fellow drifted." Sabin glanced at the door. "How's your woman?"

"It wasn't her," Teasdale said. Close up, he proved to be smaller than he'd seemed standing so defiantly against Pitchfork, a little man past forty, with a stoop to him and a small, seamed face that looked scared and rabbit-like and grooved by a perpetual hunger. "They gone?" he asked.

"For tonight," Sabin said. "You can show a light."

Teasdale called over his shoulder, and after a moment a lamp blossomed, an edge of light showing around the partially opened door, and he said then, "Come inside."

Sabin followed him through the doorway and stood in the room, expecting a rush of memories to smother him; but little here was as he remembered it. Some of the furnishings—that chair in the corner—might have been Jeff Sabin's, and the bunks were certainly the same, but the windows had calico draping them, and the stove wasn't the old one. And the people were different. That was what made the real change. The place seemed full of children, boys and girls, no two of them the same age but all of them looking alike, all of them big-eyed and scared, the smallest two clutching at the skirts of an immense, shapeless woman whose gray hair fell into her eyes. This was Ben Teasdale's family; and among them the girl sat, not belonging.

He judged that she was a tall girl, and she was not one who'd been here in the old days, not one he'd known, anyway. She had gray eyes, still and deep, and brown hair drawn smoothly away from her temples, and a face that was placid in spite of the pain that drew her lips tight. He saw the blood stain on the shoulder of her gingham dress, and he saw that she kept one of her hands to that shoulder, as though holding a pad in place. She was the one who'd been shot, yet she was the only serene person here. The aftermath of his own daring had settled upon Ben Teasdale, leaving him sick; and a great fear stood in his wife's eyes and in his children's.

Mrs. Teasdale said, "Debbie got hit by a bullet. I did the best I could for her."

The girl said, "I'm Deborah Gray, from Stirrup. I was visiting."

Sabin saw a wicker basket on the table, and he judged that it was hers and that she'd brought things in it—food, perhaps, the kind of food a squatter family wouldn't have. He didn't remember any garden in the clearing. He took off his sombrero; his hair was a sun-bleached brown, looking gray in the lamplight. "How hard were you hit?"

"It's only a scratch," Deborah said. "It bled some till Mrs. Teasdale got a bandage on it."

"She's got to be taken to Doc Hatwell," Mrs. Teasdale said firmly.

Teasdale said gravely, "I shouldn't ought to leave here."

"You rode out?" Sabin asked, looking at the girl.

She nodded.

He said, "My own horse is up the hill. I'm going to town. I'll take you."

Mrs. Teasdale said, "Clear out, you men. I'll fix her bandage tighter."

Sabin had already turned toward the door. He put on his sombrero and went striding across the yard to where the slope towered above, black and formless, and began his climbing. When at long last he reached the top, his breath coming hard and the calves of his legs aching, he made his way to the medicine tree and stood in the clearing and called, "Trenchard—?" softly, getting no answer.

He groped to his horse and saddled the mount and broke camp; but before he descended, he stood on the rim of the hill and looked out across Arrowhead. Far away the lights of Stirrup winked; between here and the town lay a lake of shadows, peaceful and silent and mysterious. Somewhere in those depths rode Pitchfork, routed and angry, edgy with remembering. Crowfoot spread was down there, and Goodnight's G-Rafter, and Star-Cross and all the other ranches that neighbored Pitchfork and Inland and lay dwarfed by the immensity of those two.

It took Sabin a long time to get the sorrel down the slope, and when he came into Teasdale's yard again, the man was awaiting him before the shack. Teasdale was staring off toward the northeast.

"They'll come back," he said.

"They'll come back," Sabin agreed. Then: "Look, friend, didn't you know this was the way to the hills? Any man taking this place might as well put up a sign: Rustler."

Teasdale said, "What would I want with their native stock? I'm breeding up good stuff, mister. Can't the big fellows understand that I have more reason for a grudge than they have? How's a man to raise blooded cattle when his neighbors let scrub bulls range all over the graze?"

He put a fervor into this that startled Sabin; and then Sabin wanted to laugh, finding a kind of irony in this rag-tag little man with his rag-tag brood of children wanting to produce a better breed of cattle. But he only said, "Pitchfork would figure your worry was your own. The hills are their worry."

Teasdale said, "You're cowboy. You'd see that part of it their way. But I'm beholden to you, almighty beholden. I hope you're riding through. Pitchfork's going to hate you right down to the ground for this." He looked over his shoulder. "I'll see if Debbie's ready."

He went into the shack; and Sabin stood waiting,

shaping up a cigarette and looking toward the cotton-wood, not seeing it at first until it crowded into his consciousness and filled it to the exclusion of all else.

That was where they'd hanged Jeff Sabin on another night when shadows had cruised the clearing and guns had spoken from the stumps; and he wondered now how it had been with Jeff and what thoughts went through a man's head when they stood him under the branch and the rope whistled through the air and scraped against the stoutest limb. Had Jeff lived his whole lifetime in that minute, the way they said a drowning man did? Had he thought about his boys, Mark and Curly, and wondered what the years would hold for them and whether they would come to such a moment, too? What kind of courage did it take to sit a saddle with your hands tied behind you and a rope cramping your neck, just the flick of a quirt away from eternity? Sabin fell to exploring all of his own experience, trying to find in it something of the last dark taste Jeff Sabin must have known, but nothing he could conjecture had the finality of tree and rope.

Jeff hadn't begged. There was that to remember; Jeff hadn't begged.

He was aware that the door had opened; and a flood of sound rolled out, the goodbyes of the children and the admonishments of Mrs. Teasdale and the voice of her husband. They came spilling into the yard, all of them, and Deborah Gray touched Sabin's elbow. She had a shawl drawn over her shoulders. She said, "I'm ready."

He looked at her. Standing, she came up to his eyebrows; her serenity was still unshaken; she would have been bovine in her serenity except that her eyes spoke of a wisdom that had stood against all the vicissitudes and given her her own kind of philosophy.

He said, "Sure you can sit a saddle? There must be a rig here of some kind."

"I can ride," she said.

Teasdale said, "I saddled for her while I was waiting for you." He went around a corner of the shack and came back leading a dun mare, and Sabin helped Deborah up. She rode side-saddle fashion, though the kak itself was built for straddling. Sabin stepped up to his own saddle and neck-reined among the stumps.

When they'd got out of the yard, Deborah Gray said, "You didn't mention a name."

"Sabin," he said. "Mark Sabin. You've heard it in Stirrup, I reckon."

"Yes," she said. "I've been there that long." She was silent for a long moment. "Now I understand why you helped against Pitchfork," she said. "There's a kind of sickness of hate in you, I think."

He said gruffly, "We've got a long ride to make."

3

Orders from Pitchfork

MIDNIGHT WAS PAST WHEN they neared Stirrup and rumbled across the wooden bridge that spanned Arrowhead Creek at a point where the creek elbowed to make a wedge of land upon which the town stood. Across the miles, Stirrup's lights had been a beacon for Sabin; and some of the lights still burned and the town was livelier than he'd expected at this late hour. Five years had made their difference; buildings stood where none had been; but he remembered the older landmarks and went unerringly to the mercantile and brought his horse to a halt in the shadows banked beside the covered stairway clinging to this frame structure. Up above were Doc Hatwell's office and quarters.

Sabin said, "Easy, now. I'll give you a hand."

He helped Deborah down from her saddle, and she reeled against him, and he hoped there was no fever in her. She'd had little to say on the long ride, but he hadn't forgotten her hurt; he'd chosen easy trails for her sake. Now he got an arm around her and guided her toward the stairs. They ascended and paused before Doc's door, and Sabin thumped lustily upon it with his free hand and stood then in a well of silence and darkness. Someone raised a shout in the street, down in the direction of the Maverick, Sabin judged, and the tinkle of the saloon's piano reached him like a ghost of sound wandering forlornly in the night.

Something stirred beyond the closed door, and shortly the door edged open, giving a narrow show of light. Hatwell held a lamp high, and Sabin saw the man's long, horsey face and tangled hair and saw, too, that Hatwell was in his nightgown.

Hatwell said, "Whatever it is, can't it wait till morning?" not angry, really, but tired of something that made an old, old pattern. He recognized Deborah then, and surprise showed in his eyes. He said, "Come in. Come in." He flung the door wide and crossed his littered office and placed the lamp atop his desk. "Wait till I get my pants," he said; and when Sabin led the girl into the room, Hatwell was whisking into his bedroom, and Sabin had an impression of a man all bony ankles and floppy slippers.

He took Deborah to Hatwell's own swivel chair, and she eased down into it, and he saw how chalky she looked in the lamplight. Pity touched him then, and a deference for her kind of courage.

"I'm all right," she said.

Hatwell came back, his pants pulled over his nightgown and only one of his suspenders in place. He looked at the girl and the man, and his long face lighted a little when his eyes searched Sabin's. "Ah, Mark!" he said and held out his hand.

"This one's your patient," Sabin said. He looked at Deborah. "I'll take care of the horses."

"I rent mine from Conover's. You know the place?"

Sabin nodded and stepped toward the door; and

Hatwell said, "You'll come back, Mark. I want to talk to you."

"And I want to talk to you," Sabin said.

He descended through the darkness and got the horses and led them along the street toward Conover's; this brought him past the Maverick, and he saw the horses standing at the gnawed hitch-rail. There was light enough spilling from the saloon for him to read the brands; all of them were Pitchfork. The shadow of a smile touched his lips, and he thought: *So they came here to lick their wounds.*

He had to do a lot of thumping at Conover's before he roused the hostler. When he'd got the man to open the livery door, he turned Deborah's horse over to him and made arrangements to stable his own, then left his blanket roll there. He came to the street again and drew a deep breath.

This was Stirrup, this collection of angular frame buildings scattered upon the basin's floor. This was home, and he supposed it should touch him, coming back like this. A nighttime silence hung over most of the town; only the Maverick stayed fully alive. The wind had a sting to it and stirred frantic little dust devils, and Sabin looked at the sky and saw that the stars were now nearly obscured. Maybe he'd been wrong; maybe it would snow after all; weather bred up that fast in Montana.

He began walking back toward Hatwell's, and he was abreast of the Maverick when Pitchfork came out upon the wooden porch and began spilling down the steps to the boardwalk. He saw Ginselling and Ginselling saw him, but the surprise was all Pitchfork's foreman's. Ginselling had a hard face to him and a rocky set of shoulders, and he was now whiskey-brave and whiskey-sullen. He said, "Whoa!" and peered hard at Sabin and said, "Damned if it ain't!"

Sabin halted and let his hands hang idle, his face showing no more than a stone shows; he felt master of this moment.

Ginselling said, "I thought I knew that voice when you shouted at Teasdale to get inside. It's been pecking at me ever since. Damned if it hasn't!"

Sabin said, "Now you know."

This rocked Ginselling as though a gust of wind had shoved at him, but Sabin knew where the man's fear lay, and he said, "She didn't die, Ginselling. You don't have to run for the brush. You can stand right there and make whatever play you have a mind to."

Ginselling said, "And have the Stock Growers' blacklisting Pitchfork?"

"You don't have to worry about that, either. Maybe I'm just a loose rider this trip."

Anger clouded Ginselling's face; he came a step forward, leaving his crew bunched behind him and making a flat downward gesture with both hands that stopped Pitchfork. "Damn you, quit needling me!" he said.

Anger came up in Sabin, too, made of more than tonight; he had only to reach out now to get a handful of Ginselling's shirt, and he did this with his left hand and brought his right fist back and smashed it hard into Ginselling's face. The blow took Pitchfork's foreman back against the saloon's steps; his spurs tangled up and he flailed the air with his arms, then fell heavily and lay stunned, not quite unconscious.

"There's your boss," Sabin said, and waited for any of them to take it up.

Ginselling's mistake had been in the gesture that had kept the others back; Ginselling had made it one man against another. A mutter ran through Pitchfork and had its moment and died. Sabin held them with his eyes, looking at no one man; someone knelt and hooked Ginselling under the armpits and tried hoisting him to his feet. Ginselling began a low, steady cursing.

Sabin turned and walked on up the street, not looking back. But he was thinking: *That kicked over the coffee pot. I'll be fair game from here on out.*

When he climbed to Hatwell's, the doctor admitted him, but the office stood empty. Sabin thumbed back his sombrero and let himself down upon a horsehair sofa that stood along one wall, and he said, "She's gone?"

Hatwell nodded. These years had put their weight on his shoulders; his face had too many creases, and there was gray in his tufted, sandy eyebrows. "Whoever took care of her first did about as much as I could do. She wouldn't talk about it. Will you?"

"Who is she?"

"Runs a dress-making shop. Thora Lantry's old enough now to want flashy clothes."

"New here?"

"From Lewistown, I think. Came in two, three years ago. She'll do."

Sabin looked around. "Curly asleep?"

Hatwell's eyes clouded. "Curly's gone."

"Gone?"

"Drifted. Six months ago."

Sabin's mouth drew hard. "Hell, Doc, I counted on you. Wasn't I sending you enough money for his keep?"

Hatwell said, "You're forgetting that Curly's eighteen now. Five years turned him from a kid to a man. This place was crowding him, Mark. What was in it for him, living with an old fuddy-duddy doctor? And he had to go throwing himself at Pitchfork; Curly never forgot that cottonwood out at the old place. On his seventeenth birthday, he chose Ginselling right out there in the street. Ginselling marked him up plenty."

"So—?" said Sabin, and looked down at the skinned knuckles of his right hand.

"I couldn't hold him after that, Mark. He was big enough to be moving, and big enough to know what he wanted. Damn it, man, I tried."

Sabin looked up at him and said, "Forget it, Doc. I owe you more than I owe any man. Who else would have kept the kid when I lit out of here?"

Hatwell said, "Should be I've got a jug stashed out somewhere."

He opened a drawer in his desk that was large enough to hold a letter file and brought from it a stoneware whiskey jug, which he sloshed. He found a couple of glasses and blew out the dust and let whiskey gurgle into them. One of these he passed to Sabin.

The whiskey bit deep into Sabin, warming him. "Trenchard?" Sabin asked then. "How about him?"

Hatwell drank his whiskey. "A big man—an ambitious man. He'll go far in the business, I think. He's got a notion. Now that the railroads have refrigerator cars, he figures he can establish a slaughter-house and meat-packing plant right here in Arrowhead, same as that Frenchman DeMores did over in Dakota."

Sabin shook his head. "You need a rich New York father-in-law like the Frenchie's got. Talk has it that DeMores' outfit is going belly-up. Still, a couple of fellows put up a meat-packing plant at Miles this summer. Got burned out, but they were rebuilding when I left." He held out the whiskey glass. "Pitchfork ship heavy this fall?"

"Not with prices down the way they are. Three bucks a hundred for grass-fed native steers! I'll bet that's got Kate Lantry worried."

Sabin said, "She'll get along. She's as much cattleman as old Morgan ever was."

Hatwell held his liquor to the light. "They're fools, all of them—Trenchard with his dream of a packing plant, this new fellow Teasdale trying to breed blooded stock, Kate Lantry running Pitchfork like this was still the seventies and a spread had all the elbow room it needed. Don't they know they're going to have something else to think about? There's white arctic owls on the range this fall, Mark. The Indians are pulling their blankets closer and mumbling about something their pappies and grand-pappies told them. Can't fool an Indian. They know we're in for a winter that will make '80-'81 look like the Fourth of July. But nobody pays heed to an Indian."

Sabin stood up. "The Austin House still taking in cash customers?"

"Room for you to bunk here, now that Curly's gone."

"I feel like sleeping the clock around, Doc. See you tomorrow."

"You're staying in Arrowhead, Mark?"

"Maybe Curly will show back," Sabin said.

The hotel had a sleepy clerk behind the desk, and Sabin got himself a room on the second floor. It was every hotel room in every prairieland town, musty and clammy and holding some intangible token of each of its birds of passage. But it had a bed. He turned the key and got out of his boots and stripped down to his underwear and rolled in, and sleep came to him quickly. The wind yammered at the window, and his last conscious thought was to wonder if he'd see snow by morning; but when the grayness woke him in spite of his need for long sleep the sun was out and the air lay quiet. The enemy still hid off to the north.

He washed up and ran his hand over the stubble on his cheeks and chin and decided that shaving could wait till later. When he came down to the lobby, a different clerk was on duty. Two men sat in chairs, reading Glendive newspapers; both were strangers to Sabin. He asked about the hotel dining room. It had just opened, so he had his breakfast and came out to the street afterward. He could have got his razor from the gear he'd left at Conover's, but he went instead to a barbershop and bought a bath and a shave and a haircut. He looked at the lettered mugs while the barber worked on him; there was one for Garth Trenchard and one for Lucius Hatwell.

Outside again, he found the town livelier; swampers swept the boardwalks and a wagon rolled along the street, a dog pacing it, barking and leaping. Pumps were creaking, and the first bonneted shoppers appeared. Sabin put his back to a porch support before the mercantile and watched the town begin its pulsing, and while he watched he saw the stirred dust at the far end of the street and made out the rider who materialized from it.

Thora! he thought, and all the years between dissolved, the years and the miles and the tangled trails and the many things to which a drifting man had turned his hand.

She had come at a hard gallop, but now she pulled her horse to a walk; there was spirit in the beast and it pranced and side-stepped and made a great show of fighting the bit. She wore a divided riding skirt and a fringed buckskin jacket, and her black hair was a torrent escaped from under her hat. She was full-bodied and supple and something like a mountain cat; and she was pretty, the prettiest girl Sabin had ever known. Before she was abreast of him, he called out to her, not meaning to, but doing this without conscious bidding. "Thora!"

She brought the horse around and rode it up upon the boardwalk until she was beside the mercantile's porch. This brought her eyes level with his, and he saw the anger in them.

She said, "You'll keep your hands off Pitchfork's men!" and she raised her quirt and brought it down hard across his left shoulder.

He said, "Stop it, Thora!" and knew that if she struck him again he would haul her from the saddle, if needs be. Something in his eyes must have told her this; she looked at him, the tempest alive in her, and then he thought she was going to cry. She'd always been a mixture of fire and ice, of cruelty and regret, quick to anger, quick to tears. She said, "Oh, why did you have to come back!" and wheeled the horse around and sent it at a hard run on up the street.

He watched her go, moved as he had not been moved since he'd come again to Arrowhead. A few townspeople had seen this little tableau; they stood about staring, until Sabin gave them a level look that closed out any questions they might have voiced and sent them walking away. He heard a new thunder of hoofs and looked up the street again, looked in the direction from which Thora had come; a dozen men were riding there, Ginselling leading them.

She had started out from Pitchfork with them, he supposed. But she had ridden faster, for such was her way.

Ginselling spied him, and Pitchfork became a milling maelstrom in the center of the street. Out of this, Ginselling edged his horse, bringing it halfway across the openness that lay between Sabin and the bunched riders. Ginselling had a shadow upon his jaw where Sabin's fist had made its mark. Ginselling said, "Mrs. Lantry wants to see you."

Sabin said, "She could have come with you."

"At Pitchfork," Ginselling said.

Sabin shrugged. "I finished all the talking I had to do with the Lantrys five years ago."

Ginselling's face turned harder. "The orders was to bring you."

"So—?"

"You coming?"

Perverseness made this suddenly a game to Sabin's liking, and he asked, "You'll drag me along if I don't?"

Ginselling said again, stolidly, "The orders was to bring you."

And now this was a colossal joke, this being summoned to Pitchfork; this was the laughter of all the little devils who fashioned the destinies of men. "What you making such a fuss out of it for?" Sabin asked and watched Ginselling's face come apart with astonishment. "I'll be along as soon as I get my horse."

4

A Woman's Wish

HE'D THOUGHT THAT THORA would ride out with them,
but some fancy held her in town; and when they
rattled the bridge and put Stirrup behind them, Sabin
was pocketed by Pitchfork, and the feeling was strong
in him that this was foolish business. Ginselling had
that mark upon his jaw and a banked anger in his eyes
and as many things to remember as Sabin had. Only
Mrs. Lantry's wish stood between them, and Mrs.
Lantry was a shadow off somewhere yonderly, yet
always there was that queer kind of loyalty in the
Ginsellings: they got an order and put their teeth into
it and held it fast. Ginselling kept his eyes away from
Sabin; and when they were through the willows on the
creek's far bank and lined out, Sabin found himself up
front, Ginselling almost abreast of him but half-a-
horse behind. And so, oddly, it was Sabin taking
Pitchfork's crew to Pitchfork.

They went riding due west. Last night Sabin had
crossed half the basin, riding with Deborah, when

he'd angled up out of the southeast. This seemed different terrain—different than it had been by night, different than it had looked, softened by distance, from the high rim where the medicine tree stood. He could see what the dry summer had done here; once this country had been good grass all the way to the Yellowstone, a land well watered and well sheltered, the hills supplying an abundance of yellow pine for fencing and building. Today autumn's brown lay upon the land, and autumn's sadness; and the breeze flowing down from the hills had a touch that made Sabin wish he'd fetched his sheepskin.

Sabin wondered how this country had looked to Morgan Lantry and to Jeff Sabin—they had come here when a man's nearest neighbor was apt to be forty miles away and a stockman built stout shutters against the Indians. They had had that in common, those two; they had pioneered. But one of them had given an order of a night, and the other had danced out his life beneath a cottonwood.

There were two gates to be opened and closed this morning, Ginselling getting down ponderously to do the chore; and one of the fences Sabin remembered, but the other was new. He supposed there'd be a lot more fencing in the next few years, and his mind shied from the thought.

Beyond the first gate he saw Pitchfork cattle, native steers all; and before noon they sighted Pitchfork's buildings and were almost upon them when they did, for Morgan Lantry had built in a shallow coulee. There was no fooforaw to Pitchfork; Lantry had built of log and built to last, not caring about looks. The house was huge and sprawling, the barn even bigger; cook shack and bunkhouse and blacksmith shop and corrals stood wherever convenience had placed them. This was Pitchfork, a monument to one man's way of life.

A man who'd built big, Sabin reflected, but it had taken only a tiny bit of lead to put that man beating his bootheels in the dust of Stirrup's street. And what were all these structures and all the cattle then?

Ginselling stepped down from saddle before the ranchhouse and clumped up the steps to its long gallery and, crossing, vanished into the maw of the house. He came back within a minute; he looked at Sabin from the top of the steps and said, "She says for you to eat." It was the first time he had spoken to Sabin since they'd left Stirrup.

Sabin said nothing; he neck-reined his horse and went with the others to a corral and put his horse there and slung his saddle over the top rail. Someone forked hay into the corral. They went walking to the cook shack, the silence still holding them; and Sabin stood in line with the others and washed himself at the bench. Afterwards, they went inside and, seating themselves, began eating; and when Sabin had finished, he stood up and made for the door, taking his time. Ginselling came after him and was at his elbow at the ranch-house steps.

Ginselling went in first, leaving Sabin on the gallery; and when Pitchfork's foreman returned, he said, "She'll see you now."

Mighty polite and formal, Sabin thought, but he didn't smile.

He had been at Pitchfork before—he could remember coming here a time or two with the old man, years back, to make talk of strays that needed cutting out of roundup herds—but he'd never been inside the house. He stepped into the place now, finding himself in a hall, and he heard her say, "Here," her voice bringing him through the right doorway. Now he was in the dining room, a long room with a table big enough to seat ten, but she had eaten alone, not even asking her foreman in. She sat at the far end of the table and looked at Sabin across the distance. No horsey, big-bodied cattlewoman, this one, given to stiff leather and heavy wool. She was tall and thin, so frail he felt he could have snapped her between his fingers. She wore a stiff black dress that came to her throat, its severity broken only by a cameo brooch; her hair was gray, her skin dead.

She said, "Sit down, Mark Sabin."

No man, save Morgan Lantry, had ever called her anything but Mrs. Lantry. Sabin took off his sombrero and placed it upon the table, hooked out a chair with his foot and seated himself, putting his hands on the table.

She looked at him; she had a parchment-like face in which only the eyes were alive, and he saw that her hands were thin and blue-veined and almost transparent. He had seen her before, of course, but not so close as this, and he thought: *Why, she was beautiful once! Beautiful as Thora.* Still he held silent, finding this moment awkward. With Thora he'd have known what to do, or with Ginselling or any Pitchfork man.

She said, "Smoke if you wish," and her voice had the same mournfulness that the wind had at this season. His hand strayed to his shirt pocket where the Durham label dangled, but he let his hand fall. "What was it you wanted, Mrs. Lantry?" he asked.

"Ginselling tells me you're not working for the Stock Growers' Association any longer."

He shrugged; his lips tightened. "I'd never have got the job if Morgan Lantry had had a loud enough voice at their meetings."

"You hate us, don't you, Mark Sabin?"

He shrugged again.

"Morgan's dead," she said. "Jeff Sabin is dead. You and I are other people. Will you work for Pitchfork?"

This came so suddenly that he could say nothing but, "Doing what?"

Her hand lifted and moved in a gesture that took in all of Arrowhead. "We lose stock. Since that Riel trouble in Canada, about seven hundred families of Crees have moved into Montana. They're starving and they live off ranch beef. I dare say you've come up against them in your work. Then, too, there are white rustlers. We didn't get them all in '84. I need a man of your cut."

"To burn out Ben Teasdale some dark night?"

"If that proves necessary."

He said, "I've seen a lot of Montana these last few seasons. Most big ranchers live and let live. Some let settlers milk range cows, so long as the calves get their share. Then the ranchers buy butter from the settlers at fifty cents a pound. Most loan horses and farm machinery to the settlers. It's a big enough country for everybody."

"Not big enough for thieves," she said, her voice suddenly a whiplash. "The Texas system of branding every calf found on the range is just one step short of mavericking. Pitchfork stands against anything that approaches cattle stealing. If Ben Teasdale is guilty, he's no better than a rustler."

Sabin shrugged again, knowing no argument against this kind of stubbornness. "You don't need me. You've got a crew. And a foreman. What about Ginselling?"

"I'm not offering you Ginselling's job," she said. "I'm offering you a half interest in Pitchfork."

This morning he'd heard the laughter of all the little devils who fashioned the destinies of men; now the peal of their laughter was so loud in his ears that it drowned out all thinking. When his mind did work, a picture came into it; he was remembering a night, and the creak of saddle leather in the clearing, and the old man reaching for the rifle that was racked over the door. He was remembering the din and the great rush of men and Ginselling's face in the starlight. Someone had laid a gun barrel above Sabin's ear that night; as he went down to his knees, his last memory had been of Curly flung to the ground, fighting and crying. Sabin had called out to the old man then, and he'd heard somebody say, "That cottonwood yonder will do." The first thing he'd seen when he'd opened his eyes was the cottonwood, and silence had held the clearing then; there was only Curly's sobbing, and the old man turning to the wind's hand, turning and turning and looking like a bundle of rags, looking like nothing.

There was still a blank between that scene and the one in Doc Hatwell's office late that same night, when he'd left the kid there.

"I'm riding out," he'd told Hatwell. "You take care of Curly for me, see. You'll hear from me."

And now he sat in Pitchfork's ranch-house, the length of a table from Mrs. Lantry, hearing her say, "I'm not offering you Ginselling's job. I'm offering you a half interest in Pitchfork."

He wanted to laugh, but that numbness of mind still held him. He said, "Half a ranch, just for chasing rustlers?"

Her fingertips touched the table; she began drumming lightly, making no more show of agitation than this. She said, after a while, "Thora meant something to you in the old days."

He wondered who could have told her; he wondered if she had eyes that pierced these walls and leveled butte and hill. "I saw her again this morning," he said, and his hand raised to where her quirt had burned him.

41

"Thora's wild," Mrs. Lantry said. "Wild as a hawk. Perhaps I failed her as a mother somehow; perhaps she's too much like me. A few more years and she'll be married and settled down. But she's got to be helped across those years. She's of a mind to marry now, Sabin. That mustn't happen."

"Ginselling—?" he asked, and found it odd that as Morgan Lantry and Jeff Sabin had had something in common, he and Ginselling had a shared thing, too.

"No," Mrs. Lantry said. "Garth Trenchard."

He didn't let his face show how that hit him; he didn't want her knowing that Garth Trenchard's name carried any real meaning to him. He said, "He's Inland's new manager, so Doc Hatwell told me. Doesn't that make him big enough to marry a Lantry?"

Her face drew tighter. "I've offered you half of Pitchfork. Do I have to name all my reasons besides? I don't want her married to Garth Trenchard. But alone I can't stop her. That's why I need you, Mark Sabin."

She'd needed Morgan Lantry across the years, he thought. She was a frail reed of a woman, and she'd leaned on the whang-leather strength of Morgan Lantry until that strength had dwindled away in the dust of Stirrup's street. For a moment pity touched him, for she was an old woman and alone; but when he read her eyes, he knew he'd overlooked something in his estimate. She was desperate, but she was not weak, so perhaps the real strength had been hers instead of Morgan Lantry's.

She said, "What is your answer, Mark Sabin?"

He stood up, reaching for his sombrero. He said, "I'll have to think about it." He supposed there should be a certain triumph in a Sabin answering a Lantry in this fashion, but the moment had no real zest for him.

He stepped into the hall and came along it to the

gallery, and Ginselling stood there waiting, and they regarded each other for a long, reflective moment until Ginselling said, "She aims to set a thief to catch a thief, is that it?"

Sabin felt the crawl of anger. "Do you listen at keyholes, Ginselling?"

"I don't have to," Ginselling said. "I know what's eating her. I saw the tally on fall roundup."

Sabin thought: *I've only got to turn on my heel and go back and speak a little piece, and this lump takes his orders from me.* It made the kind of thought that had a hearty taste to it. But his only move was to reach for the makings and fashion up a cigarette. He was slow about this, and Ginselling stood watching him. When the quirly was fashioned, Sabin dug for a match. He held the match in his hand, then reached and hooked the head inside one of Ginselling's shirt buttons and brought the match aflame. He lighted the cigarette and tipped his head back and blew the smoke straight up.

"Be seeing you," he said, and walked down the gallery steps.

He came around the house and crossed the hard-packed yard toward the corrals and saw the men who'd escorted him from Stirrup ranged beside the bunkhouse, some lolling on the benches, some with their shoulders to the log wall. They were silent as he showed himself, though he'd heard them talking and bantering a moment before. Under the impact of their silence, he saddled and swung a leg up and sat his saddle for a moment, looking at them but not seeing them.

He looked at Pitchfork, the buildings and the men and the great brown acres beyond, and heard again the pealing laughter of irony. Pitchfork could be his, not half of it but all, for there was Mrs. Lantry, overripe with years, and Thora who would succeed her and who would need a husband. That was in the bargain, too, even if the words hadn't been said.

Then he lifted his hand to Pitchfork's crew. "Be seeing you," he said, but no man made him answer. He neck-reined through the yard and took the wagon road across the burned-out grass toward Stirrup. He didn't look back.

5

The Rustler

HE TOOK TO CRUISING Arrowhead in the week that followed, riding by day and by night, sometimes sleeping in Stirrup and sometimes packing his bedroll with him and spreading his blankets under the cold stars. He seemed a man aimless, yet there was a certain pattern to his riding; he wanted first to familiarize himself with all the basin, to mark the changes that had come in the five years so that when the need arose, he'd know where each new fence stood and where the different brands grazed. He had a job to do and knew only one way of doing it: to catch a Reese Stringham, you became a Reese Stringham, knowing the country as a rustler would know it, thinking as a rustler would think.

He got a sense of timelessness with the passing days. The nights when he slept out always found him near the old place, for it was still the passage to the hills; nothing had changed, not really. At first he camped beneath the medicine tree, keeping vigil until long after the midnights and rolling in then, but later he found a place behind Teasdale's where he could be screened by timber but still watch the slot into the hills. From this new stand, a broad shelf on the slope, thick with ancient timber, he could get down into the ravine much quicker than he could have descended from the medicine tree.

Always he thought of the weather; for if the snow still held off, the threat of it was in the air and the cold crept through his blankets, and Arrowhead Creek had ice along it one morning. Sabin remembered what Doc Hatwell had said about the Indians; he remembered and was sometimes scared with his thinking.

Of a certain evening he walked Stirrup's street, knowing he should be up into saddle and off, but his patience had worn a bit thin, and he was feeling futile. He might have spent that evening with Doc Hatwell; but when he climbed the dark stairway, he found Hatwell gone on a night call, so he came again to the boardwalk. The Maverick held no enticement for him; he had lived within himself too long to need men at his elbow, and he had small taste for the aimless talk of the saloons. His hunger tonight drove deeper and was for the kind of camaraderie a man found with an old and trusted friend like Hatwell, a camaraderie that could be bridged with long silences in which the things unspoken counted as heavily as the things said. He went walking along the boardwalk, no direction to his footsteps, his breath a faint cloud before him.

He found her house near the center of the street, and he would have passed it by, not knowing, except for a glimpse of her as she moved by a lamplighted window. He paused and stood looking till she was gone from his sight. The house was little more than a shack, and he tried to remember who had lived here in the old days or what sort of place it had been. He went to the door and raised his knuckles to it, and the door opened for him. Surprise touched her.

"I wondered how your shoulder was," he said.

"Come in," she said and stepped to one side, holding the door open wider.

The room had been made cheerful in small ways, and the reflection of her was in it, in the checkered gingham curtains, in the bookcase that might have once been a packing box. This was her workshop as well as her home, for a dress dummy stood in one corner, covered with pieces of cloth held together by pins.

He said, "Looks pretty," and nodded toward the dummy.

"It's for Thora Lantry," she said. "There's a dance at Grove schoolhouse at the end of the week, you know."

He hadn't known, but he guessed now what had kept Thora in town the other morning when she had ridden in with Pitchfork's crew and then stayed on business of her own. He felt a sudden irritation that this girl, this Deborah, should toil with needle by lamplight that Thora might be prettier; and he asked, "Do you like this kind of work?"

She said, "It's a living." She had the same serenity he had marked at Teasdale's place and her face was prettier with the pain gone from it.

He asked again about her shoulder.

"Healing nicely," she said. "Won't you sit down?"

He had used up his only reason for being here, and he hesitated now, then seated himself because he liked being here; he liked being shut off from the rest of Stirrup, and there was a warmth to this girl; her serenity spread peace all around her. He lowered himself to a chair and placed his sombrero on a table, beside the lamp. He had no more ready words, but he said, finally, "You've done this kind of work long?" nodding again toward the dress dummy.

"All my life, but not always for a living. My folks ranched, over on the other side of the Judiths. They started on a shoe string, and the shoe string broke. They're both gone now. What they left was enough to get me started."

He nodded, understanding now why she'd visited the Teasdales and brought them gifts; she had lived in a shack like the one on the old place; she had had a mother and a father who had been like the Teasdales. There were things no person could truly leave behind.

She seated herself across from him and let her hands lie idle in her lap. He had the feeling, suddenly, that she knew all about him, why he was here and what he'd been before he'd left and how he'd fared in the years between. She would know things without prying; she had an eye for seeing and a mind for understanding; and he felt defenseless before her, like a man with his gun snarled up in leather at a time when he needed it. He wondered if she'd heard about Thora quirting him before the mercantile the other day.

She smiled softly. "You're a man without a religion, Mr. Sabin?"

He shrugged. "They didn't have a church in Stirrup in my day; they still haven't got one. It's a long, long ride to Lewistown."

"I didn't mean that," she said. "Most of us have our particular religion—the thing we believe in, the thing we're driving at. Ben Teasdale's is cows—blooded cattle. Mrs. Lantry's is cows, too, lots of cows, native stock that can range for itself and grow fat and pile up profits at shipping time. I suppose that my religion, if you can call it that, is to turn out a nicer dress than the last one."

He said, "I do any job that's handed to me the best way I know how."

"But tomorrow you could climb to the opposite side of a fence, is that it? And handle the new job as well as you did the old?"

He wondered if she had heard what Pitchfork had offered him, but he knew that that couldn't be so. Only Mrs. Lantry knew, and she wouldn't have talked.

He said thoughtfully, "Suppose your old man had been the sort who'd rather go fishing than put up hay. Suppose that taking the easy way kind of got to be a habit with him, and pretty soon it was easy to close his eyes when rustlers rode by his place, then take a cut for keeping shut. Suppose that he took to peddling whiskey to any man, white or Indian, who had the money to buy it. Wouldn't you get so you'd figure yourself not much account because you had an old man who wasn't much account?"

She said, "My dad couldn't pass a card game. Big or small, it was his game whenever he ran across one. I remember my mother sitting up nights waiting."

He said, "Suppose you got a notion you could show folks you were cut from different stuff than your dad. Suppose you picked the trail opposite to the one your old man took and rode that trail straight and saw to it that your kid brother rode straight, too. Do you think that in time the brand you packed would read different to folks, even though it was the same brand as your old man's?"

Her eyes shone in the lamplight, and her mouth softened and quirked just a little at the corners. "I was wrong," she said. "You have a religion."

He shrugged. He was not given to long speeches or to a show of the things that were closest to him, and tonight he'd spoken of a need he'd never before put into words, not to the Stock Growers' when they'd hired him, not to Doc Hatwell who had figured into his planning. Yet because Deborah was looking at him now in a manner that made him proud, he wanted her to understand how it really was, all of it; he wanted her to know that the need was one thing, the doing another, and that he didn't deserve what he saw in her eyes. Not yet.

"Suppose," he said, his voice harsh, "that no matter how much you wanted that brand to read different, you kept remembering that the old man had got hung and you hadn't done anything about it."

She said, "Morgan Lantry is dead, too, Mr. Sabin. Let that be the end of it."

"That's what his kind of religion got him," he said. "Cows came first—men second."

"Not at the end," she said. "I know. You see, he died in this room."

That startled him, and only then did he see the blood stain on the faded carpet; she had scrubbed that stain many times, he could tell, but still it showed.

She said, "He fell out there in the street with a bullet in his back, but there was a lot of leather to him. They carried him in here, because it was closest, and they ran for Doc Hatwell. There was no work for Doc when he got here."

He hadn't known this; it had been enough for him that Lantry was dead. Now he asked, "He talked, then?"

"He was concerned about his wife and daughter. At the end it wasn't cows that counted. Does that make things any easier for you?"

He stood up, reaching for his sombrero, his eyes bleak. "There's still Ginselling."

"Do you blame a gun as well as the finger that pulls the trigger? Ginselling's religion is loyalty to Pitchfork. I think I know why—I've seen him look at Thora."

"Ginselling never carried out any order without

making it personal," Sabin said flatly. At the door he paused, feeling that he'd drawn this girl to him tonight, then pushed her away.

She came toward him; she opened the door and said then, "You'll come back?"

"If you like," he said.

Outside, he went to Conover's and got his horse and lined out of Stirrup. The night closed around him, still and cold, and he set a straight course for Teasdale's. The moon showed itself, lifting above the eastern rim of the basin before he reached the hills. Light winked in Teasdale's shack, but Sabin skirted the buildings and rode on to that place where he could sit upon the slope and watch the slot below. He began his vigil then, wishing he'd brought along his sheepskin; for the night had teeth in it, the wind rattled the pine needles and found its way through them and stung Sabin's cheeks; the night was no longer still. The moon climbed and fingered its way through the pine tops.

Sabin found sitting here in the night and the cold a perverse thing, when he might have stayed in Deborah's house. He had squatted here on the slope many wasted nights, and he was of a mind now to turn back to Stirrup.

Then, near midnight, he heard the tumult of stock moving. He came out of his doze and stood up, stiff and sluggish, no eagerness in him. He had waited so long for this that he was empty of feeling now that it was happening.

Still, he tuned his ears to the sound, keening the night and standing silent. Those were horses being moved, not cattle, and he edged forward through the timber until he could look down into the slot. The moon rode high, and the trail was silvered with a day-like luminosity. The horses, he judged, were being driven as wide of Teasdale's place as the crowding hills permitted; there might be twenty head. He waited, hearing them come closer; he waited, and they spilled into the slot and the moonlight danced upon their backs and silvered the dust they raised. They passed below him, and the rider who was hazing them came along. There was only the one rider, and this surprised Sabin and brought a grudging admiration, for such a lone-handed foray bespoke a rare sort of daring.

He went back to his horse and climbed into the saddle and came angling down the slope, careless of sound, for the clatter of the stolen horses ahead would blanket his own movement. He came down upon the lone rustler, his gun in his hand, and was close enough to the man to touch him before the rider discovered him. Sabin said, "Up with them!" and watched the rider's hands rise; and then Sabin nudged back his sombrero and said, "You got careless, son," for this was a young one. "You shouldn't have counted yourself safe until you were well out of Arrowhead."

The youngster said, "My God, Mark! It's you!"

It was the voice that told Sabin, even though the voice had changed, for the old man had had that same high-pitched quality to his speech when he was surprised. He looked at the face in the moonlight, that handsome, go-to-hell face, and the five years' difference wasn't so much, now that he knew. He said, "Curly!" and remembered how evasive Doc Hatwell had been. He hated Doc, but only for a moment; Doc could no more have prevented this than a man could keep it from snowing.

Curly dropped his hands and angled a leg around his saddle-horn, grinning. "Heard tell you were back," Curly said. "Now you can help me with these broomtails."

Sabin said, his face showing nothing, "You didn't hear all of it, then. I'm not stealing horses."

"Shucks," Curly said, "this is different. Every one of 'em wears Pitchfork's brand."

"Get on up there and turn them around, kid," Sabin said. "They go back where you got 'em."

"No," Curly said flatly, and his face turned sullen and savage.

They looked at each other in the moonlight, these two so strangely met; and Sabin was remembering then the talk he'd had just a few hours before with Deborah, when he'd spoken of a man giving new significance to an old brand's meaning. That was what had to link him and Curly together, that same need, even in a moment like this when the edges of the kid's temper showed and the old way and the new way stood deadlocked.

He remembered, too, that night beneath the medicine tree, when he'd talked to Garth Trenchard and Trenchard had asked if he had any reason to go easy on Reese Stringham. He thought: *Trenchard knew, damn him!* He wondered if Mrs. Lantry had known, too; but he judged not, remembering the bargain she'd tried to drive.

He said, "They go back, kid. There's no two ways about it."

Curly said, "Reese Stringham will have something to say about it. He's not going to like this, Mark, not a bit. I'm riding for Reese now. You might as well get that straight."

6

Heart of the Hills

THEY SAT THEIR SADDLES, eyeing each other across the space that lay between them, and they were enemies in that moment, hating each other, looking alike because their hate made them alike, hard-featured and implacable and unbending. It was Mark Sabin who softened first, making no outward show of it, his anger tempered by the only real affection he had ever known, his tolerance kindled by a sad knowledge of how it was to be young and headstrong and alien in your own land. He started to speak but sensed the futility of speaking; the ten years between him and his brother made Sabin mute. Curly would have to live those ten years before he could understand.

Because this was so, Sabin suddenly wheeled his horse to the west. He saw Curly drop his foot solidly to the stirrup, and then Sabin was sending his sorrel up the slot, and Curly was lost to him. Sabin rode hard along this ravine until he overtook the drag of the horse herd, and then he began skirting the stolen pack, being careful not to scare them. The first edge had been worn off these Pitchfork horses, and they were more tractable than he'd expected, yet he marveled that Curly had bunched them alone.

When he'd got to the head of the herd, Sabin turned them, waving his sombrero and slapping it against his leg and letting out a wild "Yipp-ee-ee!" that was caught by the shouldering walls and went echoing. He got the bunch to a gallop and sent them streaming back down the slot, counting on the noise of their coming to warn Curly. Sabin saw his brother as he went by; Curly had pulled his own horse to the side, and the boy's face was a sullen mask, but he made no move to try to turn the horses. They went clattering out of the slot and down toward Teasdale's, and Sabin turned back then and came to where Curly waited.

He looked at the boy, and he thought: *He could have pulled a gun.* And because Curly hadn't, Sabin counted that a victory.

He said, "Most of them will head back to Pitchfork. Ginselling can comb the rest out of the draws. It will give him something to do."

Curly said, flat-voiced, "You've got awful damn' big across the britches, Mark. Too damn' big for your own good!"

Sabin crooked a leg around the saddlehorn and reached for the makings and spun up a cigarette, taking his time at it and giving the kid a chance to cool. But when he'd fired the quirly, he looked through the smoke and saw that Curly's face hadn't softened. Sabin said then, "Wasn't one Sabin at the end of a rope enough?"

"That's it," Curly said. "Somebody had to square up."

"It won't do, kid."

"Damn it, the old man never meant anybody any harm, Mark. You know that."

"The old man," said Sabin, "was guilty as hell."

"Just the same, Reese is going to have something to say about this."

"Take me to him, Curly."

Curly looked startled. "What kind of fool do you figger I am?"

"He'll want to know why you had a leaky loop tonight. I'll tell him. Take me to him, kid."

Curly thought about this for a long, reflective moment, his face still sullen. Anger sparked his voice. "By grab, I will at that! I want to see how rocky you are when you stand up to Reese and the boys."

"Hell, Curly, Reese was a friend of mine."

Curly said, "We'll see," and jogged his horse.

Sabin fell in behind him, having again that feeling he'd known when he'd ridden out of Stirrup with Pitchfork's crew, that feeling that this was foolish business. He remembered the horses running back toward Pitchfork through the night; he could hear the diminishing thunder of their hooves, and his own kind of laughter was in him.

Soon they were out of the slot's west end, into the darkness and mystery beyond; and he kept as close to Curly as he could without crowding him. He supposed they were following a game trail, and Curly must have ridden it often. The trail rose through long windings and many switchbacks, the timber pressing close all around, and the horses laboring to the climb, and the smell of pine tight in a man's nostrils. Once they came out upon a promontory and breathed their horses, and only then did Sabin realize how far they'd climbed, for he could look down upon lesser hills and Arrowhead was lost to him. He strained his eyes in the starlight, and presently he was able to give names to some of the landmarks; and he was a man come out of the mystery of the lower trail to an understanding of his whereabouts.

He thought: *This is my country,* and suddenly knew a real affection for the tumbled land, an affection that was alarming in its intensity. He had ridden many ranges these past years, never caring about the Arrowhead, for he'd counted the older days a closed page. But now he was realizing that every man must be bound to some section; and this was his, this was where his boyhood had been spent; and so the land had marked him and claimed a part of him and there was no changing that. He was tied to the land as he was tied to Curly, irrevocably and beyond any will of his own. Time and distance had given an illusion, making him feel apart; but he had ridden out a full circle and this coming back was made of more than the will of Garth Trenchard and the bidding of a man's bosses. It was made of inevitability.

Curly said, "This way," and jogged his horse.

They moved through timber again, each with an arm crooked before his face, driving deep into the hills with a seeming aimlessness until the moment came when Curly halted his horse and cupped his hands to his mouth and halloed a camp. They came out into comparatively clear country, a little mountain meadow that lay stark in the moonlight, the bushes that dappled the openness showing a metallic sheen, the trees silvery sentinels, and the moon wintry above. In the meadow's center was a log cabin with a stable; a large corral, also of logs, connected the two buildings.

Lamplight showed in the cabin's windows, and a man stood in the door, half-slouched and half-ready, until Curly halloed again and the last of the tension left the man. This one said, "Who's that with you, kid?"

Curly said, "It's Mark." He stepped down from his saddle before the cabin and said, "We crossed trails," leaving it at that. "Reese around?"

The one in the doorway said, "Inside."

The two left their horses with reins trailing, and Curly shouldered into the cabin first, Mark following him close. Four men sat around a slab table, playing poker; and Sabin could have named all of them, though Reese Stringham was the one he knew best. Reese had been a handsome man, and some said he had education. He was no more than thirty now, but his face had got flabby; he looked like a man who'd let go, yet in his long, lean body and in the ghost of his handsomeness there was a certain constant wariness. He had a smile that was warm and bright as any campfire, and he showed little surprise when he looked up at Sabin. He had a quirly pasted between his lips; he licked this from one corner of his mouth to the other and said, "How, Mark." He came up from the backless chair he'd straddled and shook hands in a loose and lazy way. "Long time no see. You know the boys?"

Sabin said, "I know them," and gave them a nod that was neither friendly nor forbidding; they came fat and thin and old and young and ruddy and dark, but there was a stamp on all of them and he had read it on many men.

Stringham said, "Heard you were around, Mark." He lifted a stack of chips and riffled them, then put them down and seated himself again, leaving his cards lie. "How did you come across the kid?"

Sabin looked at his brother. "Tell him," Sabin said.

The sullenness was still in Curly's face, but there was uncertainty besides, as though his first anger still lingered but cold logic had diluted it. He said, "I lifted a passel of Pitchfork's broomtails tonight. I ran 'em as far as the slot."

Stringham regarded him speculatively, his eyes sleepy-lidded. "All by your lonesome?"

"All by my lonesome."

Stringham's face darkened. "That was a damn' fool thing to do."

Sabin said, "I turned them back for him."

Stringham turned his glance upon Sabin, his eyes no longer sleepy but shining hard in the lamplight. "On account of the kid? Or on account of the horses?"

Sabin shrugged. "Call it both."

A chair scraped against the floor; one of the four at the table let out a raspy breath. Stringham said then, "Were you doing Stock Growers' work tonight, Mark?"

"Ginselling might have been hard behind those missing broomtails, him and his crew. I think you'd better have a little talk with Curly."

"Curly's shaping up fine," Stringham said, mollified but still guarded. "He's just too damn' chancy. I send him on an easy chore and he's got to try bringing back a hatful of horses. Time will take that out of him."

"If he's got enough time left."

Stringham's eyes squinted down at the corners, and Sabin could see how harshly suspicion was ruling Stringham; and then Stringham's grin broke wide and he slapped the table hard, rattling the stacked chips. "No need for everybody to be so edgy," he said. "The kid bit off too big a chunk. Maybe he'd have swallowed it, and maybe he wouldn't have. You showed him some sense. By grab, Mark, it's been a long time since we've frolicked together. Squinch, what are we saving that jug for?"

One of the men went to a wall cupboard and brought back the jug. Stringham got the tin cups himself and sloshed whiskey into them and passed the first one to Mark and kicked a chair toward him. Sabin took the cup in his hand and held it, waiting, still standing. When Stringham hoisted his cup, Sabin aped the motion, tipping the cup and tasting the fire of its contents.

Stringham drew his hand across his mouth. "Loose, Mark?"

Again Sabin shrugged. "Just riding. It's been quite a spell since I last saw Curly. All Doc Hatwell said was that he'd drifted."

Stringham said, "Lots of cows in the basin."

"So?" said Sabin and let it lie at that.

"It's fat, Mark. Fatter than you could guess. And safer. I could use a man with Curly's kind of nerve and your old man's kind of carefulness."

"Fat pickings—thin ropes," Sabin said.

Stringham laughed. "It won't be like '84, with the vigilantes knocking on a man's door to take him for a short walk to his own ridgepole. I've got friends, Mark." He swept his hand in the direction of Arrowhead, taking in all the basin.

"So?" Sabin said again.

"Look," Stringham said, "I know you've been riding for that Miles City bunch. That was just a job; and if you scotched snakes for them, that's no hide off my back. You want to cut in on this?"

"No," Sabin said.

Again that chair scraped, the sound strident in the complete silence, and somebody pushed at the table, spilling the chips.

Stringham said, "Easy, boys!" barking it, yet keeping it to a whisper; and Sabin let the whiskey cup drop to the floor, wanting his fingers free.

They looked at him, all of them, and he felt the impact of their stares and was braced against it when the man Squinch said, "He's still a cattlemen's law dog!"

Stringham made a spreading movement with his hand, and his smile was only on his lips. "What am I going to do about you, Mark?"

"We'll call this a howdy," Sabin said. "The next time we meet, we'll take up the real talking."

Squinch said, looking at Stringham, "We let him go, eh? Then we run out of this hideout? We give it up because he knows where we're at?"

Stringham said, "Hell, that wouldn't make sense." He said it in a flat voice, not smiling, and let the silence close down again.

Sabin was suddenly conscious that the man who'd stood in the doorway had now come inside and ranged himself along the wall; he heard this man's slight movement, and he thought: *Here it is!*

But Curly said then, "I fetched him here, Reese. I aimed that he should go back afterwards."

Sabin couldn't see the kid, not fully, for Curly was ranged to the left of him and standing a pace back, his shoulders to the log wall, his hands hanging loose. Sabin wanted to look at Curly's face and read what was there to read, yet he had to keep his eyes on those at the table; and in that moment everything stood out with the startling clarity of a sharp photograph, the room and the men and the wavering lamp and the spilled chips on the table. Somewhere out in the night a horse nickered, probably in the corral between the buildings, the sound loud.

Stringham raised his hands slowly and put them upon the table, palms down. "Next time, Mark," he said.

Sabin turned toward the door, and this gave him a full look at Curly, but the corner of his eye was upon Reese Stringham, for Stringham would have to make the move, and he put no real trust in Stringham's words. He saw Curly's face and read Curly's eyes, troubled and defiant, and he knew what this was like for Curly, this being torn between.

He took a step nearer the door and looked full at Curly and said, "Coming, kid?"

Curly glanced toward Stringham, then dropped his gaze to the floor. "I got friends here," he said.

"The old man had friends, too," Sabin said.

"Damn it, Mark!" Curly said with sudden violence. "Git while you can!"

"Sure, kid," Sabin said and walked through the open doorway and stepped toward his horse.

He had his back to the cabin as he lifted himself to saddle; he had this one unguarded moment when only Curly's ephemeral loyalty stood between him and Stringham and Squinch and the others. He hoped in that moment to hear the fall of Curly's boots, and he was taut with the knowledge that if he did he would have to turn back gun in hand, for Stringham would be a cougar unleashed. He would have accepted that danger just to know that Curly had made a real choice. But when he looked toward the cabin, no man had moved to the doorway, and in the tight silence he stirred his mount to a walk and took to the screening timber.

7

The Thin Chance

HATWELL PACED THE NARROWNESS of his office, his long, horsey face old and troubled, his hands fluttering as he made his to and fro movement and talked. To Sabin, seated stiffly on the horsehair sofa, the thought came that no task harder than the admission of defeat ever befell a man, and there was born in him a sympathy for Hatwell tempering the anger that had ridden Sabin through all this day. Beyond the walls, Stirrup stirred, the blended sounds of the town reaching into the room. This was early evening of the day after Sabin's ride to Reese Stringham's hideout.

Hatwell said, "Hell, man, I never knew for sure. Not till you told me. All the kid said was that he felt like drifting. I've heard talk, yes. But nobody ever *saw* him riding with Reese Stringham."

Sabin eased his long body full length upon the sofa, feeling tired. "He's up there now."

Hatwell ran his fingers through his sparse hair. "I

wish I knew the words to say, Mark. You left him with me. That meant more than feeding him and keeping a roof over him and seeing that he had one dollar to rub against another. I talked to him whenever I had the time."

Sabin looked at this man, this Doctor Lucius Hatwell, and thought of all the years Hatwell had followed his profession on this range and on others. He thought of the many babies born since Hatwell had begun practicing, born and grown to manhood and womanhood; he thought of the long nights and the sick-bed vigils and the patients who had slipped away in spite of all one man could do. He thought of sleepless hours and lonely roads, and he looked around him at the sum total of Hatwell's worldly goods, these meager material rewards for faithfulness; and the anger that had been with him down from the hills and through this day dissolved into humility.

He said, "You took him when nobody else would have taken him. I'm beholden, Doc. Will you forget the rest that I've said tonight?"

Still Hatwell's face was screwed tight. "When a man has a job handed him, Mark, he should do one of two things: turn it down if it's too big for him, or else handle it right. I could have turned you down that night you fetched Curly. I didn't."

"Look," said Sabin, smiling a rare smile, "isn't there something left in that jug you had stashed out?"

Hatwell moved automatically to his desk, got the jug, sloshed it, found glasses, and blew the dust from them. Then he turned his back to the jug, a man still troubled. "Mark," he said, "just one thing: are you certain sure Curly was alone last night?"

Sabin said, "Certain sure."

Hatwell passed the back of his hand across his tufted brows. "I got to tell you," he said. "I went out on a call last night. When I got back, one of Pitchfork's boys was waiting for me—that lantern-jawed fellow, Marias, they call him. I rode to Pitchfork. One of the crew was moaning and pitching in a bunk, a young kid Ginselling took on about a year ago. Somebody had planted a chunk of lead in the kid's shoulder. Somebody who was running off Pitchfork horses last night."

Sabin sat upright, his face taut in the lamplight, his anger renewed and strengthened because fear was the core of it. "It took you long enough to get around to telling me," he said.

Hatwell made a helpless gesture with his hands. "The pieces didn't fit till you told me about Curly and the horses. I wanted to keep this from you. I couldn't."

"Hell," Sabin said, "pour us that drink."

Hatwell turned and groped for the jug and tipped it. Sabin took the proffered glass and downed the whiskey fast, finding it not to his liking. He watched Hatwell drink, and then said slowly, "No wonder Curly wouldn't ride back down from the hills with me."

Hatwell said, "It's one bad mess."

"Pitchfork's boy going to pull through?"

Hatwell shrugged. "Maybe yes—maybe no. If that bullet had gone two inches lower, I'd have the answer for sure. There's a chance—a thin chance. I'll be riding out there again tonight."

"If you get shed of your work in time. Somebody's on the stairs right now."

Hatwell said, "Oh, hell," and put the whiskey jug in his desk drawer. "A man counts on three people in his lifetime—his preacher, his wife, and his doctor. So he kicks up a fuss if any of them take a drink." He turned toward the door; and when he opened it, Ben Teasdale stood there, looking so small and rabbity that Sabin found it hard to remember how this same man, only a few nights ago, had stood in the clearing before his shack, defying Pitchfork.

Teasdale said, "Good evening, Doc," and looked surprised to find Sabin here. He ventured into the office, and Hatwell said, "One of your young ones, Ben?"

Teasdale shook his head. "It's not sickness, Doc."

Hatwell waved toward a chair. "Sit down."

But Teasdale stood. He said, rushing out his words to get rid of them, "I'm going to move my beef, Doc. I'm playing a hunch. You've talked hard winter, and I'm guessing that you're right. Maybe the ridges will be kept bare while the snow piles up on the prairie. The hills are bound to be a better bet than the plains."

"But, man, you've got feed," Hatwell said. "You put land into alfalfa."

"A lot of that's pledged to Inland, Doc."

Sabin spoke up. "Hell, you might just as well turn your herd over to Reese Stringham and be done with it. How many critters do you think you'll comb out of the hills come spring?"

Teasdale said stubbornly, "It's risk them to rustlers or lose them through the winter. I'll chance Stringham. Pitchfork's my real worry. Me and my oldest boy will be gone from home while I'm moving the herd. I was hoping, Doc"—his glance swung back to Hatwell—"that you could sort of keep an eye on the missus and the young ones while I was gone."

Hatwell made his helpless gesture again. "I'm a busy man."

Teasdale said, "Maybe you could talk to Mrs. Lantry. All I want is to live and let live."

Sabin said, "The last man who asked Doc to handle his troubles lived to learn there're some things a man better do for himself, Teasdale. Sure, I know you can't set foot on Pitchfork. Let me talk to Mrs. Lantry for you. I'd like an excuse to ride to Pitchfork."

Teasdale said, "I know who you are now. Maybe I'd have less trouble if you didn't talk for me."

Sabin had to grin. "That's really looking a gift horse in the mouth."

Teasdale's nose twitched. "I ain't forgot the other night. You find yourself crowded, mister, you can come through my door any time."

Sabin's grin broadened. "With Pitchfork after me? The idea is to keep Pitchfork *off* your doorstep. Go move your cattle, Teasdale. We'll see what can be done."

Teasdale backed from the office, and as his boots hit the stairs, Hatwell said, "Mark, you're a damn' fool."

"Sure," said Sabin and arose from the sofa and started for the door. "Be seeing you, Doc. You've got a long ride to make. Leave something standing at Pitchfork that I can tie my horse to."

He might have ridden out with Doc Hatwell tonight, he reflected, but he'd got no sleep the night before, and his business with Pitchfork could wait. He went to the hotel and fell into a deep sleep, and after breakfast he started for Conover's where he'd been stabling the sorrel. A man stood on the mercantile's porch, tall and black-garbed and ruggedly handsome, and thus Sabin had his first glimpse of Garth Trenchard by daylight.

He passed Trenchard, giving no sign of knowing Inland's man, and Trenchard called then, "You, stranger! Got a match?"

Sabin turned and saw that Trenchard had his cigar case in his hand. He walked toward the man, and Trenchard's face stayed still, at once remote and ready. He gave Trenchard a match and Trenchard extended the cigar case. This time Sabin took one of the weeds; he stripped the band from it; he'd never seen this particular brand before.

"Havana made," Trenchard said. "Imported." He

clipped the end from his and scraped the match on
one of the wooden supports of the mercantile's porch.
With the flame held close to his face, he said, low-
voiced, around his cupped hands, "How's wolf hunting?"

"I've only run into whelps so far," Sabin said and
looked straight into Trenchard's eyes and saw that
Trenchard had known all along.

Trenchard said, "A man with your experience
would know which to skin and which to tame."

Sabin got the cigar alight. "The next time you send
me hunting, you call all the shots beforehand," he
said.

Anger put a shine in Trenchard's eyes and a hard
belligerency to the angle of his jaw. "Look, friend—!"
he began, then paused; bonneted shoppers were on the
boardwalk, some turning toward the store. Trenchard
tipped his sombrero to one of these, then smiled at
Sabin. "Smoke that and you'll never find another
cigar good enough for your taste. Drop out to Inland
sometime and I'll give you the name of the importer."

"I'll do that," said Sabin and went on toward the
livery stable.

When he came riding along the street, Trenchard
was still on the porch of the mercantile, but now
Thora was with him. She stood close to the man, deep
in animated conversation; she had her quirt in her
hand and she flicked it against her boot top. She
looked up as Sabin rode by; she looked startled. He
touched the brim of his sombrero, and Trenchard
made a like gesture, and then the pair was lost to
Sabin's sight.

Across the bridge, he lined out for Pitchfork, not
pushing his horse, and it was past noon when he came
down into the shallow coulee where Morgan Lantry
had done his building. Pitchfork looked deserted

today; no men loitered in the yard or at the corrals or around the bunkhouse door. But Ginselling was here. He came from the house as Sabin mounted the gallery steps. He looked at Sabin, and truculence darkened his blocky face. He said, "What do you want?"

Sabin said, "You're going to get lop-sided carrying that chip on your shoulder," and crossed to the door and put his knuckles to it.

Mrs. Lantry opened for him. She stood looking, a leaf-thin woman, and then she said, "Come in, Mark Sabin."

She led him to that long dining room where they had talked before, and pointed to a chair. He turned the chair around and straddled it; and when she had seated herself, she said, "You've brought me your answer?" and her tone told him how eagerly she awaited that answer.

He said, "I've still got to think about it."

She leaned back in her chair; she was dressed in black again today, and she looked as a queen might look who saw her empire lost. "What brings you?" she asked.

"Ben Teasdale," he said. "Your crew's gone. Is it out giving him trouble?"

She said, "I don't know if that's any concern of yours. Ginselling put the men to rounding up some of our horses."

He let his eyes smile. "Well, the chore shouldn't be too hard. They found most of them heading this way, didn't they?"

She was startled out of her usual impassivity. "How could you know that?"

Sabin crossed his arms on the back of the chair and rested his chin upon his arms. "Look," he said. "Ben Teasdale is a little fellow. He's only got a little herd. He'd like to move it into the hills. He'd like his wife and kids to get full nights of sleeping while he's gone. You'd better put Ginselling to looking for those stray horses, too, and keep him at it for a week."

She said, "A favor to repay a favor? Is that it, Mark Sabin?"

He hunched his shoulders. "The horses got headed back toward Pitchfork. There's no changing that. So you don't have to do a single, solitary thing you don't want to do."

She thought this over; he could see the care she put to her thinking. She said then, "No Lantry ever proved ungrateful. Tell your Ben Teasdale not to fret while he's away."

Sabin stood up. "I'm obliged," he said. From one of the windows of this room he could see a corner of the bunkhouse. "Doc Hatwell tells me somebody got hurt."

"The boy's doing as well as can be expected. Hatwell was out here last night. I think he'll pull the boy through. That's why you're getting your bargain, Mark Sabin. Tell your Ben Teasdale that, too."

Sabin said, very carefully, "Your boy saw Teasdale?"

"He saw nothing but the flash of a gun. Who else would have hit at Pitchfork but Teasdale? Stringham's crew? The rustler seemed to be riding alone. Stringham would have had a bunch at his back."

"So—?" said Sabin, knowing no way to shake her conviction without bringing Curly into it. He stepped toward the door, and here he paused. "Thora was in town this morning," he said. "Visiting. Maybe you shouldn't let her ride alone so much."

Her eyes probed him as though she were trying to read the meaning behind his words. She said, "Thank you, Mark Sabin."

"Be seeing you," he said, and strode out to the gallery.

Ginselling was no longer about. Sabin lifted himself to saddle, wanting mightily to pause at the bunkhouse and have a look at the wounded boy. Instead, he headed along the coulee and rose from it when the walls grew gentle, crossed openness and dropped down into another coulee. He was a quarter of a mile along this ravine when he stepped down to tighten his saddle's cinch, and it was then he heard the ring of a shod hoof striking rock. He waited for a horseman to show himself on the backtrail; and when none appeared, he mounted again and rode on, wary now. The coulee angled abruptly; and past a turn, he pulled to one side where bushes grew thickly. It was no more than ten minutes before a Pitchfork rider came into view, the lantern-jawed one Doc Hatwell had mentioned.

Sabin jogged his horse forward, blocking the trail, and said, "If you're heading to town, Marias, we might as well ride together." He said this and saw the man's guilty surprise.

Marias said, "There's room on this range for both of us."

Sabin got his gun out then, making the move quick and certain, and held his piece leveled. "Spill it," he said, his voice turning sharp. "Why are you tagging me?"

Marias' eyes shifted. "Look, this is Pitchfork land. I don't have to answer your damn' question."

Sabin said thoughtfully, "It wasn't gun work Ginselling sent you to do; you'd have tried cutting ahead of me. Turn out your pockets."

"You go to hell, mister!"

"Then strip down, right to the buff, and toss your clothes over here. I'll go through them myself." His voice tightened to a brittle coldness. "Get at it!"

"Hell," the man said, "they don't pay me to freeze to death. What's the difference whether you know or not." He dug into his shirt pocket and withdrew a scrap of paper and passed it to Sabin. "This was to go to Miles by wire."

Sabin took the paper in his free hand and got it unfolded, still holding the gun. The message was addressed to the Stock Growers' Association and read: *Inform us if Mark Sabin still employed by you and if so state nature of his business in Arrowhead.* It was signed: *"Ginselling—Foreman—Pitchfork."*

Sabin passed the note back to Marias and dropped his gun into its holster. "Better send it and earn your pay," Sabin advised. "But I could have saved Ginselling the trouble. Now why didn't he think to ask me?"

8

Death's Rendezvous

TONIGHT A RESTLESSNESS POSSESSED Sabin like that he'd known when he'd waited on the rim of Arrowhead for Garth Trenchard's coming. Again he was playing a game of waiting, but now he had nothing tangible to fix his waiting upon; he stood tied by what had happened in the hills the night before. Once his chore had been simple of purpose: he'd had to lay his loop on Reese Stringham and thus preserve the peace of Arrowhead. But Stringham had Curly Sabin with him, and that made all the difference. It left Sabin wrestling with two kinds of loyalties.

He'd gone to Pitchfork today to find out in his own way how the wounded man fared; and he'd gone, too, to keep Pitchfork off Ben Teasdale's place, and thus he'd staved off war for a brief while. He knew now that he'd done this so he might feel that he earned his pay, but it made a poor sort of compromise, leaving the taste of ashes in his mouth.

This afternoon he'd ridden to Teasdale's and found that rabbity little man already gone into the hills, his herd hazed ahead of him. Sabin had left a word of assurance with Mrs. Teasdale and her great brood, then ridden into the slot and had a look around. The signs of Teasdale's passage were here; Sabin had read these and shaken his head and afterwards ridden back to Stirrup. He should be out at the slot again tonight; he knew that. He should be doing the job to which he'd first set his hand. But there was Curly.

Last night he'd been angry with Hatwell. Now he thought: *I'm as helpless as Doc was.*

His supper under his belt, he took to cruising the street aimlessly. No Pitchfork horses stood at the hitchrails, but when he had a look in the livery stable, he found one. He knew that mount. It belonged to Marias—he whose courage had been less than his loyalty. This afternoon the south-north stage had passed through Stirrup. The Northern Pacific had a telegraph line; and Sabin smiled grimly, understanding. He wondered if Pitchfork's man, upon his return, would report to Ginselling that the message had been seen, or if Marias would keep his humiliation to himself. He decided it didn't matter.

He turned into one of the saloons and saw a broken line of men along the bar; a few stragglers from outlying ranches were bellied up, but it was a quiet night. He had no taste for liquor this evening, but he tarried for a while at the blackjack table, losing a dollar and getting it back and losing it again. The game held no zest, the dealer was listless and taciturn, and Sabin soon tired of playing.

He came to the street and stood idly, watching a Crowfoot horseman trot along the street, roiling the dust. The wind held the hint of snow, but still the snow didn't come. Doc Hatwell emerged from the covered stairway of the mercantile building and headed toward Conover's; Sabin supposed Hatwell was going out to pay his nightly call at Pitchfork.

He remembered that Thora had been in town this morning, but he had not seen her since. He thought about Thora and Trenchard, giving them only a corner of his mind. Then he turned and began walking, his bootheels striking hard against the boards, his spurs jingling; for now he had a purpose that had been with him through all his restlessness, though he had not faced it, not till now.

He came to Deborah's door and rapped upon it and waited for her rustling movement inside; and then the door opened and she stood there, her face dim and ethereal in this uncertain light. The intensity of purpose which had brought him along the street suddenly left him, and he felt awkward and at loss for words. He said, "You asked me to come back," and wasn't sure if this was exactly true.

"Yes," she said. "Come in."

He moved past her into the room's cheerfulness, and she took his hat and placed it upon the table beneath the lamp. She said, "Sit down, please," and he did so. The dress dummy still stood in the corner. He looked at it and asked, "How's the work coming?" and then, remembering a more pertinent question: "How's your shoulder?"

"Quite well," she said, and he supposed that answered both questions. She seated herself and took some sewing into her lap and bent nearer the lamp. "You don't mind," she said. "I'm behind schedule." She lifted her eyes as she said this; she had a way of looking at him that was a man's way, straight and unswerving, with no coquetry in it.

He said, "I wonder if you knew my brother Curly."

Her face turned thoughtful before she made her answer. She raised her sewing to her lips and bit off a thread. "He was still with Doc Hatwell when I came here. He lifted his hat to me a time or two on the street. I was much too old for him—a million years too old. No, I didn't know Curly—not as I know you."

This surprised him, for he felt a stranger as he sat here, and he'd wondered at his own strange need, which had brought him to her door. He said, "But this is only the third time you've laid eyes on me."

Again she gave her wise, thoughtful consideration to what he said. "You're a man who'll do any job that's handed to you the best you can. You said that yourself, remember. That told me a great deal about you. But I'm wondering if you know what your job is."

He said, "There are big men and little men and they draw sparks from each other. But there needn't be flame. Maybe I'd like to see peace in Arrowhead, now and forever. At first that was just a job. Now it's become more than that. It hit me a couple of nights back. This is home. I'm stuck with it."

She said, "I wonder if that's weakness. Or your first show of real strength."

"I wonder, too," he said.

She dropped her eyes to her sewing; the lamplight tangled in her hair gave it a reddish glint. "Is it that you think I can help you?" she asked, so quietly that he had to lean forward to hear her.

He said, "I don't know," and laid his honesty out for her to see. "I wanted to come here tonight. There was no reason for it. Maybe it was just you."

She let the sewing slip from her fingers and looked at him, and for the first time he saw her stripped of her serenity; she was scared, and she was bewildered, and he was surprised to see her so.

"Mr. Sabin," she said, "what would you do if you had the name of the man who killed Morgan Lantry?"

He stiffened, not expecting this, and excitement

crawled in him like a living thing. He said, "So he talked, didn't he? He talked to you before he died. Not only about his wife and his daughter but about the man who shot him. He knew."

"No," she said. "He never knew. He got it in the back, remember."

"Then you've guessed?" He leaned forward, placing his hands on his knees.

"You haven't answered my question yet," she said. "What would you do?"

He could be no less than honest with her, and that meant he had to be very honest with himself. That was why he didn't answer her at once. He had to turn this over carefully in his mind, but first he had to purge himself of many things—the memory of the cottonwood at the old place, and the raw antagonism of Ginselling, and the breathless beauty of Thora. He had to think of that leaf-thin old woman who ruled Pitchfork; he had to think of Ben Teasdale and Reese Stringham and Curly.

He said at last, "I haven't a shred of official power. If I laid my loop on the man, I could only turn him over to Pitchfork. They could make their choice—a court, or a cottonwood."

She was still scared. "No court would listen to what I'd have to say, Mr. Sabin. It's something I've slept with every night since. You talked about big men and little men and the sparks. There's an old saw about one rotten apple spoiling the barrel. Maybe that's the way it is in Arrowhead."

"The man—?" he demanded.

She shook her head. "I can't tell you. Maybe the thing is better left alone. Maybe his name wouldn't be any part of the real answer."

He had got so tensed up that anger came easily to him. "What was this?" he asked. "Some sort of test to see what my answer would be?"

Her cheeks colored, and her anger matched his own. "Across the street is a saloon called the Red Front. Above it is a room—an empty room. Go up there and have a look. I did. I waited night after night, knowing that sooner or later they'd forget to lock the door."

He said, "I'll have that look," and came to a stand and lifted his sombrero from the table.

She crossed the room and opened the door for him, and he strode to the boardwalk and stood looking across the street. Yonder was the Red Front, one of the smaller saloons, and on either side of it were empty lots, weed choked and debris littered. Flanking one lot was the low stand of a Chinese restaurant, flanking the other was a blacksmith shop. He knew that Morgan Lantry had gone down in the dust between the spot where he stood and the Red Front, and he knew what Deborah meant: whoever had done for Lantry had fired from the single window over the Red Front.

He crossed the street and shouldered into the saloon, finding it ill-lighted and sour-smelling and deserted save for the barkeep and a pair of saddle tramps playing an uninspired game of cards at a far table. This place got the backwash of Stirrup's trade; iniquity was in its air, and the feel of sullen violence. Sabin came up to the bar and said, "What's upstairs?"

"An empty room."

"Big enough to hold a bed?"

"Big enough to hold ten beds."

"Care to rent it?"

The apron shrugged "The man who owns this shebang lives in Helena. You'd have to write him."

"Care if I take a look?"

The apron motioned with his head toward a stairs at the back of the barroom. "You've got legs under you."

Sabin climbed the stairs into darkness and stood in the musty folds of darkness, smelling dust and hearing the quick scurrying of a rat, and he thought then of Deborah's courage; he thought of Deborah waiting her chance to come here of a night. He got a match to burning, nursed the flame and held it high and saw the huge expanse of the room, big as the barroom below. The flooring was plank, uncertain and creaky to the tread. A broken table and some chairs stood here, and a few empty whiskey barrels. At the far end, the rectangle of the window made a dull glow.

He groped toward this, feeling his way carefully when the match burned out; he felt stifled and trapped, and the darkness had a prickly quality to it. He got to the window and looked through it; there was light enough to show him the street, starlight and lamplight; and he came down to one knee and pointed the index finger of his right hand downward and knew how one man had had his look at Morgan Lantry.

How had it been? How had it been that day?

Anger and hate and an opportunity blossoming before a man's eyes and a quick pull at the trigger? But no; no ordinary business would have brought a man to this musty, empty room. Someone had waited here, perhaps day after day; someone had had Deborah's own kind of patience and had bided his time carefully, pitting such patience against the inevitable hour when Morgan Lantry would show himself and the sign would be right in all the ways. And, crouching here, Sabin knew how it had been.

There he is now. That's him, that's Lantry. Walking along like he owned the earth, and no man near him and no man watching and his back turned this way. What are you thinking about just now, Morgan Lantry? Can't you feel an itch between your shoulder blades? You've grown big and you've grown arrogant— have you grown blind and stupid as well? Turn around, Lantry! I want to see your eyes when I look at you over this gun sight!

Sabin arose, shaken and perspiring. He lighted another match and had an uncertain look at the floor beneath the window. The ancient dust upon the planking lay undisturbed except where he himself had marred it, but there'd been time enough since last spring for the wind to have sifted through this thin planking and smoothed out the dust again. In a corner of the window a spider had spun its silvery web.

He came back down into the barroom and the apron asked, "How did you like it?"

"It might do, with a little fixing. Anybody else interested in renting it?"

"Hasn't been anybody up there for a month of Sundays, mister," the apron said. "You want the boss' name?"

"Write it down."

The apron scrawled upon a slip of paper and passed it over. Sabin looked at the name and the Helena address, and neither had any meaning for him. He pocketed the slip and nodded his thanks and came out into the open air, finding it good to taste. He looked across the street at Deborah's house and saw her standing before it, awaiting him. He crossed over.

"It was done from there," he said. "Reese Stringham would have played it smart like that. He could have slipped out back easy enough afterwards, while the town was buzzing and everybody running for the doctor. In a way, it was smarter than dry-gulching from a cutbank. Lantry never rode alone on the open range."

"Yes," she said. "But it took a strange sort of courage to do all the waiting that the man must have done."

He remembered Curly and the stolen horses and the damned fool kind of courage that had taken, and was shaken by the thought. He had grown tired of thinking of Curly; he wanted to get inside Deborah's house where lay the only real serenity he had found in Arrowhead. She must have read the hunger in him, for she shook her head. "I've got to get that dress finished for Thora," she said. "That Grove dance is tomorrow night, you know."

He'd forgotten about that, but he felt again the stab of resentment that this girl should toil to make Thora more beautiful. He asked, "Are you going to the dance?"

She smiled. "No one has invited me."

"Then I will," he said, and lifted his hat to her and turned upon his heel and walked away.

9

The Enemy

HE CALLED FOR HER in a rig he'd rented from Conover's and found her ready and waiting, bundled in a cloak of some dark material that made her face the whiter by contrast; she looked like a little girl dressed up in her mother's clothes. She had fixed a box supper for both of them, and he took this from her, then handed her into the buggy and tucked a blanket around her. The night was motionless; the night had a sting to it, and no star showed. He asked her if she was comfortable and got her quick nod; he picked up the reins and wondered if any other man in Stirrup had taken her to a dance. He supposed some one must have; this was a country where women were at a premium; and he wondered about the swains who had brought a buggy around on other nights; he wondered if her serenity had closed them out so completely they'd never come back. He remembered her saying that she'd been a million years too old for Curly.

Across the bridge, he sent the horse along the westward road, and the night closed in around them and the land was formless, the far hills standing dimly etched, darkness against darkness. The clatter of hoofs and wheels made talking a hard task, and Sabin didn't try. They were a pair of people taciturn by nature, and the silence between them made its own queer bond.

He'd had no suit to wear tonight, but he'd put on a clean shirt and shaved carefully and thought twice about wearing his sheepskin. It was an ungainly garment, but he might need it before this night was done, so he'd compromised by putting it in the back of the buggy. Now he kept his eyes ahead, letting the horse find the road, letting the horse find its own pace. Around him the darkness lay; off yonder were Pitchfork and Crowfoot and Inland and G-Rafter and Star-Cross; off yonder were Teasdale's and the high hills and Reese Stringham's hidden cabin.

He had put in an aimless day, and he wondered if he had any right to this kind of holiday. Yet he could only play at waiting, not being sure what it was he was waiting for, and his feeling was that the whole world waited; there was that sort of breathless quality in the night.

At the first sharp turn, he stopped the buggy and was going to get out and have a look for a sign; but Deborah said, "South," and he remembered then. Grove schoolhouse was near the center of the basin, its location picked to make it convenient to all the big ranches. Sabin had got his own book learning there. After he'd turned the buggy, he tried visualizing the country and a picture of it came back to him. He'd been in the neighborhood of Grove schoolhouse in his studied cruising of the country since his return. He was now skirting Pitchfork's fence, and later he followed Inland's, the road paralleling the stretched wire.

After the first few miles, he saw a tiny, flickering tongue of flame against the far night, and this became for him a beacon. Sometimes he lost it as a bluff shut off the view; and each time he sighted it anew, the fire had grown larger. He knew it for what it was; and when he finally wheeled up before the school, the blaze was an immense thing in the hard-packed yard before the building, a dozen men warming themselves around it.

He maneuvered the buggy to the end of a row of vehicles and got out and unharnessed the horse and tied it behind the buggy. There were other buggies here, and buckboards, and quite a few saddle horses; and when he helped Deborah down and escorted her toward the building, he read most of the brands of the basin in the flung light of the fire.

Inside, the desks had been shoved to two of the walls and piled upon each other. Benches, flanking the walls, were filled with the women of the range, all wearing their best. Thora was among them, and, oddly, he knew her first by the dress he had seen in Deborah's house; the dress made her different; it softened her and took some of the mountain cat out of her. Her hair had been piled high, and this changed her, too; she looked queenly and imperious and altogether beautiful in a strange, new way. Most of his memories had been of her aboard a horse; he could see her now at Pitchfork's table where her mother had sat. The dress made that much difference.

He looked at her and was hungry for her; she had always done that to him.

At the far end of the room, where the teacher's desk had been pushed to the wall, a big stove stood, cherry red with much priming; and near it the musicians worked with fiddle and guitar. A few people danced with that awkward self-consciousness that always comes at the first of such affairs. Sabin stood by the doorway, watching them, until someone tapped his shoulder.

"Check your gun and the lady's wrap."

He surrendered his belt and holster and lifted the cloak from Deborah's shoulders. She wore a long dark gown of some rustling material, a bright colored shawl over her bare shoulders. The music was a waltz and he held his arms open for her. She was nothing in his arms, she danced in a light-footed fashion that gave him pleasure and surprised him as well, until he realized that she would bring her own kind of skill and serenity to all things she did. He was careful of her wounded shoulder.

He saw Mrs. Lantry as he danced, and was mildly astonished that she was here. She was seated on the opposite side of the room from Thora; she sat among people and yet was aloof from people, her parchment-like face showing nothing. At the far end of this same wall, he found Mrs. Teasdale seated, her numerous brood around her, starched and scrubbed. Mrs. Teasdale made an ungainly lump, her hands in her lap, her expression one of eager interest. He gave her as much of a nod as he'd given Mrs. Lantry and it came to him that the dance was a truce of sorts and some were here only to show that they honored that truce.

Ginselling came in—he'd been one of those about the fire—and approached Thora, and shortly Sabin saw them dancing. Ginselling was heavy-footed, and this was duty for both of them, but something more for Ginselling. Doc Hatwell was here, too, standing with his hands locked behind him, making small and polite talk to Mrs. Goodnight of G-Rafter. When the music ended, Hatwell took a stand before the musicians, lifted his arms and called for a square dance.

Sabin took Deborah to a seat on one of the benches and looked down at her. "Want this one?"

She smiled at him. "I'd rather watch."

There was room for him to sit beside her, and they watched together. Hatwell's voice rose: "Grab your partners, don't be late—swing 'em wide on the big front gate!" Deborah withdrew into her serenity, softly smiling. Sabin knew this about her now: she was at her best in the things she did alone. A square dance was for watching.

The music grew to a frenzy; the room warmed to the heat of people, and the stove threw out hot arms to encompass the room and smother it. The early self-consciousness was gone; this group had gaiety to it, yet it was a restrained sort of gaiety, the voices a little too boisterous, the laughter a little too shrill. Again Sabin had the feeling that all the world was waiting.

Someone came in and said to a friend near Sabin, "It's snowing. Just a few flakes." The other said, "It won't amount to much. It will stay open till Christmas this year. Want to bet?"

When the square dance was finished, Hatwell called for a schottische; and before Sabin could ask Deborah her will, he saw Thora cross the room toward them. She stood before them, and Sabin rose. Thora smiled and said, "Aren't you going to ask me to dance, Mark?" She had been in the square dance, and the exertion had brought her a high color.

He glanced at Deborah, and she gave him her smile and a nod, and he said to Thora, stiffly, "I'd be pleased."

Thora looked at Deborah. "I like your dress," Thora said. Deborah only smiled again, saying nothing. Sabin looked from one to the other, wondering about this, wondering if Thora's comment had been couched so that Deborah couldn't make a like comment, since Thora's dress was the product of Deborah's skill. He knew that women had their own strange way of making war, indirect and smile-bedecked, and he grew uncomfortable and held his arms open for Thora, wanting to make an end to this.

They went wheeling and dipping around the room, and in the midst of the dancing, Thora asked, "Why did you come back, Mark?"

He made a shrug of sorts. "It's home."

She said, "I'm sorry about what happened the other morning in town. I saw the mark on Ginselling's face and got the story out of one of the boys. I thought you'd come home to war on Pitchfork. That made it my fight."

"It doesn't matter."

"But it does," she insisted. "You see, Mark—" Her voice trailed away and he followed her fixed glance toward the door and saw Garth Trenchard standing there, a late comer. He hadn't realized till now that Trenchard hadn't been present. He saw the manner of Thora's look, half-eager, half-aloof; and she grew clumsy in her dancing. When the music finished, he took her to the bench where he'd first seen her tonight; and as he crossed back over toward Deborah, Trenchard passed him, saying, "Good evening," in a cool, remote voice, his smile impersonal, showing Sabin those strong, white teeth.

"Evening," Sabin said.

Deborah was watching Trenchard as Sabin rejoined her; Inland's man stood before Thora and appeared to be asking her for a dance. The music struck up a waltz again, and Trenchard and Thora went out upon the floor. Sabin looked at Deborah; she nodded, and they began dancing.

Sabin guessed it was turning colder outside; the stove was too hot to be near and the musicians had moved as far from it as space permitted, but the door end of the room was chilly.

As he glided past Mrs. Lantry, Sabin saw that the woman's eyes were following Thora and Trenchard.

Deborah said, "You knew her in the old days?"

"Thora?" Sabin said. "I knew her."

"I think she is very unhappy because she doesn't know what it is she wants."

"No religion?" he asked and wondered why she turned always to this kind of thinking.

"No religion but Thora. Some day she'll be a woman like her mother if she doesn't choose a wrong trail between."

"Does it matter to you one way or the other?" he asked and was instantly sorry for his petulance. She made him some sort of answer, but he didn't hear it, for as he turned with the dance, he got a glimpse of the doorway and the man who stood there, his eyes searching. Sabin knew this one: it was the Pitchfork hand Marias, who'd been sent to send a wire to Miles City.

Sabin lost the man as the dance wheeled about him again; and when he next glimpsed Marias, the Pitchfork man had found Ginselling and was crossing toward the stag line where Ginselling stood, big and solid. Marias made talk, a man visibly excited. Ginselling's glance lifted and sought out Sabin among the dancers, a hard shine to Ginselling's eyes in the lamplight.

Sabin thought: *Now he thinks he knows!* He had anticipated that someone might make just such a move as Ginselling had made, and so he'd left instructions at Miles City when Trenchard had stressed such great secrecy in the letter that had fetched Sabin to the medicine tree rendezvous. Thus Miles City would have wired that Mark Sabin was no longer employed by the Stock Growers' Association, and this falsehood was now being relayed to Ginselling, giving him greater arrogance.

Sabin thought of the gun he'd checked, but he judged that Ginselling wouldn't push this, not now. Ginselling would play cat-and-mouse with the news Marias had fetched; Ginselling would have Sabin marked for fair game, and the next move would come when Ginselling felt ready. Maybe tonight, when the dance was done. Maybe tomorrow. Maybe next week.

Some tension born from the run of his thinking must have transmitted itself to Deborah, for she looked at him sharply. "What is it?"

He shook his head. "Nothing."

At the end of this dance, Hatwell held up his hands, commanding attention. "Supper hour will be early," Hatwell said. "It's snowing hard, and we've got to break this up sooner than we expected. Some of you have a long way to go."

Talk buzzed then, excited and meaningless, and some went to the door for a look. Boxes were brought out and the smell of coffee soon rose from the stove. Deborah said, "I left my box in the buggy," and Sabin rose to fetch it and saw Mrs. Lantry come walking toward him. There was no haste to her, not any outward show of it at least; but he sensed her desperation, just as he'd sensed it once at Pitchfork.

Mrs. Lantry looked at Deborah and said, "My apologies," and then she looked at Sabin and said, a strange sort of breathlessness to her voice, "I asked you a question not long ago. Have you had time to make up your mind?"

He said, "I think so. The answer is no." But he was remembering that wounded man in Pitchfork's bunkhouse, the one who'd been laid low by Curly Sabin's bullet.

Mrs. Lantry said, "Thora and Trenchard have gone."

Sabin looked around, startled, and saw that she was right; the last time he'd seen the two they'd been dancing, and he'd been concerned thereafter with the coming of Marias in search of Ginselling. He said, "Gone where?" and knew how stupid that sounded.

"To Inland, I suppose. And then to Lewistown. There's no preacher in Stirrup."

He felt a surge of pity for her, and he put his hand to her elbow and found that she was trembling. "It's not as bad as that, likely," he said. "Maybe they went out to see how hard it's snowing."

"No," she said. "I've seen this coming. I've fought against it the best I knew how. Sabin, will you go and fetch her back for me?"

"Why?" he asked bluntly.

"Because you were in love with her once."

He colored, not liking this being paraded before people. "She's old enough to know what she's doing."

"Please," Mrs. Lantry said, "it's Pitchfork he wants, not Thora. You must believe that! Do you know what it will do to her when she wakes to find that out?"

He said, bluntly as before, "It's no concern of mine."

"Must I beg?" Mrs. Lantry asked. "Is that what you want?"

"Send Ginselling," he said.

"Ginselling isn't cut out for this kind of work. He'd turn it into a war between Pitchfork and Inland. Sabin, will you please go while there's still time?"

He remembered Deborah saying once that there

was a sickness of hate in him, and he looked at Mrs. Lantry; he looked at this frail, leaf-thin woman who had only her pride to live for and who was humbling herself now, and then he looked at Deborah; and she nodded.

He saw Doc Hatwell from a corner of his eye, and he swung around and beckoned to the man. Hatwell came to him, and Sabin said, "How did you get here?"

"Saddle horse, Mark."

He remembered that Hatwell had never favored a fast horse but all of his had had staying power. He said, "I got a rig from Conover's. Now I've got to ride to Inland. I'll need your horse. Will you see Deborah to town?"

Hatwell's eyes flicked from one face to another, looking at Sabin and Mrs. Lantry and Deborah. He said, "Yes, Mark. Of course. My horse is at the far end of the hitchrack. The one you saw me leaving town with this morning."

Sabin turned toward Deborah and spread his hands apart, asking her understanding but having no words for it.

She said, "Do whatever it is you think you must do, Mark."

"Thanks," he said and stopped at the door long enough to get his gun-belt. He flung this around his middle and latched it, then got the door open and stepped outside and felt the sting of snow against his cheeks, hard snow, wind-driven and already sheeting down so thickly as to make the yard obscure. The fire still burned, giving him light; he would have to get the sheepskin from the buggy.

He thought: *This sets me against Trenchard,* and he thought of Ginselling, ripe with news that freed his hands, and he thought: *Enemies everywhere.*

But the real enemy was here, in this yard, in this

night, the enemy out of the north, the foe whose presence he had felt on the rim of the basin that first night. For this was no unseasonable snowstorm, come to give its threat and leave again. This was a blizzard in the making, and another hour would feel the full force of it.

10

White Darkness

SABIN GOT TO THE BUGGY and got his sheepskin from it and shrugged into the heavy coat, wondering the while if he might need a pair of woolly chaps before this night's riding was done. People were beginning to spill from the schoolhouse, bending into the wind and heading for the wagons, and he supposed he might borrow a pair of chaps, but he didn't want to take the time. He found Hatwell's horse and pulled himself aboard the animal and took the road north toward Inland. When he looked back, only a few minutes later, the schoolhouse was lost in the snow's curtain, but he could still see the fire; it was a wild thing, wavering and ragged, raveled by the wind.

That wind was from the north, and it blew intermittently, so that sometimes the snow was like mica flung in Sabin's face, and sometimes, when the wind lulled, the snow was soft to his cheeks and the flakes were large. He knew that he must keep the wind in his face, for that way he could be sure he was heading north.

After a mile or two he came upon a fence corner; the wire ran north and west; this was one of Inland's corners. The fence gave him a feeling of security; he could dimly make out the posts as he paralleled them; he must follow them many miles to the gate and then turn west, inside the fence.

The snow had not yet piled deep enough to impede the horse, but it was coming down hard, and the morning would find the land shrouded and formless, all the basin blanketed. He kept Hatwell's horse plodding onward, not looking for the tracks of Trenchard and Thora, for they must of necessity have gone this way. They'd have to get to shelter fast, and the closest shelter was Inland, unless the two chose to go on to Stirrup and take the coach to Lewistown from there. But Trenchard would be too wise for that; Trenchard would probably choose to sit out the storm. Trenchard hadn't counted on anything like this when he'd talked Thora into running away from the dance.

The schoolyard fire was long since lost to Sabin's sight, and he ceased looking backward. After a while he realized that the wind had taken a new voice; it had ceased its high, shrill yammering and become a low moan; and his face stiffened to the driving snow and his eyes squinted down. Soon the fence was lost to him, and he could only be sure that he was staying on the road by keeping the punishing wind full in his face.

He was encompassed in a world of white darkness that had suddenly narrowed down to the pocket in which he rode; he had the sensation that though he constantly strove to move forward he was really standing still. He put this thought from his mind, knowing it would lead to panic. Soon he dismounted, and holding fast to the reins, he leaned into the wind and fought the force of it, groping laterally till his hands touched the fence. He had veered a little from it, but now that he'd found the wire he was reassured and piled into the saddle and moved onward.

He was Montana reared, and he had known how quickly a storm could rise to blizzard fury, but the temperature was dropping faster than he'd supposed it would, and he wished now that he'd taken time to borrow chaps. He could feel the cold through the wool of his trousers; and his feet, in the stirrups, soon felt like blocks of wood.

He got out of the saddle again and led the horse for a while, stomping hard as he set each foot to the snow-covered ground. When the sting of restored circulation told him his feet were not frozen, he rode again; but he was to get out of the saddle time after time in the next hour. He unknotted his neckerchief; the wind snatched at it and threatened to tear it away, but he managed to get the cloth tied over his ears, knotting it beneath his chin.

He thought: *I've got to get out of this!*

He wondered about the people at the dance. Some of them had great distances to go, but many would have the storm at their backs on the homeward trek. Those whose risk would be the greatest would probably elect to stay inside the school; they would have fuel and food and could weather through, if the storm didn't last too long. He worried about Deborah, though Doc Hatwell was wise in the ways of blizzards; he had fought many of them in his day. Hatwell was a good man for any job. Perhaps the buggy was not far behind now.

The snow was piling deeper, and each step was becoming a struggle. When Sabin dismounted to stomp life into his feet again, he found it hard slogging. His breath came hard, and once he stumbled and went down to his knees, the reins slipping from his hands. This was his worst moment; it held a wild desperation that left him weak.

He lumbered to his feet crying, "Whoa, boy! Whoa, boy!" knowing he couldn't make himself heard over the storm. He went lurching, his arms widespread and panic in him; he found nothing. He turned and lurched at a right angle and careened into the horse and clung to it, fumbling for the saddle-horn.

The task of raising himself to the leather seemed a mighty one; he had been doing too much night riding since he'd come back to Arrowhead, he decided. He would have liked to lie down in the snow and sleep for a while. This seemed an overpowering temptation until some shard of his consciousness alerted him to the danger of this kind of thinking. He heaved mightily and got himself into the saddle and pressed onward.

Now his world had narrowed down so that he couldn't see his hand when he held it before him. He began to fear that he might plunge into a coulee or over the rim of a cutbank, and he took to dismounting more often, not only to restore circulation but to make sure he hadn't lost the fence. Each time it was a harder task to mount again. The cold ceased to bother him as much as it had; he had grown used to the cold, but he was very hungry and wished he'd taken supper at the schoolhouse before starting this trip. He wondered if his cheeks were frozen and fell to rubbing them, ungloving one hand at a time and not leaving his fingers exposed long.

He had lost all track of time and distance; he seemed to have been floundering through this white darkness forever, and now a new panic came to him. Suppose he had passed Inland's gate. By all the calculating he could do, he shouldn't have come to it yet, but he couldn't be sure. And from this first suspicion, the great worry grew. He summoned all his

knowledge of the basin from the old days and all that
he'd learned in his riding since coming home, and he
knew that somewhere in these miles of fence was the
gate, and that from that gate a road drove westward a
short mile to Inland's buildings. He made a mental
map and placed Grove schoolhouse upon it, and
Stirrup, with Inland between them; but this gave him
no real assurance as to how far he'd traveled since he'd
left the school. The fear persisted that he'd passed the
gate; the fear grew.

He might have turned around and started following
back along the wire; this would mean that he would no
longer be facing into the storm, and if his fear was
unfounded and the gate was still to the north, at least
he would get back to the schoolhouse. Only stubbornness kept him going forward. He'd taken on this task,
and he would follow it through. He was sure now that
Thora and Trenchard would indeed be at Inland; only
a madman would have risked trying to reach Stirrup.

Dismounting again, he wrapped the reins securely
around his left forearm and groped to the fence and
began following it northward afoot. Now his progress
was so painfully slow that he despaired again. He took
to counting fence posts; this gave him a sense of
achievement. He thought: *If I come to where the fence
joins Pitchfork's, I'll know.* He wondered what he
would do if the fence suddenly abutted Pitchfork's,
for this would be sure proof that he'd passed Inland's
gate. He wondered if he could find a cutbank's shelter
somewhere and get a fire going in this gale. Panic
began creeping into him again, and he put his mind
away from this kind of thinking.

And then the wire was no longer taut in his hand,
and at first he could not understand why it sagged, and
then he sobbed aloud, for here was the gate.

It took him an interminable time to fumble with the

wire loop and get the gate open, and a longer time to close it again, after he'd led the horse through. He might have left the gate open, but here was a rangeland edict stronger than the need to save his strength; cattle drifted with a storm and the gate must be closed. Now that he was inside the fence, his most hazardous task lay before him, and he stood in the wind-driven dark and peered hard, trying to see the lights of Inland and knowing the futility of trying. The buildings were due west, but there would be no wire to guide him, and the road was buried in the snow; if he veered from the road, he would be hopelessly lost.

He must keep the wind to his right cheek. This would mean he was heading west, but if he got off on even a slight tangent he might miss Inland's buildings by a quarter of a mile. In blizzard time Montana ranchers often strung ropes from house to barn, for cattlemen had got hopelessly lost in making even so slight a traverse as their own yards. But now the grim gamble remained; he had no choice; and he pulled himself aboard the horse and headed into the nothingness of wind and snow and night.

In this kind of dicing with chance, the horse's savvy was as good as his own, so he gave Hatwell's mount its head, tugging on the lines only when the snow no longer stung his right cheek. He moved forward with that old sensation of standing still; he covered distance and got nowhere. He hoped that the wind hadn't veered; for now that he had no fence wire to keep him headed straight, the wind was his compass.

He peered hard, still searching for a glimmer of light; this went on forever until the old panic came again to him, that feeling that he'd gone too far. Suppose the ranch buildings were now behind him or to his left or his right! He shouted, not meaning to; the storm caught the sound and smothered it. He drew his gun sluggishly and fired twice, then twice again; and the fitful explosions were also lost in the wind. And then he saw the lights.

He couldn't be sure whether they were real or something he'd so longed for that his fancy had conjured them up. Then he realized that the horse had stopped, and he fell down out of the saddle and groped forward, floundering in snow until he sprawled across steps. He climbed these on hands and knees and was on Inland's gallery. He crawled blindly and found the door and raised his fist to it and then slumped face forward. He knew only vaguely that the door opened; the glare of lamplight was punishment to his eyes and heat smote him and he wanted to sleep.

Someone said, "My God!" and it was the voice of Garth Trenchard, sounding far away. Then: "Cliff! Come here and give me a hand!"

There were two of them then, tugging at Sabin's armpits and hauling him to his feet, and he was fetched inside and the door was closed; he stood teetering, his legs trembling beneath him. Warmth was here, and light, and the opulence of a big room rich in furnishings, rich in rugs; but the great Franklin stove was all Sabin had eyes for.

He said weakly, "My horse . . ." and Trenchard again shouted, "Cliff!" and the door opened and closed behind Sabin; the Inland hand who'd helped him inside was gone to tend to the horse.

Trenchard said, "Sit down," and Sabin fell into a chair, and Trenchard was gone somewhere in the great house, his voice calling out. He came back with a steaming cup in his hand. He said, "Drink this," and Sabin took the cup. It was coffee, hot and black and laced with brandy; it warmed him inside and out, it brought strength back to him, it made him alive again. He looked up at Trenchard, thanking him with his eyes. He looked toward a doorway giving into this room, and Thora was standing there.

They'd been far enough ahead of him, Thora and Trenchard, that they'd had their time to get thawed out. He could tell that.

Thora came toward him with a cry. She said, "Mark! What brought you here?"

Trenchard said, "Caught in the storm," but Sabin shook his head, not wanting the man to misunderstand.

"No," he said. "I came to fetch you back to Pitchfork, Thora."

He stood up and shrugged out of the sheepskin and moved nearer the stove, holding out his hands to it and putting his back to the pair of them, not knowing the run of their thoughts, or caring, until Trenchard said stonily, "You saw us slip out of the schoolhouse?"

Again Sabin shook his head. "Mrs. Lantry sent me."

"You're working for Pitchfork?"

"It makes no never mind," Sabin said. "Thora's going home."

He turned and faced them then, feeling master of himself again, feeling renewed. He saw the stormy look in Thora's eyes; he saw the set of Trenchard's features and knew then that here would be a hard man to cross. But he had done too much tough battling tonight to want to deal in subtleties.

Thora said, "I'm not going!"

Trenchard said, "This is no affair of yours, Sabin. We'd be on our way to Lewistown right now if the blizzard hadn't closed down on us. We're going to be married."

Sabin looked at Thora and asked, "Is that so?"

"Yes," she said.

He crossed to her then; he took her in his arms and drew her hard against him and pressed his lips against hers, making the kiss fierce and compelling. He released her and stepped back; she looked stunned.

He said, "Are you very sure, Thora?"

Trenchard said then, slowly, not showing anger but only a careful calculation that made his eyes hard in the lamplight, "I had the feeling at the medicine tree that I'd made a mistake about you, Sabin."

He met Trenchard's gaze; he was remembering that Mrs. Lantry, at the schoolhouse, had said that it was Pitchfork Trenchard wanted, not Thora. He hadn't quite believed that then, and he'd had no time to think about it since. But now he knew that Mrs. Lantry had been right, and knowing, he had a full consciousness of how he stood between Trenchard and Trenchard's desire.

The truth stood naked in Trenchard's face; and Sabin, seeing it, thought: *He could knock me over the head and dump me out yonder in the snow, and who'd know the difference?* And in this moment, with Trenchard his enemy and himself at Trenchard's mercy, he knew that the real danger of the night had not been out there in the white darkness from which he had been lately delivered, but dwelt here in this house, in this sanctuary.

11

A Man's Choice

WHEN THE DOOR OPENED and closed, letting the breath of the blizzard into the room, Sabin had turned and was facing the stove again, and he thought: *That's Cliff.* Cliff had been nobody to him, an Inland rider, a pair of hands at his armpits when he'd collapsed on the gallery, a man to take care of a horse. Now Cliff was suddenly someone to back Trenchard, another enemy in a nest of enemies; and Sabin let his hand move toward his gun, trying to remember how many shots he'd fired out there in the storm and whether the gun was now empty.

Thora said, "Mother!" and in the instant that the single ejaculation was wrung out of her, it seeped into Sabin's consciousness that there'd been too much commotion for one man's making. He turned to see Mrs. Lantry in the room, her back to the door, Ginselling beside her. Snow powdered the buffalo coat Mrs. Lantry wore; she looked drawn, she looked staggering tired. Even the edge of Ginselling's vitality had been blunted. Pitchfork's foreman stood swaying on his feet, his blocky face withered by the cold, his face crazy angry. Sabin felt a moment's kinship to him, knowing what Ginselling had fought through to get here.

Trenchard was at once the host, moving toward the two and saying, "Sit down! Sit down, please!"

Ginselling fixed a blind look upon Trenchard and then thrust out his arm, pushing at Trenchard's chest, pushing Trenchard aside. Ginselling lurched straight toward Thora and got his hands on her shoulders and shook her hard. "You're coming home!" Ginselling roared. "You're coming home, do you savvy!"

Trenchard, his handsome face hard as Ginselling's, took a step toward them and tugged at Ginselling's arm, saying, "None of that!"

Mrs. Lantry looked straight at Sabin. "He was fetching me home from the schoolhouse," she said, her voice harassed. "The crew was along, with lanterns. At Inland's gate, Ginselling insisted on turning. I couldn't reason with him."

She rushed the words out, making them a flat statement of the facts that was at the same time an appeal that reached through to Sabin. He remembered her at the schoolhouse saying, "Ginselling isn't cut out for this kind of job. He'd turn it into a war between Pitchfork and Inland. . . ."

Trenchard was still tugging at Ginselling; and Ginselling elbowed him aside savagely, his face all fury. Sabin made his move then, crossing the room and driving between the two men, almost spilling Thora in his rush. He pushed against Ginselling with his left arm, and at the same time he brought his right fist up in a long looping blow. His fist made a small explosion of sound against Ginselling's jaw; the man's knees wavered and his eyes turned glassy; he went down hard and lay crumpled and senseless.

Trenchard looked at the fallen man and said, very thoughtfully, "That's just what I was going to have to do to him in another second."

Sabin said, "Yes, and you'd have had every Pitchfork hand riding against you once the storm blows over."

He glanced toward Mrs. Lantry and thought she was going to fall.

Trenchard got to her first and took her by the elbow with a great gentleness and eased her into a chair near the stove. Thora stood rooted, her eyes wild and her face puckered, and then she came quickly to her mother and knelt beside her and began chafing Mrs. Lantry's wrists. Trenchard went thundering about the house, calling to the cook, and came back with coffee for Mrs. Lantry. She drank this; but when she looked up, it was Sabin she thanked with her eyes.

Cliff came in; he was a small and grizzled man with the stamp of Texas upon him. He said, "Boss, there's a wagon in the yard. I just put a Pitchfork team in the barn—" He saw Ginselling then.

Trenchard said, "We'll carry him out to the bunkhouse. Tell the men to watch him when he comes out of it. He may be full of fight."

They toted the unconscious Ginselling from the house, Sabin closing the door after them and putting his back to it. He looked at the Lantrys and said, "We're all stuck here till the blizzard blows itself out."

Mrs. Lantry stirred in the chair. "You're coming home then, Thora?"

"No," Thora said.

Sabin looked at his bruised knuckles. "Then he'll have two of us to fight—me and Ginselling. Because you're coming if I have to drag you."

Thora smiled at him; her smile was a barbed spear. "Is it that you're such a poor loser, Mark?"

He remembered kissing her; he was sorry now that he'd done that. He said, "Oh, hell!"

Trenchard came in, bringing the wind and the cold with him; he strode toward the stove and held his hands out to it, then turned and smiled upon the three of them. "We'd better go to bed," he said. "I can put all of you up here in the house." He crossed to a table and picked a lamp from it. "The stair is this way."

He was the host again, putting all his charm to the task; but when Sabin stood in a dark, unheated upstairs bedroom a short while later, he reloaded his gun before he crawled into the blankets. And he slept with that gun on the floor beside him and a chair propped under the doorknob.

This was the beginning of the armed truce that held in Inland's house while the blizzard shrilled across the crusted range and the cold fingered its way through the walls, the white cold that had been born in Canada. They met at table each day, the four of them, Sabin and Trenchard and Thora and Mrs. Lantry; they slept beneath Inland's roof, with the storm screaming under the eaves and the world beyond the windows blotted out. They put in their days in idleness, crowding the stove, making small and useless talk, and waiting . . . always waiting.

They spoke of cattle, guessing at the losses from this storm; and Trenchard, still playing the host, spoke of his packing plant dream. This was no secret with him; he had gathered facts and figures and presented them with a certain enthusiasm. And Sabin, listening, recalled Deborah's saying that each man had his religion.

Ginselling kept to the bunkhouse; Ginselling ate with Inland's crew and showed himself not at all. Sabin wondered how Ginselling felt about that clout on the jaw and regretted it a little, remembering that

Ginselling's coming had been his own reprieve. He felt edgy within these walls and was glad when a morning came when white silence lay upon the range and the blizzard was gone.

They stayed at Inland that day and another, while Inland's crew floundered knee-deep in snow, digging out the road to the gate. After that, Trenchard said, "There's been some travel on the main road," telling them in this manner that they could make it to Pitchfork. The wagon that had fetched Ginselling and Mrs. Lantry was brought around, and the four stood in the room where Sabin had felled Ginselling.

Sabin looked at Thora. "We'll be going now."

Her eyes moved from him to Trenchard, and she fought her own silent fight. "Yes," she said.

Sabin wondered if it was the knowing what might ensue if she refused that had made her choice, or if it had been things her mother had said in those nights when the two had bedded together. He put no trust in Thora's tractableness; he was only glad to have scored this much of a victory. When they left the house, he handed her up into the wagon and tied Doc Hatwell's saddler behind and got to the seat, Thora between himself and Mrs. Lantry. He raised his eyes to Trenchard, who stood on the gallery, bundled up in a buffalo coat and looking immense. He met Trenchard's steady gaze and said, "Thanks for everything."

Trenchard lifted his arm and smiled, showing his teeth. "Don't mention it," he said; and Sabin knew that they were enemies now, knew that they would hate each other until one of them lay dead.

Thinking thus, he lifted the reins and started the wagon moving.

Ginselling came lumbering across Inland's yard, leaving slovenly tracks in the snow, and climbed aboard the end of the wagon and sat there with his legs dangling, his back to the three on the seat. Ginselling said nothing.

They went floundering along, the horses fighting the snow and all the range lying around them, an endlessness of white, shrouded and alien and cold, the sky above lead-gray, the sky a curtain against which the sun dimly fought. They got to the gate, and Ginselling opened it and let them through. It was easier going on the main road as they drove north, and presently they skirted Pitchfork's fence. They reached Pitchfork's gate in midday and came to the buildings an hour later. When Sabin headed the team toward the wagon shed, he saw the livery stable buggy there.

Ginselling came down off the wagon as Sabin was helping Mrs. Lantry to the ground. Ginselling looked from Sabin to Mrs. Lantry and said, "Is he welcome here?"

"As long as he wants to stay," Mrs. Lantry said.

Ginselling strode toward the bunkhouse. Before Sabin had unharnessed the team, Ginselling came out with a packed war-sack. He left this on a bench before the bunkhouse and walked toward the corrals, a lariat over his arm.

Sabin went toward the ranch-house, following the tracks Mrs. Lantry and Thora had left in the snow. He came into the house and found the two women in the dining room. Deborah was here, also, and Doc Hatwell.

Hatwell said, "How, Mark." He looked tired, as if he'd lost sleep. "We got this far the night of the blizzard and decided not to try for Stirrup. I had work here anyway. That wounded boy. I moved him into the house."

Deborah sat with her hands folded in her lap; the dress she'd worn at the dance had been discarded for jeans and a flannel shirt, and Sabin realized that these garments must belong to Thora. Deborah looked smaller, garbed thus; she looked elfin. Sabin said hello to her and walked to a window and rubbed a hole in the frost. He peered out and saw Ginselling riding across the yard, his war-sack tied behind his saddle.

Sabin turned to Mrs. Lantry. "You've just lost your foreman, I think."

Hatwell shuddered and said, "Did you ever see anything like that blizzard? You can bet the Pikuni-Blackfeet are praying to Aisoyimstan, the Cold Maker, these days. And here it is only November."

Deborah said, "We'll be leaving for town today."

Mrs. Lantry came to Sabin's shoulder and peered through the hole he'd rubbed in the frost. Cold was here, in the house; cold was everywhere. Mrs. Lantry's lips thinned down, and she said, "I could call him back. But from the moment he found Thora and Trenchard gone from the dance, he wouldn't listen to me. He quit being foreman then."

She turned to Sabin and said slowly, "I made you an offer once. I put a string to it, and I don't think that was to your liking. I'll make you another. Will you be Pitchfork's foreman?"

"With every man in your bunkhouse hating me from the old days?"

She said, "It's the cattle I'm thinking of. Ginselling was a good hand. Ginselling's gone."

Hatwell said in a strained voice, "Mark, that boy's going to go, I'm afraid. It's this damn' cold that's licking him. It takes vitality to fight a bullet wound and vitality to fight the cold. He just hasn't enough to go around."

Sabin looked at Hatwell, knowing what Hatwell was trying to tell him and knowing, too, why it couldn't be put into more direct words. Then he thought of the enemy, the real enemy, and of the steers that would stumble across the buried plains to die in the drifts and beside the frozen streams. He asked himself then where a man's real duty lay; but if there were two things to be served, then here might be the way of serving both. He turned this over carefully in his mind, making his choice. Then he said to Mrs. Lantry, "I'll take the job." But as he said it, he felt tired and all his thinking was gray-clouded, and he could hear again the laughter of the little men.

He found then that Deborah had been watching him intently. Her eyes drew him; but when he looked at her, her glance moved to Thora, who had flung out of her coat and seated herself and was studying him with a thoughtful petulance. Deborah's face was unreadable, and in Sabin was the protest: *No, it's not as you think!* He wanted to say this to Deborah; he wanted to shout it; yet he couldn't be sure if it was true, not when he remembered kissing Thora at Inland.

Deborah's glance moved to Hatwell. "We should be getting back to town."

"Yes," he said and sighed. "There may be another storm." He came to a stand.

Thora said, "Bundle up well. Deborah, you can keep my things. I'll not be needing them."

Pitchfork's crew had converted the buggy by replacing the wheels with bobs, and when it was brought around, Sabin walked to it with Hatwell and Deborah and handed the girl up and waited while Hatwell fumbled with robe and whip and reins. One of Pitchfork's men, at Mrs. Lantry's orders, hitched Hatwell's saddle horse behind the buggy. Hatwell called Sabin's name, and Sabin came to the doctor's side.

Hatwell said guardedly, "I figured you'd want to be around if that boy goes."

Sabin said, "Thanks."

Hatwell shook his head. "Ginselling's had the hiring and firing here since Morgan died. That makes the crew handpicked. You won't find it a friendly bunkhouse."

Sabin said, "I don't expect to."

Hatwell said, "Well, good luck."

Sabin came back to Deborah's side of the buggy and stood there, and in him was a need to say something that must be said, but still there were no words for it.

Deborah leaned toward him then, smiling faintly, smiling sadly. "Goodbye, Mark," she said.

"I'll be in Stirrup again," he promised.

She hesitated; he could see her lips tremble, and then she said, "It won't be easy, the job you'll have to do. If you ever think it's going to throw you, come to me. Perhaps I'll be able to help."

He didn't understand her, not really, but he stored her words away for remembering; they were to be his crutch if he needed one. He thanked her with his eyes and stepped back from the buggy and watched Hatwell turn it around and send it into the drifted road. And Sabin turned then toward Pitchfork's gallery, as befitted Pitchfork's foreman, his breath a cloud, and the cold driving at him, the cold a weight upon him.

12

The Voice of the Enemy

SABIN HAD HIS LOOK at the boy who'd been laid low the night Curly had run off Pitchfork's horses. The youngster had been moved to the ranch-house at Doc Hatwell's orders, and he lay listlessly in a spare bedroom; he lay upon a tick filled with "Montana feathers," fragrant sweet grass cut in the summer meadows and left to dry. He was no more than Curly's age, this boy, a fuzz-faced youngster, a transplanted Texan, perhaps, or a Wisconsin farm boy who'd come west with a cattle train, wanting a taste of the woolly life, wanting adventure.

Sabin looked at him and thought: *Well, son, you got it!* He saw the feverish eye, the labored breathing, and he understood why Hatwell had given the boy up as lost.

Sabin came out of the house and went then to the bunkhouse, a savage fury riding him, not thinking of Curly consciously, yet hating Curly and feeling sorry for Curly all at the same time. He came into the bunkhouse and closed the door and put his back to it. The heat of the stove smote him, and the smell of wool and leather and men was here. Pitchfork's crew lounged about in the bunks; four of them played listless cards at a makeshift table; all came to sullen alertness as he stood there watching them.

He looked these men over; he looked at men young and old, fat and lean, a whang-leather breed, burned by sun, burned by wind, and there was this one sameness to them: they knew him for their enemy. Some had stood beneath the fruitful cottonwood at the old place that long-gone night; some had seen Ginselling felled in front of the Maverick when Sabin had come again to Arrowhead.

Marias was here, the same Marias who'd fetched the word that Sabin was fair game to Pitchfork's guns. It was he who made himself spokesman, rubbing his lantern jaw and looking at Sabin slantwise and saying, "Well—?"

"I'm foreman now," Sabin said.

Marias shrugged. "So she told us."

Sabin said, "I didn't come to preach. We've got cattle to pull through a winter. It will be quite a chore. All I'm asking of you is a good day's work. If anybody wants to draw his pay, now's the time to do it."

They moved slightly, shifting their feet, shifting their bodies. They muttered; there was no coherency to it. He looked at them, knowing how deep loyalty was ingrained in them, knowing how deep hatred could drive, for he had lived a long, long time with hatred. He waited them out, watching Marias, for this one was the shifty shadow of Ginselling. He could feel his own face flaming to the heat of the stove, and the cold seeping through the door, driving at his back. A stick popped in the stove, making a small explosion in the piled-up silence.

Then Marias shrugged again. "Foremen come and

they go. Drop around when you've got orders for us. Keep out of here meantime. Likely they've fixed up a bed for you in the house. Leastwise the girl will have."

The implication was there, not so much in Marias' words as in his eyes, and it brought the fury rising in Sabin. He crossed the room in one lunging stride and slapped Marias, striking that out-thrusting jaw with the back of his right hand. He sent Marias reeling against a bunk. Sabin wondered in that moment if he would find all of them on his back and didn't much care; he'd itched for a fight ever since he'd stood looking down upon that wounded boy in the house.

Marias cocked his fists, then let his hands drop. "Hell," he said, "I don't have to take that. I'm drawing my time." He crossed to the door and yanked at it, letting the winter in. He pulled the door shut behind him.

Sabin looked around. "Anybody else?"

Again there was that shifting of feet and bodies, that deep-chested angry mutter. Sabin gave them their moment and then he said, "I've got one order for you. Just one—and it holds from now until the chinook wind blows. Save the cattle. I want every man into saddle at the crack of dawn tomorrow."

He walked out then, walked out to watch Marias saddle up and ride toward Stirrup.

And that was the beginning. . . .

Once, three years earlier, after Christmas of 1883, a shining mist had formed over the Rockies' northern ramparts, and the Blackfeet had lifted their faces to their savage god of cold and prayed that they be spared from calamity. Day by day they had cowered in their lodges, praying to Aisoyimstan; they had implored their agent for extra rations, while the sun was a pale ghost setting far to the south, and the cold stayed. At long last, freighters bucked the drifted trails to bring food to the far reservation, and they found a

tribe thinned down by starvation, six hundred needing burying. That had been a winter men talked about.
That should have been a warning, but the cattlemen
had let it pass unheeded. And now a more savage
winter was upon them.

December. . . . December came without Sabin's
knowing it, for he paid no heed to the days. Each he
took as it came: each was a frosty morning when a
man piled into two suits of heavy underwear and two
pairs of wool socks and drew on, over these, wool
pants and overalls and leather chaps and two woolen
shirts. Wool gloves were worn under leather mittens.
Blanket-lined overcoats and sheepskins and fur caps
cluttered the pegs in Pitchfork's bunkhouse, and
Sabin made the men walk in snow in their bare feet,
then vigorously rub their feet dry before donning their
socks. The older hands knew this trick, and another:
they stood in water after pulling on their riding boots,
then stood outdoors until their boots were sheathed in
ice, made air-tight with ice.

That was the way each day began; and always, out
yonder, were the waiting cattle.

Always, off yonder, were the waiting blizzards.

Two struck Arrowhead in December, and the native
stock stumbled across the drifted range to die by the
frozen banks of Arrowhead Creek, though some had
strength enough to strip the bark from the willows.
Gaunt-eyed riders, their faces smeared with lamp-
black to fend off snow blindness, fought with the
cattle, trying to keep them from the treacherous
air-holes in the creek, trying to herd them into the
sheltered ravines. Here was man-killing work, endless
work, beginning before the brief daylight, lasting long
into the night, with Sabin lashing the crew on, cursing
them and being cursed in turn, hating them and being
hated, and the cold always pressing them, rasping at

their lungs and deadening their arms and legs and turning their faces numb.

Night. . . . The men in the bunkhouse rubbing at frost-bitten cheeks and hands and feet. . . . Night, and Sabin stumbling wearily into the ranch-house to make his mumbled report to Mrs. Lantry and to gulp his supper and sprawl out upon his waiting bed and let the weariness claim him. Night, and Thora petulant by lamplight, Thora with her vast, feverish energy shackled by the winter, sitting unmoving, yet in her very immobility beating against the walls with her fists, beating blindly against the winter.

Sometimes, when the weather lifted enough to make it possible, Doc Hatwell was there, come out of Stirrup to look in on his patient who got no better and no worse, but who sometimes babbled in the night, his feverish voice roaming through the house, vying with the wind that screamed under the eaves. Doc Hatwell standing with his hands to the stove, trying to store up warmth against the long trip back. Doc Hatwell talking to Sabin, but Sabin not hearing him really, a man too tired to care about another's troubles, a man drugged with tiredness.

Sometimes Sabin wondered about Deborah. He thought: *Who the hell will be wanting a fancy dress these days?*

When the blizzards made it suicide to ride, he could only haunt the house, listening to the blizzard, listening to the constant voice of the enemy. Pitchfork had saved some hay, and this was rationed out carefully when the weather permitted. The cattle knew about the hay; they ringed the fenced stacks day and night, bawling piteously, shoving at the fences with their gaunt bodies, fighting the wire. Their bawling blended with the wind and rode with it and thrummed at the nerves of a man, making him edgy, making him want to run from the wind when there was no place to run. Not for a cattleman.

The white arctic owls were on the ranges; and the native birds and animals had long since fled south. So had the Cree, for the Cree were from the Height of Land in Northern Canada, the place where the weather was born, and they knew what this meant; they knew the voice of calamity.

To Sabin, hauling a starving steer from a drift in a lull between the storms, the thought came that the cattlemen didn't own the cattle; it was the other way around. Thus he and the hundreds like him must stay here in the cold and storm, stay because these cattle owned them and they had to minister to the cattle until the last cow was gone.

He found himself laughing at this notion, laughing hysterically, and he was sobered by his own hysteria. *You damn' fool!* he thought. *You act like you're drunk!*

He would walk into the bunkhouse and the men would have no word for him; the men would stare at him, hating him with their eyes, telling him with their eyes to get the hell out of there. He would go back to the house, to pace the rooms that were both shelter and a prison, to watch Thora in her sullen brooding, and to hear the fevered, plaintive voice of that boy who was taking so long at dying.

Once he found Thora up into saddle, fighting the drifts along the road that led to Pitchfork's gate. He was coming back to the ranch headquarters after a day with the cattle and there was no patience in him nor any real emotion; he was too tired for that. He merely took her reins and led the horse back to the barn; and Thora, too, hated him with her eyes then. But she said nothing as she went stumbling to the ranch-house, and she said nothing afterward. He thought to speak to Mrs. Lantry about Thora's attempt, but Mrs. Lantry had worries enough.

He too had more to think about than Thora and her wilfulness; he had the wolves to think about.

Those large gray timber wolves had come down out of the hills and ran in packs of from twenty to thirty, with a dog-wolf captaining them and providing the cunning for all of them. The wolves Sabin knew from old; they had troubled Jeff Sabin in his day, and every Arrowhead rancher. The cowhands had carried strychnine with them at all times, spreading it on bacon rinds and poisoning not a few wolves that way. But now the wolves were too numerous, and it was like emptying the sand out of a boot and trying to fill a coulee that way to fight against the wolves with anything so puny as a handful of strychnine. The wolves ravaged the weakened cattle, and more than once Sabin found a cow bitten upon the flanks or came upon one defending her calf from the gray, vicious circle. Sabin was to spend many rifle shells against the wolves and feel the futility of an endless fight.

And so it went, the everlasting struggle, with the voice of the enemy singing always its paean of triumph and Thora brooding and the men hating him and the winter roaring endlessly, the winter taking its toll and gaunting him down and keeping him going until there was no resting; there was merely nightmare when he did tumble into his blankets, the nightmare of re-living the days.

Christmas came and was just another day of riding and struggling and looking toward the western horizon for that arch of black clouds that might spew forth what the Indians called the black wind, the chinook wind. He wouldn't have known it was Christmas, save that Hatwell came out that evening and told him. Hatwell brought Sabin's own sorrel from Stirrup's livery, and this was Sabin's Christmas present. The doctor had whiskey on his breath, but there was no festive spirit in Hatwell. The winter had thinned him, too, and dulled him.

The day after, Sabin came into the bunkhouse and found Ginselling there.

At first he saw Ginselling only with his eyes, not being aware of him really; and then Ginselling came into his full consciousness, a block of a man sitting sullenly, a man finding his own kind of triumph in this moment.

Ginselling said, "I come back."

"Yes," Sabin said. "You came back."

"I figgered," Ginselling said, "that I made it too easy for you, riding off and leaving it to you. You're in the saddle, bucko, but I'm going to get you some day. And I'm going to get you good!"

Sabin said wearily, "I don't give a damn why you went or why you came back. If you stay here, you're a forty-a-month hand. Now get out there and get to work."

But afterwards, when he got to thinking about Ginselling's return, it came to him that something useful might be shaped out of it, and he sought out Ginselling then and gave him a special job.

"You keep an eye on Thora," he told Ginselling. "Not long ago I caught her heading toward Inland. I can't be around to watch her all the time. That's your chore, mister."

He didn't wait for Ginselling's answer. He didn't care how Ginselling felt about it. They were enemies united in the doing of a job, and Thora was part of the job. That was the size of it.

13

Bitter Hours

NOW IT WAS JANUARY, but the Indians had another name for it; the Indians called it the Moon of Cold-Exploding Trees. When nine of its days had dragged themselves by, a cold wind blew out of the north, and Sabin remembered what the Crees had said when this kind of wind came down from Canada: "Kissin-ey-oo-way'o—it blows cold." This was the voice of the ancient enemy, soft with remembered grief, rising to a wail of despair. Snow came on January ninth, and there was sixteen hours of it. Sixteen inches of snow fell upon the levels in those hours; and when Sabin looked at the thermometer tacked to Pitchfork's log wall, he saw that it registered twenty-two below zero. He shook his head.

Still it snowed, and still the temperature dropped. By January fifteenth it was forty-six below zero, and Arrowhead lay locked by storm and cold.

After that there was a week in which the snow held off, the sky a sullen bleakness with a dim sun showing;

and again Sabin lashed Pitchfork's crew to its work. Now there was more work than before. Cattle which had been pushed north of the Missouri River to better graze in the summer and fall were drifting back; some of these bore Crowfoot's brand and some Star-Cross; and all of them were listless from cold and gaunt from hunger and they roamed blindly in a blind world of white; they careened into the strung barbed wire and fell and perished. They floundered in drifts that were belly-deep; they died in these drifts, standing stolidly and waiting for death, waiting for the wolves.

And Sabin, fighting to save these cattle as well as Pitchfork's, fought Pitchfork's crew, fought their sullenness and their hatred for him, and found them loyal, after their fashion. Even Ginselling took orders and slaved in the saddle, his blocky face lampblackened, his bulky body looking bulkier, swathed in many clothes. It was dawn till dark riding; it was man-killing, and it turned them to animals, stolid and hopeless as the cattle. But Sabin kept them going, sparing no one of them, sparing himself least of all.

They had ceased to be just so many faces to him; they had become men with individual personalities and names, and in another bunkhouse he would have liked most of them and found himself akin to them. There was the inevitable Tex, old and grizzled and warped by the saddle. There were a Joe and a Pete and a Buck, and men who bore the names of rivers and trails—Yellowstone and Chisholm and Cimarron. And there was the inevitable Kid; always, in any crew, there was one called the Kid. The Kid was the one who lay in the house, taking so long at dying.

This was the crew; these were the men with whom he toiled through the unceasing days; and out of their adversity was born a queer kind of association, the eternal armed truce of necessity. Yet once, when Sabin fought through the last of a day's light, bucking the drifts, a rifle whammed in the dusk, the bullet splintering Sabin's saddlehorn. He came down off the horse on its off side, fumbling woodenly for his gun and peering hard, but no second shot came. Ginselling—? Sabin couldn't be sure, but he rode with a constant wariness in the days that followed until the incident dimmed in his memory.

The winter became endless, claiming all of a man's consciousness until the thought of other seasons was like a dream remembered, and rest was a thing yearned for as food is yearned for by a hungry man. Once, heading a few Crowfoot steers south, Sabin got a glimpse of Grove schoolhouse, snow-buried and forlorn, and remembered the music, and the fire burning in the yard; and this was like dredging up a recollection from childhood or a tale told by an old man, an experience so remote that it must needs have belonged to someone else.

He thought of Deborah then; he remembered how light she had been in his arms.

Sometimes, in the lulls between snowstorms, he looked to the hills so sharply etched in the clear, cold light, thinking of Curly, thinking of Reese Stringham, neither of whom he had seen since that long-gone night when he'd ridden boldly to Stringham's hideout, hoping to lure Curly from it. Stringham's men had been afraid that night, thinking he might lead a posse back there; and Sabin had to grin now, thinking of that; for the hills were locked in snow and Stringham's men were jailed men, jailed by the winter, unless they'd got out of there after that November storm. Sabin wondered what crossed the agile mind of Reese Stringham these days; he wondered what Stringham thought about the future. *There won't be any cattle left to rustle!* Sabin reflected.

He also wondered how Curly fared these endless weeks; he thought of Curly playing listless poker with the others; he thought of Curly pacing that narrow cabin and beating blindly against its walls in his mind, even as Thora beat against the walls of Pitchfork; and he thought: *This will give the kid time for thinking.* He found some hope in that reflection.

The winter might put Curly to a test and bring out the best in Curly; still it might be too late—one bullet too late, or perhaps two, for Sabin remembered the man who had waited above the Red Front Saloon.

The winter was testing all of them, making Ginselling more sullen, making Sabin bitter; even the great spirit of Mrs. Lantry bowed before the constant cold. In the evenings Sabin saw her sitting close to the fire, sitting dazedly, contemplating with vacant eyes the doom of cattledom. He pitied her then. She had watched a boom build and been part of it; she had seen the great migration north out of Texas to Montana's virgin graze; she had seen Pitchfork transplanted and had made Pitchfork her religion and her life, living by the whang-leather principles of Morgan Lantry even after Lantry had gone down into the dust.

Now all of it was finished; all cattledom was a single cow stuck in a snowdrift.

Only Thora still cherished a dream, but the winter blocked her; and she brooded, too, not with the hopeless brooding of her mother but with calculated patience, with cunning; and Sabin reminded Ginselling again of the special chore assigned to him. Sometimes Thora's face frightened Sabin in the evenings; its beauty was still there, but there was a hardness to it, an implacability, as though the winter had frozen it.

He watched her of an evening and knew suddenly that her old magic was gone for him; he looked at her beauty and was unmoved. He supposed there should be some sadness in him with this perishing of what had been; his only real thought was that next day he must ride again.

Sometimes in his day's riding, Sabin came across horsemen from Star-Cross and Crowfoot and G-Rafter and Inland, and they were all men united in a common cause; they were men battling the great cold, counting the winter's kill. He asked them of Ben Teasdale, but no men knew of Ben Teasdale, for none had worked that far south in the basin. The town, attainable between storms, had no word of Teasdale, either, when Sabin asked those who had ridden to Stirrup. So Sabin wondered and worried, promising himself he would have a look in at the old place when the weather broke a little; but it never did.

On January twenty-eighth, the full fury of this worst of winters broke upon Arrowhead in a great blizzard which roared down upon them. For three days and three nights the storm screamed, and a man could see less than fifty feet in any direction. Ropes were strung from house to bunkhouse, from corrals to barn, and the thermometer dropped to sixty-three below. Hatwell put in no appearance; the whole world was a prisoner; and the boy in his sickbed grew worse and made the nights and days wild with his babbling.

The cold broke suddenly and the wind shifted, giving promise of a chinook. This promise permeated all of Pitchfork; men smiled who had forgotten how to smile, and Mrs. Lantry stirred to life before sinking into hopelessness again. For the storm started all over and carried them into February. The last of the hay had been used up, but still the cattle ringed the ranch-house, bawling piteously.

There were more storms in February, and while these were not so severe, they came at a time when the cattle were so weakened from the cold months as to be easy prey to the new onslaughts. Doc Hatwell was again able to reach Pitchfork, coming out in a cutter; he brought them news from a world beyond their own white horizon; he brought them the unconsoling word that all the West suffered as they suffered, that all cattledom was dying in the far-flung draws.

Now the cattle were into the towns, Hatwell said. Native stock, heavier coated than the pilgrim cattle or the longhorns fresh out of Texas, had hung on by eating sagebrush and cottonwood twigs, and Hatwell told tales of their gnawing tar-paper from ranch shacks. Some had drifted into Stirrup like gray ghosts of the storm, rooting for garbage, stripping the trees, dying before the doors of Stirrup's citizenry. And Hatwell also brought tales of human suffering, of cattlemen who'd ridden from their ranch-houses never to return, of men lost between their own houses and corrals.

He left a Bismarck paper behind him on one of these trips, and Sabin looked at it by lamplight, the words dancing before his tired eyes: "Serious apprehension . . . there will be an appalling loss of human lives in Montana and western Dakota . . . most stage roads are entirely closed up and trains are running at irregular intervals, some being four and five days apart . . . the supply of fuel is becoming almost exhausted. . . . More people have frozen to death this winter than for a quarter of a century. . . ."

He flung the paper aside, not wanting more of this; he had lived too long with the winter.

And across the room Thora regarded him with lackluster eyes, and Mrs. Lantry drew closer to the fire, a shawl tight across her bony shoulders.

But always there was another morning and another donning of heavy clothes and another grueling day in the saddle, the world white and formless, and the wolves reaping their red harvest, and the sun lost in a sullen sky.

He got so he looked forward to Doc Hatwell's comings, for these were breaks in the monotony of a treadmill existence. Sometimes he told Hatwell how it was, the work, the futility of the work, and sometimes he spoke of the people, the crew and Thora and Mrs. Lantry. He told how he'd found Thora heading for Inland that one day, weeks back, and how he had put Ginselling to watching her.

On a later trip, Hatwell said, "I told Deborah about Thora's running away. She says Thora will try it again. Probably she's right. I don't know whether Thora loves the man, or whether it's just stubbornness that drives her. No one ever crossed that girl in all her life. Now somebody's going to pay for that."

And it was the next day that it happened.

Sabin came back to the ranch-house in the last of the afternoon, glad for a day when the range stood clear and cold and white, no snow in the air and no instant threat of it. He came back, needing Ginselling for a task; he had left Ginselling at the ranch. He found him in the bunkhouse face downward across the floor near the stove, but the fire had almost died out; it had been that long since Ginselling had last fed it.

At first he thought Ginselling was dead, and then Sabin saw the piece of firewood on the floor close by and understood how Ginselling had been laid low. He got his hands hooked under the man and half-lifted, half-dragged him to a bunk. He was surprised that there wasn't more poundage to Ginselling; the man was mostly clothes. But he supposed that Ginselling had lost weight this winter.

He got snow from the doorway and rubbed Ginselling's face with it until the man's eyes fluttered open. Ginselling looked about stupidly, and Sabin waited until there was some show of intelligence in the man, and then he asked, "Thora—?"

Ginselling looked about wildly. "Gone!" he decided. "To Inland."

Sabin said, "You fool!" not putting much rancor into it.

Ginselling said, "She came out here and pleaded with me, wanting me to ride there with her. She was afraid she might not make it alone, with the roads drifted. I told her no."

"And then she clouted you."

A savage anger possessed Ginselling, and his eyes showed it. "At first she was fighting mad," he said. "Then she warmed up to me. She came close enough to put her arms around my neck. I should have known; she'd picked up that piece of firewood and been fiddling with it." He swung his legs to the floor and came to a tottering stand. "I'm going after her!"

"You fool!" Sabin said again and pushed at him, pushing him back into the bunk.

He walked out of the bunkhouse then, lifting a rope to take along; and he went toward the corral, wanting a fresh horse for the ride he had to make. He walked without anger, a man going about his job. This, too, was part of it.

14

An Old Fire Dies

Across the snow's crusted surface, the tracks of Thora's horse stood out plainly in the last of the day's light; and Sabin followed these, not pushing his horse. He might have to do much riding before he returned to Pitchfork; he might need the mount's last reserve. He'd said no word to Mrs. Lantry before he'd left; Ginselling could do that much.

At first he'd not been angry, but fury built in him as he rode along, a fury that left him insensate to the bitterness of the day. He felt his anger for its core, wondering if it was made of jealousy, for Thora had accused him of being a poor loser. Yet he felt more like a father in pursuit of a recalcitrant child than like a jilted lover. His anger, stripped bare, was impersonal. He had cattle to tend to; he had a winter to fight, and Thora had given him this additional task when he needed his strength for the real work.

So thinking, he came to Pitchfork's gate. Beyond it, Thora's tracks pointed toward Stirrup, though he'd expected them to swerve south to Inland. He grinned a brittle grin at her sagacity; she had told Ginselling she was going to Inland, and now, anticipating pursuit, she was avoiding Inland. Was it her plan to escape from Arrowhead, possibly to Lewistown or Helena, and then make contact with Trenchard? Or had she made rendezvous with him in Stirrup? Sabin decided the first notion was more likely. Thora could scarcely have got word to Trenchard these past weeks; Thora had been a prisoner of the winter.

He pushed on in the gathering dusk, the bitter dusk, and soon Thora's tracks were lost to him; the night came down and left the land a glimmering ghost beneath the faint stars. He had given up any notion of overtaking Thora on the trail; he could only guess at how much start she'd had. He'd find her in Stirrup. Suddenly possessed with a fear that she might elude him, he tried to recall the stage schedules out of Stirrup. But the stages weren't running on schedule, not with new storms always in the making.

He saw Stirrup's lights in mid-evening, and it occurred to him as he crossed the bridge over frozen Arrowhead Creek that it had been three weary, man-killing months since he'd been in Stirrup. Other Pitchfork hands had made it to town, bringing out supplies in the lulls between storms. Snow banked along the buildings, and the windows were dead eyes, sheeted with frost; and he found gaunt cattle wandering aimlessly in the street. He went directly to Conover's, liking the livery's warmth as he stiffly dismounted. He saw a horse in one of the stalls and recognized it as Thora's. He looked for an Inland brand on the other mounts and found none.

"Any stage go out this afternoon?" he asked.

He learned that none had, and he came to the street and walked to the mercantile and climbed the stairs to Hatwell's quarters. The medico wasn't in. Descending, Sabin crossed over to the post office, seeing a light burning there, and found no one in the building but the postmaster. He asked if Thora Lantry had been in.

"Ain't seen her," the postmaster said. "Say, there's a letter for you."

This surprised Sabin, and he thought: *Miles City,* but when he had the letter in his hand, he saw a Helena postmark. He read the brief note enclosed, before he remembered the next to the last night he'd been in Stirrup, the night he'd gone to the Red Front and had a look in the upstairs room. The barkeep had given him the name and address of the Helena owner of the building. He'd written the man that night.

Now he had the answer: "Mr. Garth Trenchard of Inland Ranch has been acting as my business agent in Stirrup. You may negotiate with him if you are interested in any of my holdings. . . ."

He thought: *Trenchard again!* and pocketed the note, forgetting it.

Out upon the boardwalk, he stood for a moment, aimless in his thinking, knowing only that Thora was here and he must find her. The hotel? But Thora had expected pursuit and would not leave herself so open to discovery as to put up at the hotel. She had friends in Stirrup, of course, but who were they? He began walking; he came along the street to Deborah's door and rapped upon it. She opened the door and stood looking at him; surprise was in her eyes, but he chose to read a quick gladness there as well.

"Come in," she said.

He stepped into the room and moved automatically toward the stove. It was the same room as of yore, cheerful and quiet and serene as this girl; and when he peeled out of his sheepskin and seated himself, it was as though the room dissolved all the time that lay between, the weary weeks of cold and blizzard and dying cattle and men hating him. The dress dummy still stood in one corner; the gingham curtains were on the windows.

"You're thinner," Deborah said.

He looked up at her. "Yes."

"It's been hard out there." She stared toward the west.

He nodded.

She came close to him; she put her hand on his shoulder. "I thought perhaps you'd come. I've hoped for it and dreaded it. What is it I can do for you?"

"Thora," he said. "She's run off from Pitchfork. To meet Trenchard, I suppose. She's somewhere in town. Where, Deborah? Where?"

She looked sad. "Thora means a very great deal to you, doesn't she?"

Suddenly the fury he'd known on the trail possessed him again, having a new core. He'd taken this girl to a dance once and left her there because of Thora. He'd found Deborah again at Pitchfork, when the first blizzard had blown itself out, and again he'd left her because of the Lantrys. He had watched Deborah's eyes that day; he had understood what she thought. He knew what she was thinking now. It wasn't to his liking.

He said, "There's a saying that a cat can look at a queen. I used to see Thora often in the old days; we'd meet in secret and go riding into the hills. Maybe it made me eight feet tall, having a girl as pretty as Thora, a girl that every man in Arrowhead was trying to spark. Then again, maybe it was my slap at Pitchfork, meeting Morgan Lantry's daughter on the sly. Lantry knew about it; so did Ginselling. They made Arrowhead too hot to hold me."

"But you came back," Deborah said.

"Not because of Thora. Once I tried to tell you what it was that really fetched me. Maybe it wasn't straight in my own mind. The night of the dance, it was partly because of Thora that I took her trail. That was then. The winter has brought out a lot of things. I can face the truth now. It's not because of Thora that I'm in town tonight; it's because of Trenchard but more because of Mrs. Lantry."

Deborah said, "Then the old fire has died?"

"Frozen to death," he said.

"You might have been good for Thora, Mark. You might have changed her."

"No," he said. "Nobody will ever be first with Thora but Thora. You knew that before I did."

She drew in a long breath; she was making her decision and Sabin waited her out, remembering what she'd said the day she'd left Pitchfork with Doc Hatwell, wondering what strange knowledge she possessed.

She said then, "There was an Eastern girl who came out here last summer for her health. She kept a room at the Austin—room seventeen, upstairs. I know; I made a couple of dresses for her and went to the hotel to fit them. When the winter closed down, she went back East. But she's keeping the room. Thora was a good friend of hers. Thora might be in room seventeen."

He came to a stand and donned his sheepskin and plucked his sombrero from the table. "I'll have a look," he said. He paused, remembering that once he'd seen her terrified. "Is there anything else you want to tell me?"

Her eyes clouded. "I can't. Not yet, anyway."

She stepped to the door and he paused there before she opened it; he stood searching her face, trying to read it, trying to understand what it was that always fetched him here, and then he thought he knew. He said, "You live for other people, not for yourself. Isn't that so?"

She smiled. "I'll be a prouder woman the day that

that's true." She opened the door. "Good luck, Mark."

He walked up the street to the Austin House and went into the familiar lobby and climbed the stairs. He found room seventeen; it wasn't many doors from the room he'd occupied those first nights in Stirrup. Lamplight seeped under the door, and he raised his knuckles and knocked. There was a faint stirring; a sudden silence fell, and out of it a voice said, carefully, "Who's there?"

And because it was Garth Trenchard's voice, Sabin put his hand to the knob. When it didn't give to his fingers, he stepped back a pace and hurled his shoulder hard against the door, hurled it with cold fury. The flimsy lock gave, and he catapulted into the room.

Trenchard was here, his buffalo coat thrown carelessly across the bed beside Thora's outer wraps; and Thora was here, too, standing close to Trenchard and staring with widening eyes at Sabin.

Sabin said, "Get your things. You're coming home, Thora."

He was thinking that no Inland horse had been at Conover's, but he was remembering, too, that there was a lean-to behind the hotel where horses were sometimes stabled. He hadn't thought to look into the lean-to. He could only guess how these two had made rendezvous; perhaps some Inland rider, storm-harried, had reached Pitchfork one of those days when Sabin had been out on the range, and perhaps such a man had carried a message back to Trenchard, naming a time and a place. Perhaps Trenchard had just happened to come to Stirrup today and met Thora on the street. Sabin was never to know, and it didn't matter; it only mattered that he had found them here together. A great disgust was in him, and the last flicker of an old fire dying.

Thora said, "No, Mark! I'll only run away again!"

Sabin said, "Then I've got to tell you: It's Pitchfork he wants, not you. Can't you see that it's part and parcel of this meat-packing scheme of his? He's only a hired hand at Inland; he needs cattle of his own, lots of cattle."

Trenchard's strong face lost some of its color. He took his cigar case from his pocket, being very careful about this. He fished out a cigar and held it in his hand, then suddenly snapped the weed between his fingers, letting the broken pieces fall. "Sabin," he said, "I'm damned tired of your interfering," and his hand went under his coat again and came out with a gun.

Sabin looked at the gun; the first night he'd met this man, Trenchard had denied an ability with a gun and he'd known then that Trenchard lied.

Trenchard said, "Get out, damn you!"

Sabin turned to the ravaged door and opened it wider, then he spun on his heel and lunged toward Thora and grasped her wrist. Jerking her past him, he flung her out through the door, so hard that she fell on her knees in the hallway; and Sabin slammed the door shut and put his back to it. The gun sounded at that moment, thunderous within these walls; the bullet splintered the door close to Sabin's shoulder, and the lamp winked, the flame fighting to live.

Sabin's face screwed up, and he put the fingers of his left hand over his right shoulder and took a stumbling step forward. Trenchard watched him, the gun sagging slightly and a wild sort of triumph in Trenchard's eyes. And in this unguarded moment, Sabin lurched another step forward and his right fist shot out, striking for Trenchard's jaw.

The blow was only a glancing one, for some instinct, learned a second too late, moved Trenchard's head. But Sabin, dropping all pretense of hurt, went chopping at Trenchard's right wrist with the fingers of his left hand. The gun fell to the floor; and Sabin got at

Trenchard's jaw, a good, clean hit, straightening Trenchard and shaking him as the wind shakes a tree. Sabin shrugged out of his sheepskin and hurled it aside.

Then Trenchard's whole weight swept at him, and it was Sabin's grim thought that Trenchard had lost no poundage during this dismal winter. He put up his guard against Trenchard and gave ground; he let Trenchard bear him backward until his shoulders touched the door. He could retreat no farther, and Trenchard's fists were everywhere, bringing Sabin to his knees. But as Sabin went down, he got his arms around Trenchard's knees and yanked hard, spilling the man.

For a moment they tussled wildly upon the faded carpeting, but Trenchard broke free, got to a stand and lurched to one wall. Here stood a bureau with its pitcher and bowl. Trenchard grasped the pitcher in both hands and lifted it, hurling it hard at Sabin's head. Sabin pulled his head aside, letting the pitcher strike the far wall and break; and Sabin laughed with an unholy joy in all this, knowing now that he had been born to fight this man, knowing that there was a reason for their fighting but that the reason didn't matter. They were one breed of man pitted against another, and this fight was inevitable and had been inevitable since their first meeting.

He closed with Trenchard and they stood toe to toe in the room's center, slugging hard and making no effort at defense. Sabin became dimly aware of a commotion in the hall, of raised voices and thudding boots. That first shot had aroused the hotel as a hornets' nest is aroused by a thrusting stick; the door burst inward and Sabin got a sidelong glimpse of startled faces. He shouted, "Keep out of this!" He shouted it angrily, not wanting to be robbed of this.

Trenchard got his arms around him then, and they

wrestled mightily, each striving to bring the other to his knees. They went over together, falling across the bed and crashing it to the floor with the hard impact of their combined weights. Rolling free of the wreckage, they fought upon the floor; and Sabin feared his ribs were going to give to the tightening of Trenchard's arms. Then Trenchard's grip relented, and Sabin felt Trenchard's thumb trying for his eyes. He bit at the thumb, sinking his teeth deep; and in the midst of Trenchard's yowl of anguish, Sabin broke free and got to a stand.

Trenchard came up, too, groping blindly for Sabin. He plucked at Sabin's shirt front and tried getting his arms around Sabin again, but Sabin fought him off, taking Trenchard's blows. His head sang, but Trenchard was wavering; Trenchard's strength had been worn down. So had Sabin's, and Sabin knew that he must make the next few minutes count. He tried making a target of Trenchard's face; he saw that face as something bloody and grimacing, a frightful mask that whisked about before him. He supposed his own face looked like that.

And then Trenchard broke, and the manner of his breaking was a wild rout, a sudden giving up of hammering at Sabin and a dive for the gun that lay upon the floor. Trenchard put everything into reaching for that gun; he stooped, throwing himself off balance, and Sabin found the man's jaw again. He battered at that jaw, striking it with his left fist and following with his right, and Trenchard crumpled, going down to sprawl grotesquely. But still he tried for the gun. His fingers flexed; his hand became a crawling crab, inching across the floor, a thing separate from Trenchard, having a will of its own.

Sabin took a blind step forward and brought his boot heel down hard on Trenchard's wrist. He took another step and kicked at the gun; it slithered across the floor and hit a far corner and skidded at a tangent. Sabin reached and picked up the gun, holding it like a hot thing, then suddenly hurling it through the window. As the broken glass fell, Trenchard turned slowly over on his back and flung out his arms and sighed, and the consciousness went out of him.

Sabin stood with his legs trembling, wanting mightily to fall down there beside Trenchard. He drew his sleeve across his forehead and heard the sweat spatter against the wall. He picked his sheepskin from the floor and got into it and reeled through the doorway, the onlookers breaking before him. He saw the desk clerk, and he said, "Figure up the damage."

He saw Thora, her back to the far wall of the hallway, her face horrified. "Get your things," he told her.

She said, "I hate you! Do you hear? I hate you!"

He looked at the desk clerk again. "Send your bill to Pitchfork. One yearling ought to about pay for it. Maybe there'll be one yearling left, come spring."

15

"Now It's Happened!"

BY THE TIME HE got his horse and Thora's from Conover's, Sabin's step was steady enough, but his body protested when he lifted himself to the leather, and he wondered if he should stay the night in Stirrup. He decided against this, not wanting a night of playing sentinel over Thora. She had come silently from the hotel, waiting only until Trenchard had been lifted to a bed in another room, and she came silently with Sabin as they spanned the frozen creek and lined out for Pitchfork. She was to hold her silence thereafter, making of it a hateful thing. Once, when they were forced to dismount and lead their horses through a heaped drift, he offered his hand to help her and it was brushed aside.

The night lay clear and bitterly cold around them, the land glimmering and the far hills standing etched, making a landmark of sorts. Breathing was labor, and the cold stiffened their faces; and Sabin's fear was that another storm might swoop out of the north. He wondered again about the wisdom of striking for home at this hour, but he slogged onward, Thora toiling with him. He was concerned with her comfort, and he stopped often for rest, thus forcing her to stop. But the cold made its insidious inroads whenever movement ceased, and the night became an endlessness of fighting fatigue. Sabin had taken severe punishment from Trenchard, and he was dead tired when at long last they dipped down into the coulee that sheltered Pitchfork's buildings.

The night was nearly gone, yet a light showed in the ranch-house; and when Sabin had put the horses away and come inside, Thora, who'd preceded him, had gone to her room, but Mrs. Lantry sat by the stove. She sat there like the ghost of herself, gaunt and drawn and gray; and Sabin, looking at her, wondered where she'd found the energy to withstand the winter. He moved to the stove and held his hands out to it, and Mrs. Lantry lifted her eyes to him. He knew she was seeing what Trenchard's fists had done to his face; he knew she was drawing her own estimate from this.

At last she said, "Thank you, Mark Sabin."

Sabin said, "The next time she lights out of here, I'll let her go."

Mrs. Lantry lifted one of her blue-veined, transparent hands and brushed a lock of hair from her forehead. "Ginselling told me. Ginselling would have gone after Trenchard with a gun. I'm very grateful to you, Mark Sabin."

He looked at his skinned knuckles; they'd begun to swell. "I'll need hot water."

She went to the kitchen and fetched back a basin of steaming water, and he plunged his hands into this and let them soak. He kept at this a long time; she brought him fresh water; he could hear her moving about the kitchen, stoking up the fire. Then she brought him hot coffee. It tasted of brandy. He grinned at her over the mug; he was beginning to feel human again. She smiled back; and with their eyes meeting, he was struck with the thought that he'd never been so close to any woman as he was to this one, this Mrs. Lantry.

"Sometimes I think we're alike, Mark Sabin," she said, and he wondered how she'd divined his thoughts. "We both stick by whatever it is we're trying to do. Morgan was like that, too."

"Yes," he said and remembered the old place and the cottonwood again, and his eyes grew bleak; the camaraderie was lost from this moment.

"You'd better get to bed," Mrs. Lantry said.

But still he fussed with his hands for another half hour, not knowing why this was so very important until he realized that his fingers would have to be supple for the work ahead. *Next time it will be guns,* he thought, reflecting upon Trenchard; and he kneaded his hands, one in the other.

When he climbed into his blankets, he thought: *I wonder how Trenchard feels!*

He fell into a fuzzy sort of sleep, pain-wracked and wild with dreaming; and when the morning came, he found himself too stiff to get out of bed. He pitted his will against his muscles, making the try, and gave up, groaning. He lay there; he flexed his hands and found that they would at least obey him. He listened for the voice of the wind, the voice of the enemy, but it was a still day, a cold day, with the cold seeping in through the walls. He wondered what time it was. He knew he should be out with the cattle, and he knew he couldn't make it. Not today.

No, the others would have to do the riding—Ginselling and old Tex and Pete and Joe and the rest of them, those who'd worked so valiantly all the winter. Only the Kid was entitled to the luxury of a bed, but the Kid had a good excuse; he had a bullet hole in him. Sabin listened for the Kid's babbling; he didn't hear it, and this fretted him. He had lived with the Kid's voice for a long time; it was part of the winter, like the wind and the bawling cattle.

Mrs. Lantry tapped on his door a little later and looked in. He felt like a new-born babe, lying here not able to get up off his back, and he made his protest, but she silenced him. She fetched him hot broth and he spooned it into himself and felt better. She fetched him coffee. When she came to take away the dishes, he asked about the crew. They were out working, she told him. Then he asked about the Kid.

She looked grave. "Worse. Much worse. He's taken a turn. I've sent for Hatwell."

"Ginselling?" he guessed and thought what would happen if Trenchard were still in town.

"No, Tex."

When she'd left the room, he meant only to lie still for a short while, soaking up rest; but presently he slept; and when he awoke again, he guessed that it was late afternoon. He lay there, listening for the sounds of the house; the house was quiet—too quiet. He began worrying about this; he got out of bed and stood in his underwear, his body shrieking as he made this demand on it. He began kneading his muscles, working himself over carefully; and soon he was able to climb into his trousers.

Doc Hatwell came in then, very quietly. Hatwell said, "How, Mark."

Sabin grinned at him. "I don't need you, Doc. I can make it the rest of the way."

Hatwell shook his head; he looked old and slow-moving, as though the winter had congealed all the sap in him. "That isn't it, Mark. The Kid's gone. I lost him half an hour ago."

Sabin stood holding his shirt in his hand, hearing this but not believing it, not at first, remembering that once Hatwell had said the boy stood a thin chance, remembering that Hatwell had given the boy up that day after the first blizzard. Hatwell had said the winter made one too many to fight. But still the Kid had lived; he had shouted off death; he had battled death and the cold and held triumphant through all the weary winter. Now he was gone; and as the truth forced itself upon Sabin, his only thought was that they wouldn't be able to bury the Kid, not till spring. They'd have to wrap him in blankets and put him in a snowbank. Only blasting powder would budge the ground.

Hatwell said, "The crew will be in before long. They'll have to know. I wanted you to know first. You've held on all the while, Mark, waiting for this. Now it's happened! Can you stop the boys?"

Sabin said, "I don't know. I don't know," and he was thinking of Curly; he was thinking how Curly was lost forever.

"They've always had it in their craws that it was Ben Teasdale," Hatwell said.

Sabin nodded. "I know. Mrs. Lantry thought so, too. The sign read that way."

He finished dressing automatically, his mind as sluggish as his body, groping for the sort of answer he needed and not finding an answer he could face. Hatwell, his long, horsey face somber, stood watching him.

"Trenchard still in town?" Sabin asked.

"He was when I left. I did a patching job on him this morning. What did you work him over with, Mark? A whipple tree?"

"How's he taking it, Doc?"

"Some men blaze when they get mad. Some turn cold. Trenchard's the cold kind. I don't like to think of the look in his eye. He says that as soon as the weather breaks, he's coming to Pitchfork with his crew. He's taking Thora away from here."

"Oh, hell," Sabin said. "Everything at once."

He came out to the huge room where Mrs. Lantry sat huddled by the stove. She didn't look up at him. Thora was not here; Sabin's eyes went questing for her, the old alarm faintly stirring in him; and Doc Hatwell tipped his head toward the closed door of Thora's room.

Mrs. Lantry said in a toneless voice, "Some of the boys have ridden in. I've told them."

Sabin thought, startled, *Why, she's grieving!* Mrs. Lantry had lived a long time with the Kid's voice, too.

He said, "I'm hungry again," and went into the kitchen and fixed himself food. Hatwell followed after him; he stood with his bony shoulders to the wall, saying nothing, just watching Sabin. Presently Hatwell sighed. "I've got to be getting back to town," he said. "Another storm's in the offing, if I'm any kind of guesser."

"Yes," Sabin said. "Another storm."

And then, because there was no sense putting it off, Sabin got his sheepskin and left the house and walked toward the bunkhouse, the snow crunching beneath his boots, making its cold sound, his breath fanning out before him.

There was little left of this day; winter's dusk had come down upon the basin blurring all things; and the buildings were looming shadows, the bunkhouse clearly marked by the squares of light that were its windows. He came into the bunkhouse and felt the heat of its stove and closed the door and was reminded of the first time he'd entered this building, the day he'd taken Pitchfork's foremanship. Those of the crew who'd ridden in were about the room, and they came to the old sullen alertness as he stood watching them. The difference was that Ginselling was here this time.

Sabin said, "Well—?"

Ginselling lifted his eyes to him; Ginselling's eyes hated him. "You know about the Kid?"

Sabin nodded.

Ginselling's mouth tightened. "You're Pitchfork's foreman. You've played it high, wide and handsome. What are you going to do about the Kid?"

"Bury him, when the ground loosens up."

They made that slight movement of feet and bodies; he heard again their incoherent mutter. He remembered how he had recognized their loyalty that other time; now that loyalty was the thing against which he must pit himself, and he was weary with the thought; he was weary of fighting.

Ginselling said, "We'd have burned out Teasdale once, if it hadn't been for you. It ain't too late. The snow's still holding off. We can beat our way that far south."

Sabin looked them over, his face showing nothing. "That goes for the rest of you?"

They muttered. This was their answer, and Sabin knew how it was with them. There was Ginselling, making it personal, liking having a man on a hook. There were the others, following Ginselling because they had followed him so long, loyal to his cause because they were loyal to the Kid, who'd been one of them. All of it was Pitchfork, and Sabin felt alien, and the combined animosity of these men rose and filled the room and made it stifling. And there was one thing only that he could use to turn them.

"Look," he said. "Suppose you're wrong. Suppose it wasn't Teasdale."

Ginselling said, "Oh, hell."

"I was riding that night," Sabin said. "Mrs. Lantry will tell you that. Who do you suppose turned those stolen horses and got them headed back toward Pitchfork?"

Ginselling's belligerence sharpened. "What's that got to do with it?"

Sabin said, "Just this: It wasn't Teasdale who put a bullet in the Kid. It was someone else. And I know his name."

Now he had them; they leaned forward, their faces hard in the lamplight, their eyes on him, and there was only one thing left to say now, the one thing that would keep them out of saddles, keep them off Teasdale.

"I'll go after that man," Sabin said. "Will that satisfy you?"

Ginselling said savagely, "You've ridden both sides of the fence since you come back. How the hell do we know which side you're riding now?"

"Twenty-four hours," Sabin said. "Give me twenty-four hours."

He was as near to begging as he could ever come; he looked at them, wondering what counted now, the old days and the old hate or the weary months when he had worked with them, worked for Pitchfork. He had taken Pitchfork's foremanship because inevitably there was to be such a moment as this. Now he was at their mercy.

Old Tex stirred himself. Old Tex said, "Let him have his chance. Mebbeso, he won't show back. If he doesn't, we can still ride against Teasdale."

Again there was that shifting of feet and bodies and that mutter, but in it now was grudging approval of

Tex's stand. It came from all of them but Ginselling. Ginselling's eyes were angry, and he fumbled at his clothes and drew out a huge watch. He snapped this open and had his look, and he said then, "Twenty-four hours. Not a minute more. Then we ride, Sabin. You can make up your mind about that."

16

At Teasdale's

SABIN WENT FIRST TO the house; and finding Mrs. Lantry still sitting beside the stove, alone with her stony grief, he awaited her attention; and then, growing tired of this, he said, "I've got a ride to make. Tonight."

She lifted her eyes. She looked toward the room where the Kid lay. "On account of him?"

Sabin nodded. "The boys want it squared. Otherwise they tromp on Teasdale. The man who did it is in the hills."

Mrs. Lantry turned alive. "The snow must be twenty feet deep up there!"

"Hell," Sabin said, "I know that. I figure I can make it to Teasdale's by horse. After that I'll try snowshoes. They've given me twenty-four hours."

Her parchment-like face stiffened, and she said, "I told you once how I felt about Teasdale. He's nothing to me one way or the other unless he's put a scar on

Pitchfork. The way my crew feels about it is the way I feel. But you'll have your twenty-four hours."

Sabin made an impatient gesture. "I didn't come to ask a favor. I just wanted you to know I'd be riding."

He turned then and strode toward the door, and her voice gave him pause as his hand was on the latch. She was standing now, small and frail, but with the look of eagles to her. She said, "I'm a wretched old woman, but I'm all that's left of Pitchfork. When you think of me, try to understand that. Good luck to you in your riding, Mark Sabin."

"I'll be back," he said.

Outside, he looked toward the bunkhouse; he thought of the crew waiting. He got gear onto a fresh saddler and lashed a pair of snowshoes behind the saddle and made other preparations; he worked with a certain feverishness, making the minutes count; but once he'd lifted himself to leather, he had to take it slow, for there was no pushing a horse along the trail he followed.

He got to Pitchfork's gate and turned south and realized then how tired he was and how much toll Trenchard's fists had taken. But the real weight he shouldered was his own thinking, for he was a man with the devil's work to do. He had made his choice, and there was no turning back. Not now.

The cold was constant; the cold drove at him and numbed him, and he was often out of the saddle and leading the horse, though there'd been enough travel on the road to keep it fairly open. He knew now that he should have spent the night under Pitchfork's roof and waited for daylight with its slight rise of temperature, but he'd been afraid to squander the hours. Time had become a priceless, pressing thing. Yet there was only so much he could ask of himself. When he'd passed Inland's gate, he knew what he must do. He pushed on beneath the cold stars until Grove school-house loomed before him.

The building stood darkly huddled, banked high by snow; the yard where once a festive fire had burned was now a trackless expanse. He floundered to a lean-to behind the school and put his horse inside. He had fetched feed in a saddle-bag and he doled this out carefully to the horse, then closed the lean-to's door as tightly as he could and plowed his way to the school-house. He knew that it would be unlocked lest any wayfarer need a night's shelter, but the cold had stuck the door, and he had to put his shoulder against it.

Inside, he lighted a match and held it high; the desks were still shoved against the wall as they had been the night of the dance. The stove was long unused, but there was kindling in the wood box, and he fumbled in his pockets for paper and found the letter he'd got from Helena and used this to start a fire. When it was burning well, he soaked up some of its warmth, then went back to the lean-to and got an armload of firewood from a stack there. With the fire crackling, he slipped out of his sheepskin and spread it on the floor before the stove.

Now he was ready to sleep, and he needed sleep; but the torment of thinking kept him awake. He lay in the darkness with the fire flickering through the cracks in the stove, the fire dancing a mad dance upon the floor, and the frosted windows showing dimly, and he remembered this room alive with gayety and Deborah dancing with him, the music wild in the room.

But his memory drove deeper than that, for he'd gone to school here; and so had Curly.

Curly had been a mighty poor speller, he recalled, but pretty fair at figures. They'd had all the grades in this one room, and the teacher had put the older boys to the back; Curly had sat up front, there to the far left side, next to young Clint Baxter from Star-Cross, who'd stuttered. Sabin had fetched Curly. They'd come bareback on one of Jeff Sabin's horses, an old pensioner that could fall asleep in a thunderstorm and smell an oat-sack through a stone wall. He'd fetched Curly, but there hadn't been much enthusiasm in Curly, and Sabin had talked loudly of the joys of schooling.

"Look," Sabin would add, "you don't want to grow up ignorant, do you?"

And thinking of this now, Sabin thought: *If I can't get into the hills, I can't.* And he faced it then; he knew how mightily he wanted to be shed of this task.

Then he slept.

He was awake with the dawn. The fire, replenished a time or two during the night when the creeping cold had forced him to the task, had burned itself out again; the room was gray and dismal and cold. When he stirred, he found that his body had stiffened. He got to a stand, rubbed his hand over the stubble on his cheeks, pulled on his sheepskin, and was riding southward within fifteen minutes.

The day was clear and cold, with the storm that Hatwell had dreaded still holding off; the hills loomed much closer; the hills seemed within reach of his hand. He saw many dead cattle as he worked his way toward Teasdale's. The snow lay deep here in the south end of the basin; he often had to lead the horse, and more than once he thought he would have to abandon the animal and take to the snowshoes. He knew now with a mingled hopelessness and elation that the hills were closed to him, and he thought: *What about that?*

He weighed all the factors and found himself with only one course left open: he would reach Teasdale's and wait there for Pitchfork's coming; he would wait gun in hand, as he'd done on that autumn night when Pitchfork had first come.

So thinking, he presently found himself in the first of the timber; and soon Teasdale's was before him, the old place looking lost in the snow. But smoke lifted from the chimney of the shack; and when he'd stabled the horse and floundered to the door, Mrs. Teasdale opened for him, her smile a hearty welcome. "Come in! Come in!" she urged. He stepped through the doorway into the familiar interior and saw Teasdale's numerous brood huddled around the stove, and saw, too, that a man was sitting here.

He looked and was stunned with surprise and was neither glad nor sad; he hadn't bargained that Curly might be here, but that was the way of it. And he heard again the impish laughter of the little men.

Curly lifted that go-to-hell face of his and grinned and said, "How, Mark." Sabin's face still showed bruises. "Somebody run over you with a wagon?"

Mrs. Teasdale was moving about, asking Sabin whether he'd eaten, urging him to strip off his coat and get nearer to the fire. He heard her voice as something distant, for she had ceased to exist and so had the children; there were only Curly and himself in the old place, and Sabin thought: *Why does it have to happen here?*

He said, "You can get into your duds, Curly. We'll be riding."

Curly shook his head. "Not me. Not in your direction, anyway."

Sabin said, "One of the crew died at Pitchfork yesterday. He took a long time at it. He had a bullet hole in him since last fall—since the night he tried to stop you from running off some horses."

Curly said, "I'm sorry he cashed in." Then his face turned sullen. "I never held it against you for being a lawdog for cattlemen, Mark. But now you're doing Pitchfork's chores. Is that it?"

Sabin said, "You damn' fool! Can't you savvy that

they've pegged it onto Teasdale? Pitchfork will be here before another night's through."

Curly leaned back in his chair and thrust his legs out. "And what the hell am I supposed to do?"

Now the question had come, and there had to be an answer for it. Searching for that answer had churned all of Sabin's thinking since the moment when Doc Hatwell had walked into his room at Pitchfork and told him the boy was gone. There were some things no man could ask of himself at any price. But Sabin had the answer now; he had a compromise between two kinds of loyalty.

He said, "Pitchfork would hang you to the handiest tree ten minutes after I got you there. A jury would likely let you off with a prison stretch, all things considered. Doc Hatwell will testify that the winter as much as the bullet killed that boy. We're riding as far as Pitchfork's gate together, Curly. Then you're going on to Stirrup and catch a stage to Lewistown. When you get there, you're going to surrender to the law. And you're going to give me your word right now that you'll do it. You never broke a promise to me, not that I recollect."

Curly said, "You're loco, Mark! I'll be right here when Pitchfork comes. There'll be one gun they're not expecting. I'm not sticking my head into any noose."

Sabin crossed the room and slapped Curly's face then, slapped it hard, almost knocking Curly from the chair. He saw Curly's startled look; he saw Curly raise his hand to his cheek, his eyes turning cold. Sabin heard Mrs. Teasdale's startled gasp; one of the children began whimpering.

"You're coming, Curly," Sabin said. "I spent a winter being ready for this to happen. You're coming so that Pitchfork will keep off this place; I'm counting on being able to hold them by giving my word that you're on the way to the law. I have a few friends in that bunkhouse. But I've got a deadline and I haven't time to argue with you. Now get your things."

Curly said slowly, "I thought you were about the biggest man in the whole loco world. I was prouder of you than an Injun is of a paint hoss. But you'd send your own brother off to jail to keep Pitchfork happy!"

Sabin said wearily, "Can't you see that there's only one way out of this thing? There's more to it than Pitchfork and Ben Teasdale. There's *you*, kid. You've got to square up."

Mrs. Teasdale said, "He ain't going! We'll fight for him when Pitchfork comes. He's our hired hand."

Sabin said, "How's that?"

"He's our hired hand."

Curly said, "The bunch broke up after that first storm last November. We all got cabin fever, holed-up together with the blizzard blowing, and some fights started. Squinch and the boys headed south when it cleared up. I'm not sure about Reese. I lit out on my own. I found Teasdale holding his herd back in the hills. He needed a hand, and he made me a deal—no pay till shipping time next fall and none then if the winter wipes him out. I took him up on it."

Sabin said, "Then you've been working all through the winter?"

"Hell," Curly said, "this was our place, wasn't it? I just come in this morning to get some grub to pack back to Ben and his oldest boy."

Sabin said, "And when you get paid off—?"

"I figgered to stay with Ben," Curly said. "I remembered what you told Reese about fat pickings and thin ropes."

Sabin felt feathery in his stomach then, not knowing how to take this; it had come too all-of-a-sudden; but in him was the fiercest joy he'd ever known, and the greatest regret. He remembered Stringham's hideout and the time he'd ventured there for Curly's sake. He'd thought his sowing that night had been on rocky soil, but now he reaped the harvest. Out of his crowding thoughts, one stood foremost; and he said, "I'm mighty sorry about that slap, Curly."

"Forget it," Curly said.

Sabin shook his head. "It still leaves Pitchfork waiting, boy."

Curly said, "Then I'm going to have to tell you. You can take them off us. Give them Trenchard."

"Trenchard!"

"Sure," said Curly. "He's the one who dusted that Pitchfork hand."

Sabin said, "You'll have to come again on that one!"

"I wouldn't be talking if it was just my own hide, Mark. You know that. Reese told you he had friends in the basin, remember? He meant Inland. He was working with Trenchard, running off Pitchfork stuff. Trenchard let him cross Inland, coming and going, and that made it easy. Trenchard didn't give a hoot about the cows Reese lifted; Reese didn't even have to cut him in. Trenchard just wanted Pitchfork ruined so Pitchfork would have to sell out to him."

Sabin said, "You sure about this, Curly?" and he was remembering that meeting at medicine tree and Trenchard setting him against Reese Stringham.

Curly nodded. "That night you met me, Reese had sent me to carry word to Trenchard about a raid we were planning. I went with Trenchard to scout Pitchfork. We found those horses roaming loose. Running them off was my own fool idea. One of Pitchfork's boys skylined himself. He was almost on top of Trenchard. It was Trenchard did the shooting."

Sabin said, "Trenchard—always Trenchard," and began to see how it all fitted.

Curly said, "I want you to savvy how it was, Mark. That deal with Trenchard kept me riding with Reese, because Trenchard was against Pitchfork and I was against Pitchfork. But the choice now is him or these kids. That's why I've spilled it."

Sabin felt as though all the weariness had been sloughed off him, and he looked at Mrs. Teasdale. "I'll have a bait of grub, if you can spare it. Then I'd like the loan of a fresh horse. I've got to be back to Pitchfork by deep dark. And I've got to stop on the way."

The woman began bustling about the stove, and Curly said lazily, "Ben and his boy will have to go hungry a day. I'll stick here till tomorrow morning at least. Maybe Pitchfork *will* show up."

Sabin looked at him and was proud of him; Curly had got his real learning at long last.

"You play your end of it any way you want," Sabin said. His mouth tightened. "Me, I've got another ride to make."

17

The Screaming Night

SNOW FELL BEFORE SABIN reached Grove schoolhouse on the return ride, the flakes coming down huge and soft and the temperature rising. If this was the storm Hatwell had been dreading, it was a puny thing, soft climax to the roaring blizzards of these past months. But Sabin, Montana wise, was not deceived. Let the wind rise and the temperature fall, and a single hour could bring on a blizzard. As it was, the snow might choke the roads, leaving Arrowhead stricken again; and Sabin was at once concerned lest he be blocked off from Pitchfork before the deadline. Ginselling had the kind of stubbornness that would take him out in this, Pitchfork's crew behind him, and Ginselling's stubbornness might beat a trail through to Teasdale's.

Still, Ginselling would likely take the road south rather than strike overland, and Sabin met no other riders as he urged his borrowed horse north. Only cattle roamed the whiteness. At Inland's gate, Sabin peered through the snow's thick curtain, knowing he must turn west here and that Ginselling might pass along the road while he, Sabin, was at Inland. He made a guess at the time and decided there were a few hours left. He could only hope that Ginselling would wait out those hours. He thought of old Tex; he pinned all his hope on Tex.

Then he dismounted and struggled with Inland's gate as he had done in another, fiercer storm.

Inland's crew had cleared the road leading to the buildings, and he followed this road west and came to Inland's huge ranch-house and hallooed the house, sitting his wet saddle with the powdery snow a weight on his shoulders. He sat thus till Cliff appeared at the door.

"Trenchard here?" Sabin called.

"In town," Cliff shouted back.

Sabin had pinned everything on Trenchard's being here, and he felt lost and sick with the knowledge. "Staying in town?" Sabin asked.

"He didn't say." Cliff peered harder, his eyes searching Sabin's face and seeing the marks Trenchard's fists had made. "So it was you, eh?" he shouted. His voice held the grudging admiration of one fighting man for another, tempered by a cowhand's loyalty to his boss.

"It was me," Sabin said, and turned his horse and headed back into the storm.

He had now a feeling of desperate disappointment that left him empty of purpose. He hadn't known as he'd sat his saddle before Inland's gallery how he was going about the task he'd undertaken; he'd thought vaguely that if Trenchard were there he would throw a gun on the man and take him away under the very noses of his crew. He hadn't even estimated his chances on such a plan; he had been too desperate for that. Now, with Trenchard gone, he only knew that the last sands were running out on him and he would not be able to deliver a man to Pitchfork as he had promised.

He got back to Inland's gate and tussled with it and looked for tracks on the main road, hoping to tell whether riders had passed southward. But the snow had fallen thickly in the half hour and more it had taken him to reach Inland's buildings and return; the snow blotted out any signs of passage. He looked toward Stirrup and made his estimate of time and distance and knew how futile such thinking was. He faced into the north, a vague hope stirring in him, born of his desperation.

Early dusk lay upon the land when he got to Pitchfork's gate, and the lamps showed dimly through the snow when he reached the buildings. He stabled his horse and saw that lights burned in the bunkhouse and smoke rose from its chimney and horses stood huddled in the corrals, their rumps to the storm. Pitchfork's crew was still here, and he wondered how many times Ginselling had looked at his watch in this last hour.

Climbing to Pitchfork's gallery, he stomped his feet and brushed snow from his shoulders and knocked it from his sombrero, then put his hand to the latch. He came into the big room and saw Mrs. Lantry by the stove and saw, too, that the door to Thora's room was still shut. He stood there, feeling all the miles he'd ridden, feeling his long fight against the clock; and he heard the first faint moan under the eaves; the wind had come.

Mrs. Lantry lifted her eyes to him. "Sit down, Mark Sabin," she said.

He shook his head. "I've got to ride again."

"You came back empty-handed?"

He nodded. "My man is in Stirrup."

She let her surprise show briefly in her eyes. "His name?"

"Garth Trenchard."

She thought about that for a long, reflective moment. "Yes. Of course," she said then.

He told her all of it then; he told her of Curly and Reese Stringham and that night he'd ridden into the heart of the hills after turning Pitchfork's horses back. He spoke of his recent trip southward to Teasdale's and of finding Curly there and learning what Curly had become and hearing what Curly had said. He told her of stopping at Inland.

This last roused her. "You went there alone after Trenchard, Mark Sabin?"

"What else was there to do?"

"And now you're going to Stirrup?"

His lips thinned down, and he had that same feeling of inevitability he'd known when he'd fought Trenchard in the Austin House. "He's in Stirrup," he said.

"Then take the crew with you," Mrs. Lantry urged. "Tell them what you've just told me."

"No," Sabin said. "It's between me and Trenchard. You can savvy that."

She nodded, her own face hardening. "Yes, I can. What is it I can do for you?"

"I didn't ask a favor last night, but I'm asking one now. I need something to eat, and after that I'll need a fresh horse. I've got to hurry and hit the trail before the wind really whips up. While I'm getting ready, you can go to the bunkhouse and tell the boys they'll have to wait another twenty-four hours."

"I'll tell them."

He remembered how, after the Grove schoolhouse dance, one of her crew had put his own wishes above

158

her command; so he asked, "What about Ginsel-ling—?"

She came out of the chair, clutching her shawl about her, and crossed to her own bedroom. He heard her rummaging in drawers; she came back bearing a Colt's forty-five, blue-barreled and black-butted, which looked immense in her fragile hand. She laid this on the table, and he knew without being told that it had been Morgan Lantry's.

"Ginselling will wait with the rest of them," she said.

He grinned at her. "You're a good girl."

"I'm a wretched old woman, Mark Sabin. But Pitchfork still pays its debts."

He tried picturing her using that gun and the picture was so incongruous that he banished it, yet he knew she *would* use the gun if needs be; and his thought was that here was his winter's wage, here was his pay from Pitchfork. It made a decent bargain.

He went into the kitchen then and began preparing food, and he heard her donning heavy shoes and the buffalo coat; he heard the door shut as she left the house. She was back before he'd finished eating; when he came again to the big room, the gun was once more on the table. He got into his heavy outer clothes and opened the door; the wind caught it and wrenched it from his hand. The wind had risen that much, and the snow was splinters of glass flung in his face.

He thought: *Hatwell knew what was coming after all!*

He shouldered into the wind and crossed to the barn; the bunkhouse was still lighted. He got himself a horse and took the trail to Pitchfork's gate; but before the buildings were out of sight, he wondered at the wisdom of this departure as he felt the rising fury of the storm. They'd never get to Teasdale's now, those

Pitchfork men, even if Mrs. Lantry's order failed to hold them. And Trenchard would have to wait in Stirrup for this new storm to spend itself. Sabin might bide his time, with the winter freezing all of them where they were, the winter suspending the feeble efforts of men. But he had to finish this; he had to finish it tonight.

So thinking, he forced the horse onward until the bullet snapped at his sombrero brim.

The gun's report was only a distant cough in the rising wind. Sabin hauled the horse to a stop and came off the saddle, losing his balance and floundering in the snow as the gun spoke again. The horse flinched; the shot had been that close. Sabin got out his own gun and waited for a tell-tale flash, peering hard into the driving snow and feeling the swift rush of anger. The flash came, and he fired in the direction of it and sensed that he'd missed. He waited again, knowing now that it was Ginselling out yonder shooting at him, knowing that it had been Ginselling who'd fired at him that day, weeks before. None of the rest hated him this much, not after the weeks they'd worked together. Ginselling, who had disobeyed before, was running true to pattern.

Now there came an aloneness of wind and snow and darkness with Sabin holding firmly to the reins with his left hand and keeping the gun ready in his right, wondering if Ginselling were circling out there. No more shots came. Sabin waited endlessly, the waiting a hard rasp against his nerves. At last he mounted and urged the horse forward. He made it to Pitchfork's gate and wondered then if he had indeed missed or if Ginselling lay in the snow, wounded or dead. Or had Ginselling turned back to Pitchfork, having small stomach for a game at which two could play? He found he didn't much care.

Soon he was on the main road that drove straight eastward to Stirrup, and his job was to keep to the road. At first it wasn't difficult; the wind lulled at times and the snow turned soft and warm again. But the temperature began dropping; he could notice a considerable difference in an hour; and the wind grew to greater fury. He began finding it difficult to keep to the road; this was like that first winter night, the night he'd gone to Inland from Grove schoolhouse. He had to guide himself by following a fence that paralleled the road; he had to keep the wind to his left cheek to be sure he was veering eastward.

The fence gave him the old sense of security, and he dismounted many times to fight against the wind and snow and feel for the fence and make sure he hadn't strayed from it. Also, he had to dismount to keep his circulation restored. He was dressed more warmly than he'd been that first night, and he'd put a winter behind him of fighting the cold; he'd learned to know the enemy well. But before half the journey was behind him, he began casting a mental map of Arrowhead and locating the ranches upon it, his thought being to turn in at one of the ranches and sit out the storm.

He gave this notion up; the old stubbornness drove him onward, plus a feeling that his only real security lay in staying with the road and the fence. If he turned in at a gate, he'd have to flounder across openness to some man's buildings; and there was the chance that in even so slight a traverse he might become hopelessly lost.

Then he climbed down to go struggling in search of the fence again and this time he failed to find it. He had a panicky moment when sheer fright took all the strength out of him until he realized he'd passed a fence corner. Now there was only open range between here and Stirrup, open range and the snow-heaped road; but this was a good road with an embankment on either side, and he gave the horse its head, hoping the mount would stay with the road.

Sleepiness became a weight upon him; his mind turned fuzzy, and fantasy had its way with him. The storm was now a personal thing, the last fling of the winter, the last onslaught of the enemy. He had battled the winter and almost won through. He had learned the wiles of the winter and had been smarter than all the cold and all the wind, but now the winter was winning this last fight. He cursed the winter then, defying it; and the wind took his words and scattered them; the wind laughed.

The storm was a whirling demon which danced around him and blotted out all the world, and he moved through the storm blindly; he moved through the screaming night, relying on chance now and knowing a moment of utter astonishment when the horse's hoofs made a hollow sound, until he realized they were on the bridge spanning Arrowhead Creek, just outside Stirrup.

He got across the bridge and into the town, but he might have been upon the naked prairie, for the storm was everywhere; the storm obliterated Stirrup. He dismounted and began leading the horse, staggering and lurching, and saw, dimly, a lighted window and veered toward it. The wind struck at him; he careened into a building and felt along its wall for a door and identified the place by the width of the door; it was Conover's. He thumped upon the door; he beat endlessly before it was opened and he stumbled into the warmth and blinked at a lantern that was thrust in his face.

He said, "Put up my horse," and turned the reins over to the hostler and went outside again, heedless of the man's calling voice. He didn't want to linger around the livery's stove lest he might not find the courage to leave it.

He walked a few paces, his head bowed, one hand gripping the brim of his sombrero, his elbow crooked before his face. He fought against the storm and lurched into some solid bulk. He thought he'd veered upon a hitchrail, until the bulk gave way before him and he realized it was one of the starving steers that had drifted into town. There were more of them here; they moved about aimlessly; they made another hazard for him.

He began recasting the town in his mind, using the livery stable as his focal point. He got to what should have been the Austin House and found that he'd erred; this was the furniture store. He turned in his tracks then; the mercantile was just on the other side of this place. He groped into the familiar covered stairway and, out of the wind, stood catching his breath.

Then he started climbing the stairs; it took him forever, and he knew how near to the last ragged edge of his reserve he had come. He reached the head of the stairs and raised his fist to Doc Hatwell's door, then put his hand to the door and lunged into the room. Hatwell was here; the doctor stood looking at Sabin in astonishment; but Sabin brushed past him, gravitating toward the stove.

Hatwell said, "My God, Mark, I'm glad you're here!"

It was the desperation in Hatwell's voice, rather than the words, that reached through to Sabin, and he turned toward Hatwell, his eyes asking questions. Yet he didn't care what alarmed Hatwell, not really; he only cared about crowding close to that stove and letting the heat of it seep into him, and then he wanted to stretch out on the horsehide sofa and doze a little till he found the strength to lift a good stiff slug of whiskey.

"It's Deborah," Hatwell said.

"Deborah—?" He looked at Hatwell, and it came to him that he'd never seen Hatwell so desperate as now.

18

Winter Kill

HATWELL BLINKED AT HIM. "Mark, how long does it take to get to know a person? Take Deborah. I had her pegged and pigeonholed and pressed in a book like an old flower. Then she up and pulled this one!"

Sabin realized that Hatwell was more than a little drunk; it told in the thickness of his tongue; and Sabin said, a dread anxiety growing in him, "Don't talk in riddles, man! What are you trying to tell me about Deborah?"

Hatwell's face screwed up. "She sat there in her house day after day, minding her own business, making dresses for women who couldn't have touched the hem of her own. She lived inside herself, Mark, and you'd have thought she didn't know the rest of the world went on around her. And now she's braced Trenchard. How do you figure it, Mark?"

Sabin said, "Trenchard!"

Hatwell looked at him owlishly and seemed to find him here for the first time. "My God, Mark, I'm glad you're here," he said again. "Trenchard's the one who killed Morgan Lantry! He waited in a room up above the Red Front till he got old Morgan in his sights. Deborah knew that. She figured out how the trick had been done, and she waited till they left the saloon unlocked. Then she had her look in that room."

Sabin fought an urge to shake this man into coherency. "I know about that, Doc! I had a look up there myself. But how did she hang it on Trenchard?"

Hatwell said, "After you mauled Trenchard the other day, it got around that he intended to take his boys to Pitchfork and pluck Thora right out of the house. Deborah came to see me today. She said she'd hired one of the saloon hanger-ons to carry a message to Trenchard at Inland. That was before it started snowing. She sent him a letter saying that if he didn't clear out of Arrowhead on the next stage, she'd give the law evidence that he'd killed Lantry."

Sabin said slowly, "She was doing that for me," and he grew humble with the thought, and desperate, knowing now the secret that had terrified her from the first, knowing what she'd meant that day at Pitchfork when she'd said, "It won't be easy, the job you'll have to do. If you ever think it's going to throw you, come to me. . . ." Saying that when she'd thought he was staying at Pitchfork to keep Thora and Trenchard apart.

Hatwell said, "She had the evidence, too. She brought it to me this morning and asked me to keep it safe. She was afraid Trenchard might come after her, instead of running. I've got it here."

He crossed to his desk, staggering a little, and opened a drawer and took from it a tiny object which he held in the palm of his hand. It was the cigar band from an imported cigar, and Sabin had seen one like it only once before—on the day last fall when

Trenchard had given him a cigar in front of the mercantile.

"Trenchard made just one mistake," Doc said. "His nerves got the best of him, and he smoked while he was waiting up there for Lantry."

Sabin said, "Where's Deborah?" and put a grim patience to waiting out the answer.

Hatwell shook his head. "That's it! That's what's driving me crazy! She's gone. Her house is locked, and no smoke is lifting from the chimney. Trenchard came to town today; he's still in town. He's waiting."

"At the Austin House?"

"He put up there. I don't know where he is now. But what's become of Deborah? There was no stage out today, and she didn't rent a horse. I asked a few questions around town before the storm blew up. She's somewhere in town, I tell you. That's what's keeping Trenchard here. And I've had to sit and wait and listen to that damn' storm scream! Mark, it's been like slow dying!"

Hatwell sat down then, looking as though he wanted to cry, his long, horsey face falling apart. He said, his voice suddenly sober, "I can bring a brat into the world and watch him grow up to gut-shoot a good man. I can sew a fellow together after a shotgun's cut him in two. I can take care of a whole range. But what good am I at a time like this? Tell me, Mark, what the hell good am I?"

It came to Sabin that here was a man who always inherited the troubles of others and bore them valiantly until he could bear them no longer, and he saw now that Hatwell was both a good man and an old man. He moved nearer to the stove; he took his gun from leather and held it close to the stove, letting the oil limber up; and he said then, "I'll be going, Doc," and moved toward the door.

Hatwell said, "Think of it! Trenchard!"

"Yes," Sabin said. "Trenchard," and he understood everything now. He was remembering that Mrs. Lantry hadn't been surprised when he'd told her it had been Trenchard who'd put a bullet in the Kid. How was it Deborah had once said it? "There's an old saw about one rotten apple spoiling the barrel. Maybe that's the way it is in Arrowhead. . . ."

He forced the door open. Descending the stairs, he turned up his coat collar, dreading the waiting storm. His mind pushed him desperately to the task ahead; his body had soaked up just enough heat at Hatwell's that it rebelled against going out into the cold and the wind. He shouldered into the night and made for the Austin House, but a few paces beyond the covered stairway he was in that blinding maelstrom of snow and wind and darkness, and he had to feel his way along from building to building.

He got to the Austin and stumbled into the lobby; he had his look at the register and saw where Trenchard's room was. He climbed the stairs and got out his gun before he put his hand to the room's door, not knocking. The door was unlocked; the room was dark, and he lunged into that darkness with as much wariness as his urgency permitted, knowing now the full measure of Trenchard's formidability and Trenchard's desperation. But the man wasn't here.

He stood in the room, wondering if he should wait for Trenchard, but he couldn't afford waiting. He came out to the street again, fighting the wind, knowing that he must search the town. A steer came lumbering past him, a dying steer. He stepped aside for it. He groped aimlessly along; he thought of the saloons; Trenchard would be where it was warm. He thought of Deborah; she was in one of these buildings, too. But which one? Then it struck him hard that if

Deborah had intended to seek sanctuary within another's walls, she would have stayed with Doc Hatwell. It was to Hatwell she'd entrusted that damning cigar band.

He fought his way toward her house, hoping he'd find her returned, but when he neared her place, it was dark. He thought to pound on her door anyway, but she wouldn't dare answer the door for fear that he might be Trenchard. He remembered that Hatwell had said that no smoke showed. That made proof enough that she was elsewhere. He stood then with the wind whipping at him, trying to reason this out, trying to put himself in Deborah's shoes. Slantwise across the street a light showed dimly in the Red Front, as though only a single lamp burned. He stood in the cold feeling hopeless, and with the feeling he knew how it had been with Hatwell this long day.

He went struggling back toward the mercantile building, not knowing where to direct his footsteps; he went through the swirling night, his mind groping as aimlessly as his feet. And then understanding came to him, for he knew now how Deborah had reasoned, and the fullness of understanding gave him a new purpose. He tried hard remembering how the inside of the Red Front had looked that one time he'd visited the saloon, and he recalled a back door. He turned and groped his way till he was sure he was in the debris-littered vacancy between the blacksmith shop and the saloon. He found the saloon's side and felt along it with his gloved hands, the wind shoving him and the driven snow needling his cheeks.

He seemed to feel along forever in this manner, but at last he came laboriously to a rear corner of the building, and he followed the back wall till he found the door. He paused and wrenched open his sheepskin; the wind caught at the coat with eager hands.

He'd freed his gun; now he wanted his fingers free likewise; and he stripped off his gloves and tried to stuff them in the pockets of his sheepskin. The wind was threshing the coat wildly, so he dropped the gloves and pulled hard at the door. It gave to his hand; he stepped into the back of the barroom.

He stood for a moment in the dim light, in the warmth, looking the length of the barroom at the two men who crouched to the fore of the building before the front window, where they'd rubbed holes in the frost to keep their vigil. He looked at them and saw their surprise; one was Garth Trenchard, the other was Reese Stringham. They were alone here; even the bartender had gone.

Sabin took two steps toward them, and Trenchard's face lost its surprise and took on hardness, and Reese Stringham said, "Oh, hell, Mark!" He had a certain regret in his voice, and an edge of excitement; but there was no fear in Stringham, not with the odds as they were.

Sabin hadn't counted on Stringham. There were words he could have said that would have driven these two men apart, pitting them against each other instead of against him. But there wasn't time for those words, for both of them were reaching for their guns.

He got his own gun into his hand, and he sensed now the final inevitability of all this, himself looking through smoke at Trenchard and the gun speaking without his will, the gun kicking back against his palm, and the acrid smell of powder smoke a stench in his nostrils. He got Trenchard with one of those shots; Inland's man broke in the middle and the gun dropped from his fingers and Trenchard reached out as though to get a hold on air. Sabin thought of that other time when Trenchard's hand had seemed detached from him. Then Trenchard hit the floor, not crashing hard, but settling down easy as though to take his rest. His fingers flexed once; the hand was dead, and so was Trenchard.

But Stringham still fired, the beat of his gun steady and thunderous in the room, blotting out the voice of the wind and making the single overhanging lamp blink. Something struck against Sabin's left thigh with the force of a gigantic fist, but he had no consciousness of pain; he went down to one knee, still firing. He had his taste of regret; he had broken bread with Reese Stringham at Jeff Sabin's table; he had drunk with Stringham, but Stringham had taken one trail and he another, and Sabin supposed there was an inevitability about this, too.

He saw Stringham move forward from the window, and suddenly the window wasn't there; the glass had fallen before one of Sabin's bullets. Stringham came toward him grimacing, looking as though he had something very funny on his mind, something that was tickling him to death, and he wanted to get closer to Sabin so he could tell him about it. Stringham took three steps, small, mincing steps, and turned about on his heel and went down like a felled tree.

Only then did Sabin, struggling to stand, truly know that he'd been hurt.

The winter was in this room, blowing through the broken window; snow sifted Trenchard with white powder. Sabin lurched past Stringham, walking stiffly, wondering how long his left leg would carry him; he almost stumbled over Trenchard. Then he crawled through the broken window, and his one thought was that he must head straight across the street; he must get to Deborah's door.

Pain clouded his thinking as he made that traverse, and he had to hold grimly to one thought—the thought that Deborah was there, in that fireless, darkened house. For once he'd got the pattern of Deborah's thinking, everything had been clear to him. Deborah would have gone to no one, not with Trenchard hunting her. That was why she hadn't stayed with Hatwell. Sabin had known this about her: she always placed others above herself, and thus she'd have jeopardized no friend. When he'd remembered that, he'd realized, too, where he'd find Trenchard, who had not known Deborah so well. Trenchard was bound to be posted where he could watch the house, awaiting Deborah's return. Sooner or later Deborah would have stood on her own doorstep, and Trenchard had known that—Trenchard, who'd been patient once before.

Now the snow and the wind seemed a wall against which Sabin pushed futilely; his hands felt numb before he'd crossed half the street. He had fought the winter through all the weeks; he fought it now feeling lost, feeling done in. He was lunging against Deborah's door before he was aware that he'd reached it; he pounded; he cried out: "Deborah! Deborah! It's me! Mark!"

He thought vaguely: *Suppose I figured it wrong!* and was sick with the thought; it was an eternity of distance to Doc Hatwell's.

He slipped to his knees and pounded weakly; he called her name, and he realized then that he had turned blindly to this door again and again since he'd come back to Arrowhead.

Then the door gave before him, and he fell across her floor; he fell into the darkness, the cold darkness where she'd waited, not daring to let a stove's smoke show. He felt her tugging at him; he sensed that she was dressed as for outdoors. He heard her voice in his ear; she was crying his name. He wanted to tell her that there was nothing to fear now, that all the fear was gone forever, but he began laughing at a new thought. *Hell,* he told himself, *you've just squared up for Morgan Lantry! For Morgan Lantry!*

Another kind of darkness closed in on him and blanked out all thinking, but he went into this darkness unafraid, knowing he was in her hands. . . .

19

Soft Wind Blowing

OUT OF FEVER, out of pain came the many bits of remembrance, some fuzzy with the long sickness, some sharp from the lucid days. He had to lie endlessly in bed while his wound healed, and he got so he knew every item in the bedroom, but it took him a long time to place the room itself. These were Hatwell's quarters, and he'd never been beyond Hatwell's office. It worried him for a while where Doc was sleeping, and then he realized that there must be two bedrooms and this was the one Curly had had.

Curly came to see him two or three times. He could never be sure about the count, for he might have dozed while Curly sat beside the bed and thought that an awakening was another day and another visit. Curly had done a lot of talking, but Sabin couldn't remember afterward what Curly had said; it had something to do with cattle, with Ben Teasdale's herd. Sabin had been troubled at first by finding Curly here in Stirrup; there was some reason why Curly should be lying low, but Sabin couldn't quite put his finger on it. Then he remembered that Reese Stringham was dead and that Curly was forever beyond Stringham's reach.

After that, Ben Teasdale was on his mind; he had feverish nights when he searched frantically for Teasdale, groping through tangled dreams and shouting a warning to the man. Teasdale was to watch out for Pitchfork—that was it! But daylight brought Sabin the memory of Mrs. Lantry and her gun, and he had no fear then for Teasdale.

Deborah came to visit him, too, sitting quietly in the room and bringing him peace by her very presence. Later, as he mended, he got out of her the story of how she'd left him lying on the floor of her house and fought her way through the screaming night to Hatwell's. He had no recollection of being toted to Hatwell's. He got so he looked forward to Deborah's coming and fretted when she was delayed. He had never before put such dependence upon another person.

Once it seemed that Thora was in the room, but he was having a bad time of it that day, and he couldn't be sure afterwards whether she was something conjured out of delirium. He might have asked Hatwell about it, but he didn't. He told himself he'd dreamed it; Thora would hate him forever now that Trenchard was dead by his hand. No one thanked you for smashing an illusion.

Thus were his days and nights made from mingled realities and dreams, and he grew tired of the room and the bed and became a difficult patient. Often the window was frosted, and that told him the winter was still here; there was the one enemy yet to be vanquished. And perhaps another, for he remembered Ginselling shooting at him that night he'd left Pitchfork. He had his old habit of listening for the wind, the voice of the enemy; he had lived so long with the wind that he missed its threnody. He thought of the cattle and knew he should be up into saddle. Some days in his fever, he rode, laying his tongue to old Tex and the others, making the room wild with his cursing.

One day Doc Hatwell let him sit up in a chair, and later Sabin took to walking the room, limping a little; and there came a time when he felt fit to ride.

He had a look at himself in a wall mirror that gave back a distorted face, but he could see that he was thinner, much thinner. At least the havoc wrought by Trenchard's fists had healed. He wondered what month it was, and Hatwell told him it was March. He borrowed Hatwell's razor and shaved himself, then dressed and got down the stairs to the boardwalk. It was good to draw in the clear, cold air. Stirrup looked shabby, a town gaunted down by the winter.

He'd been going to take a walk around and test his strength, but suddenly he wanted a horse beneath him; this became a crying need made of his long rebellion against the bed. He went to Conover's; the Pitchfork horse he'd left there was as fiddle-footed as himself. He did his own saddling and would have sworn that the kak had doubled in weight. He got up into leather and found this to be real medicine; he felt like himself again. He gauged how much daylight was left and made his estimate of the miles, then headed across the bridge and lined out for Pitchfork.

The creek was still ice-bound, and this was one of those sparkling days with the range white all around him and the serrated skyline over the western hills looking as if it might be harboring a chinook. But he'd waited so long for a chinook that he'd ceased hoping. He rode slowly, sometimes so light-headed that everything was beyond reality, sometimes feeling like a man let out of jail. He saw dead cattle, and his face hardened. He came to a fence and felt friendly toward that fence; it had guided him into Stirrup that bitter night.

Lamplighting time had come when he reached Pitchfork; the bunkhouse windows were aglow and smoke rose from the chimneys. He put up his horse and found himself drawn toward the bunkhouse; but he'd been told once, long ago, to keep out of there, and he had no real business with the crew tonight. Yet he now felt a queer affection for the bunkhouse and those hard-riding hands who held forth there, and he would have liked to look in. He thought: *They'll see my horse in the stable,* and his lips thinned down with the old pride and the old way of thinking. Let them come to him!

He climbed to the gallery and entered without knocking and found Mrs. Lantry in the long dining room. This was like the first time he'd come here; she was wearing that stiff black dress and the cameo brooch, and the temperature had risen enough that she no longer needed the shawl. He felt strangely like a man come home and considered that odd, for this was Pitchfork. He spoke to her and saw kindliness in her eyes.

"Sit down, Mark Sabin," she said.

He took a chair and turned it around and straddled it, facing her. Morgan Lantry's gun still lay on the table, precisely where it had been when last he'd left this room. He looked about; he looked toward Thora's door, not asking the question.

"Thora's gone East," Mrs. Lantry said. "She has a friend back there, a girl who came out to Stirrup last year. I supposed you knew she was gone. She said she'd see you in town before she left."

It hadn't been a dream then! He turned this over in

his mind, wondering what to make of it. His thinking was as slow as his movements; he'd been a long time sick.

He raised his eyes to Mrs. Lantry. "I've a lot to tell you."

Her hands moved, those hands so thin and blue-veined and transparent; he grew fascinated by her hands, thinking that with these she'd tried to hold a range together.

"Hatwell was out a couple of times," Mrs. Lantry said. "He told me about Trenchard. And Stringham."

He shook his head. "I should have seen Trenchard's play from the first, but there was just one part of it that fooled me and that was his sending for me to run Stringham out of the hills. His game was as old as greed and grass. He was a man who dreamed big, not caring who got trampled by his dreaming. His scheme was to start a packing plant. So he needed cows—lots of cows. Pitchfork had them."

"And that's why he had to have Pitchfork. I knew that much, Mark Sabin. I didn't know the rest of it. I was blind, too."

Sabin nodded. "First he made a deal with Stringham to rob Pitchfork blind. That was supposed to bring Morgan Lantry to his knees. But Lantry chose to fight, so he laid for Lantry; Trenchard could go in and out of the Red Front as he pleased and nobody paid any attention; he was handling the place for the owner in Helena. But after he'd killed Lantry, he still had you to fight. He hadn't counted on that. You stood between him and his scheme to marry Thora and so marry Pitchfork."

She said, "I only knew it was Pitchfork he really wanted, not Thora. A woman always knows."

"He sent to the Stock Growers' for a man," Sabin went on. "He asked for me. He didn't know me. Just knew I had reason to be packing a grudge against

Pitchfork. That made me the perfect tool, no matter which way he chose to use me. But mostly he wanted to use me against Stringham. You see, he didn't need Stringham any more, not when he had Thora willing to ride off and marry him. Any cows Stringham lifted from Pitchfork from there on out would be cows Trenchard counted on owning. The time had come to double-cross Stringham. Reese died without knowing that; he died siding Trenchard. I feel sorry for Reese when I think of him."

Mrs. Lantry said, "There was a coroner's inquest while you were flat on your back. Stringham's being with Trenchard at the end spelled something to the jury. Did Hatwell tell you they'd cleared you?"

Sabin tried remembering, and he supposed that maybe Hatwell had told him, or Deborah. He said, his eyes dreaming, "Deborah knew who'd waited above the Red Front for Morgan Lantry. She didn't have the courage to point her finger at the killer. Do you understand? She was human enough to be afraid. But she'd have spoken up before she'd have let Morgan Lantry's daughter marry him. Not for Thora's sake, but for mine. She thought I was in love with Thora. At the end, she did point at Trenchard."

Mrs. Lantry said, "You marry that girl, Mark Sabin. You're a fool if you don't."

He spread his hands. "What have I got to offer her? Months of waiting at home while I larrup around for the Stock Growers'? Maybe there won't even be an Association after this winter."

"I offered you half of Pitchfork once," Mrs. Lantry said. "That was a desperate old woman talking, but I'd have made good. But what is half of nothing? Ride out tomorrow and see what you see in the draws and coulees. The winter kill. It will sicken you as it's sickened me; I never want to see another cow again; I never want to own an animal I can't feed. I'm going

East, too, in a week or so and join Thora. I'd like to think she went to Stirrup that last day to thank you; Hatwell told her who'd waited over the Red Front. But she'll never come back here, not with all the things there are to remember. Maybe she'll need me now. Do you want to try keeping Pitchfork going? On shares?"

Here was a bargain a man could make without selling part of his pride, and he grew warm with the thought. He said, "I'll think about it."

They fell silent then, each of them dreaming, and the silence made a communion between them greater than words had. They'd come to know each other this well; they had been valiant, both of them. When the silence broke, the intrusion caught Sabin unawares; he'd been thinking of Thora, feeling a vast pity for Thora that would be the veneer of all his thinking of her hereafter. It was the end of it.

He heard the door open and felt the gust of air at his back, and he supposed, without thinking consciously about it, that one of the hands had come to report to Mrs. Lantry. He didn't recognize his danger until he saw it in her eyes.

He hurled himself sideways then, reaching for his gun as he fell; and this was pure reflex. As he went down, he saw Mrs. Lantry snatch at that gun on the table; he saw her lift it. Her gun spoke, and another, behind Sabin; the gun, so tremendous in Mrs. Lantry's frail hand, bucked hard and fell from her fingers. Sabin was rolling across the floor, still trying to untangle his gun, and he had no knowledge that Ginselling had been hit until he heard the crash of the man's body.

He got to his feet and stood looking at Ginselling dead in the open doorway, the gun Ginselling had fired still clutched in his hand. Incongruously, the only important thing seemed to be to close the door against the winter, and he limped over and shut it. He turned to see Mrs. Lantry wavering in her chair, her face bloodless, and he hurried to her, his fear rising that Ginselling's one shot had found her.

She said, "I'm all right," and he realized then that shock had undone her.

He tugged at Ginselling's body and drew it through the doorway to the gallery and let it lie there; the gunfire had not carried through the log walls to the bunkhouse. He came back into the house and got a dipper of water and held it to Mrs. Lantry's lips. Color came back to her slowly.

She said then, her voice dead, "He was loyal in his own way, and he was a good hand with cattle. But he always disobeyed when there was something Ginselling wanted. That night five years ago, Morgan Lantry sent him with orders to run Jeff Sabin off your place. The hanging of Sabin was Ginselling's own idea. It was you he hated, because of Thora, but he didn't dare go so far as to hang you, too. Now you know."

He said, "You should have told me the first day I came to Pitchfork."

She shook her head. "I needed Ginselling, too. I needed him because, against Trenchard, he'd have sided Pitchfork any time. The only real job was to keep him in hand."

He looked at her, knowing that she had been faithful always, in her own fashion; and knowing this, he forgave her whatever was left to forgive. He said, "I'd be dead now but for you. He figured the only sure way was to get me in the back."

He thought of Ginselling's body out there on the gallery, and he said, "I'll get a couple of the crew to give me a hand."

He walked outside; but when he reached the gallery again, reaction hit him and he stood trembling, fighting nausea. He fumbled with the makings and twisted a quirly into shape and got it lighted and stood drawing in the smoke. He realized then that something had changed; he felt the wind and found it from the west, a soft, warm wind. He had a look at the thermometer, holding a match toward it, and was surprised how much the temperature had risen in the last hour. He thought: *There'll be water dripping from the eaves before the night's over!*

The chinook had come, but he remembered what Mrs. Lantry had told him he'd find in a day's riding, and he knew that the chinook had come too late. He stood there feeling the wind's caress and seeing the ancient enemy vanquished, and he was empty of feeling. This, too, was the end of it.

20

All the Days to Come

ON A DAY WHEN the wild flowers were showing and spring's softness lay upon the awakening land, Sabin rode southward on his own sorrel, leading the horse he'd borrowed from Teasdale's that day he'd found Curly there. He rode overland, following the banks of Arrowhead Creek, which had been swelled by the melted snow. He rode slowly, sick with what he saw.

Coulees and draws were filled with dead cattle, and the few survivors stood stark-ribbed, mere shadows of steers. In the recent spring round-up, Pitchfork's crew, hoping against hope, had ridden whole days without seeing a living steer. The creek had become a moving graveyard with dead cattle swept downstream amid the ice and debris; the creek carried the winter kill along its course, the flotsam of tragedy. Seeing this, Sabin knew how Mrs. Lantry had felt when she'd said she never wanted to see another cow again, and he remembered the sadness of her face as he'd handed her aboard the eastbound stage the evening before.

The spring tally had told its tale; Pitchfork was indeed ruined; Pitchfork was a name, and a brand registered upon a book, and a lost glory of the yesterdays.

Sabin rode now with a sickness in him greater than any brought by Trenchard's fist or gun, and a weariness weightier than he had known in all the winter's riding. He rode listlessly, tired of dead cattle, tired of blasted hopes.

He came in due course to Teasdale's and saw the smoke rising from the chimney of the old place and many of Teasdale's brood playing about the yard. Curly was here, too, splitting wood. Curly looked up as Sabin dismounted; and after Sabin had turned the borrowed horse into a corral, Curly set the axe aside and wiped his hands on his pants. He grinned and said, "How, Mark."

Sabin looked over his shoulder, back to the north. "I never want to see another range like that one."

Ben Teasdale came ambling from the shack and crossed the yard to the pair. He stood listening to their talk, and then he said, "I'm the exception which proves the rule. You're going to call me a liar, but I branded more calves this spring than last. That was a lucky hunch, moving the herd into the hills. The wind did keep the ridges bare, and there was grass up there that had never been grazed."

It came now to Sabin that Curly had done some talking about Teasdale's wintering through in fine shape, but Curly had had his say while Sabin had lain feverish in Hatwell's bed, and Sabin hadn't got the sense of Curly's talk then. Now Sabin said, "Pitchfork branded four hundred this spring; three thousand last year." Yet he felt heartened, hearing Teasdale; he felt the first flicker of hope. All cattledom hadn't died after all.

Curly grinned. "I've got into Ben so deep for wages

that he wants to put me on shares. He'd have room here for you, too, Mark, I reckon."

Teasdale said, "You betcha."

Sabin shook his head. "I've got a deal with Pitchfork. It will be slow going at first, but I'll make something out of that brand. You ever need a riding job, Curly, you come to me."

Curly frowned. "Pitchfork!" he said and put the old rancor into the word. "Still, I guess it was really Ginselling I hated the most. Doc Hatwell came by a few days back and told us what happened to Ginselling."

Teasdale nudged Sabin. "Stay for supper."

Sabin looked at the sun. "I'll be getting on back toward Stirrup." He looked across the yard; something was changed here, but it wasn't till he'd swung up into leather that he realized the cottonwood was gone. He spoke of this.

"Used it up for firewood," Teasdale said. "With the winter as tough as it was, it was mighty handy having a tree so close. It was an unsightly old thing."

"Yes," Sabin said. "It's better gone."

He rode away then, cutting northward and coming at last to Grove schoolhouse. There were children in the yard; he wondered how the children felt about the winter's ending. They'd had a mighty long vacation. He sat his saddle watching them for a moment; in the shrill voices of children there was something soothing, something that helped erase the memory of cattle bawling around a depleted haystack.

He rode on and passed Inland's corner and paralleled the fence northward; here was another fence that was his friend, for this fence, too, had served him well one night. He saw Inland's smoke lifting and wondered what would become of Inland, whether it would get a new manager or whether the investors would give up the place after the winter kill. A lot of those big outfits all over the West had gone belly-up. He guessed that Inland would be sold, section by section; probably there'd be a lot of small places like Teasdale's, and a lot of barbed wire. He was a little sad with that thought; he'd known the old days.

At Pitchfork's gate he turned east and came in late afternoon to Stirrup and left his horse at a hitchrail, meaning not to linger here too long but to make it back to Pitchfork by deep dark. He climbed the stairway to the mercantile building, hoping he'd find Hatwell in his quarters; and he was there, a lot of newspapers spread out around him. Hatwell looked as if he'd put on a little weight lately.

He said, "Sit down, Mark," and Sabin settled himself on the familiar horsehair sofa and fashioned up a cigarette.

"I've been over to Miles," Hatwell said. "Gave the Stock Growers' your resignation. They hated to lose you, boy. Joseph Scott told me to tell you so."

Sabin said, "Then they've still got an Association?"

"They let me sit in at their meeting. Scott pointed out that if the winter had continued another twenty days there wouldn't have been any stockmen left. But they've got hopes, Mark. Scott said they were meeting to revive the industry, not to bury it."

Sabin glanced at the scattered newspapers. "It was tough all over."

Hatwell sighed. "That Scotch financed outfit, the Swan Cattle Company, down in Wyoming, went bankrupt. Nelson Story had a seventy-five percent loss. That French marquis closed up his packing plant at Medora and they say he's gone off to India to hunt tigers. Yes, it was bad all over—Dakota, Wyoming, Colorado, Montana. Some of our own papers are trying to dodge the facts."

"But some spreads pulled through," Sabin said, remembering Teasdale.

"Shucks," Hatwell said, "it will turn out to have been a good thing in the long run. Figure it out for yourself, Mark. All that snow is going to mean rich new grass this spring; you can see it coming up already. The cattle business was overexpanding till it was heading for a bust. The hard winter merely hurried the inevitable. There's just going to have to be a new type of operation, that's all—the kind Ben Teasdale preached: fewer but better cattle, limited but better range, supplemental feeding. We had to learn the hard way about the dangers of open-range feeding and cluttered acres. You've heard about a man ending up sadder but wiser. It happened to a whole industry. It was a costly lesson; maybe it will be a remembered one."

Sabin said emphatically, "I'll never raise a cow on Pitchfork that I won't be able to feed."

Hatwell ticked off his points on his fingertips. "Smaller herds—more careful control—shelter for the weaker animals—hay for emergency feeding. Those things will do it."

Sabin stood up and crossed to the cold stove and put the remnants of his cigarette in it. He smiled at Hatwell. "You're a good doctor for this range; you know all the cures. Too bad they wouldn't listen to you last fall. You're a good man, Doc."

"Oh, hell," Hatwell said. "Where's that jug? There must be a drop or two left in it."

But Sabin wasn't of a mood for drinking and he left then, returning to the street. At once he found himself aimless, and he was crossing to where he'd left his horse when old Tex ambled out of the mercantile. They met in midstreet and paused, neither of them ready with words; and it came to Sabin that he'd scarcely had time for speaking in the rush of that tragic spring round-up.

Old Tex squinted at him now and said, "I been

meaning to tell you that I aimed to get in and see you when you was sick at Hatwell's. We was pretty busy with the cattle about that time."

"Sure," Sabin said. "Sure."

Tex fumbled at his Durham tag and got out the makings and built up a cigarette, taking a great deal of time at it. "Smoke?" he invited then and extended the sack to Sabin.

The taste of the quirly he'd smoked in Hatwell's office was still strong in Sabin's mouth, but he took the sack and fashioned a cigarette. They shared a match, and Tex said then, "I'll be gittin' along. You ridin'?"

Sabin shook his head; Tex took a step or two, then turned. "The boys never did hold none with backshooting."

Sabin said, "It's over and done."

"You show your face in the bunkhouse," Tex said dourly, "and you're going to get cleaned at blanket poker like you never got cleaned before, mister."

"Hell," Sabin said, "my old man invented the game."

He watched Tex top a horse and ride out to the west, a gnarled man in the saddle, but there were a lot of seasons left in old Tex. Sabin stood on the edge of the boardwalk and found the sun warm and the breeze soft to his cheek, and there was a mellowness in him; it was as though he'd had that drink with Hatwell. He put the quirly out carefully; he looked at the brown smear of tobacco crumbs on the boardwalk, and he said then aloud, very slowly, "By grab, they got so they like me!"

He remembered all the cussings he'd given old Tex and all the cussings he'd taken. When it came to bluestreak profanity, old Tex could give the best of them lessons.

Still he stood, and it hit him that he was queerly happy; he prodded this happiness for its core and knew then that it was made up of Curly, and the cottonwood being cut down at Teasdale's, and Doc Hatwell talking of a new hope, and old Tex offering him the makings. It was made of all those things, and it held a strange victory come out of disaster. And as he thought of this, the winter became a receding thing, driven back into the north and vanquished; the winter was just a beginning of new seasons to come, not the end of everything.

He thought: *That's it—a new breed of cattle, a new way of doing things. Shucks, we're just getting started!*

He wanted to share his mellowness with someone, to tell that someone how it was with him now, how he'd learned the hard way, just as all cattledom had learned the hard way, that no man or no idea is vanquished so long as there are seeds of faith to burgeon under a new sun. Hatwell was up there yonder above the mercantile, but he turned instead toward Deborah's door; he came along the street to her house and knocked at the door.

She opened for him. She said, "Come in."

The room was the same as always; the dress-dummy still stood in the corner, and Deborah was at work; sewing lay piled on the table. She bade him sit down, but this time he stood; he wanted the full feel of this room he had come to know so well; he wanted to look across it at her. She stood regarding him with all her serenity manifest in her face, this tall, gray-eyed girl. She smiled faintly.

He said, "Did you know? They cut down the cottonwood at the old place."

She nodded. "I knew. I wanted you to find that out for yourself." Her breath came with a quick indrawing. "I told you once that there was a kind of sickness of hate in you. I was so very wrong, Mark. Now I know why you rode out from Grove school-house the night of the dance, and why you took Pitchfork's foremanship with all the long winter ahead of you. It was because you came back to do some good for Arrowhead, wasn't it? That was what really brought you home, not hate."

He turned his sombrero brim in his fingers, at a loss how to explain himself. He said, "I spoke once of showing folks I was cut from different stuff than my dad. Jeff Sabin would have let them all go to hell. But I told you, too, that there were some things I kept remembering and one of them was that he'd got hung and I hadn't done anything about it."

She said, wonderingly, "Are you trying to excuse yourself with me when all those months I knew about Trenchard and was afraid to face him with the truth?"

He said, "I suppose that if you took any person apart, you'd find somewhere one weakness in him. Each of us had ours. Each of us licked it. I think that's the thing to remember, Deborah."

She said, "And now—?"

"I'm running Pitchfork. Up till today I didn't think that made anything to offer you. Now I see it different-ly. It will be small pickings the first few years."

She seemed to hold her breath and then she said, her eyes wide with understanding, her eyes misty, "You want me there?"

He had no answer for this other than to open his arms. She came into them with her face lifted, her lips soft and expectant. He had dreamed how her kiss would taste, embodying all of her serenity, all the balm she had ever brought him. He found her lips fiercer than he had imagined, and that was good, too; the fire had been there, for the man who could kindle it. Now he knew that the last loneliness was forever driven out of him, and the last hopelessness. They had crossed to each other and no traverse could ever be too long for them in all the days to come. . . .